Sunday Times #1 bestselling author Kimberley Chambers lives in Romford and has been, at various times, a disc jockey, cab driver and a street trader. She is now a full-time writer.

Join Kimberley's legion of legendary fans
on Facebook/kimberleychambersofficial
and @kimbochambers on Twitter.

Also by Kimberley Chambers

Kimberley CHAMBERS

The Victim

HARPER

Harper
An imprint of HarperCollins*Publishers*
The News Building
1 London Bridge Street
London SE1 9GF

www.harpercollins.co.uk

This paperback edition 2017
2

First published in Great Britain by
Preface Publishing 2010
Published by Arrow Books 2014

Copyright © Kimberley Chambers 2010

Kimberley Chambers asserts the moral right to be identified as the author of this work

A catalogue record for this book is available from the British Library

ISBN: 978-0-00-822870-5

Set in Times New Roman PS by Palimpsest Book Production Limited, Falkirk, Stirlingshire

Printed and bound in Great Britain by Clays Ltd, St Ives plc

MIX
Paper from
responsible sources
FSC™ C007454

In memory of a wonderful man and publican

Lou Smith

(The Corner Pin, Tottenham High Road)

ACKNOWLEDGEMENTS

Firstly, I would like to thank my publisher Random House for giving me the initial opportunity to get my books and my name out there. A special mention to Ruth Waldram, who has been a fantastic publicist to work with, and Nicola Taplin, who has always been so wonderfully efficient.

As per usual I would like to thank my fabulous agent, Tim Bates, who I am sure would like to strangle me at times, and my amazing typist and friend, Sue Cox.

I have purposely left my editor Rosie de Courcy until last, as this special lady deserves her very own special mention. Thanks for everything, sweetheart. I will never forget you and will always love you loads xxx

A strong, successful man is not the victim of his environment. He creates favourable conditions. His own inherent force and energy compel things to turn out as he desires.

Orison Swett Marden

PROLOGUE

Trussed up like a dead chicken, the man was in agony as he lay on the cold, concrete floor. His left arm was definitely broken, and he suspected his right leg could be as well. As his captor picked up the gun and pointed it at him, the man shut his eyes. His colourful life had finally caught up with him; there was no way out this time. Images of his family flashed through the man's mind. He pictured his beautiful wife and children whom he loved so very much. He wasn't afraid of death – he never had been – but he was very afraid of never seeing his family again.

Laughing at the man, his captor aimed a kick at his head and put the gun back down on the floor. The captor had waited years for this moment and he wanted to torture his prey as much as possible before he finally killed him off.

The man opened his eyes again. Every second that passed seemed like a minute and every minute like an hour.

Out of the shadows, the captor's accomplice reappeared. 'You not killed him yet? What you waiting for?' he asked.

The captor laughed, his tone full of evil. 'I was waiting for you. I thought you'd wanna watch the cunt take his last breath an' all,' he replied, picking up the gun once more.

The man clenched his eyes firmly shut as he felt the steel of the metal barrel pushed into his temple. This was it now, and with his past sins, he wondered if God would accept him in heaven or banish him to hell.

The captor put his finger on the trigger and ordered the man to open his eyes. He wanted to feel his anguish, see his fright.

'Wanna make one last wish?' he said mockingly.

1

'Go fuck yourself,' the man croaked. He had never bowed down to anyone in his life and he wasn't about to start doing it on his deathbed. If he was going to die, then he would die the way he had lived, with pride.

Hearing four gunshots, the man shut his eyes and prayed. He was no Bible-puncher, had never really believed in God, but what choice did he have now? Surprised that he wasn't feeling even more pain, the man wondered if he was already dead. Did the pain start to leave your body as your spirit left the earth? he wondered.

Frightened to open his eyes in case he came face to face with the devil, the man froze as he heard a familiar voice. It couldn't be! He must be dreaming – he had to be. He opened his eyes and gasped. This was no dream and, in that split second, the man realised that there must be a God after all.

CHAPTER ONE

1993

Eddie Mitchell's mind was working overtime as his motor crawled towards his aunt's house in Whitechapel. The A13 was chocka with roadworks, as per usual, and the five miles an hour he was able to drive gave him plenty of time to ponder over his decision.

For the first time since his father had been murdered and Eddie had taken control of the family firm, he'd been stumped over what he should do. He knew what he wanted to do – he wanted to wipe out every single one of the bastard O'Haras but due to what his dickhead brothers had done, that was now impossible for the time being.

Rubbing his tired eyes, Eddie thought back to the past. The feud with the O'Haras had originally started in 1970. At the time, Ed's father Harry was running an extremely successful pub protection racket in the East End of London, until one day a bunch of travellers turned up out of nowhere and tried to muscle in on their patch.

Ed and his brothers, Paulie and Ronny, had all worked for Harry at the time and an all-out war with the travellers to take control soon followed.

The O'Hara firm was run by the old man, Butch, but it was his son, Jimmy, whom Eddie despised the most. Ed still bore the scars of his tear-ups with Jimmy, but at the time he'd got his own back by putting Jimmy in hospital for a long spell. Not many moons later the O'Haras disappeared. Harry, Ed's father, finally got rid of them by shooting Butch in the foot. Ed thought he'd seen the last of them but, unfortunately for him, he hadn't.

It was many years later, when Ed was living in Rainham with his beautiful wife, Jessica, and their twins, Frankie and Joey, that Jimmy O'Hara reappeared. He bought a house nearby, so they became neighbours. A kind of truce was called and was sort of kept until Ed's daughter Frankie began dating Jed, Jimmy's youngest son. Then all hell broke loose.

The ringing of his mobile phone snapped Eddie out of his daydream. It was his fiancée, Gina, whom he'd sent away for safety reasons while he sorted things out. 'All right, sweetheart? How's tricks?'

'Oh, Ed. Claire's gone back to work today and I'm so bloody bored. I miss you so much and I swear I can look after myself, so please let me come back home. If I leave now, I could be back by teatime.'

Eddie sighed. He missed Gina dreadfully and the decision he'd made was partly because of that. 'Listen, I'm nearly at me aunt's now. I've come up with a plan that I'm gonna put to the lads and hopefully that will set the ball rolling so you can come back home. It won't be today though, babe. Stay put for now and hopefully you'll be home by the weekend. I have to be sure we're all safe first, so just trust me on this one, Gina.'

Eddie and Gina continued their conversation until he pulled up outside his Auntie Joan's gaff. When Ed's father was alive, he'd always insisted that any important meetings should take place in a room upstairs in Joanie's house and Ed had continued that tradition.

'You can never trust too many eyes and ears,' was Harry Mitchell's motto.

Ed said goodbye to Gina, then hugged his aunt as she opened the front door. She'd been baking, as usual, and the smell of her house was always a comfort to him. Joanie had brought him up as a kid after his mum had died of TB, and she was very special to Eddie.

'I've made you two plates of sandwiches and some rock cakes. Now you go on up, 'cause the boys have been waiting ages.'

Eddie took the stairs two at a time and entered what he called their office. The room hadn't been decorated since the seventies and Ed liked it that way, as it reminded him of the good old days when his old man was still alive. A large mahogany table sat in the centre of the room, with eight mahogany chairs around it. An old-fashioned bar stood in the right-hand corner and, apart from a massive picture of Harry Mitchell, which Eddie had blown up as a tribute and had placed on the main wall, the room had little else in it.

'What time do you call this?' Gary asked jokingly.

Eddie sat down at the head of the table. The firm at present only consisted of four of them. Himself and Raymond, who was Jessica's brother, and his two eldest sons from his first marriage, Gary and Ricky.

Ricky poured everybody a neat Scotch and then opened the door so Joanie could bring in the sandwiches and cakes.

'Well, what you decided?' Gary asked as soon as the door was shut.

'Let's eat first and talk after,' Ed replied.

Raymond studied Eddie carefully. He knew Ed better than anyone, probably even better than Eddie's sons did. When Eddie had mistakenly shot and killed Jessica, Ray had never envisaged being good pals with Ed again or returning to the firm, but he had done both, and was now raring to go. In Raymond's eyes, Jessica's death had been Jed O'Hara's fault, not Eddie's, and for the sake of his sister's memory, Raymond now wanted revenge. Not even remotely hungry, Ray slung his sandwich back onto the plate.

'For fuck's sake, Ed, spill the beans. What we gonna do?'

Eddie pushed his plate away and sipped his Scotch. 'I've thought long and hard about this and I think I should go round to Jimmy O'Hara's house and call a truce. I shall tell him he can do what he wants with Paulie and Ronny. It's the only way forward – for now, at least.'

Raymond was gobsmacked and Gary and Ricky looked at their father in complete and utter horror. Gary was the first to break the silence.

'Have you fucking lost your marbles or what, Dad? How can you go round O'Hara's house and shake his hand when he's responsible for our whole family falling to pieces? Not only is Jessica dead because of them cunts, Frankie's in

Holloway and her kids have been kidnapped by the pikey bastards. You'll mug us right off if you call a truce – O'Hara'll think we're a proper bunch of pricks.'

'I agree with Gal. What about you?' Ricky asked Raymond.

'I want to get revenge for Jessica, but we have to get them kids back before we do anything else. She would have loved them grandchildren of hers and getting them home safe and sound would have been her priority.'

Eddie held his palms face up. 'Hold your horses for a minute, the lot of ya. I run this firm and I make the decisions.'

Gary shook his head. 'How can you offer your own brothers up on a plate, Dad? I know they're a pair of fucking idiots, but they're still our flesh and blood.'

Eddie's eyes clouded over. He immediately stood up, picked up his glass and threw it at the wall, purposely missing Gary's head by only inches. 'Do you think I really want my brothers dead? No, they might be a pair of bell ends, but they're still family. Remember, they're in Belmarsh at the moment, and I know every face in there who'll keep an eye on 'em for me. Use your loaves, lads, O'Hara is a fucking pikey and all he probably knows is two bob mugs in there. He ain't gonna have many pals in a cat-A nick like Belmarsh, is he? If, by hook or by crook, O'Hara does somehow get to Paulie and Ronny, then that's life, but I'm confident he ain't got the brawn. But if he has and he wanted to do that, he could do it without my permission anyway. It's our safety I'm more concerned about now. I want Gina back home with me and yous boys alive. Raymondo has got a nipper on the way – he don't need the grief – and let's not forget about Joey. Who's to say that O'Hara wouldn't try to top him? He's an easy target, ain't he? The way I see it, lads, is by pretending to hand Ronny and Paulie to O'Hara on a plate, we won't have to look over our shoulders.'

Raymond immediately nodded his head in agreement. Gary and Ricky just stared at one another.

'Do you think O'Hara will swallow it?' Ray asked Eddie.

Eddie shrugged. 'I don't see why not. It weren't us that killed his son or his grandkid, it was Ronny and Paulie. He knows I ain't had fuck-all to do with my brothers for years, so why shouldn't he swallow it? You gotta remember, Jimmy might be fuming, but he's also grieving. He's already lost two of his family and if he won't accept my handshake, he knows the rest of 'em, including that rotten, fat, ugly wife of his, are in danger.'

Gary shook his head. 'I think we're all forgetting something 'ere. What are we meant to say to Frankie, Dad? She's tried to kill Jed, he's got her kids, so what do we do? Tell her that you've shook hands with his father and everything is fucking hunky dory now?'

Ordering Raymond to top all their drinks up, Eddie gave a false chuckle and, for the second time that day, his eyes clouded over. 'Son, you've got a lot to learn about me. For now, what I propose we do is just a temporary answer to our current problems. Then we start planning, and I mean properly planning. We'll take our time, we have no choice.'

Pausing momentarily, Eddie stood up and stared at his dead father's photograph. He then placed his hand against his heart and turned to Gary and Ricky. 'I swear on your grandfather's grave, that one day I will get revenge for what the O'Haras have done to this family.'

He then turned towards Raymond. 'And I promise you, Raymondo, that I will also get revenge for Jessica's death. Believe me, I will personally fucking kill them pikey cunts one by one, and may God be my judge if I fail.'

CHAPTER TWO

Frankie sat bolt upright as the piercing screams of the new girl disturbed her wonderful illusion. She'd been dreaming of Georgie and Harry. They'd all been at the funfair together, and the reality of waking up and finding out that it wasn't real filled her with sadness. Frankie had been banged up for stabbing her then-boyfriend, Jed O Hara. On finding out that Jed was responsible for murdering her grandfather, Harry Mitchell, Frankie had tried to kill her evil ex and apart from now being parted from her chidren, the only regret Frankie had was that Jed had managed to cling to life.

'The fucking snakes, there's a load of 'em! Get the bastards off me!'

Closing her eyes, Frankie lay back down and pulled the covers over her head. There were no snakes of course, the new girl was just having withdrawal symptoms, which seemed to be a common occurrence on the hospital wing.

It was three weeks to the day since Frankie had had her second bail application rejected. In her first week in Holloway she'd been bullied something chronic, so she'd taken her father's advice, acted doolally and got herself put in the hospital wing.

As the girl in the next bed started screaming again, Frankie put her hands over her ears. The days she could handle, but she hated the nights. Most of the other inmates were heroin addicts. They were given methadone to suppress their withdrawal symptoms, but Frankie soon realised that the alcoholics were the worst. It was usually them that kept her awake all night with their hallucinations.

Aware that somebody had arrived to deal with the distressed

inmate, Frankie pretended to be asleep. It was daylight now, but all Frankie wanted to do was shut her eyes and picture her beautiful children again.

'Wakey wakey, Mitchell. Get up and pack your stuff. I've just been informed there's a space waiting for you on the maternity wing. Sort yourself out and I'll come back to collect you as soon as I get the OK from the powers above.'

Frankie immediately leaped out of bed and, for the first time in days, smiled. She was just over twenty weeks pregnant now and the baby inside her was the only thing that had kept her going over the last few weeks. She had been doing buttons to move to the maternity wing. Surely in there she would meet some other nice inmates and they could discuss their kids and stuff.

With a spring in her step, Frankie packed her belongings up. She was done and dusted in ten minutes flat. She sat back down on her bed, rubbed her swollen tummy and whispered to her bump. 'Your father might have taken your brother and sister away from me, but he'll never get his evil hands on you. I still don't know if you're a little boy or a girl, but whatever you are, your mummy will love you dearly and you will belong to her.'

Unaware that his sister was about to be moved, Joey Mitchell opened the front door and gave his father a hug. He had barely seen his old man since Frankie's last court case and, seeing as they'd only recently been on good terms again, Joey had missed their new-found closeness.

Eddie kissed his son on the forehead and then shook Dominic's hand. Dom was Joey's boyfriend and when Ed had originally found out about his son's sexuality, he'd gone apeshit. Being a notorious East End gangster, Ed just couldn't deal with the fact that his sperm had produced a homosexual son, and it had taken a lot of pride for him to step down off his anti-gay soapbox.

Now things were different and even though Ed still couldn't quite understand his son's preferences, he'd learned to live with them. It also helped that Dominic was a lovely fella – so much so that Eddie often felt guilty for turning up at his flat that time and threatening to cut his cock off.

When Joey's Chihuahua ran into the hallway to greet him, Ed picked the dog up and kissed her on the nose. He'd always loved animals, especially dogs. 'Hello Madonna, my little darling,' he said, laughing.

Dominic grinned. 'I hope you're hungry, Ed. I've just made a big pot of chilli for lunch. I've used lean steak mince, of course. It's a wonderful recipe; my mother gave it to me.'

Eddie smiled. He was anything but hungry – he felt too worried to eat – but he didn't want to be rude. 'I could do with a drink first, actually. Listen, I need to speak to yous boys, so get us all a drink and we'll chat before we have any grub.'

Joey sat down nervously on the sofa. His dad wasn't his usual jovial self and he hoped that whatever was wrong didn't involve Frankie. His twin sister had been through hell already and it would be awful if she had been beaten up in prison or something.

Dominic handed Eddie and Joey a bottle of lager each and sat on the armchair.

'Please tell me that nothing bad's happened to Frankie, Dad. I couldn't deal with her having any more bad luck.'

Eddie shook his head. 'Frankie's OK. She rang me yesterday. Look, I don't want you to worry about this, because it's probably just me being paranoid, but yesterday I went round to Jimmy O'Hara's to try and sort things out. Someone has to try and shovel up the mess your uncles have created, so I thought I'd offer him a truce.'

The colour drained from Joey's face. 'He didn't threaten you, did he?'

'No, he wasn't even there. The whole place was locked up, no one was there, so I rang Pat Murphy, who informed me that the O'Haras have gone away and they've been missing for over a week. Georgie and Harry are obviously with them, but no one seems to know where they've gone. I don't trust O'Hara – he's a snake, always has been – so I just want you and Dominic to be extra vigilant, in case they're planning any repercussions.'

'What! And you think they'd come here?' Dom asked anxiously.

'No, I don't. If Jimmy or Jed want anyone's blood, it's mine, not yours, but just watch your backs. I shouldn't think for a minute that they even have a clue where you live, but I don't trust the pikey bastards. They're scum, the lowest of the low and I would never put anything past 'em.'

When the room fell silent, Joey picked Madonna up and held her to his chest. 'If anyone tries to hurt you, I'll kill them,' he whispered in her ear.

Aware that his boyfriend was worried, Dominic broke the ice. 'So how's Gina, Eddie? And when are you both going to let me and Joey take you to that fabulous new restaurant we told you about?'

'Gina's fine. She's staying at her mate Claire's at the moment, but as soon as I sort things with O'Hara, she'll come back home. To be honest, I really miss her; I'm rattling around like a lost sheep in that cottage on me own.'

Joey handed Madonna to Dominic. 'Take her outside for a wee-wee, Dom. I need to have a quiet word with my dad.'

When Dominic left the room, Joey closed the door and turned to Eddie. 'I didn't want to say too much in front of Dom 'cause, unlike our family, his parents are so normal, but what I don't understand is how is Jimmy O'Hara going to accept a truce when Uncle Ronny and Paulie have killed his son and blown his grandchild to pieces?'

Eddie was a little taken aback. Unlike his other two sons, Gary and Ricky, Joey had rarely taken any interest in the family business or asked any questions in the past. Ed downed the rest of his lager and decided to be truthful with Joey.

'I'm going to offer O'Hara Ronny and Paulie on a plate. Tell him that what happened was fuck-all to do with me and if he wants revenge, it's all right to do whatever he wants to do to them. And before you call me a wrong 'un, Ronny and Paulie are in Belmarsh, where I know plenty of people who will watch their backs for me so O'Hara's henchmen can't get to 'em. What else can I say to the man, Joey? I have no choice.'

Joey had steel in his eyes as he faced his father. When he was a child, he'd been a proper crybaby and even now he'd sob at the drop of a hat, especially if it was a sad story or film where someone was nasty to an animal. But at the end of the day, he wasn't a boy any more, he was a man. He might be gay, enjoy a normal life and detest violence, but he was still his father's son.

'Paulie and Ronny are both a pair of arseholes, always have been. I've never liked them and neither has Frankie. They haven't exactly got many good points, have they?'

Eddie threw an incredulous glance Joey's way. He couldn't quite believe what he was hearing and for a second he wondered if his son was taking the piss out of the callous way he'd sometimes behaved in the past.

'Are you having a laugh with me or what, Joey?'

'No, Dad. I'm deadly serious.'

Eddie scratched his head. It was a habit of his when he was struggling for the right words. 'Look, I know what you're saying, and yes, your uncles are both arseholes, especially Ronny, but they're still our flesh and blood, son. Even though I'm gonna tell O'Hara it's OK to fucking top 'em, I don't think he has the power to do it. Once they come out of Belmarsh he might, but they're looking at life and until then, I think they're both safe. Whatever my or your opinion of 'em, I grew up with 'em, and you know how much I loved your grandad Harry. I can't, in reality, order a hit on me own, Joey, it ain't done in my circles.'

Joey faced his father with a nonchalant expression on his face. He walked towards him and placed his hands on Eddie's shoulders. 'Listen to me Dad, and listen carefully. I might not be part of your world, but I'm not stupid. If I was, I wouldn't be working in the Stock Exchange. I'm worried about us. Me, you, Frankie, Dom, Nan and Grandad. And let's not forget about Dom, Gina, Gary and Ricky. Mum's death toughened me up and I've thought about your world a lot since. Do you honestly think that if you offer O'Hara Paulie and Ronny and then he can't get to them, he's gonna fall for that? He won't. I barely know the man and even I know he won't. Frustration at not getting his own back will set in and then he'll look for other targets. You seem to be more concerned about Jimmy, but I know that Jed is the worst out of the lot, Dad. Frankie didn't tell me too much, but I know he's evil and he won't let something like this rest. Don't ask anyone to protect your brothers in prison. It's all their own doing, aint it? Let the

O'Hara's have their revenge. If you don't, you're putting all our lives at risk.'

Frankie's good mood evaporated as she walked into the dormitory and saw who she'd be sharing with. The girl that had bullied and humiliated Frankie on her arrival at Holloway had been black and this girl was the same colour. Fearing the worst, Frankie smiled and nervously held out her right hand.

'Hi, my name's Frankie.'

As the girl stood up, Frankie was shocked by how short she was. She was no more than five feet tall, if that. With a mass of bushy afro hair and enormous breasts, she almost looked as though she was about to topple over. The girl smiled, and as she did, her face lit up. She had one of the most beautiful smiles that Frankie had ever seen, and perfect white teeth. As she began to speak, her voice had a slight Jamaican lilt to it.

'Thank you, Lord. I prayed last night that I wouldn't be saddled with another head case, and he must have listened because he sent me you. My name's Barbara, but you can call me Babs. Me and you, Frankie, are gonna get along just fine.'

Eddie arrived home, poured a large Scotch and sat at the kitchen table. The cottage seemed dismal and lonely without Gina's presence and he couldn't wait for her to return. Unable to stop thinking about what Joey had said earlier, Ed mulled over his words once more. The boy was right: if O'Hara couldn't get to Paulie and Ronny, he'd get his revenge elsewhere. With his conscience pricking him, Ed topped his drink up. If he ordered nobody to watch his brother's backs in Belmarsh, he was sure O'Hara could find somebody to get to them. The question was, could Eddie order his own brothers' death sentences? He was temporarily saved from feeling like an executioner by the shrill ring of his phone.

'Ed, it's Pat. Just a quick call to let you know that Jimmy's home. They're all back, including Jed and your grandkids. Apparently they'd spent the week with poor Marky's wife and kids.'

'Did you tell Jimmy that I wanna speak to him, Pat?'

'No. To be honest, I don't really want to get involved, mate.

It's awkward, because I'm friends with the both of yous. Having said that, I do think you need to sort it, Ed. I know you're no man's fool, but if I was you I'd get this shit sorted fast. Jimmy ain't a man to be messed with, you know.'

Eddie ended the call and sat back down at the kitchen table. He could sense the threat in Pat Murphy's voice: O'Hara had said something to him, that part was obvious. Furious with the decision he was now faced with, Ed slammed his glass down so hard that it shattered into pieces. The O'Haras were the bane of his life and he would never be truly happy until they were all dead.

Over in the maternity wing in Holloway, Frankie and Babs were getting along rather well. Frankie had been suspicious of Babs' warm welcome at first, but the more she'd chatted to her, the more her earlier distrust had evaporated. Babs was six months into her pregnancy and, like Frankie, she was also the mother of two other children, a boy and a girl. The only subject they hadn't yet discussed was how they'd both come to end up in prison. Frankie was the first to broach the subject.

'So when is your court case, Babs? And how long have you actually been in Holloway?'

'My trial is probably next year sometime. I've been in here four months, but I know I'm gonna get life.'

Frankie was gobsmacked. Babs seemed so nice, but she must have done something really bad to be looking at life. Sensing Frankie's reluctance to ask her what she'd done, Babs started to open up. In the four months she had already spent in Holloway, she had never really talked about her crime. The other inmates all knew what she'd been charged with, but nobody knew why she had done it. Her usually bubbly expression disappeared and was instantly replaced by a look of sadness.

'My first boyfriend, Dennis, was a bastard to me. He's the father of my daughter, Matilda, and I met him when I was fifteen. As soon as I fell pregnant, the beatings started. He nearly killed me one time; pushed me down some concrete stairs and I was in hospital for nearly two month. He was Jamaican, like me, and involved with the Yardies, into drugs, prostitution, the works. Once he even made me sleep with a mate of his while he filmed it.'

'Oh my God, that's awful,' Frankie said, shocked.

Months of not speaking about what had happened came bubbling to the surface and Babs was determined to share her burden with Frankie.

'That's nothing compared to what happened next. I contacted one of those women's refuge places and they were brilliant. They put me in one of their safe houses and me and Matilda were so happy until Dennis turned up one day and set fire to the place with us inside. We managed to escape through a back window, but it were such an awful experience, Frankie. Even to this day, a whiff of smoke is enough to frighten the living daylights out of me.

'The police never caught Dennis: he went on the run, and he knew the right people to protect him. Me and Matilda got moved again, this time to Surrey, but I could never say we were happy there. I used to sit in the dark most nights in case Dennis had found out where we were. Then, one fine day, a copper knocked at the door. Dennis had been found dead on the streets of Brixton. He'd OD'd on drugs, crack cocaine, and the police reckon he'd died in a house or flat and had been dumped on the pavement after his death. I was so happy. All I wanted was to move back near my family and friends, but Dennis dying just seemed too good to be true. I insisted on viewing his body – I needed to know it was definitely him – and when I saw his evil face in that morgue, I danced for joy, as I was finally free.'

'So, how did you end up in here? The police didn't accuse you of injecting him or something, did they?'

Babs shook her head. 'Dennis died over ten years ago and I vowed never to get involved with any other man, but I was desperate for a brother or sister for Matilda, so I had a fling until I got what I wanted. Jordan's dad was a guy called Brandon. I barely knew him, and I never told him Jordan were his son. He seemed an OK sort of dude, but he lived with a girl. I doubt he would have been happy about it, as I'd told him I was on the pill. Me and the kids were then given a council house in Streatham and that was the happiest I've ever been in my life. There was a park nearby and because I never had much money, I used to buy a cheap loaf of bread and take the kids there to feed the ducks. Then one day I got talking to this guy. I'd seen him there before and he seemed so nice. He was great with the kids, especially Jordan.'

When Babs began to cry, Frankie sat on the bunk next to her and put a comforting arm around her shoulder. 'If it's too upsetting for you, don't tell me any more,' Frankie whispered.

'I want to. I need to tell someone,' Babs sobbed.

Trying her hardest to pull herself together, Babs continued her story. 'Unlike all my ex-boyfriends, Peter was a white dude. He was a bus driver and seemed such a kind, honest, down-to-earth person. I didn't rush into anything. I met him loads of times at the park before I agreed to go out on a date with him.'

'Ssh, it's OK. He can't hurt you no more, nobody can,' Frankie soothed, as Babs began to cry once again.

'I went out with Peter a whole year before I let him move in with me. He'd play football with Jordan, help Matilda with her homework, he seemed like the ideal stepfather. Then one day I was meant to be taking Jordan to his friend's birthday party. Peter had offered to look after Matilda and I told him I'd be back in a couple of hours. When I got to the party, they'd had to cancel it because the child's grandma had died suddenly. Jordan was upset, so I said we'd go home and Peter would take us all to the Wimpy. As I opened the front door, I could hear Matilda crying. I thought she'd fallen over and hurt herself, but as I listened more carefully I realised it was something much worse. "Please stop, Peter, you're hurting me," she was pleading. Twelve years old, that's all she was.'

'Oh my God,' Frankie whispered. She had guessed what was coming next.

'I told Jordan to be quiet and sit in the living room, then I took the dagger out of the drawer. It had once belonged to Dennis, but I had always kept it after I split up with him, as it made me feel safe. I crept upstairs and saw the bastard with my own eyes. Matilda was naked from the waist downwards and Peter was raping her. I tiptoed into the room and then I stabbed him in the back over and over again, until the breath and blood seeped out of him.'

Frankie was crying herself now. She thought she'd had it tough with Jed, but it was nothing compared to what poor Babs had been through. 'You won't get life. If you tell the jury the truth, they'll let you off, I know they will.'

'I can't. Apart from you, I've told nobody. I told the solicitor I killed Peter because he used to beat me up.'

A good judge of character, Frankie now decided that Babs was the real deal, totally genuine. She urged her to listen to what she had to say. 'I'll have a word with my dad if you like. He'll find you a good brief to represent you. Babs, you must tell the truth for the sake of your children. I know your mum is looking after them, but they need you, especially Matilda.'

Babs shook her head furiously, then put her hands protectively on her rounded stomach. 'I will never put my Matilda through a court case and let's not forget, I'm carrying that evil bastard's child. I love my children more than anything else in the world, and to protect them, I'm willing to keep my trap shut and do life.'

Eddie Mitchell stared at the clock on the kitchen wall. He had promised himself he would make a decision by midnight and he had ten minutes left to do so. He poured himself another Scotch and stared at the now empty bottle. Jessica used to hate him drinking the stuff, said it changed him as a person and made him violent. Well, tonight he'd done at least three quarters of a litre, but he wasn't drunk and had only been drinking to help him make a decision. Picking up his glass, Eddie walked into the lounge. A big photograph of his dad was on the opposite wall to Jessica's. It had been taken on his dad's sixtieth birthday at the restaurant where they'd all celebrated and Harry looked as large as life, with a big grin on his face and a fat cigar in his hand. Ed stared at the photo and smiled sadly. He still missed his dad dreadfully and he would never rest until he found out who had murdered him so brutally. One day Ed would find out, that thought kept him going, and when he did, he would torture those responsible before he actually killed them. He began to speak, his voice full of emotion.

'I've had to make a decision, Dad, and I want you to know that it's been the most difficult one of my life. I would like to shoot every O'Hara tomorrow. I could easily kill the fucking lot of 'em, but I can't because of everything that's happened and I would hate to see Frankie's kids end up in care. I'm gonna plan my revenge carefully. Last time when I tried to kill Jed, I went at it like a bull in a china shop and look what happened – I lost my beautiful Jessica and I'll never forgive myself for that. This time around, I need a proper plan. Things have to be perfect and, when they are, I'll use my loaf, keep my wits about me and strike. I hope you can forgive me for what I'm about to tell you, but there's a good chance Ronny and Paulie will be arriving at the Pearly Gates soon. I don't want that to happen and I'll be devastated if and when it does, but I really do have little choice in the matter. Ronny and Paulie have dug their own graves, unfortunately, and I have to put the safety of my children first and also Gina and Raymond, who both mean the world to me. Please forgive me, Dad, and if you see Ronny and Paulie before me, tell 'em I love 'em and I'm sorry.'

CHAPTER THREE

'Mummy! Come back, please, Mummy. Don't leave me! I promise I'll be good.'

Harry O'Hara woke up and rubbed his tired eyes. At three years old, Harry was eighteen months younger than his sister, Georgie. To look at they were chalk and cheese. Harry was a pale-skinned, chubby blonde boy, whereas Georgie was very tall for her age, skinny, with long, dark hair and dark skin. Harry got out of bed, toddled over to his sister and prodded her arm.

'Georgie, what a matter?'

Georgie sat bolt upright and began to cry. She kept having the same awful nightmare. Her mum would come back home, then she would walk out and leave her again.

Harry clambered onto his big sister's bed. Georgie was the only one who would give him a cuddle these days. His mummy used to give him loads, but whenever he asked his dad, nanny Alice, or grandad Jimmy for one, they all laughed at him. 'Stop being such a sissy, Harry. You're a big boy now and big boys don't need cuddles. Cuddles are for babies and girls, you dinlo,' his dad would tell him.

Georgie and Harry huddled together in silence. The last month had been awful for both of them. Firstly, their mum had disappeared, then on the day they'd found out that they had a brother called Luke, he'd had his brains blown out in front of them.

'Are you thinking of Luke?' Harry whispered.

Georgie shook her head. 'I was thinking of Mummy.'

'Can we go see her, Georgie?'

Georgie didn't answer immediately. Nanny Alice had told her that her mum was in prison because she'd tried to kill her

19

dad, but Georgie didn't believe it. Her mum would never do something like that, she was too nice. Hearing movement on the landing outside, Georgie turned to her brother, so her mouth was next to his ear.

'If I tell you something, you won't tell anyone, will you, Harry?'

'Promise, Georgie.'

Ever since Georgie first learned to walk, she'd had a habit of running away and exploring. Once, when her uncle Joey had taken her to a pub, she'd hidden in the woods, climbed up a tree and watched the police search for her. She loved an adventure; it was part of her nature.

'You know yesterday when Grandad drove us home?'

Harry nodded.

'I think I saw Nanny Joycie's and Grandad Stanley's house. It wasn't far from here, so maybe we can run away and they can take us to see Mummy.'

For the first time in weeks Harry's eyes lit up. He liked Nanny Joyce and Grandad Stanley and, most importantly, they always gave him cuddles. 'Can we go there now?' he whispered.

About to reply, Georgie was stopped in her tracks by the bedroom door opening.

'Up you get, yous two. Come on, now. Nanny Alice is gonna do us all a nice big fry-up. Bath first, then breakfast after.'

When her nan turned her back, Georgie put her forefinger to her lips to warn Harry to keep schtum. She then held his hand and led him out of the bedroom.

Jimmy and Jed O'Hara had got up at the crack of dawn and gone over to the fields to check on the horses. It had been cousin Sammy's job to feed them and keep an eye on them while Jimmy and Jed were away, but by the looks of the stallion lying on the grass, he hadn't done a very good job.

Neither Jimmy nor Jed could be described as animal lovers. Jimmy owned a goat that he rather liked, but he'd sold all the dogs now, and the horses were just a way of making money.

Jed knelt down and looked into the stallion's eyes. 'He don't look good, Dad. I think you'd better ring a vet.'

'Nah, he's had it, boy. It'll be cheaper to shoot him meself,' Jimmy replied.

As they headed off to get the gun they kept hidden nearby, the conversation turned to Alice.

'She seems much brighter now, Jed. Did her the world of good spending time with Tina and the kids.'

Jed agreed. Tina was his brother Marky's wife. The last month had been awful for all of them, none more so than himself. Marky had been murdered, then Jed's son Luke had been shot by mistake. The bullets had been meant for Jed, and Lukey boy had died in Jed's arms. Jed had thought he would never smile again at the time – he wished he was dead instead of his boy – but, unlike the boy's mother, who had literally fallen to pieces, he'd had to pick himself up and carry on. As a proud travelling lad, he had no choice other than to put on a brave face, but what had happened was eating away at him inside, like a fast-spreading cancer, and he would never be truly happy until he got revenge for his brother and Lukey boy.

'What's happening with Sally? Why don't you invite her round for dinner, that'll cheer your mother up no end,' Jimmy suggested.

Jed shrugged. Sally was Luke's mother, and she was also pregnant with their second child. Unlike Frankie, whom his mother had despised, Sally got on like a house on fire with Alice.

'Why you shrugging? You ain't split up with her, have you?'

'Nah, but I've barely seen her since Lukey boy died. I've only met up with her twice since her father came round and poked his fucking oar in. She's still staying at his, and when I rang her earlier to tell her I was home, she came out with some cock and bull about having gut ache. I reckon her old man has told her to keep away from me.'

'Or she could be telling the truth, Jed. Perhaps the girl ain't well. How far gone is she now?'

Jed smirked. 'I dunno. Men don't take much notice of dates and times, do they? She's probably about three month, at a guess, but what with that slag Frankie being pregnant at the same time an' all, I didn't really listen.'

As they reached the field again, Jimmy turned to his son

and smiled. 'I know it's been a tough few weeks for you, boy, but you'll get through this, I know you will. None of us will ever forget Lukey boy, he was a little diamond, a chavvie to be proud of, but you and Sally will have plenty more chavvies. Take my advice and look after that Sally – she's a good girl, your mother likes her and you could do a lot worse.'

Without waiting for a reply, Jimmy marched over to the stallion, put the gun to its head and dispassionately shot it.

Eddie Mitchell was not in the best of moods. He'd drunk far too much Scotch the previous evening and even though he hadn't felt drunk at the time, this morning it had made him feel sluggish and heavy-headed. Even a shower hadn't made him feel any better; it had actually made him feel worse. Ed got dressed and studied himself in the mirror.

With his six-foot frame, his couple of days' trademark stubble and his short dark hair, which he'd recently started to wear slicked back to cover the odd strands of grey, he looked good for fifty-three and he knew it. He'd always been broad-shouldered, but when he'd been banged up for accidentally killing his wife Jessica, he'd trained a lot in prison through boredom and he'd walked out of those gates with the toned body of a thirty-year-old.

Turning his head slightly to the right, Eddie fingered the scar down the left-hand side of his cheek. Women had always loved it – they said it made him look rugged – and men had always been jealous of it, wishing they had one to make them look as manly, but he'd always fucking hated it. It wasn't the actual scar itself: if someone other than Jimmy O'Hara had put it there, he would have probably been quite proud of it, but the fact that his worst enemy had scarred him just reminded Eddie every day how much he hated O'Hara.

The shrill ring of the landline interrupted Eddie's foul mood. It was Stuart, his old cellmate from Wandsworth.

'One week to go. One week to go. I'm counting down the hours, and I can't fucking wait,' Stu sang to the tune of 'Here Comes the Bride'.

Despite his own problems, Eddie had to laugh. Stu had

recently been moved to an open prison and he seemed to have the use of a phone morning, noon and night.

'What's been happening, mate? How's Gina?' Stuart asked.

'Yep, everything's fine and Gina's just popped to Tesco,' Eddie lied. He wasn't one for talking over prison phones and he hadn't told Stu any of the recent gossip. He would tell him everything when he picked him up next week. 'Listen, Stu, I've gotta shoot out, I'm running late as it is. Bell us later if you can and don't worry, your bed's all made up here and Gina insists you can stay as long as you like.'

Ending the call, Ed wanted to smash the phone against the wall as the bastard rang again. 'What?' he screamed into the receiver.

'Ed, it's me. Are you OK?' Gina asked.

'Sorry, babe. I thought it was one of the boys.'

'When can I come home, Ed? I'm pulling my hair out here through boredom.'

'Soon. I'm going to sort things out right now – that's if I ever get off this poxy phone,' Ed said sarcastically.

'Oh, sorry, go on, you get off and ring me as soon as you get things sorted. I can't wait to see you again. I love you, Ed.'

Eddie returned the compliment, apologised for being snappy, then ended the phone call. The thought of what he was about to do next was making him feel physically sick. What type of man signs his own brothers' death warrants? he pondered, as he searched high and low for his keys. He found them down the side of the armchair and, as he stood up, he came face to face with his father's photograph.

'I'm so sorry. Please forgive me, Dad.'

Alice O'Hara was feeling more positive than she had in weeks. Her son and grandson being murdered had knocked her for six, but visiting Marky's widow and his two sons had somehow helped her come to terms with her grief. Her daughter-in-law, Tina, was a tough cookie and she had given Alice a serious talking-to. Tina had made her realise that no amount of screaming, crying and self-pity were going to bring Marky or Lukey boy back and, for the sake of the rest of the family, she needed to get her act together.

Singing along to Hank Williams' 'Lovesick Blues', Alice carried two large china plates over to the kitchen table. On one there were sausages and bacon and on the other black pudding and fried bread.

'Get stuck in and I'll bring the eggs and beans over in a tick,' she said.

Georgie stared at the two big plates in horror. The meat was swimming in grease and she hated that black stuff and the horrible bread that her nan cooked.

'Nan, can me and Harry have Rice Krispies instead?' she asked.

'Don't start, Georgie. You need to get some meat on them bones of yours, so you eat what Nanny gives you,' Jed shouted.

'Oh, for fuck's sake,' Jimmy said as the doorbell rang. He hated being disturbed at mealtimes; it pissed him off big style.

'You eat your breakfast, Jimmy. I'll answer it and tell whoever it is to take a running jump,' Alice insisted.

With the spatula still in her hand, Alice stomped into the hallway and, as she opened the front door, very nearly had a fit. 'Gertcha, you murdering mother's cunt. Get off my property before I kill you,' she screamed, as she lunged at Eddie with the greasy spatula.

Eddie held his hands in front of his face to stop the stupid bitch from blinding him. 'I ain't come here to cause no trouble. I need to speak to Jimmy. I wanna make amends for what happened.'

'Amends! Fucking amends! Gonna bring my Marky and Lukey back from the dead are you, you animal?'

Hearing a commotion, Jimmy and Jed ran to the front door.

'You no-good shitcunt,' Jed yelled as he lunged at Eddie.

As his son grabbed Mitchell around the neck, Jimmy waded in to pull Jed away from him.

'Look, I've come here to apologise, not fight. I know nothing can make up for the stupidity of my brothers, but what happened was fuck-all to do with me. I wanna try and sort this mess out for good,' Eddie said.

Georgie O'Hara was brighter than most four-year-old girls and as soon as everybody had left the kitchen, she'd scraped her and Harry's greasy breakfasts into the bin and covered the evidence with her nan's tea-towel. Now she'd led Harry into the hallway to see what all the fuss was about.

Because Eddie had been in prison for virtually all of his grandchildren's lives, neither Georgie nor Harry knew him that well. Both had visited him in Wandsworth with their mum, but it was Harry who had seen him more recently than his sister, and recognised him first. Thinking that his grandad had turned up to take him and Georgie home to their mum, Harry let go of his sister's hand and ran towards Eddie.

'Grandad, can we see Mummy?' he yelled excitedly.

Eddie had been too busy arguing with Jed to notice the kids were there and he felt really emotional as he laid eyes on the pair of them. Georgie looked skinnier than the last time he'd seen her and Harry seemed a few inches taller.

'Get away from them chavvies. They're nothing to do with you or that whore of a daughter of yours any more!' Alice screamed.

'I want my Mummy!' Georgie sobbed, as Alice roughly dragged her and Harry back towards the kitchen.

'Grandad, can we come home with you?' Eddie heard Harry shout just before the door was slammed. Eddie felt completely useless. He could tell the kids were unhappy – it was written all over their little faces – and he needed all his self-restraint to stop himself from putting them in his motor and taking them home with him.

'You ever come near my kids again, I'll fucking cut you to pieces,' Jed yelled, lunging at Eddie once more.

Jimmy grabbed his son by the hair. 'Get in that kitchen with your mother and make sure them kids are OK.'

'No! Why should I? That bastard killed my son and . . .'

Grabbing Jed by the neck, Jimmy marched him into the kitchen. 'You leave this to me and if you come back out this kitchen, I shall clump you so hard you'll see fucking stars,' Jimmy warned as he slammed the door and marched back to where Eddie was standing. He walked out into the cold December air, shut the front door and marched Eddie over to where the stables were.

'You've got some fucking nerve turning up here, I'll give you that much,' he spat.

Unlike Eddie, Jimmy O'Hara was no oil painting. He was six feet two, had dark, greying, wavy hair, thick lips, a beer belly and a big bulbous nose that splattered over to one side of his face. Jimmy opened the stable door, let Eddie inside and turned to him with a look of hatred.

'So, what do you want?'

Eddie was finding it increasingly difficult to keep his cool. Jed had attacked him and had ripped his Armani shirt, he hadn't been able to speak to his own grandchildren and now he had this big, ugly prick looking at him as if he were some kind of faeces he'd trod on. Taking the advice of his probation officer, who had told him to take ten deep breaths whenever he felt as if he was about to lose his rag, Eddie spoke in the most sympathetic voice he could muster.

'I came here to apologise for the deaths of your son and your grandson.'

Jimmy gave a sarcastic chuckle. 'Well, that's fucking big of ya. We'll forget all about it and be best buddies then, shall we?'

'Just drop the sarcasm and hear me out will you, Jimmy? It weren't fucking easy for me to come round 'ere today, so the least you can do is listen to what I've got to say. If you don't, then I'll walk away now and we all know what will happen next, don't we? You'll shoot a couple of my family and then I'll shoot a couple of yours. And so it goes on Jimmy, like it always bastard well has done, until we're all laying six feet under.'

'Go on then, talk, I'm all ears,' Jimmy spat.

'I've come here today not only to apologise, but also to offer you a deal. You know as well as I do that I had sod-all to do with what happened. I've had sweet fuck-all to do with my brothers for years – they might be my flesh and blood, but they're mugs, the pair of 'em. I ain't stupid; I know you're gonna want revenge and so would I if I'd gone through the same as you had. So I'm gonna give you permission to go ahead, do what you've gotta do with Paulie and Ronny and when you do, I promise they'll be no repercussions from me or my family.'

'I think you've forgotten something, Mitchell. Your cunting

brothers happen to be in Belmarsh with a lot of your old pals and I know for a fact that you'll say one thing to me, then have their backs watched for ever more. Don't insult me, by treating me like some dinlo, please.'

'I promise you, Jimmy, I won't get involved. My brothers fucked up big time and now they have to pay the price. I'll keep out of it, I swear I will.'

Jimmy was thinking of the bigger picture. He would never truly rest until all of the Mitchells were dead, especially Eddie, but if he agreed to this deal now, it would give him plenty of time to plan the rest of their executions properly. Neither Eddie nor his sons were any man's fools, and Jimmy wanted that fucking Raymond dead as well. Doing life in prison didn't appeal to Jimmy one little bit and if Alice ever lost her beloved Georgie girl over his rash actions, she would never forgive him, and would probably leave him for good.

'Well?' Eddie asked impatiently.

Determined to make his biggest enemy sweat, Jimmy glared at him. 'Hold your fucking horses, Mitchell. This is heavy shit and I need five minutes to think.'

Jimmy knew quite a few traveller lads in Belmarsh and even if Eddie's heavies were looking out for Ronny and Paulie, Jimmy was sure he could bribe someone to get to them for him. He turned to Eddie; he was determined to have the last laugh, even today. 'I'll agree to the deal on one condition.'

'What?'

'I know two lads who will sort out your brothers, but they ain't gonna do it for nothing. I want thirty grand off you so I can give 'em fifteen each.'

Eddie was gobsmacked. This was getting silly now. 'No way. It's bad enough I know my brothers are gonna die without paying for some bastard to do it. I can't do that, Jimmy, it's fucking despicable.'

For the first time in weeks, Jimmy felt like really laughing out loud, but he managed to hold it back. 'Well, that's my terms, so take it or leave it.'

Feeling as though his head was about to burst, Eddie sat down on a bale of hay. He hadn't told Gary, Ricky and Raymond that he was coming to see Jimmy today and now he could never tell them. With images of his kids, his grandchildren and Gina flashing through his mind, he stood up. Their safety was his priority right now.

'OK, you've got a deal. But it's between me and you, and if you blab to anyone, including any of your family, the deal's off.'

'Cushti. When will I have the wonga by?' Jimmy asked.

'Friday. I'll meet you in the car park of the Optimist at twelve noon.'

Jimmy smirked. 'We gonna shake on this then?'

Eddie reluctantly shook Jimmy's hand, and then took a slow walk back to his motor. Paying for his own brothers to be killed literally made him feel like the Devil in disguise. Picking up pace, Ed broke into a jog. He knew O'Hara had made a complete mug out of him today, but he could hardly refuse his terms; his hands were tied for now.

Feeling as sick as a dog, Eddie started his motor and drove at speed towards home. When he reached his own driveway, he got out of the Range Rover, leaned against it and pictured Ronny and Paulie's faces. He then vomited like he'd never vomited before.

CHAPTER FOUR

Stanley Smith smiled as his lady friend, Pat, handed him a mug of steaming coffee with a big dollop of cream on top. They had only known one another for six weeks, but it felt more like six years.

Pat, or Pat the Pigeon, as she preferred to be called, had recently moved to Orsett in Essex from the East End of London. Stanley had met her in the Orsett Cock pub and there was an instant spark between them. They had since become great friends and Stanley often popped round Pat's for a cuppa and a natter. Joyce, Stanley's wife, had no idea of his special friendship. There was nothing untoward going on, but Joycie would probably chop his testicles off if she found out he'd been sitting in another woman's house on a regular basis.

Unlike Joycie, Pat was a good listener. She had a caring nature, a heart of gold, and Stanley felt able to pour his problems out to her. Jessica, his daughter, had been murdered by her villainous husband Eddie Mitchell, and Pat was the only one who truly understood Stanley's despair and heartache.

'You're not your usual chirpy self today, Stanley. What's bothering you?' Pat asked in a sympathetic tone.

Stanley stared wistfully out of Pat's conservatory window. Unlike the house he now lived in with Joycie, Pat's was only a two-bed semi-detached, but it was homely and it always reminded him of his and Joycie's old property in Upney.

'I'm OK, love. I just hate that bloody house I live in so much. I miss me old house – I was happy there.'

Pat the Pigeon nodded her head understandingly. Stanley had told her that Joycie had forced him to live in the house

29

that had once belonged to his daughter, Jessica. Apparently, Eddie Mitchell had given the house to Joyce as some kind of compensation for accidentally shooting her and Stanley's daughter.

'Well, you know my views on that house, Stanley. How your Joycie can live there with everything that's happened, I don't know. I don't like to speak ill of people I haven't met, but your Joycie must be as hard as old boots. I could never have taken a gift off a man who had murdered my daughter.'

'Well, that's my Joycie for ya, Pat. Full of airs and graces, and I ain't gonna change her now, she's too long in the tooth. She loves that big house, lords it over her friends, she does, and she'll never move, not a cat in hell's chance. We were at it hammer and tongs arguing again this morning – drives me bleedin' bonkers, she does. That money we've got left in the bank from the sale of our old house, she wants to buy a flash motor with it. Not a second-hand one, a brand bleedin' new one. I like me old Sierra – it might not look a picture, but it drives like an angel. I mean, what do I want a poxy Mercedes at my age for? I only want a run-around to get me from A to B and to cart me pigeons about in.'

Pat smiled and nodded in agreement. She had been terribly lonely since her husband Vic had suddenly passed away, but meeting Stanley had brought some sunshine back into her life. His wife Joycie sounded like a right domineering old dragon and Pat just hoped that one day Stanley would leave Joyce, move in with her and they could live happily ever after.

'I made a nice date and walnut cake this morning, Stanley. Shall I make us another coffee and cut you a nice big slice?'

'Thanks, but I'd best not stuff me face, Pat. In fact, I'm gonna have to make a move in a minute. It's Jock's granddaughter's twenty-first birthday and I promised him that I'd accompany him to the restaurant this evening. They're having a little surprise do for her.'

Pat knew Jock. She had met him at the pigeon club a few times. 'Oh, a birthday party sounds lovely. Where's it being held, Stanley?' she enquired, hoping for an invite.

'Jock still lives in Barking, but his granddaughter lives in Rainham, not that far from me. They're holding it in a poxy

Chinese by the Cherry Tree somewhere. Shame it ain't a steak-house. I don't really like foreign food.'

When Stanley stood up, Pat stood up as well. 'Well enjoy yourself, love. Is Joycie going with you?'

'No, I mentioned it to her last week, but I don't think she fancied it.'

'Oh well, never mind. I'm sure you'll have fun anyway. Why don't you pop round and tell me all about it tomorrow? I can wrap the cake in foil and you can have a piece then if you like.'

Stanley smiled. Pat really seemed to enjoy his company as much as he enjoyed hers. 'I'd like that, Pat. I'll pop round about midday.'

Even when she was a young girl, Pat the Pigeon had always loved sex. She couldn't help it; it was in her nature. She had been married to her husband, Vic, for many years and their sex life had never dwindled. When Vic had died, Pat never thought that she would fancy another man or ever have sex again. Then she'd met Stanley and, for her, it had been love at first sight. The problem was, she could tell that Stanley was a shy one and she didn't want to put him off by being too forward. Pat ushered the object of her affections towards the front door and, as she usually did, gave Stanley a gentle peck on the cheek.

'Bye, Stanley. Look forward to seeing you tomorrow, love.'

Over in Holloway, it was visiting time, and Joey had just given his twin sister a loving hug. 'I'm really sorry I'm late,' he said as he sat down opposite her. Because she was on remand, Frankie was allowed plenty of visits, but Joey's hectic job meant he could only get up to visit her a couple of times a week.

'So how's the Stock Exchange? Still doing your head in, is it?' Frankie asked. She liked to wind Joey up, but she was extremely proud of his high-flying career.

'Brain damage, per usual. Half-eight I left the bloody office last night. No wonder most of my colleagues have cocaine instead of food for lunch; at least it keeps 'em awake.'

'You ain't taking cocaine, are you?' Frankie asked suspiciously.

31

'Don't be daft. Dom would bloody kill me. There are a lot of blokes at work on it, though. Most of them are real big drinkers as well. I'm fine, I can handle the pressure and stress, but you'd be surprised how many men can't, especially the macho, straight ones. Anyway, enough about me. How are you? You look much happier than when I came up last weekend.'

'Well, now I'm out of that awful hospital wing, I'm sleeping so much better. The maternity wing is quite nice compared to the rest of the prison. The staff are polite and my new cellmate is lovely. Her name is Babs, she originally comes from Jamaica and we get on really well. I've only known her for a short while, but it feels like we've been mates for years.'

Joey was pleased by the change in his sister. Her mood had been so low on a couple of his previous visits that he hadn't really known what to say to her. He'd cried once as he had left the prison because he'd felt so bloody helpless.

'So, what's your friend Babs in here for? Is she convicted, or on remand like you?'

Frankie leaned forward so nobody could hear what she was saying. 'Babs is on remand and she's in here for stabbing her boyfriend as well. He died and now she's looking at life, poor cow.'

Horrified that his sister was sharing her cell with a murderer, Joey clasped her hands in his. 'Be careful, Frankie. Watch she don't turn on you.'

'Babs is one of the most sweet-natured people I've ever met in my life, Joey. Her bloke was far worse than Jed and I don't blame Babs for killing him. Any woman would have done the same in her situation.'

'What did he do? I won't say nothing, I promise,' Joey said in a hushed tone.

Frankie leaned over and covered her mouth with her hand. 'He raped her twelve-year-old daughter, the fucking nonce. The bastard deserved to die, don't you think?' she whispered.

Joey nodded dumbly. This conversation was getting a bit heavy for him and he was desperate to change it. 'Dad popped round the other day. He didn't stay long; I think he's got a lot on his plate over what Paulie and Ronny did. He's even sent

Gina away to stay with her mate. I think he's lonely in that cottage on his own.'

'What! Is he living with her then?'

Cursing himself for putting his foot in it, Joey lowered his eyes and looked sheepish. 'I thought you knew they were living together. Gina's really lovely, Frankie. If you gave her a chance, I know you'd like her.'

Fuming that her father had forgotten to mention that he'd moved his old tart in, Frankie glared at Joey. 'Unlike you, I'm loyal to our mum. You might wanna be friends with the old slapper, but I don't. She probably only got her claws into Dad 'cause she knows he's a face and he's worth a few quid.'

Joey shrugged. He wasn't about to argue, because when Frankie had one of her cobs on she could be a complete bitch. He changed the subject yet again. 'I wonder how Georgie and Harry are coping? Do you reckon Jed and Alice are looking after them properly? Dom and I miss them dreadfully, so I hate to think how you must feel.'

Frankie's face hardened. She'd spoken about her children to Babs and she couldn't help constantly dreaming about them, but at all other times she tried not to think about Georgie and Harry as it upset her too much. Knowing the O'Haras had custody of her children was pure torture and Frankie could not deal with it. 'I don't wanna talk about the kids, Joey. I can't, OK?'

Noticing tears in his sister's eyes, Joey gently squeezed her arm. 'You'll get them back one day, I know you will, Frankie.'

Frankie ignored his comment. 'How's Nan and Grandad? Have you seen them lately?'

Joey shook his head. 'What with being so busy at work and visiting you up here, I haven't had much chance to pop round there. Nan rang me at work the other day, invited me and Dom to dinner this Sunday, so we'll see them then. She was ranting and raving about Grandad on the phone, something about a new car. You know what they're like, Frankie, they don't change.'

Frankie smiled. Her grandparents had never got on, but it was her nan who threw all the insults – her poor grandad had never had the guts to retaliate.

Desperate to get an answer to what had been playing on his mind, Joey leaned forward. 'Kerry rang me late last night; she wants to come and visit you. I spoke to her for ages and even though she wouldn't tell me much, I know something really bad happened, Frankie. Why did you really try to kill Jed? We've never kept secrets from one another before, so please tell me the truth.'

Frankie's heart urged her to open up to her brother, but her head told her not to. Joey was close to her father again. He was also a gossiper, especially in drink, and if he blurted out the truth, all hell would break loose. Her dad's life was probably already in danger because of what her uncles had done to Jed's family and if she told Joey that Jed had tortured and murdered their grandfather, Harry, carnage would be sure to follow. Frankie knew just how evil Jed was and the thought of her dad or brothers getting killed was enough to make Frankie keep schtum for ever more. Relieved that the bell was ringing to signal the end of visiting time, Frankie stood up and hugged her twin brother.

'You take care and give my love to Dom,' she said.

Joey pulled away from her and stared deep into her eyes. 'You haven't answered my question yet, Frankie.'

'I wish I could answer it, Joey, but I'm sorry, I can't,' Frankie replied. She then walked away without a backward glance.

Stanley Smith was not having the best of evenings. When he was a lad he had been taken to one of the first Chinese restaurants ever to open in London. He had no memory of whereabouts exactly it was, but he did remember that he had been taken there because it was his Auntie Agnes's fortieth birthday. The evening itself was nothing to write home about, but what did stick in Stanley's mind was that he was forced to eat some kind of fish heads, then on the way home he got a clip round the earhole from his mother because he spewed his guts up over some poor bloke on the train. Ever since that day, Stanley had avoided eating Chinese food like the plague.

'So what do you fancy then, Stanley?' Jock said, handing him a menu.

Stanley glanced at the menu and immediately felt queasy.

'Don't they do any English food, Jock? I ain't a lover of rice or bleedin' noodles, mate. I had food poisoning on this shit once.'

Jock laughed and called one of the waiters over. He explained Stanley's predicament and the waiter turned to Stanley. 'We do very nice omelette and very nice chip.'

'Yeah, that'll do, mate,' Stanley said politely.

As Jock chatted to his granddaughter, Stanley studied the rest of the company. They were all bloody youngsters and he felt about as out of place as a Nigerian at a National Front march.

'You remember my daughter Louise, don't you?' Jock asked, as he excused himself to go to the toilet.

Stanley hadn't seen Jock's daughter for a good few years and she had put on that much weight he would never have recognised her unless Jock had told him who she was.

'Hello, love. You look well,' Stanley lied.

'Ah, thanks Stanley. How are you keeping? Your Joycie still looks well, don't she? I saw her recently in a pub.'

'What pub? She never said, where did you see her, Louise?'

Louise sat down on the chair next to Stanley. 'In the Bull in Romford. I work behind the bar in there at lunchtimes. To be honest, I didn't speak to her, Stanley. I've put on a lot of weight recently, so she probably wouldn't have recognised me anyway. Not only that, she was with Eddie Mitchell and I didn't wanna make meself busy.'

About to swallow a sip of his beer, Stanley very nearly choked. He spat the beer back into the glass. 'Eddie Mitchell! It couldn't have been my Joycie. We've had nothing to do with him since my Jessica died.'

'It was definitely Joyce. I was always round your house years ago and she still looks the bleedin' same. I could hear her chatting and laughing with Eddie. There ain't many people got a full-on laugh like your Joyce has, Stanley.'

Feeling the colour drain from his cheeks, Stanley grabbed Louise's arm. 'Are you sure it was Eddie with her? Think carefully, because this is important.'

Louise was rather merry. She also wasn't the brightest of girls and didn't even realise she'd said the wrong thing.

'Of course I'm sure it was Eddie. Everyone knows who Eddie Mitchell is, don't they? Blimey, Stanley, my mate Carol went out with him before he got with your Jess, so I know what he bloody well looks like. He even bonked Carol in the back of his car once while I was sitting in the passenger seat like a bloody gooseberry.'

'Whatever's the matter, Stanley?' Jock asked, as he returned to the table and clocked his pal's deathly white face.

Stanley ignored him and turned back to Louise. 'How long ago did you see them in the pub together?'

'About six or seven weeks ago,' Louise replied, necking the rest of the wine in her glass. She had just sort of realised that something was amiss when her dad had shaken his head frantic-ally behind Stanley's back and she didn't fancy any agg with Eddie Mitchell. She stood up and smiled. 'Perhaps I got it wrong, Stanley. My eyes play me up terrible sometimes. In fact, I'm going to have an eye test next week to see if I need glasses.'

Stanley knew without a doubt that Louise was lying. He stood up just as the waiter reappeared.

'Omelette and chip, sir.'

Filled with anger and betrayal, Stanley pushed the waiter, who then unfortunately dropped the plate on the floor.

'Stanley!' Jock yelled, as he chased his friend out of the restaurant.

'Leave me alone, Jock,' Stanley warned. 'You knew about this, didn't ya? Go on, fucking admit it.'

Jock at least had the sense to look shamefaced. 'I'm so sorry, Stanley. I didn't wanna get involved, I knew how you'd react and I didn't wanna cause no trouble between you and your Joycie.'

Stanley turned to Jock with a look of pure hatred on his face. 'You were meant to be my poxy mate!' he screamed.

'I am your mate, but everyone knows what Eddie Mitchell is capable of and like most people, I don't wanna cross him. I've gotta think of my own family's safety, ain't I?'

As Jock turned to grab his arm, Stanley roughly pushed him away. He then walked towards him and, as Jock backed into a wall, Stanley pointed his forefinger into his face. 'Me and you are finished, Jock and don't you ever fucking contact me again.'

Full of pent-up rage, Stanley turned on his heel and stormed over to his car. He had been betrayed by the two people closest to him in the worst possible way and he would never forgive either of them until the day he died.

CHAPTER FIVE

'Are you OK, Frankie? You been ever so quiet since visiting time. Did your brother upset you or something?' Babs asked her cellmate.

Frankie sat down on the edge of her bed. 'I'm OK, it's just I've been thinking about my kids a lot today. I try not to as a rule, because it upsets me too much, but sometimes you just can't help it, can you?'

Babs stood up, walked over to Frankie's bed and sat down next to her. 'Look, don't feel you have to, but I feel so much better inside for telling you my story, so if you wanna tell me yours, I'm a good listener. Like me, you're a lovely person, Frankie, and I know something bad must have happened to you as well.'

Frankie bowed her head and stared at her feet. Her dad had always told her to be careful to whom she told things. 'Tell no bastard nothing, Frankie, especially someone you've only known five minutes', he'd always say.

Frankie turned to Babs. She might have only known her new friend for what her dad would call 'five minutes', but gut instinct told Frankie that she could trust her. Not only that, she was desperate to share her burden with somebody, so she took a deep breath and started right at the beginning.

'I met Jed on my sixteenth birthday in a club in Rainham called the Berwick Manor. I was there with Joey and my friends and it was the first time we'd been to a proper nightclub. We usually just went to a local pub, but the Berwick held these rave nights and we were all desperate to try it 'cause everyone had said how good they were. Anyway, I met Jed at the bar and I was instantly smitten by him. He was good looking, confident and charming and he had the most beautiful bright green eyes that I'd ever seen. We got chatting, he bought me a drink and it wasn't until we swapped names that I realised who he was. Apparently, we'd met once before when we were kids.'

'Whaddya mean, who he was? Was he famous or something?' Babs asked, intrigued.

Frankie shook her head. 'He was the son of my dad's biggest enemy. My dad's a bit of a face, you know, a sort of gangster, and for years he had this feud going with a bloke called Jimmy O'Hara. Well, it turned out that Jed was Jimmy's son.'

Babs knew a lot of drug dealers like her ex, Dennis, who were into prostitution rackets and similar stuff, but most of them were scumbags. She didn't know any real gangsters. 'So, is your dad like the Krays or something?'

Frankie shrugged. 'Sort of, I suppose. He's a moneylender and he's got his fingers in loads of other pies. He comes out of Canning Town originally, but he's quite famous all over. I don't know too much about the businesses he runs, but I do know everyone's shit-scared of him. Every school me and Joey attended, everybody wanted to be our friend because of who our dad was.'

'Wow, that's well cool,' Babs said, in awe.

'Anyway, getting back to Jed. Knowing who he was, I should never have got involved with him in the first place. I knew if and when my dad found out there'd be murders, but I was so young and naïve, I just couldn't help myself. Jed was so sexy and I'd never felt that way about any boy before. To be honest, I'd never really had a proper relationship before Jed.'

'So, what happened next?'

'Well, we started dating and we both fell in love. With everything that's happened since, I do often wonder if Jed ever really loved me at the time, or if he was just trying to get one over on my dad, but I don't think he was. At first, I'm sure Jed really did love me.'

Babs was fascinated. When she was at school, she'd been in the play *Romeo and Juliet* and the way Frankie was telling her story reminded Babs of it in some strange sort of way. 'Tell me more,' she said, as she put a comforting arm around Frankie's shoulder.

'I fell pregnant with Georgie within months of meeting Jed.

I didn't know what to do, so I told my brother. Joey advised me to have an abortion. He said Dad would go mental, but I couldn't do that, Babs, so I told Jed about the baby.'

'What did he say?'

'Jed was really pleased. He's a travelling boy, you know, a gypsy, and they all have their kids young. He even proposed to me, but when my dad found out, everything went dreadfully wrong.'

'So, what did your dad do? Did he beat Jed up, or what?'

Frankie shook her head. 'As a kid I was always a daddy's girl. Joey was very close to my mum, he never used to get on that well with my dad, but I did. My dad adored me. Because Jed was Jimmy O'Hara's son, I couldn't face telling Dad what I'd done. He would have been so angry and disappointed in me, so I took the coward's way out. Jed and me, we hid behind a bush until my dad went out, then I went indoors and told my mum. My Uncle Raymond was there, he worked for my dad, and he went mental and tried to lock me in the house, but Jed confronted him, then we legged it back to his. Jed only lived down the road; he had his own trailer on his father's land.'

Frankie paused. She didn't even want to think about Jed, let alone remember her romance with the evil bastard, but she had to carry on now and once she had told Babs, she would never tell anyone ever again. 'It was Jed's idea to go to Tilbury. His dad had a trailer there on an old scrapyard and Jed said my dad would never find us there, but he did.'

'What did your dad do, Frankie?'

Reliving the memories as though it was yesterday, Frankie started to cry. Her mum had died that night and, looking back, she now realised it was all mainly her fault. When Frankie's cries turned to painful sobs, Babs held her friend's shaking body to her own. She soothed Frankie by stroking her long, dark hair.

'Sssh, it's OK, sweet child. You have a lie down and get some rest. If you wanna talk again later, we can, and if you don't, then that's fine by me.'

Joycie Smith was thoroughly enjoying the latest episode of her favourite soap. She always prerecorded *EastEnders* and watched it when Stanley wasn't about, as his constant jibes and criticism of the programme often resulted in an argument.

'Load of old bleedin' codswallop. Ain't nothing like the real East End. I should know, I was born within the sound of Bow bloody Bells,' Stanley would constantly chirp.

Sipping a drop of sherry, Joyce put her glass down and clapped her hands in glee as her current fancy man appeared on the screen. Up until recently, Joycie's only love interest had been that Eamonn Holmes off GMTV, but since that dishy David Wicks had appeared in *EastEnders*, Eamonn had taken a back seat in her affections.

Fantasising that David Wicks was snogging her instead of the actress playing his girlfriend, Joyce was annoyed as she heard Stanley's car pull up outside. 'Bleedin' nuisance,' she mumbled as she pressed pause.

'What are you doing home? I thought you were going for a meal with Jock,' Joyce shouted as she heard his key in the lock.

Stanley marched into the room, his face as black as thunder. He walked towards his wife and stared at her with a look of pure repugnance. 'How could you, Joycie? How fucking could you?'

Joyce was stunned. What was she meant to have done? Surely Stanley didn't think she was having an affair or something. 'Whatever you on about? You silly old sod.'

Stanley had never hit a woman in his life, but he'd been made so furious by his wife's betrayal that he could have quite easily knocked her from one side of the room to the other. Restraining himself, he instead pointed a finger in her face. 'You have been fraternising with the enemy, Joycie. I know all about you meeting Eddie Mitchell in the Bull in Romford. How could you sit there laughing and joking with that bastard when he obliterated our daughter? You absolutely repulse me. In fact, I fucking hate your guts.'

Shocked by her husband's contorted expression and harsh words, Joycie decided to be truthful with him. 'It's not what you think, Stanley. I only met up with Eddie the once to sort things out between him and Joey. It's what Jessica would have wanted and I did it for her.'

'Don't you dare say you did it for our daughter. I know

41

exactly why you met up with him – 'cause you love being associated with the villainous bastard, you always have done. You only encouraged our Jess to marry him because he was a face and that gave you something to brag about. In that warped, fucked-up mind of yours, our daughter ending up with a notorious gangster gave you the street-cred you'd always craved. Well, let me tell you something, Joycie, you are a nasty little nobody, and none of them people you used to brag to even fucking liked you. Even your friends Rita and Hilda can't bastard well stand ya – no one can. You're an evil old dragon; everybody knows exactly what you're like.'

Livid that Stanley had brought her friends into the argument, Joyce knocked his dumpy finger away from her face, stood up and gave him a dose of his own medicine. 'You wicked, bald-headed old bastard! How dare you call me a nobody! If anybody's a nobody in this house, it's you, Stanley. You have no style about you, no bloody class, and that's why you always hated Eddie Mitchell from the word go, because he was something that you wasn't. I loved my Jessica more than I've ever loved anyone, and if I can accept that what happened was an accident, then why can't you? Both Frankie and Joey have forgiven their father – they know how much he loved their mum – but no, not you, you have to be the odd one out, Stanley. Bitter, twisted and full of grudges, that's what you are.'

Unable to control his boiling temper any longer, Stanley lifted his right hand and slapped Joyce fiercely around the face. 'You are poison, Joycie, and I'm leaving you. In fact, I want a divorce.'

As Stanley stomped out of the living room, for the first time in donkey's years Joyce was left totally struck dumb.

Back in Holloway, Frankie had stopped crying and was now ready to continue her story. 'Where was I?' she asked.

'You and Jed had fled to the trailer in Tilbury,' Babs reminded her.

'Oh yeah. Well, my mum rang my mobile, said that my dad was on the warpath and she asked if she could come and see me to sort things out. She was so sweet, my mum, she was beautiful and everybody loved her, Babs. Anyway, I gave her the address, but not long after she'd turned up, my dad and uncle Raymond turned up as well, so my mum hid under the bed. My uncle kidnapped me; he bundled me into a car and drove off. He didn't know that my mum was there, but he'd put tape over my mouth and my hands were tied up, so I couldn't even tell him. Finally he realised something was wrong and he stopped the car. When I told him that my mum was in the trailer, his face went white and he drove straight back there. But, we were too late. By the time we got back there, my beautiful mum was already dead.'

As Frankie began to cry once more, Babs rested her young friend's head on her shoulder. 'If it's too upsetting for you to talk about your mum's death, just tell me what happened with Jed,' Babs suggested.

Frankie nodded, then wiped her eyes with the cuff of her sweatshirt. Talking about her mother's demise was still far too raw and she couldn't relive it – it was too awful for words. 'Well, after my mum, you know, died, my dad got put in prison and I moved in properly with Jed. Things started to go downhill almost immediately. I hated his mother and I couldn't adapt to what he called "a traveller's way of life". By that time I was trapped, though. I was pregnant with Georgie, my mum and dad weren't there to help me, and I wasn't even speaking to my grandparents. Jed was a bastard. He knew I couldn't run away 'cause I had nowhere to run to, so he did exactly as he pleased. I was so naïve, Babs. I used to think that he was actually working when he stayed out all night, but he was out shagging other birds. Jed was such a convincing storyteller, even God would have believed his lies.'

Babs squeezed Frankie's hand. 'Don't beat yourself up for believing him. They're all lying bastards – trust me on that one, honey.'

Frankie smiled gratefully, then carried on talking. 'Looking back now, apart from right at the beginning, I can't believe that I ever really loved Jed. I mean, how can you love someone who tries to strangle you and gives you black eyes regularly? And I'm sure the night Harry was conceived, Jed practically raped me.'

43

'You can easily love an evil man like that, because I did it also, remember?'

'He even got another girl pregnant while we were together and I still forgave him, but one day I woke up and I felt differently. The love I'd had for him had turned to hate and I wanted him out of mine and my children's lives.'

'So, is that why you stabbed him then?'

Frankie fell silent for thirty seconds or so. Apart from her friend, Kerry, nobody knew the real reason that she had stabbed Jed, and she was weighing up whether she should tell Babs or not. She turned to her cellmate. She had barely spoken to Kerry for weeks and she had to tell somebody the secret that was burning a hole in her heart.

'My grandad was a legend in the East End. Harry Mitchell was his name, and I think he was one of the biggest villains to ever come out of Canning Town. He wasn't the best grand-father in the world – me and Joey rarely saw him – but obviously I still loved him 'cause he was my dad's dad. Anyway, a few years ago my grandad got murdered. It happened on Christmas Day and it was awful for my dad. Well, to cut a long story short, I found out that it was Jed and his cousin Sammy that had killed him and that's why I tried to kill Jed. That and everything else, I suppose. I just lost it.'

Babs eyes were like organ stops. Her own sorry tale was just about druggies like Dennis and nonces like Peter, but Frankie's sounded like something out of one of those gangster movies. A bit like *Once Upon a Time in America*.

Babs caught her breath and asked the all-important question. 'Are you sure it was Jed that killed your grandfather?'

'Absolutely positive. I recorded the evidence on tape, but Jed's cousin ran off with it, so I have no proof.'

Both girls stared at one another. Neither knew what to say next, but it was Babs who broke the ice by laughing. 'Wow, man, that is some heavy gangster crap, but Frankie, my sweet child, if we don't laugh about the shit God threw at us, we will go mad and fucking cry.'

Pat the Pigeon was having one of her nostalgic, melancholy evenings. In the daytime she was quite a happy person. She would spend time with her family, tend to her pigeons and she had the added bonus of Stanley's habitual visits. However, once darkness fell, Pat's mood changed. It was only then that she realised what a lonely fifty-five-year-old woman she really was.

Flicking through the TV channels, Pat stared at BBC1 with a glum expression on her face. *Waiting for God* was on, a programme about people like herself who had no spouse and ended up in one of those poxy retirement homes, sitting in their own piss and shit. About to turn the depressing programme off, Pat was stunned to hear the doorbell ring. She glanced at the clock, it was just gone half-nine and nobody ever visited her at this time of the evening. Pat put on her fluffy slippers and cautiously walked towards the front door.

'Who is it?' she shouted nervously.

'Pat, it's me, Stanley.'

With her heart leaping out of her chest with excitement, Pat undid the chain-lock and opened the front door. 'Are you OK? Whatever's the matter, Stanley?' she asked as she clocked the dismal expression on poor Stanley's face.

Stanley nodded to the suitcase beside him. 'I'm really sorry for turning up here this late, Pat, but I didn't know where else to go. Joyce has betrayed me in the worst way possible, so I've left her. I've got the pigeons in the back of the car. I couldn't leave 'em at home 'cause she's such a wicked old bag. She threatened to cook 'em in a pie once. Is it OK if me and the birds stay here for a few days? We'll be out of your way in no time, I promise.'

Pat looked into Stanley's distressed eyes. She rubbed his arm and smiled. 'Of course it is, my love. My home is your home, Stanley, and you're welcome to stay here for as long as you like.'

CHAPTER SIX

Eddie Mitchell was having another little bout of insomnia. He had to meet O'Hara at lunchtime to hand over the dosh and the guilt he felt at what he was about to do was eating away at him. Picturing his brothers' faces once more, Ed turned onto his side and forced himself to think about Gina. He'd sent his fiancée away to her friend's house while he sorted out the sorry mess his brothers had made, but she was coming back home this afternoon and Ed couldn't wait to hold her in his arms and tell her how much he loved her.

At thirty-four years old, Gina was nineteen years younger than Ed. They'd originally met when he had found her in the Yellow Pages. Gina was a private detective and Ed had hired her to follow his son, Joey. It was through Gina that Ed had found out the truth about his son's homosexuality and his relationship with Dominic.

Months after Ed had got arrested for murder, Gina had written to him in the nick and stood up in court as a witness at his trial. They'd sort of got together soon after that. Gina became a regular visitor to Wandsworth Prison and they'd planned their future in the odd hour they snatched together every week. It was a gamble coming straight out of the slammer and moving in with a bird he barely knew, but the gamble had paid off. They had originally rented, but had since bought the cottage in Rettendon and, until all this shit had kicked off with the O'Haras again, had been as happy as two pigs in shit.

Picturing Gina's naked body, Eddie smiled. Facially she was a ringer for the famous Page Three girl, Linda Lusardi, everybody said so. She was tall, with long, dark hair, legs up to her armpits and a pair of tits to die for. Feeling himself getting harder, Ed lifted the quilt, looked underneath it and smiled. He might be fifty-three, but his king-sized attribute was still in fine working order. Seconds later, Ed heard an enormous crash coming from downstairs. His erection deflated like a burst balloon and he gingerly got out of bed and grabbed the baseball bat he kept underneath it. Ever since he'd been a young man, Ed had slept with a gun nearby, but recent events had made him hide it away from the cottage. Another long stretch for a firearms charge was the last thing he needed.

Eddie put on a pair of shorts and crept down the wooden stairs. He held the bat firmly in his right hand, ready to strike if need be. Daylight was just breaking, so he could easily see where he was going without falling arse over head. The front door was shut, so Ed moved cautiously towards the kitchen. He could have sworn that he'd heard the sound of breaking glass and, if that was the case, the kitchen was the easiest form of entry for an intruder. He checked the windows and door; there was nothing untoward, so he headed into the lounge. Ed's stomach lurched as he spotted the culprit. His dad's framed photo that hung on the wall opposite Jessica's had, for no apparent reason, fallen onto the floor and smashed.

Eddie sat on the sofa and put his head in his hands. It must be a sign, a sign that his father disagreed with his decision-making. Well, he couldn't go through with what he had arranged now, not after this, and if it turned out to be his own poisoned chalice, then so fucking be it.

Joey Mitchell dried himself with a towel, then looked at his watch in dismay. He liked to have a strong coffee in St Paul's before he ventured into work, but he was running late this morning, so wouldn't have bloody time.

Dominic had an important meeting with an investor up in Hammersmith at lunchtime and was still lying in his pit. As the phone rang, Dom answered the one in the bedroom.

'Joey, it's your nan,' he shouted.

'Tell her I'll ring her later,' Joey yelled back.

Stark bollock naked, Dominic ran out of the bedroom with

the phone in his hand. 'You'd better talk to her now, Joey, she sounds in a right old state.'

Silently cursing his dysfunctional family, Joey snatched the phone. 'What's the matter, Nan?'

'Your grandad's gone. He went last night.'

Feeling his legs go from beneath him, Joey sank onto the bed. 'Oh my God! What did he die of?' he whispered, tears forming in his eyes.

'He ain't bleedin' dead, although I wish the bastard was. He's gone, left home, wants a divorce, the silly old sod. You're gonna have to come over, Joey. I can't stop in this house on me own. I've already had a large brandy and I'm worried I'll do something silly and end up back in that nuthouse again.'

'I can't come over, Nan. I'm really busy at work at the moment and I need to go in.'

Joyce was an expert at making people feel guilty – she'd practised for years on Stanley. 'Oh well, if your job's more important than your poor old nan, best you get off. But, if and when something bad happens to me, don't you dare come crying round my grave. If you do, I shall come back and fuckin' well haunt ya.'

Joey felt his conscience pricking him. 'Can't you ring Raymond, Nan? My boss will kill me if I don't go in today.'

'Already rung him. Since that tart of his has been up the spout, he's had no time for his poor old mum whatsoever. He says he's got an important meeting with your father. Knowing what a lying bastard Raymond is lately, I bet his important meeting is at one of them poncy antenatal clinics with that stuck-up prat he married.'

Joey sighed. The last time his grandad had left home, his nan had completely lost the plot and ended up in Warley Hospital. If that were to happen again, Joey knew he would never forgive himself for not being there when she needed him. 'Don't drink no more, Nan. I'll ring work, tell 'em I'm ill and I'll be with you within the hour.'

After he'd found his father's photograph lying horizontal on the living-room carpet, Eddie had knocked back a large brandy to calm his fragile nerves. He had then taken it upon himself to call an emergency meeting. None of the lads were very happy at being woken at 7 a.m., but that was tough shit; he was the boss and he called the shots.

As per usual, Eddie had ordered the meeting to be held at his Auntie Joanie's house. These days he would never chance any of their important gatherings being held anywhere but. He was too worried about the Old Bill; they weren't so backward as they used to be. The filth had been well pissed off when the jury had found him not guilty of the murder and manslaughter charges against Jessica. He'd still done bird for unlawful possession of a firearm but knowing how desperate the rozzers were to lock him up and throw away the key, Ed would never put it past the bastards to bug his, Gary's, Ricky's or Raymond's home addresses. Joanie's house was by no means foolproof, but it was definitely the best for security purposes and also better than meeting in a café or some poxy boozer.

Ed had called the meeting for 9 a.m. He had to meet O'Hara at twelve in Upminster, so he'd had no choice but to call it on so early. Due to the decrepit state of the A13, Eddie arrived at his aunt's at twenty to ten. Joanie answered the door and, pushed for time, Ed gave her a quick peck on the cheek and darted straight up the stairs.

'Shall I make you a pot of tea and some sarnies?' Joanie shouted out.

'No thanks, Auntie. We're fine, sweetheart,' Eddie replied.

Raymond, Gary and Ricky were already sitting around the big mahogany table with glum expressions on their faces. Gary and Ricky had both been on the piss until the early hours and felt like crap, and Raymond had had an earful from Polly, as he'd had to tell her that something important had cropped up and he couldn't attend the antenatal clinic with her.

'This better be fucking important, Dad,' Gary said, thoroughly pissed off that he'd been woken so early then his old man had had the audacity to turn up late.

Eddie grabbed a bottle of Scotch from the bar and ordered everybody to drink one.

'For Christ's sake, Ed. It ain't even ten o'clock. I was meant to go somewhere with Polly and she'll annihilate me if I go home smelling of booze.'

Not in the mood for Raymond's marital issues, Eddie knocked back his drink in record time and slammed the empty glass on the table. 'Fuck Polly, this is business and what I've got to say is far more important than anything your old woman will say to ya later.'

Raymond immediately shut up and, as Ed began to tell the story of what he'd agreed with Jimmy O'Hara, Gary and Ricky sat open mouthed.

'So, when your grandfather's picture fell off the wall, I just knew I'd done the wrong thing. Call it fate, but I know now I can't go through with it,' Ed said remorsefully, concluding the tale.

Ricky knocked back his Scotch and looked at his father in outright disgust. 'How could you pay to arrange your own brothers' deaths in the first place? That is sick, Dad, fucking proper sick. Say O'Hara gets to them somehow?'

Gary shook his head in disbelief. 'I know Paulie and Ronny are a pair of useless cunts, but they're still family, Dad.'

'Yes, I know they're family, but they ballsed up, not us. All I was trying to do was keep the rest of us safe. O'Hara ain't gonna let this rest, you know. If he can't get to them, he'll come for us, I just fuckin' know he will.'

Gary gave a sadistic smirk. 'Worried about your new fancy piece, are ya?' he asked sarcastically.

As Eddie grabbed his eldest son by the neck, Raymond intervened and dragged Eddie away. 'For fuck's sake, arguing and fighting amongst ourselves ain't gonna solve this, is it? Let's get a grip and sort this out sensibly, shall we?'

Ray turned to Gary and Ricky. They were good lads, but they were also playboys. Gary was twenty-nine now and Ricky twenty-seven. They were both handsome boys, but neither had settled down. Therefore, they had no idea about what it was like to worry about a wife or kids.

'Your father has got a point, you know. If anything happened to my Polly or the baby, I couldn't deal with it. Yous two are single: once you settle down and have kids of your own, you'll understand where your dad's coming from.'

Gary shrugged. He had no intention of settling down. Tarts were a pain in the arse and 'love 'em and leave 'em', was his motto. 'So what happens now, then? Are you just not gonna turn up to meet O'Hara?'

Eddie rubbed the stubble on his face. He used slow movements from his cheeks to his chin like he often did when he was deep in thought. 'I've got the dosh on me. I think I should still meet O'Hara and pay him the thirty grand. It sounds big bucks but it's peanuts to me. Let him think he's still got a deal. He won't get to Ronny and Paulie, not if I put the word about.'

'And how you gonna stop him fuckin' getting to 'em?' Ricky asked wisely.

'Ginger Mick, Lee Adams, Scouse Lenny – they're all banged up in Belmarsh and they all owe me a favour or two. I'll get word to Paulie and Ronny to spend as much time as possible inside their cells. Any time they come out, I'll have someone watch their backs.'

'It's an impossibility to get someone to watch over Ronny and Paulie all the time, Dad. I mean, how do you know that your pals are even on the same wing as them?'

'Because I made phone calls on the way here. Flatnose Freddie knows everything; he also told me that Paulie and Ronny are sharing a cell. He reckons if they hadn't have spilled their guts to the filth, the system would have definitely split 'em up, but they did, so no one cares. Also, the screws don't wanna be bothered clearing up Ronny's shit and piss. They ain't got a lot of time for cripples, I know that for a fact. That poor raspberry who was a few cells away from me in Wandsworth, the one that had strangled his mother, he was left to rot. That's why Paulie is sharing with Ronny; the authorities want Paulie to take care of the cunt, save them a job.'

Raymond was worried, very worried. 'Jimmy O'Hara ain't no mug, Ed. I know he's been out the frame for a few years, but don't underestimate him. His son and grandkid have been killed, for Christ's sake and he ain't gonna be happy if he can't get revenge of some kind.'

Eddie poured himself another large Scotch. 'Look, these pikeys are backward bastards deep down. There is no way O'Hara will think I've parted with thirty grand if I ain't in agreement of the deal. Yes, in the end, chances are he will clock on, but for now the dough should be enough to keep the mug sweet.'

Raymond shook his head. He had the same feeling as he'd had the night that Jessica had died. This was a bad idea and he half-wished he'd stuck it out in the jewellery trade and never come back to the family firm. 'When Jimmy O'Hara finds out you've crossed him, he'll come gunning for you, Ed,' he warned.

Eddie looked at his watch and stood up. 'Not if I go gunning for him first, he won't.'

Gary smashed a fist onto the table. 'Why are we giving these pikeys the time of day? Why don't we just get rid of the whole lot of 'em in one fell swoop, Jed included?'

'Because of them kids. Once Frankie is out, we can do what we want, but if we strike now, not only will the Old Bill know that we're behind the O'Hara's disappearance, there's a good chance Georgie and Harry will be taken into care. The filth have got it in for me big time, they always have had, and more so since Jessica's death. James Fitzgerald Smythe reckons he can get Frankie off her charge and I believe him,' Eddie replied.

'You're off your head. Frankie admitted to what she'd done and won't even tell no one what really happened. She's going down, I know she is,' Ricky reminded his father.

Eddie stood up. He truly believed that it was not the snapped string on the frame that had caused his father's photograph to crash to the floor; he believed it was a sign from above. It was Harry Mitchell's way of telling him that what he was about to do was wrong and, with his dad's guidance, Ed knew things would work out OK. 'I've gotta go and meet O'Hara now. We'll talk again later in the week.'

Full of his usual self-assurance, Eddie ignored the worried looks that were being thrown his way and bowled confidently out of the door.

Joey snatched the glass of brandy out of his grandmother's hand. He darted out to the kitchen, poured it down the sink and then gave her what for. He hadn't lost a day off work to watch her drink herself to death.

'Drink is what sent you loopy the last time, Nan. Now tell me exactly what happened and I'll help you find Grandad,' he said kindly, as he sat back down on the sofa.

'I don't wanna find him. I hope the nasty old bastard rots in hell,' Joyce replied dramatically.

Joey smiled. He could see through his nan's façade, her hard exterior. Deep down she loved his grandad and even though she rarely had a good word to say about him, she was a lost soul without him.

'Shall I ring Jock? My guess is that Grandad's stopping with him. What happened anyway? You haven't even told me yet, Nan.'

Joycie finally broke down as she repeated what had happened and the names Stanley had called her. 'I only went to meet Eddie so I could sort things out between you and him. I wanted you and your dad to get on 'cause I know your mum would have wanted it,' she wept.

Joey put both of his arms around his nan and held her tightly. Stanley Smith was a weak man and his nan would never have lasted that many years married to a man with more balls. She was a woman who liked to have the final say, make the decisions, and a stronger man would have divorced her yonks ago.

'I'll ring Jock now. Is his number in your address book?' Joey asked.

Joyce nodded tearfully. 'He must be at Jock's, 'cause he took them stinking, bastard pigeons with him,' she said.

Joey released his nan's grip, stood up, flicked through her address book and dialled Jock's number. 'Hiya Jock, it's Joey, Stanley's grandson. Is my grandad there? Only I'm at my nan's house and she wants to speak to him.'

Joey listened to Jock's reply and instantly felt rather nauseous. He couldn't leave his nan alone until his grandad returned, and he had his own bloody life to be getting on with.

'Well, can you make some phone calls, see if you can find out where he's gone, Jock?' Joey thanked Jock for his co-operation, then replaced the receiver and turned to Joyce.

'He's not there. Jock said they had a big row at some restaurant and he hasn't seen or heard from Grandad since.'

Joyce shot off the sofa as though someone had put a bullet up her arse. She had noticed Stanley acting strangely a lot recently; he kept disappearing at lunchtimes, saying he was going for a 'little drive', and she could have sworn blind she'd smelled women's perfume on his clothes two or three times in the past few months. She walked over to the drinks cabinet and poured herself a brandy for the shock.

'Please, Nan, don't drink any more,' Joey pleaded.

'Don't fuckin' drink any more! I need a bastard drink. Your grandfather has gone and got himself a bit of fluff, Joey, and when I find out who the old slapper is, I'm gonna wring her bleedin' neck until her tits fall off. Little drive! I'll show him what a little drive is when I drive that knife straight through his bollocks.'

Eddie Mitchell grinned as he heard Gina's car pull up outside. He deemed himself too cool to run outside to meet her, but he was no good without a woman by his side and to say he had missed her was putting it mildly.

The handover with O'Hara had gone to plan. There had been few words exchanged. Jimmy had pulled up in a pick-up truck, Eddie had got out of his own motor, handed him the dosh, then walked way and driven off. O'Hara had smirked when the dosh was handed over to him, Ed had clocked that, but he wasn't worried, as he knew he would have the last laugh. 'Good things come to those who wait,' his dad used to say.

When the front door opened, Ed walked into the hallway.

'I have missed you so much, Eddie,' Gina said, as she threw herself into his arms.

Eddie grinned, then kissed her passionately. He only had to look at her to feel his dick go rock hard. 'Let's go to bed, eh?' he whispered.

Usually, Gina would have run up the stairs, but not only was she ravenous, she also had something on her mind that had been plaguing her for the last few days. 'As much as I fancy you Ed, we need to talk first. I'm also starving. Have you been shopping or shall we get a takeaway?'

Thrown by the matter-of-fact tone in Gina's voice, Eddie lifted her chin with his hand and stared deep into her dark-brown eyes. 'You ain't gonna fuck me off, are ya? Don't tell me the first bit of agg we've had, you're bolting, babe.'

Gina looked at Eddie's handsome face. No, she wasn't

impressed by being shoved off to her friend Claire's house for weeks, but she loved Ed dearly and would never leave him, no matter what he did.

'Ed, I love you more than I love myself. How can you even ask such a thing?'

Eddie pushed her long, dark hair away from her forehead. 'Something's wrong, I know it is. Tell me.'

Gina smiled. Nothing was wrong, everything was right, but for once it wasn't just herself she was having to think about, it was another little person. 'There's nothing wrong. I'm pregnant, Ed.'

CHAPTER SEVEN

Terry Baldwin sat in the Thatched House in Barking with a glum expression and a pint of Guinness. His wonderful grandson's murder had left Terry stunned and heartbroken. He'd fucking loved that kid, idolised every hair on his little head.

Purgatory would be the best way to describe the six weeks since Luke had died. Terry's daughter Sally had been distraught, in absolute bits and, even though she was pregnant, had hit the bottle big style.

'You're gonna be burying another baby if you carry on like that,' Terry had warned her only yesterday.

'I'm so unhappy living here. I need to move back in with Jed. Please say I can, Dad. You can't keep me away from him for ever. I love him.'

Sick of watching Sally necking the wine night after night, Terry had reluctantly agreed that she could move back in with her no-good, pikey arsehole of a boyfriend. When Luke had first been murdered, Terry had turned up at the O'Haras' and ordered Sally to return home so she was safe and they could grieve and cry together. Terry had hoped that she would leave Jed for good, especially when she learned from the police that Frankie was also pregnant in the nick with the toerag's child, but it wasn't to be. The silly little cow was going back to him for now, until Terry found a way to get the piece of shit out of her life for good.

The pub door opened and Terry nodded as Jamie Carroll sat down opposite him. Jamie was a fixer and whether you wanted a firearm, a dodgy motor got rid of, or some bastard assassinated, Jamie could fix it for you.

'What you having to drink?' Terry asked.

'Nothing, I've gotta be in Shoreditch in half an hour. You got the boodle?'

Terry nodded. 'Shall I give it to you here?'

'No. I'll leave first; you finish your beer and meet me outside in five minutes. I'm in a silver Jag.'

Obeying Jamie's orders, Terry sipped his pint. He then stood up, checked nobody was watching him and left the pub. He spotted the Jag at the far end of the car park and walked towards it.

'Shall I get in while you count it? It's in bundles of a thousand.'

Jamie shook his head. He'd done bird with Baldwin and knew he was sweet. 'I trust ya. As soon as I get the nod, I'll let you know,' he replied. He started the engine and sped out of the car park like a racing driver.

Terry watched him go and then got into his own car. There was no going back now, not now he'd called it on. Nothing would bring Lukey boy back, but as the child's grandfather, Terry saw it as his duty to do whatever he could for Luke's memory.

Georgie and Harry O'Hara sat silently on the sofa as their dad fondled Sally on the armchair. Neither child particularly disliked Sally – she had always been quite kind to them and given them lots of attention when Luke was alive – but today she was solely focused on their father and had barely spoken to them all afternoon. Noticing that her dad had put his hand up Sally's short skirt, Georgie grabbed Harry's hand.

'Come on, let's play in the other room,' she said.

Thrilled to have Sally back and also desperate for a leg-over, Jed was happy to let his children do their own thing. His mum had gone to do the weekly shop, his father had driven her there, and when she got back he would leave her in charge of the kids while he took Sally upstairs for a good seeing-to. It would do them good to spend some time alone; they could have sex, then talk about Lukey boy.

'What you doin', Georgie?' Harry asked, as his sister stood on a chair and removed items from the fridge.

'Ssh,' Georgie warned. She didn't want her father to get wind of what she was up to.

Harry watched his sister in awe as she buttered the bread, spread some Marmite over it, then put big lumps of cheese in the middle. Georgie placed the sandwiches into her Mister Blobby lunchbox. She then placed four cans of Pepsi and four packets of crisps in a carrier bag.

'You hold the lunchbox, I'll carry the bag 'cause it's heavier,' she whispered to Harry.

Georgie put her Puffa jacket on, helped Harry into his, opened the front door and urged Harry to follow her outside. She could hear her dad making strange noises in the living room, so she left the door slightly open in case he heard it click shut.

'Are we going for a picnic, Georgie?' Harry asked excitedly.

Georgie held Harry's hand and urged him to run towards the nearby fields. 'No, we're running away to Nanny Joycie's house.'

Unaware that his great-grandchildren were on their way to his old abode, Stanley Smith finished the last of his rabbit stew and puffed out his cheeks.

'Have some more,' Pat the Pigeon ordered, as she leaped out of her seat to bring the large saucepan over.

'Christ no, I'm that bloated I can't even move.'

Pat smiled. She knew how to take care of a man – her mother had instilled it into her from a very early age. 'Patricia, all you've got to do in life is learn to cook like an angel and act like a whore in the bedroom. If you can successfully master those two acts, no man will ever leave you – why would he?' her mum used to insist.

'I've made a rhubarb crumble, but if you're stuffed we'll eat that later for supper, Stanley. My Christine lent me a film the other day, reckons it's bloody brilliant. It's called *Thelma and Louise*. Have you seen it?'

Stanley shook his head. 'Well, you go and make yourself comfortable in the living room while I wash up and then we'll have a couple of cans of bitter to wash that dinner down and watch our film.'

Stanley grinned and did as he was told. Unlike Joycie, who had always treated and spoken to him like something untoward on the bottom of her shoe, Pat was kind, she respected him and Stanley could get very used to that indeed.

Back in bitterly cold Rainham, Harry O'Hara was shivering, tired and had just fallen over on the uneven ground and grazed his knee. 'Can you pick me up, Georgie? My knee hurts,' he asked with a tremor in his voice.

Seeing headlights approaching, Georgie pushed Harry behind a bush. The only way to Nanny Joycie's house was via the road and because it was a country lane there was no pavement to walk on.

'Why do you keep pushing me?' Harry wept.

Aware that Harry's teeth were chattering, Georgie gave him a hug. She opened her Mr Blobby lunchbox, gave Harry a sandwich, then handed him a can of Pepsi out of the carrier bag. It was dark now, pitch black, and as they nibbled on their sandwiches they could barely see what they were eating.

'I'm sorry I pushed you, Harry, but if we don't get out the way when a car drives along, we might get run over.'

Harry nodded tearfully. He didn't like the dark, had always been afraid of it. 'When will we see Nanny Joycie's house?' he asked.

'Soon, but you have to walk quicker, Harry. I can't carry you.'

They finished their sandwiches in silence, then Georgie stood up and grabbed her brother's hand. She knew they were going the right way. Her teacher had taught her how to tell her left from her right and she knew her nan's house was this way, because she'd spotted it from her grandad Jimmy's truck. Georgie didn't miss going to school at all. She hadn't been back since her mummy had disappeared and she was pleased that she didn't have to sit cooped up in a classroom every day. Not only that, she didn't want to leave Harry indoors on his own. If she went to school, her brother would have no one to play with.

Feeling herself shiver, Georgie turned to her brother. 'It's nearly bedtime now, so we must run before Daddy finds us.'

Not wanting to be found by his daddy, Harry ignored the pain in his bruised knee and did as he was told.

Alice O'Hara had had a pleasant afternoon. Her Jimmy rarely took her out, but on the way back from Tesco, he'd suggested they have a meal in a local pub. For the first time since Marky and Lukey boy had died, Alice had laughed and smiled. She'd even drunk five pints of Guinness and it was good to forget her troubles, even if it was only for a day.

'I wonder what the chavvies have been up to?' Alice asked Jimmy. She was dying to get home now to have a little cuddle with her Georgie girl.

'I dunno, but you'll soon find out,' Jimmy replied, as he pulled up outside their house.

'I'll kill that Jed, he's left the poxy door open, the house'll be bloody freezing,' Alice moaned as she marched into the hallway. 'Georgie, Harry, Nanna's home,' she yelled.

The silence immediately unnerved Alice and left her with her usual feeling of doom and gloom. 'Jed, where are you?' she screamed. He had to be here, his Shogun was outside.

Hearing his mother's dulcet tones, Jed got out of bed, put his pants and jeans on and walked to the top of the stairs. 'I'm up 'ere. Sally's home, so we've been getting reacquainted, if you know what I mean.'

'Are the chavvies up there with ya?' Jimmy asked.

Jed felt the colour drain from his face. He'd got so used to his mum looking after the kids, he'd sort of forgotten she wasn't there. He ran down the stairs like a lunatic. 'Georgie! Harry!' he yelled.

Alice ran back into the hallway. She'd checked all the rooms and looked out the back. 'You stupid, selfish little bastard. The front door was open, you dinlo.'

As Alice began pummelling her son's bare chest with her fists, Jimmy searched for his mobile. He'd forgotten it earlier when he'd gone out with Alice. 'We'd better call the gavvers,' he yelled.

Alice stopped hitting her son and chased her husband into the lounge. 'No, dordie, no. If the gavvers get involved, we'll have social services knockin' on the door and they'll take the chavvies away from us. We gotta find 'em ourselves.'

Fuming that after such a good day his Alice was now in floods of tears, Jimmy grabbed his youngest son around the throat. He tapped his forehead with his free hand. 'You wanna start thinking with that rather than this,' he said as he kneed him in the bollocks.

'For fuck's sake, Jimmy, fighting ain't gonna find 'em. Let's go search for 'em,' Alice cried.

The house had automatic lights at the front and back, but Jimmy grabbed a couple of torches. Georgie was four and Harry was only three, so they couldn't have got far.

'You don't think the Mitchells have snatched 'em do you?' Jed asked, still holding his private parts.

'No chance, with Frankie still inside. It's more than they dare do,' Jimmy replied confidently.

'What's going on?' Sally asked, as she appeared at the top of the stairs.

Jed ignored her and pushed his parents out of the front door. He felt tearful now and sick with fear. He'd already lost one child and losing his other two didn't bear thinking about.

Stanley sat open-mouthed as Thelma and Louise prepared to drive off the cliff. It wasn't the film that was causing his state of shock, it was because Pat the Pigeon had just laid her head on his shoulder and put an arm across his belly.

Even as a lad, Stanley had been no lothario. Women had never liked him, full stop, and apart from the rare fumble with Joycie, he'd had fewer sexual encounters than a monk.

Willing Thelma and Louise to get on with it and drive off the bastard cliff, Stanley was relieved when they did so and as the credits rolled, he immediately faked a yawn and stood up. 'Oh well, that's me done for the night. Them bitters have knocked me out.'

'What about your rhubarb crumble?' Pat asked, sitting up straight.

'I'm still bloated from that stew, love. Is it OK if we eat it tomorrow?'

Pat the Pigeon was a five-foot-two, voluptuous and big-breasted blonde. She was in her mid-fifties, but still had a lovely complexion and an extremely pretty face. With her hearty laugh and sexy smile, men had always fallen at her feet and even when she'd been married to Vic, she'd had to fight off unwelcome advances from her army of admirers. Stanley was a different kettle of fish and as desperate as Pat was to get him into bed, she knew she had to play the waiting game.

'Slowly, slowly catchee monkey,' her wise old mum used to say.

'Yes, of course it's OK to eat it tomorrow, Stanley. You get off to that nice comfortable bed in the spare room and I'll see you in the morning, lovey.'

Desperate for his nan not to go off her head or get drunk and smash the house up like she did the last time when his grandad left home, Joey had offered to stay the night with her. Dominic, being the best partner a man could wish for, had just arrived with a big bag of fish and chips for them all.

Pleased that his nan was tucking in, Joey offered her another pickled onion.

'I bet that's the old bastard. He's probably too frightened to use his key,' Joyce said as the doorbell rang.

Positive it couldn't be his grandad, as they hadn't heard his car pull up, Joey put his plate down and stood up. He opened the door and could barely believe his eyes. Georgie was standing on a plant pot, which she'd used to reach the doorbell, and Harry was standing next to the pot, shivering and crying.

'Oh my God. Get inside, you're both freezing,' Joey urged his niece and nephew.

When the children walked into the room, Joyce dropped her dinner on the floor in shock and burst into tears. 'Oh, my little darlings,' she said, as she knelt down and hugged them both.

Dominic looked at Joey in astonishment. 'How did they get here? Did Jed drop them off?'

Joey knelt down, it had been raining for the past half an hour, so he took the children's coats off and ordered them to sit next to the fire. Harry was still sobbing and, overcome by emotion, he clung to his Nanny Joyce. Her cuddles reminded him of his mummy.

Joey knelt down and held Georgie in his arms. 'Who brought you here?' he asked her.

'No one. We ran away.'

As Georgie then burst into tears as well, Joey turned to Dominic. 'What are we gonna do?'

Dominic knelt down next to Joey. 'This is important, Georgie. Why did you run away? You must tell us what happened.'

'Because we wanted to see our mummy,' Georgie cried.

Joyce was the next to break down in tears. 'How did you find Nanny's house?' she wept.

''Cause I saw it when I was in Grandad Jimmy's truck.'

'Where is Mummy? Don't wanna live with Daddy no more,' Harry exclaimed, hiccupping.

Joyce held both children tightly to her chest. They were frozen stiff, the poor little mites. 'Shall Nanny make you something nice and hot to eat and drink? It will warm your cockles, I promise.'

Georgie and Harry both nodded. They had chucked the rest of their sandwiches away and, after their marathon walk, were now both starving.

Joyce walked out into the kitchen and urged Joey to follow her. 'What are we gonna do? We can't keep them 'ere, we'll get ourselves arrested. Should we ring the police?'

Joey thought momentarily, then shook his head. 'Not yet. I'm gonna ring Dad, he'll sort it out.'

Hearing Georgie and Harry chatting in the other room to Dominic, Joyce placed the sausages in the frying pan. She had missed her great-grandchildren so much and perhaps now they had run to her in their hour of need, something good might come out of this. Perhaps the authorities might let her have some kind of access to them.

Joyce made two mugs of hot chocolate and added some cold water so the poor little ha'porths didn't burn themselves. 'There you go, me little angels,' she said, handing the mugs to them.

'Can we see Mummy soon?' Harry asked innocently.

'Mummy isn't here, love. But she told me to tell you that she can still see you from where she is and she loves you both very much.'

'Daddy says Mummy is in prison and Nanny Alice says she

is an evil old shitcunt,' Georgie said, not quite understanding the meaning of her words.

'If anyone is evil, it's your Nanny Alice, not your mother,' Joyce said standing up. She could smell the sausages burning.

Joey ended his phone call and walked into the kitchen. 'Me dad said don't do nothing till he gets there. He's on his way.'

CHAPTER EIGHT

Eddie Mitchell rang his trusted solicitor Larry, then hit a ton as he zoomed along the A13. Gina announcing she was pregnant had been a big enough bolt out of the blue, but finding out that his grandkids had run away and turned up at Joycie's had literally knocked him for six. What was God trying to do? Give him a fucking heart attack?

Hearing his dad pull up outside, Joey opened the front door and ran outside to greet him.

'How are they? Are they OK?' Eddie asked, concerned.

Joey nodded. 'Nan's just made 'em sausage sandwiches and given 'em a hot bath. They was in a right state when they arrived though, Dad. Their clothes were soaked and they were frozen stiff. They could have been snatched by some pervert or anything.'

Eddie nodded, then put an arm around Joey's shoulder. 'Have they said why they ran away?'

'Yeah, they wanted to see Frankie. They said they missed their mum.'

As tough a man as he was, Eddie felt his eyes well up as he walked into the lounge. Georgie and Harry were sitting either side of Joycie. They both had big white bath towels wrapped around them and were munching on a bowl of crisps that was positioned on Joycie's lap.

'Look, Grandad Eddie's here. Go and give him a cuddle,' Joyce urged them.

Harry loved a cuddle, so he immediately stood up, and held his arms wide open. He didn't care that his towel dropped to the floor.

Eddie picked up Harry's naked little body and swung him

around in the air. 'Hello, me little bruiser, Grandad loves you, you know,' he said, planting kisses on his face.

Georgie sat motionless on the sofa. She knew she had a Grandad Stanley and a Grandad Jimmy, but she didn't really remember her Grandad Eddie. She was sure she had heard her mum mention him, but he didn't look familiar to her.

'Give your Grandad a kiss, Georgie,' Joyce ordered.

Eddie sat Harry on the sofa next to his sister, then knelt down in front of the pair of them. Apart from a quick glance when he'd knocked at O'Hara's house, he hadn't seen Georgie for well over a year, but still felt hurt that she didn't seem to remember him. He spoke gently. 'I know neither of you really know who I am, but that's my fault because I had to go away somewhere. I'm your mum's dad, your Grandad Eddie.'

Georgie and Harry glanced at one another. Within seconds, Georgie had worked it all out. 'What, like my dad is Jed and you are Eddie, Mummy's dad?'

Eddie smiled. 'That's right, and being your mum's dad makes me your grandad.'

Georgie smiled and then hugged him. If this man was her mum's dad, then she liked him.

'Can we see Mummy now?' Harry asked again.

'Hopefully you can soon, but you have to do what I tell you to do, is that OK? Will you do that for me?'

Georgie and Harry both nodded excitedly. They couldn't wait to see their mum.

'In a little while a man and a lady are going to come here. You must tell them that you ran away from home because you miss your mum so much. The lady will ask you some questions and you must tell her that you don't like living with your dad, Nanny Alice and Grandad Jimmy. Tell her you want to live with Nanny Joyce, Uncle Joey, or me.'

'Will she take us to see Mummy then?' Harry enquired.

'Not tonight, but hopefully very soon,' Eddie replied.

'Why did Mummy leave us?' Georgie asked sadly.

Eddie stroked her long, dark hair. 'Your Mummy didn't leave you. She would never do that because she loves you and Harry more than anything in the world. Something happened between your mum and dad and the police took your mummy away for a little while.'

Georgie chewed her fingernails. 'Is Mummy in prison? Daddy says she is and Nanny Alice says she's an old shitcunt.'

Eddie could barely believe what he was hearing. He was no angel, but how could any grandmother teach her four-year-old granddaughter that type of language? 'Your Nanny Alice needs her mouth washed out with soap. Tell the lady that as well, Georgie, tell her what Nanny Alice said about your mum. Don't forget, will ya?'

'She said Mummy is an old shitcunt,' Harry repeated proudly. Neither child was old enough to understand the meaning of such awful language.

'Good boy,' Eddie said, patting Harry on the head. Larry and the social worker would be here soon, and they needed to get this right. 'Now, I want you to pretend that I'm the lady and when I ask you a question, you are to answer it like I told you to. Can you do that for me?'

Both children nodded.

'So, why did you run away from home?' Eddie asked.

Joyce, Joey and Dominic all smiled at one another as the children repeated what Ed had told them to say. Georgie was especially convincing, as she answered every question in detail with the answers her grandfather had given her.

'Was that your idea or Larry's, Dad?' Joey asked, impressed.

'A bit of both really, but it was Larry's idea to get the social worker involved. She's got a lot of sway, apparently.'

'I can't believe the O'Haras ain't knocked here. I mean, surely they know the kids are missing,' Joyce said, perplexed.

'They're scum, what do you expect?' Eddie replied.

Dominic turned to Georgie and Harry. 'Where was your dad, nan and grandad when you ran away? Were they all at home?' he asked.

Both children shook their heads. 'Nanny Alice and Grandad Jimmy went out and Daddy was in the front room with Sally, making funny noises,' Georgie replied.

Eddie glanced at Joey, shook his head and knelt down again. 'Tell the lady that as well. Tell her that when you ran away, Daddy was making funny noises with his girlfriend in another room.'

Georgie grinned and nodded eagerly. She really liked her Grandad Eddie; he was cool and treated her like a big girl. 'Can we live with you, Grandad?' she asked hopefully.

Feeling himself getting all emotional again, Eddie stood up. Anything could have happened to those kids today, absolutely anything. Say some nonce-case had spotted them and abducted them? The O'Haras wanted shooting and the fact that they'd put his grandchildren in danger made Ed want to be the one to pull that trigger even more.

'Where you goin', Grandad?' Harry asked as Eddie bolted from the room.

'Toilet,' Eddie lied. The truth was, he was struggling to hold back the tears and it wasn't in his nature to show weakness, not even in front of his own.

Alice O'Hara was inconsolable. Crying one minute, screaming, ranting and raving the next. She was losing the plot, especially with Jed, and Jimmy knew it. They'd all spent an hour searching on foot, but there was neither hide nor hair of Georgie or Harry. It was as though the kids had disappeared into thin air. Knowing they had to widen their search, Jimmy had now called reinforcements in. His nephew Sammy had already arrived and his son Billy was on his way and was bringing another four blokes from his site with him. Pat Murphy had offered to help as well. He'd got here within minutes of Jimmy's phone call, as he only lived down the road.

'Don't just fucking stand there, then!' Alice screamed at everyone.

Jimmy grabbed hold of his wife and held her shaking body close to his chest. 'We're just waiting for Billy boy, love, and then we'll jump in three or four motors and we'll find them. They'll be OK, I promise you that.'

'You promised me Marky's funeral would be OK and look what happened there. As for you,' Alice yelled, breaking free from her husband and punching her youngest son in the side of his head, 'you ain't fit to be a father, you selfish, no-good cunt.'

As Sally tried to cuddle him, Jed pushed her away. He blamed his girlfriend entirely for what had happened. It was all her fault; he'd been happily watching the telly with the kids until she'd started rubbing his cock. She should never have done that, not when she knew he had to look after Georgie and Harry.

'Do yourself a favour and go back to your father's tonight, Sally. I ain't in the best of moods, OK? If you hadn't have come round 'ere today, none of this would have happened.'

Sally looked at Jed with an incredulous expression on her face. None of this was her bloody fault. How could he even say that when the reason her beautiful son was dead was because of him?

'You bastard! My Lukey boy died because somebody was trying to shoot *you*. How can you blame me for this, Jed? After everything we've been through, how could you be so callous?'

'Don't you dare blame that girl,' Alice yelled at Jed.

Desperate to get back into his mother's good books, Jed did what he was best at and lied. 'You don't know the fucking half of it, Mum. I told her to leave me alone, but she kept touching me in front of Georgie and Harry. I didn't want them to see all that shit, that's why we went upstairs. I mean, I ain't had sex for weeks, so what was I supposed to do?'

Jed had always been the apple of Alice's eye and she was now glad she had an excuse to stop hating him and blame somebody else. 'Go home, Sally, and don't fucking come back until you learn how to behave,' she screamed viciously.

Jed pushed Sally towards the front door. 'Wait at the end of the drive. I'll order you a cab and ring you tomorrow.'

Sally was in floods of tears. Her dad was right, the O'Haras were scumbags and Jed was a lying, cheating, no-good bastard.

Seeing his brother Billy pull into the drive, Jed waved his hand for him to stop, then ran over to Sally.

'I'll bell you when the chavvies are home,' he said, attempting to peck her on the cheek.

Sally turned her head and, seeing Jed for what he really was for the first time ever, boldly spat in his face. 'Drop dead, you shit-bag. And I swear, if you ever try to contact me again, I will make sure my dad fucking kills you!'

Larry Peters arrived at Joycie's at 9 p.m. He had represented the Mitchell family and had been on their payroll for many decades, hence his quick response to Eddie's phone call. When asked by some of the snobs in his profession about his relationship with the notorious clan, Larry liked to describe himself as a family friend. He had been especially close to Harry, Eddie's father, and had been devastated when Harry had met his maker in such awful circumstances.

Larry turned the ignition off, got out of the car and opened the passenger door for Carol. Larry had known Carol Cullen for many years. She had done him a few favours in the past and vice versa and he knew she was the right person to be involved in an incident like this. If anyone could pull some strings for him in social services then that woman was Carol.

Eddie opened the front door, shook Larry's hand and was then introduced to Carol. 'Thank you so much for visiting us at such short notice. My grandchildren have had the most awful ordeal and I'm very concerned over their future well-being. They miss their mother enormously,' he said, laying it on as much as he could.

Carol shook his hand, then walked into the living room and smiled at Georgie and Harry.

'Hello, my name is Carol. Wow, don't yous two look nice and snug with them big bath towels wrapped around you?'

'Can you take us to see our mummy?' Harry blurted out.

Carol hated making promises if she couldn't keep them. 'Hopefully, I can organise a visit so you can see your mum, but first I need to ask you some questions, is that OK?'

Georgie and Harry both nodded. Their grandad had now told them numerous times what they had to say and his words were firmly drummed into their little brains.

'Do you mind if I speak to the children alone? It's the usual procedure,' Carol asked Eddie.

Larry had prewarned him that Carol would probably ask to speak to the kids alone, so Eddie nodded and he, Dominic, Joey and Joycie left the room.

'I hope they remember everything you told them,' Joyce whispered.

'Of course they will. They ain't silly kids, especially Georgie. Bright as a button, she is,' Eddie said confidently.

Larry joined the quartet in the kitchen. 'Did you have a chat with 'em, like I told you to, Ed?'

Eddie nodded. 'So what happens next, you know, after she's spoken to 'em?'

'I briefed Carol about everything that has happened in the children's lives on the way down here. Once she has finished speaking to them, she will inform the police that they are here, so it gets noted. I have a feeling that when the O'Haras realised they were missing, rather than involve the police, they have probably been searching for them themselves. You know what travellers are like, Ed, they hate the police and everything they stand for. If my theory is right and they haven't contacted the authorities by the time we do, that will go very much in our favour to getting some kind of access. I should imagine the children will almost certainly be allowed to visit Frankie on a regular basis. She is their mother, after all. Now, if you'll excuse me, I am in desperate need of a visit to the lavatory.'

'Where's Stanley, Joyce? Out the back with them birds of his?' Eddie asked.

Joyce had barely given her husband a second thought for the past few hours. She wasn't worried – she knew Stanley too well – and was positive he would be back home in the next couple of days with his tail between those knobbly knees of his.

'Stanley's stomped off in one of his tantrums, the silly old bastard. He found out that I'd met you in the Bull that time and threw all his toys out of his pram,' Joyce replied.

'Oh, I'm sorry, Joycie. How did he find out?' Eddie asked.

'No idea, he was too busy asking for a divorce to tell me that vital piece of information,' Joyce said, laughing.

Dominic glanced at his watch. He had an early meeting in the morning with a potential billionaire investor. 'Do you mind if I make a move, Joey? I've got that meeting early tomorrow morning with that American guy I told you about. I would stay here with you, but I've no change of clothes and Madonna will need to be fed and watered.'

Joey put a casual arm around his boyfriend's shoulder. 'You get off, Dom. I'll stay here with Nan tonight. Perhaps pick me up tomorrow when you finish work. I'll have to call in sick again, I'm afraid, but it can't be helped.'

Eddie shook Dominic's hand. 'Thanks for being there for my Joey, mate. You're a good lad.'

Joycie grinned. Sod Stanley's sulks, Eddie had now fully accepted Joey and Dominic's relationship and that was all that mattered.

In the lounge, Carol was still talking to Georgie and Harry. Both children had spoken candidly about why they had run away, and their love for their mother was clear to see. 'So, has your daddy explained why your mummy had to go away for a while?' she asked.

Remembering her grandfather's words, Georgie nodded. 'Daddy told us that Mummy was evil and Nanny Alice said that Mummy was in prison because she's an old shitcunt.'

'Nanny told me that, too,' Harry chipped in. He was determined to do his bit for the cause.

Carol was horrified. She was used to dealing with children that came from deprived homes, but what sort of grandmother was Nanny Alice to use vile words like 'shitcunt' to children so young? Carol stood up; she had made plenty of notes of her conversation with the children and now it was her duty to call the police.

'Can we see Mummy now?' Harry asked her again.

Carol smiled and ruffled his hair. 'Hopefully, you can see your mummy soon and I promise I'll do my best to make sure that happens.'

Eddie looked at Carol with expectation as she walked into the kitchen. 'Well, did they answer all your questions OK?' he asked.

'Yes, they did, and they have given me plenty of insight into the family they are currently living with. I am going to ring the police now and they will collect the children and take them back home. I shall then submit my report to my husband, who is in charge of this entire area.'

Joyce was gutted. Having the children at home had made her forget about all her other problems.

'Do they have to go back to the O'Haras? They obviously aren't happy living there and I'm willing to look after them,' she pleaded.

'I'm afraid the law says they do have to go back to their

father, for now at least. I do understand how worried you are for their welfare, but these things take time. The one thing I am sure about is that I can arrange a regular visit for the children to see their mother. My husband, Phillip, is actually in charge of social services in this area, and I can make sure that definitely happens. As for the children being taken away from their father, with the circumstances of their mother's plight, that might prove to be quite difficult.'

'Go and sit with the kids,' Eddie ordered Joey and Joyce. 'Why is it so difficult to take them away from the scumbags they're currently living with?' he asked Carol. 'I'm willing to look after them and even if my police record puts the kibosh on that, Joyce will have them until Frankie comes home.'

Larry gave Eddie a warning look. His voice was raised, and if he lost his cool, it could balls everything up.

'I'm sorry, Mr Mitchell, but it's just not that simple. Now, if you will excuse me, I really do have to call the police now,' said Carol.

Realising that his adorable grandchildren were about to be carted off back to what he fondly described as 'pikey hell', Eddie stomped into the lounge and crouched down in front of them.

'Did you tell the lady everything I told you to?' he whispered.

Georgie and Harry both nodded. 'Can we see Mummy now?' Harry asked, his voice filled with hopeful innocence.

Joyce and Joey both had tears in their eyes as Eddie explained that the police were coming round and the children would have to be taken back to live with their father.

Georgie and Harry started to cry. It had been a long day and they were both physically and mentally drained. 'But we don't want to live there, we want to live with you, Grandad,' Georgie pleaded.

Eddie leaned forward and held both sobbing children close to his chest. He had rarely cried after he'd reached the age of ten, but for once he couldn't control the tears rolling down his cheeks.

'Everything is gonna work out just fine. Your grandad will make sure of that, I promise.'

CHAPTER NINE

Harry O'Hara was first to wake up the following morning. His Nanny Alice had ordered his Grandad Jimmy to sleep elsewhere, so that he and Georgie could share the bed with her. Harry was careful as he prodded Georgie. His nan was snoring like a disgruntled pig and he didn't want to wake her. He actually preferred her when she was sleeping.

Georgie sat up, rubbed her eyes and smiled at Harry. Neither of them had wanted to come home last night, but the police had made them. Both children had cried themselves to sleep, but this morning, they felt brighter. The nice social worker lady had promised she would arrange visits so they could see their mum. She even said she would try to sort it so they could see their Nanny Joyce again as well. They had asked her if they could see Grandad Eddie also, but she hadn't answered that question.

'My legs hurt,' Harry mumbled, remembering his ordeal from the day before. He wasn't used to long walks and his knee was grazed and scabby from where he had fallen over.

'I'm hungry. Shall we get some breakfast?' Georgie whispered.

As the children quietly got out of bed, Alice sat bolt upright. 'What you doing? Where you going?' she asked fearfully. She immediately presumed they were about to do a runner again.

'We're hungry, Nanny, we want some food,' Georgie replied.

Alice leaped out of bed and put on her slippers and dressing gown. She was so relieved to have the children home safe that after the police had left last night, Alice had vowed to Jimmy to move heaven and earth to make them happy again.

'Nanny'll cook breakfast for you. What do you want? How 'bout a nice fry-up?'

Georgie glanced at Harry and both children shook their heads. Since Marky and Lukey boy had died, nobody had been very nice to them. Everybody had virtually ignored them, even their dad, and Georgie instinctively knew that running away would change all that. Their escape could only make life better for them.

'Me and Harry don't like your fry-up. We like toast with Marmite and cheese on top, that's what Mummy used to cook us,' Georgie said brazenly.

Alice ignored the mention of Frankie, crouched down and hugged both children close to her chest. She had been so wrapped up in her own grief, she had sort of neglected these two and they needed her, needed her badly.

'From now on, yous two cheeky little chavvies can have whatever you bleedin' well want. Your Nanny Alice loves you both very much.'

Eddie had woken up early, made love to Gina, then ordered her to have a lie-in while he cooked the breakfast, for a change. Watching his grandkids being carted off back to the O'Haras' last night had upset Ed immensely. He had spoken to the police and demanded answers as to why the O'Haras hadn't reported them missing in the first place.

'They should be with us, a normal family who would love and care for them, instead of living with a load of two-bob pikeys,' he'd insisted.

The two coppers had very nearly burst out laughing. Neither had ever had any personal dealings with the Mitchells before, but every police force in England were well aware who they were, what had befallen them in the past, and they were anything but bloody normal.

When Ed had got back home last night, he'd poured himself a large Scotch and had a proper heart-to-heart with Gina about the upbringing of their baby. Eddie had insisted that she must give up her job for good and be a full-time mum and, as luck would have it, she had seen sense and agreed.

'I always told myself that the day I fell pregnant I would walk away from it all. I loved being a private detective but it's a job for a childless woman, not a mother,' Gina admitted, not wanting Eddie to think she was jacking it in just because he wanted her to.

As he was about to scramble some eggs, Eddie's mobile rang, so he took the saucepan off the hob. It was Gary. He had had a problem with a geezer who had done a bunk. 'What does he owe?' Eddie asked, when Gary finally stopped talking.

'Well, he borrowed twelve grand and promised he would pay it back in six weeks, so me and Ricky did a deal with him. He was desperate for it that day, so we said yes, but only if he paid us back sixteen. We said we'd take ten in a month, then give him the extra two weeks to pay the odd six. It was a month yesterday since we lent it to him, so we went round to his gaff to pick the ten up. When we got there, we found out he'd done a runner. It didn't take us long to find out where he was. We gave his mate a proper good dig and then he gave us the address. I tried to ring you all last night, but I couldn't get hold of you. Where was you?'

'What's the cunt's name?' Eddie spat, ignoring the question. He'd been in the money-lending game for years now and because of his reputation, people rarely dared take the piss out of him.

'Colin Griffiths, but he sometimes uses Simmons as his surname as well. He used to be a publican, ran a couple of dives in Barking and a couple more in East Ham. I think he might have even ran the Central at one point.'

Eddie was fuming. He and Raymond had a meeting with a geezer over in Whitechapel who owned boozers in the East End and wanted to pay protection to get rid of an Asian gang who had been making a nuisance of themselves. Ed made his decision and smashed his fist against the wall in annoyance. Twelve grand was peanuts to him, but it was the fucking principle, not the money. 'I'll tell Raymond to go to our meeting alone and I'll pick you and Rick up in an hour, Gal.'

Over in Holloway, Frankie was in a far happier mood than her father was. The prison had organised an antenatal class for anyone on the maternity wing who wanted to attend, and she and Babs had put their names down for something to do.

In the maternity ward there were a lot of young girls who were first-time mothers, and their faces were a picture as the woman was describing 'how to give birth in the correct manner' out of some textbook she was reading from. The woman's posh voice wasn't doing her any favours, either. Most of the girls in Holloway were as common as muck, and they had never heard anybody who spoke the way she did; she sounded as if she had a plum in her mouth, and even Frankie was shocked by her upper-class accent.

When the woman picked up a doll, put it in a plastic bath and said the word 'vagina' as she was washing it, nearly all the lags burst out laughing. In their world it was called a noony, a snatch, a cunt or a fanny.

As she and Babs were giggling, Frankie noticed a girl with dark hair staring at her. She had seen the same girl looking at her earlier. 'Don't look now, but there's a girl that keeps looking at me. She's got a black cardigan on, curly shoulder-length hair and she's on your left. Look in a minute and see if you know who she is.'

Babs did as Frankie asked, then nudged her pal. 'Never seen her before. Perhaps she's a lezzie and fancies you.'

'Don't say that, that's all I'm short of,' Frankie said worriedly.

Laughing, Babs gently punched Frankie on the arm. 'I'm only winding you up. If she was a lezzie I doubt she'd be preggers, would she? And even if she was one of them bisexual bitches, you've no worries, 'cause Babbsy will look after you, sweet child.'

When the posh woman ended her speech with, 'May God bless each and every one of you,' Frankie stood up with the rest of the girls. The girl who had been staring at her immediately approached her.

'Are you Jed O'Hara's girlfriend?' she asked.

Frankie was instantly on her guard. The girl was obviously a traveller; she had the same strange accent as Jed and his family.

'Who wants to know?' she asked boldly.

The girl held out her right hand and smiled. 'I'm Katie, Katie Cooper. I don't know if Jed ever mentioned my sister, Debbie. She went out with him for a year when he was fourteen. Debs was older than him, she was sixteen at the time.'

Frankie shook her head. 'No, he didn't and Jed's not my boyfriend, he's my ex.'

Katie shook her head understandingly. 'I heard what happened, news travels fast in our community. Jed's a bastard and I don't blame you for what you did to him. I wish I'd had the guts to do the same to him and that cousin of his myself as payback for what he did to me and my sister.'

Frankie looked at the girl suspiciously. 'All travellers stick together,' Jed had always told her.

'Mitchell, move, come on, and you, Lewis, back to your cells,' the screw shouted at Frankie and Babs. Babs stared at the screw. She was going nowhere without her friend.

'Come on, let's go,' Babs said, urging Frankie to move away from the girl.

Frankie allowed herself to be led away. She didn't like Katie – she was a traveller and Frankie had never met a decent one yet. Glancing around to make sure Katie wasn't behind her, Frankie turned to Babs.

'I don't trust her. She's probably one of Jed's spies and he's told her to befriend me.'

Babs put a comforting arm around Frankie's shoulder. She could tell that speaking to that girl had upset her, reminded her of the past. 'There ain't many people you can trust in here at all, honey.'

Frankie linked arms with Babs. She trusted her with her life. 'Especially travellers. I fucking hate 'em, Babs.'

Back at the O'Haras', Georgie and Harry were both being thoroughly spoiled rotten. Their dad hadn't left their side all morning, neither had Nanny Alice or Grandad Jimmy and they'd been playing games with them, which was unheard of in the past. Usually Georgie and Harry were expected to amuse themselves.

Alice heard a car pull up outside and looked out of the window. 'Oh dordie, it's the gavvers and they've got some woman in a smart suit with them. They ain't taking the chavvies away, are they?' she asked, petrified.

Jimmy put a comforting arm around his wife's shoulder and ordered Jed to answer the door. 'It'll be OK. They probably just wanna check that Georgie and Harry are OK,' Jimmy assured his wife.

'What's the problem?' Jed asked, as he opened the front door. There was a male and female copper and also an important-looking woman in a smart grey suit.

'Are you Jed O'Hara, Harry and Georgina's father?' the policewoman asked. Carol Cullen had asked the police to accompany her, as she suspected a breach of the peace could take place.

Jed nodded. He hated the Old Bill, wanted to tell 'em to fuck off, but he knew that kind of behaviour wouldn't do him any favours. 'Georgie and Harry are absolutely fine. They're in the living room playing with their grandparents,' he said politely.

'I'm DS Fletcher and my colleague is PC Hughes. Could we come in, Mr O'Hara? Mrs Cullen needs to speak to you about the children.'

Jed immediately started to panic and dropped his politeness. 'Who is she?' he asked, pointing at the woman in the smart suit.

'I'm Mrs Cullen,' the woman said, holding out her right hand.

Jed ignored the gesture, 'Who are you, then? What do you want? We ain't committed no crime.'

'I'm a social worker and I need to speak to you regarding your children's welfare.'

Jed unwillingly led the trio into the lounge. If they could see the kids were happy, with a bit of luck they would piss off and leave his family alone.

Alice was shaking like a leaf as Jed handed out the introductions. The gavvers always scared her, but today the social worker accompanying them was scaring her more.

'Hello,' Georgie said beaming, as she spotted the nice lady who had come to Nanny Joycie's house the previous evening.

'Can we see Mummy now?' Harry asked bluntly.

Carol crouched down and patted both children on the head. 'How are you both today?' she asked.

'OK. Daddy, Nanny Alice and Grandad Jimmy have been playing cowboys and Indians with us,' Georgie replied happily.

'That sounds like fun,' Carol said, as she stood up and turned back to the adults.

'You ain't takin' 'em away. I won't allow it,' Alice said, tears streaming down her face.

'Stop worrying. Nobody's taking the children away from you,' Carol said kindly.

DS Fletcher cleared her throat. She had only recently been promoted to DS after being in the force for many years and she took her new role extremely seriously. 'Why didn't you report the children missing yesterday?' she asked.

Jed felt his hackles rise. 'I explained all this last night. We were searching for 'em ourselves. Us travellers are a close-knit community. I had my own reinforcements, so there was no need to bother you. I knew they'd turn up alive and well anyway, kids always do.'

DS Fletcher looked at Jed in disbelief. Any nutter could have picked up those poor children yesterday. 'Do you not realise the seriousness of not reporting the disappearance of children so young? They could have been abducted by a paedophile, run over – anything could have happened to them.'

Jed was beginning to lose his temper now. What was the bitch insinuating – that he was a bad parent? 'All kids run away. I did it loads of times when I was their age. It's all part of growing up, ain't it? Anyway, I've had a good chat with them and both Georgie girl and Harry have promised me faithfully that they will never do anything like that again.'

Jed turned to his children. 'Go on, you tell the policewoman that you won't run off again, like you told me.'

'We promise we won't run off again,' Georgie said.

'I won't, 'cause my legs hurt,' Harry mumbled.

'We idolise them kids and you can see that they're clean, loved and well fed,' Alice said proudly.

Jimmy put a comforting arm around Jed's shoulder. If his son lost his temper, which he was quite capable of, the kids might be carted off there and then.

Carol Cullen turned to Jed. 'Could I speak to you alone for a minute?'

Jed led her out to the kitchen. He'd seen his mum give him a warning look and he knew he had to learn how to control his temper more, especially when dealing with the authorities. 'I'm sorry if I've been a bit snappy, but what with my brother being killed and then Luke, my son, it's been a tough time lately,' he explained.

Carol nodded understandingly. 'The reason I've come here to see you today is about access for the children to visit their mother. I spoke to Georgie and Harry at length last night and it is clear that they miss their mother dreadfully and, in my opinion, it would be in their best interests if they were to have contact with her.'

Jed stood with his mouth wide open. He couldn't quite believe what he was hearing. 'Are you serious? Frankie is a loony, a proper nutter. She tried to kill me, for fuck's sake. Would you want your kids seeing a potential murderer? I love my chavvies and I don't want them anywhere near that monster of a mother of theirs.'

'Calm down, Mr O'Hara. If you keep behaving like this, I will have to write a bad report on you and chances are you will lose your children for good.'

Telling Jed he might lose his children was like waving a red rag at a bull. 'Get out of my house, you fucking shitcunt!' he shouted as he tried to bundle Carol Cullen towards the front door.

Jimmy, Alice and the two police officers heard the fracas and ran out to the kitchen.

'Whatever's going on? Leave my boy alone,' Alice screamed, as the two Old Bill grabbed hold of Jed.

'Calm down, you dinlo,' Jimmy yelled, as Jed tried desperately to free himself.

Georgie and Harry had followed everybody else and were now standing at the kitchen door, holding hands.

'They wanna let my chavvies visit that slag in prison,' Jed shrieked.

'Over my dead body are they visiting that evil whore,' Alice yelled.

Guessing that they were discussing her mum, by the words 'visit' and 'prison', Georgie put her two penn'orth in. 'But me and Harry want to see Mummy. That's why we ran away, 'cause we wanted to find Mummy.'

As Jed began to scream at Georgie, Jimmy shoved him and Alice out of the back door and locked it. 'Jed don't mean to get angry. He's so stressed at the moment, what with his boy being murdered,' he explained.

'One more outburst from your son and he's nicked,' Fletcher replied meaningfully.

Carol felt dreadfully sorry for Georgie and Harry. Life with the O'Haras seemed even worse than she'd anticipated it to be.

'Can we see Mummy now?' Harry asked her innocently.

Carol led them into the lounge and sat down next to them on the sofa. 'I'm going to take your case to something called a civil court and then hopefully you will be able to see your mummy again.'

Eddie Mitchell was not in the best of moods. Driving to Milton Keynes to extract money out of some prick who had under-estimated him was one reason, and the other were the looks on Gary and Ricky's faces when he'd just told them that Gina was pregnant.

'Fucking hell! Anyone would think that I'd just told you someone you were close to had died. Ain't you happy for us, or what?'

Gary glanced at his brother. Both were thinking about their future inheritance. 'Yeah, course we are, but a newborn baby's a lot to take on at your age, ain't it?'

Eddie slammed his foot on the brake and mounted the kerb. 'I'm fifty-three, not eighty,' he yelled angrily.

'Does Frankie know yet?' Ricky asked. His half-sister was not going to be pleased; she hadn't even come to terms with her dad being with Gina yet.

'I'm visiting Frankie tomorrow, so I'll tell her then. Joey, I'll ring tonight. I saw him yesterday, but with all the chaos over Georgie and Harry, it was neither the time nor the place. Now check that map and see where we are. It's Bradwell village we're looking for.'

Ricky gave him directions. Five minutes later, they'd found where they were looking for. 'This is it. Do a right here, then first left and it's number sixty-six.'

Eddie pulled up a few doors away from the address. He

glanced around to make sure nobody was about, then got out of his Range Rover. 'Does he live here with anyone?' he asked Gary.

'Dunno. The geezer never said.'

Ed grabbed his baseball bat from under the back seat. It was a standing joke between him and the boys that they carried the full baseball kit around with them. They even had catcher's mitts and a helmet complete with ear flaps. They'd got tugged a good few years back, just before Ed had got put away, and the filth had swallowed the lie that Gary was training to become a professional baseball player. They'd cracked up for days over that one.

'You knock,' Eddie ordered Ricky, as he stood to the side of the porch and placed the bat beside the wall.

'Is Colin in?' Ricky asked, as a plump, dark-haired bird with big knockers answered the door.

'No, I think you've got the wrong house. My fella's called John,' she said.

'This is definitely the right address,' Ricky insisted.

The woman shook her head. 'We're not from round here, we're from East London. We only moved here two weeks ago, so maybe you're looking for the previous tenant.'

Eddie poked his head around the porch door and smiled. The mention of East London had given it away; Colin was obviously using a different Christian name and was now calling himself John. 'Where is your bloke, out of interest? Can I have a word with him? You never know, he might have a forwarding address for Colin. We need to contact him because his mum has died and it's her funeral on Friday.'

'Are you three policemen?' the woman asked.

'Yes, love,' Ed said politely.

'You'll find my John in a pub called the Victoria Inn. Spends half his life in there since we moved here, he does. His surname is Griffiths,' the woman said laughing.

Eddie grinned at the woman, then walked away. 'Thank you, you've been most helpful, and I'll tell you something else, if I had a pretty woman like you indoors, I wouldn't be spending all my time in a pub.'

The woman giggled, waved and closed the front door.

Eddie, Gary and Ricky walked back to the Range Rover. They all knew that John Griffiths was actually Colin. The dickhead was even using his own surname.

'We passed that boozer on the way 'cre, it's only a couple of minutes down the road. What I suggest is yous two go in and bring the cheeky cunt outside. I'll wait in the motor and then we'll take him for a nice little ride.'

Eddie watched the boys walk into the boozer, then collared a man walking his dog. 'Excuse me, is there any forestry or woods around here? My son has taken our dog for a walk and has rung me and asked me to pick him up. We're new around here, so he's a bit lost, I think.'

The man nodded, then gave directions. 'Come on, Poppy,' he said, as he toddled off with his faithful friend by his side.

Seconds later, Eddie saw Gary and Ricky walk out of the pub alone. 'Where the fuck is he, then?' Ed asked as they got in the motor.

'Gary'll explain,' Ricky said, leaving his brother to do the talking.

'The bloke who lives at the house we knocked at *is* called John Griffiths. He was in the boozer; we've just spoken to him. He's just moved here from Custom House.'

Ed glared at Gary. 'You've gotta be havin' me on.'

'It ain't all bad news. The geezer knew Colin, says he drinks in that pub an' all. He reckons he lives at number six, not sixty-six. I must have misheard that arsehole we gave a dig to and took the address down wrong, unless he gave me a dodgy one on purpose.'

'Well, let's go and knock at number six then.'

Gary shook his head. 'Colin has gone to the Canary Islands, Gran Canaria apparently. He ain't due back until Saturday week. That John hates him, said he's a right mouthy prick. He told me that Colin gets in the boozer at twelve on the dot every lunchtime.'

Eddie smashed his fist against the steering wheel. His bad mood had just doubled. Not only had he had a wasted trip to Milton Keynes, and now had to come back there again, but the shit-bag that had ripped him off was now pissing his money up in sunny climates, the cheeky bastard.

Eddie started the ignition and sped off like a loony. 'I tell you something, and I mean this. When I catch up with Colin Deadman Griffiths, not only am I gonna make him pay me twenty-five grand back, I'm also gonna disfigure the cunt for life. No one takes the piss out of me and gets away with it, and I mean no one!'

CHAPTER TEN

Jimmy O'Hara met his contact in the Derby Digger in Wickford. Bobby Berkley was a lifelong family friend and was also the brother of Pete Berkley, who was coming towards the end of a ten stretch in Belmarsh. Pete was willing to carry out the killing of Ronny and Paulie alone for the sum of twenty grand.

At first Jimmy had ummed and aahed over the wonga Pete demanded. He knew a few travellers in Belmarsh who would probably do the job a lot cheaper, but in the end, he had decided to stump up the cash. Mitchell had given him thirty, so whatever he shelled out, he was still in credit and that thought made Jimmy smile. Mitchell paying him to kill his own brothers while giving him a good drink on top was the stuff that dreams were made of.

Bobby Berkley stood up and shook Jimmy's hand. 'What are you drinking, pal?'

'I'll have a pint of bitter,' Jimmy said, sitting down at the table.

Bobby returned with the drinks and the men got straight down to business.

'As agreed, there's five up front and you'll get the other fifteen when the job's done,' Jimmy said, as he handed Bobby an envelope under the table.

'I'm visiting Pete on Wednesday and will tell him it's all systems go. He's on the same wing as Ronny and Paulie and he's already been watching their movements,' Bobby said.

'I don't care how he does it, I just want 'em both dead and I want it done before Christmas.'

Bobby nodded understandingly. 'Don't worry. Pete won't let you down.'

Back in Rainham, Joycie Smith was starting to get very worried. She still hadn't heard a dickie bird from Stanley, and had no idea of his whereabouts. When Stanley had had his little tantrums in the past, he'd always gone to Jock's or their old house in Upney. He was at neither this time, as he'd fallen out with Jock and their old house had now been sold.

Joyce made herself a brew and sat on the sofa feeling desperately sorry for herself. Their house was in the middle of nowhere, down a country lane, and without Stanley and the car, Joyce felt like a prisoner in her own home. There wasn't even a bus stop nearby. Stanley always drove her to and from the nearest one if she wanted to go into Romford or somewhere. Knowing that she would need to go food shopping in the next day or two, Joycie's worry quickly turned to fury. She debated whether to ring Joey and Dominic and ask them to take her to Tesco tomorrow, but immediately decided against it. The poor little sods lived miles away and it wasn't fair to keep spoiling their weekends. Getting more angry by the second, Joyce picked up the phone and dialled Jock's number.

'Jock, it's me, Joycie. Have you found out where that senile old bastard is yet?'

'I haven't, Joycie. I ain't heard a word from him, love.'

'Well, I need you to do me a favour. I've got hardly no food here and I need to do a shop, so you're gonna have to go to his little drinking haunts and find him for me. I need him to come home now, Jock.'

'I don't think Stanley's gonna take orders from me, Joycie. The best I can do is pop up to where the pigeon club drinks and see if I can find out where he's staying. If so, I'll get the address for you.'

'Thank you, and if you get no joy, let me know and I'm calling the police. The old goat could be lying dead in a ditch for all I know. Then again, I doubt I'd be that lucky.'

Jock laughed at Joycie's warped sense of humour. 'I'll go

and see if I can find out anything now and I'll bell you as soon as I have any news.'

Eddie held Frankie close to his chest. Her hair had been styled, she had make-up on and, even though she was pregnant, she looked a damn sight better than she ever had when she was with Jed.

'Wow, you look well. Been having a makeover in here, have ya?'

Frankie grinned and sat down. 'My cellmate Babs made me up. She's well cool, Dad. Babs is Jamaican and we get on so well. You know when you meet someone and just click? We're gonna be friends for life, I know we are.'

Eddie frowned. Joey had told him all about this Babs bird and he wasn't happy at all that his beautiful daughter was sharing a cell with a murderer. 'You shouldn't get too friendly with this girl, Frankie. Joey mentioned her to me. She's up for murder, ain't she?'

Frankie was instantly annoyed. She knew her dad was only concerned about her welfare, but he could be an irritating bastard at times. 'Look, I know you're worried about me, but give me a bit of credit, will ya? I know a wrong 'un when I meet one, living with Jed taught me that. I am currently in Holloway, Dad, so I'm hardly going to be sharing my cell with a nun or a good Samaritan, am I? Babs is truly lovely and I was gonna tell you a bit about what happened to her, but now you're being a stroppy arsehole, I ain't gonna bother.'

Eddie held his hands up in an 'I surrender' gesture. Frankie was a fiery little cow, she took after him and he hadn't come here to argue with her. 'I'm sorry, babe. I just worry about you, that's all.'

'Well, you've no need to worry. I am quite capable of choosing my own friends and I also know how to look after myself. You really do wind me up sometimes, Dad. When you were inside, you shared with Stuart, who was also a murderer, yet he was the greatest thing since sliced bread. And what about our family? I mean, we're hardly the fucking Waltons, are we?'

Eddie grinned. His daughter most definitely had the Mitchell sense of humour. 'So, how's your pregnancy going? Is everything OK?' he asked, cleverly changing the subject.

The mention of her unborn baby was enough to make Frankie calm down. 'Everything's fine. Me and Babs went to this antenatal lesson the other day. This posh woman took it and we had such a laugh. I feel a bit fat, but other than that I feel fit and healthy. I've had hardly no sickness with this one at all.'

Eddie nodded. He was dreading telling her that the kids had run away, but she was their mother and needed to know because of the civil court case that was being arranged. 'I've got some news for ya, but I don't want you to panic, 'cause it's created some good as well.'

Frankie's face turned deathly white when her father told the story of Georgie and Harry's little escapade. 'So they ran away to find me?' Frankie asked, bursting into tears.

Eddie took his daughter's hand in his. He was desperate to comfort her, but he didn't really know how to. 'Look, don't cry. The kids are fine, honest, and I think they're gonna be allowed to visit you up here now. That social worker Larry got involved is taking the case to court. She reckons it's in their best interests to see you regularly.'

Frankie's eyes shone with a mixture of tears and happiness. 'Oh Dad, I've missed them so much. When do you think I can see them?'

'We've gotta wait for a date for the court hearing first, but it should be soon. The social worker reckons they might be able to have some sort of contact with your nan, as well.'

'Did Nan make a fuss of the kids? How are she and Grandad?' Frankie asked.

'The same as ever. Stanley weren't there when I went round. Joycie and him have been rowing again, but she was over the moon to see Georgie and Harry.'

'So how did Georgie and Harry look? Did they look clean and well fed? You know how fussy Georgie is with her food, do you think she's been eating OK?'

The kids had turned up at Joycie's door in an awful state, but Eddie wasn't about to tell Frankie that, as a lot of it was down to the trek they'd endured. 'They both looked well and they ain't 'arf got big. Georgie's really tall now and they're definitely being fed OK, as Harry's shot up and looks as sturdy as a bull.'

Frankie thought of her two beautiful children and smiled. She then bombarded her father with lots more questions about them. Not wanting Frankie to worry unnecessarily, Eddie answered her as honestly as he could. He didn't tell her that the O'Haras hadn't even reported the kids missing, as he knew that would play on her mind.

'So, who else has been up to see you, apart from Joey?' Ed asked, changing the subject again.

'Kerry's coming up next week. I haven't seen her since that day I was last in court.'

Remembering that he'd promised himself what he would tell Frankie, Eddie began to fidget in his seat. Telling his daughter the news of his impending fatherhood was not something he relished, but it had to come from him. 'There's something else I need to tell you. It's about me and I know you ain't gonna like it.'

'I'll have a guess, shall I? You're getting married,' Frankie said sarcastically.

'Well, yeah, but not yet. Gina's pregnant,' Ed said bluntly.

With images of her poor mother flashing through her mind, Frankie stood up, walked towards a screw and asked to be taken back to her cell.

'Frankie, what you doin'? Don't be like this, babe,' she heard her dad shout.

Turning around, Frankie glared at him. 'You make me fucking sick!' she screamed.

Over in Orsett, Stanley and Pat the Pigeon had had a lovely day. Firstly, they'd had lunch in the Halfway House and then, on Pat's insistence, they'd popped into the Orsett Cock pub, where the pigeon club congregated.

'Don't you worry about bumping into that bloody turncoat, Jock. He's the one in the wrong, not you,' Pat had maintained.

Although still fuming over Jock's betrayal, Stanley wasn't one for confrontation and had been relieved that Jock wasn't in the pub when they'd arrived.

About to take a sip of his pint, Stanley nearly choked as

Pat muttered the words he'd been dreading hearing. 'Here he is, just walked in, the bloody Judas. I feel like giving him a piece of my mind, Stanley, I really do.'

Stanley looked up, locked eyes with his once best friend, scowled and looked away. 'Don't bother saying ought to him, Pat. He ain't bleedin' worth it, love.'

Under no illusion that Stanley was anything other than still mad at him, Jock walked over to the bar where Brian and Derek were standing.

'What's happened between you and Stanley? I asked him where you were earlier and he nearly bit my head off,' Derek asked.

'It's a long story, but I've had Joycie on the phone, worried sick about him. Stanley's left her and she was going to call the police and report him missing.'

Brian started to laugh. 'He's all right, is our Stanley. He's moved in with Pat, she was telling me earlier. I bet they've been at it like rabbits.'

Jock glanced at Stanley and Pat in horror. How was he meant to tell Joyce this piece of news? She would blow a fuse.

Unlike Frankie, who was currently sailing through her latest pregnancy, Sally Baldwin was indoors, crippled up with stomach pains. The stress of splitting up with Jed was taking its toll and the constant threats he kept making weren't helping matters either. He'd been ringing her all day and at first he'd been quite pleasant.

'Please come back. I didn't mean to talk to you like I did. I'm such a dinlo and I really miss you,' he'd begged.

Sally's father had then grabbed the phone and had given Jed a right mouthful. Terry Baldwin was sick of seeing his daughter upset and was at the end of his tether.

'If you ever come near my Sally again, I swear I will fucking kill you,' he'd warned Jed.

Jed, being Jed, hadn't taken any notice of the warning and had since left tons of threatening messages on the landline answerphone, the last being, 'If you ain't fucking back 'ere in one hour, Sally, I'm gonna come round there and cut your shitcunt of a father to shreds.'

Sally winced as her father entered the room and put a cup of coffee down next to her. The pains were griping and she was desperate to go to the toilet.

'How do you feel now?' Terry asked, concerned. Sally was as white as a sheet and he wondered if he should call an ambulance.

'I'm OK, but I must go a loo,' Sally replied, as she half staggered from the room.

Seconds later, Terry heard an almighty scream.

'Dad, there's blood everywhere, I think I'm losing the baby,' Sally cried.

Not one to drink too much when he had to drive from Orsett back to Barking, Jock had four pints and set off home. He felt sick with worry about Stanley's unusual behaviour. Not only had his old pal looked very drunk, but he and that Pat had looked far more than just friends, and Jock didn't have a clue what he was now going to say to Joyce.

Within seconds of walking indoors, Jock heard his phone ringing. He glanced at the clock. It was 4 p.m. and his daughter usually rang him at this time most days. He picked up the phone and was horrified to hear Joyce on the other end.

'Well, did you find the old bastard?'

'Aye, but I didn't speak to him, Joycie. He's still really angry with me, I could see it in his face.'

'So, where is he then? Where did you see him?'

Aware of how irate Joyce sounded, Jock chose his words carefully. He didn't want to get his old mate into too much trouble, but if he didn't give Joycie some information, she would be sure to call the police and find out Stanley's whereabouts anyway.

'He was in the Orsett Cock pub. He's staying with a friend who lives up that way, I think.'

'Friend! What friend? Apart from you, my Stanley has never had any bleedin' friends. What's the bloke's name he's stopping with?'

'I've no idea,' Jock replied untruthfully.

Joyce instinctively knew that Jock was lying. Stanley had definitely been behaving oddly for the last couple of months.

He disappeared regularly, usually at lunchtime. He'd put on weight, but ate smaller meals at home, and she could swear she'd whiffed women's perfume on his clothes and it certainly wasn't her Estée Lauder. It all added up now, every single, last, sordid detail.

'What's the old tart's name, Jock? I know it's a woman, so don't you dare fucking lie to me.'

Jock felt like a rabbit caught in the headlights. 'I swear, it's not what you think, Joycie. Him and Pat are just friends, that's all. Your Stanley has decent morals, love,' he stammered.

'Well, I'll give him morals and I'll give her fucking Pat. What's the old bag's address?' Joyce screamed down the phone.

Jock was petrified of Joyce at the best of times. 'I don't know, I swear I don't. All I know is she lives in Orsett,' he said, his hands shaking.

'Well, I'll be taking a little trip to Orsett and when I find that dirty old bastard I married, I'm gonna chop his fucking bits off and feed 'em to his pigeons.'

Unaware that his old woman was on his tail and currently spitting feathers, Stanley and Pat were rather inebriated and cuddled up on the sofa. They had left the pub about an hour ago and they must have sunk at least ten or twelve drinks while they were out. At one point, Stanley had even felt his legs start to buckle.

'Do you wanna watch a film, Stanley, or shall we have an early night?' Pat asked him expectantly.

Not getting the gist of what she was asking, Stanley smiled at her. Unlike Joycie, Pat was a loving person and he sometimes liked it when she put her arms around him. It made him feel manly and wanted. 'You watch a film if you like, love. I'm knackered, though, so I think I'll have an early one.'

Desperate to get Stanley into her own bed rather than the one in the spare room, Pat edged towards his lips and placed her own there.

Feeling Pat's tongue inside his mouth, Stanley leaped from the sofa as if he had a bullet up his arse. 'Night, love,' he shouted, as he ran from the room and bolted up the stairs. He was desperate for the safety of the spare room. He and Joycie hadn't kissed for years and even when they used to, there were no tongues involved. Petrified that Pat was going to come into his room, Stanley finally stopped shaking as he heard her footsteps plod past. 'Thank you, God,' he mumbled gratefully.

Terry Baldwin sat in a corridor in Harold Wood Hospital. Sally had been rushed to the maternity unit and he'd been waiting ages for some news. Putting his head in his hands, Terry cursed the day his daughter had ever set eyes on Jed O'Hara. The little shit had already robbed him of one grandchild, his beloved Luke, and if Sally were to lose another because of Jed, Terry would have no choice but to top the little bastard.

Saying a silent prayer to God that all the blood Sally had lost would turn out to be no more than a false alarm, Terry heard his name being called. He stood up and looked into the doctor's eyes.

'I'm so sorry, Mr Baldwin, but I'm afraid we were unable to save the baby. On a positive note, your daughter is stable and we have given her something to sedate her so she can get some sleep. She was, understandably, very upset, so we would like to keep her in for observation.'

Overcome by grief for the second time in weeks, Terry let out a muffled cry and slumped back onto the chair. This would be the end of his Sally and he knew it.

CHAPTER ELEVEN

Joycie Smith was still seething the following morning. Never in a million years would she have guessed that Stanley would ever leave for some old slapper. Her husband was certainly no Richard Gere and Joyce could not understand how any other woman would even like him, let alone fancy him.

Pacing up and down the living room, Joycie glanced at the clock on the wall. 'What time did Dominic say he'd get here?' she asked Joey. Patience had never been one of Joycie's virtues and she was doing buttons to get to Orsett and confront her philandering husband and his bit of fluff.

Joey sighed. He'd been working late last night when his nan had rung and told him what had happened. She'd gone bananas on the phone and, worried about her sanity, Joey had come straight over from work. He and Dom had made plans themselves today and, as much as Joey loved his nan, he was getting a bit sick of her interfering in his life. Whenever there was a drama it was Joey she called and in Joey's opinion, her own son Raymond got away very lightly indeed.

'Where you going?' Joyce shouted as Joey picked his mobile up and stomped out of the room.

Ignoring her question, Joey opened the back door and punched in a number. 'Raymond, it's me, Joey. Listen, you need to get over to your mum's ASAP. Your dad's run off with another woman and I don't know what to do.'

'I can't come over. I'm with Polly and we're on our way to visit her parents,' Raymond said bluntly.

Joey was fuming. Who did Raymond think he was, Lord Fucking Fauntleroy? Sick of taking shit from people, Joey gave it to him good and proper. 'Joycie might be my nan, but she's your bloody mother. She needs you, so best you ring Polly's parents, tell them you have to cancel, then turn your car around and get your arse over here. I've already lost my mum, Ray, but you've still got yours, so instead of avoiding her, make the fucking most of it.'

Raymond was astounded by his nephew's little speech. Joey no longer sounded like a feminine little gay boy – he sounded just like his father.

Eddie Mitchell smiled as he ended his phone call. His plan to keep his brothers safe had worked like a dream so far. Worried that Jimmy O'Hara's henchman would get to them, Eddie had ordered someone to give both Ronny and Paulie a pasting.

'Don't go too heavy, but make it look bad. Aim for their faces and make as much mess as you can without actually hurting 'em,' had been Ed's exact words. He'd then got word to his brothers via another inmate to tell them the score. 'You must insist that you're frightened for your lives and demand to be moved either to solitary or another nick. With Ronny being a cripple, the guvnor should swallow it.'

He'd also told his ally to warn them that under no circumstances must they contact him. 'If they ring me or send me any silly fucking letters, they're on their own,' he said.

Ed smiled as Gina walked into the room and put her arms around his waist from behind.

'Dinner's nearly ready,' she said lovingly.

Eddie turned around, tilted her chin and kissed her tenderly. He was picking Stuart up on Monday, so this was the last weekend that they'd have the house to themselves for a while.

'After we've eaten, let's have an early night, eh, babe?'

Gina grinned. 'Only if you promise to ravish me.'

Eddie grabbed the cheeks of her arse and rubbed his rapidly growing erection against her groin. 'Oh, I shall ravish you all right. In fact, I'm gonna shag your brains out all weekend.'

Gina giggled. She adored Eddie talking dirty to her. Her fiancé's vulgarity was her ultimate turn-on.

* * *

Raymond dropped Polly off at her parents' house and drove towards his mother's. Joey's words had somehow struck a chord, and even though Joyce drove him mad at times, Raymond realised he should make more of an effort to be there for her.

'You took your time. I thought Polly's parents had moved over this way,' Joey said as he answered the front door.

'Essex is a big place, Joey. If you drove, you'd know that Polly's parents have moved to Loughton, which isn't exactly spitting distance from here, is it now?' Raymond replied sarcastically.

Ignoring his uncle's sarcasm, Joey began to give him the lowdown on exactly what had happened between Joyce and Stanley.

Sick of waiting for a lift, Joyce had been necking the Baileys as if it were chocolate milkshake and was now in an extremely vicious mood.

Raymond walked into the room and sat down on the sofa next to his mum. Feeling awkward, he hugged her. 'Don't worry, we'll find Dad and then he'll come back home. I'm sure this woman is only a friend, whoever she is.'

'Friend! I'll give her fucking friend. Do you know where that Orsett Cock pub is, Raymond?'

Ray nodded.

Joyce stood up. 'Come on then, let's go and find the dirty old pervert who fathered you.'

Joey glanced at Dominic and smirked. His earlier outburst had obviously hit home and now that Raymond had turned up and taken over, their weekend could continue as planned.

Eddie Mitchell smiled as he rubbed Gina's slightly swollen naked stomach. He might be fifty-three, but he didn't look it and in his mind he was still only twenty-one. He couldn't wait to be a dad again. When the twins were born he'd left all that baby stuff to Jessica, but this time he wanted to be part of it. 'So what we gonna call this little beauty then?' he asked tenderly.

Gina turned her head towards Eddie and grinned. She would be thirty-five by the time the baby was born and she had never been so excited about anything in her life before. There was a time when Gina had given up on meeting Mr Right and becoming a mother, but meeting Eddie Mitchell had changed all that. From the first moment Gina had laid eyes on Eddie, she had known he was the one and now he had made all her dreams come true.

'I like Michaela for a girl and Bradley for a boy,' Gina suggested.

Eddie pondered over her choices, then turned to her. 'I like Rosie, be a nice tribute to me mum. Michaela's OK, though. My Frankie's real name is Francesca and Georgie's birth name is Georgina, so like both of these, Michaela will be shortened to Micky. Micky Mitchell, yeah, sounds proper. I dunno about Bradley though, sounds a bit poofy to me and, as much as I love Joey, I don't want two gay sons.'

'Bradley don't sound poofy! What about Gavin, do you like that?' Gina asked.

Eddie shook his head. 'Gavin Mitchell sounds like a fucking accountant who drinks piña coladas and plays squash at weekends.'

Gina playfully punched his arm. Eddie could be such a comical bastard at times; his sense of humour was second to none. 'You pick some boys' names then,' she urged him.

Eddie propped himself up on his elbow and thought carefully. If they had a son, he wanted him to have an old-fashioned, masculine-sounding name. He hated all that trendy bollocks. 'I like Lenny. Lenny Mitchell, whaddya think?'

Gina smiled. She wasn't struck on the name Lenny, but she quite liked Rosie. 'If it's a girl, you can call her Rosie, after your mum. If it's a boy though, I choose. I quite like Aaron as well.'

Eddie held out his right hand. 'You got yourself a deal, babe. Now can I fuck you again?'

Gina giggled as Eddie rolled on top of her. 'You're insatiable, Eddie Mitchell, has anybody ever told you that before?'

Thrusting his penis inside her, Eddie smirked. 'Of course, therefore you should think yourself one lucky girl to have got me, babe.'

*   *   *

Raymond pulled up outside the Orsett Cock pub. His mother had had verbal diarrhoea for the entire journey and he now had the stirrings of a headache.

When Joyce went to leap out of the car, Raymond grabbed her arm. He knew she'd had a few drinks and he didn't want her showing herself up, nor him, for that matter. 'You stay 'ere for a minute, Mum. Let me go in first, see if Dad's in there. If he is, I'll bring him outside, if not, I'll get this old bird's address.'

Determined to catch her husband red-handed, Joyce pushed Raymond's arm away, got out of the car and marched towards the pub. Opening the door, Joyce immediately spotted Brian. He was a member of the same pigeon club as Stanley and was standing at the bar alone when Joycie walked over. Brian recognised her immediately. Who wouldn't? With her bouffant auburn hair, five-foot-nine frame and big mouth, Joycie was very hard to miss indeed.

'Where is he?' she screamed.

'Who, Stanley?' Brian asked dumbly.

'Yes, that dirty, stinking, cheating, bastard of a husband of mine.'

Totally embarrassed that the twenty or so customers in the pub were all looking their way, Raymond ordered his mum to sit down and led Brian towards the gent's toilets. Once inside, he turned to him.

'Sorry about that. As you can imagine, my mum's very upset over all this. You know my dad well. Tell me what's going on with him and this Pat woman.'

Brian didn't want any aggravation, so tried to be as diplomatic as possible. Everybody in the pigeon club knew that Stanley was a harmless old soul, but they were also aware that his son was a bit of a rogue and worked for the notorious Eddie Mitchell.

'Her name is Pat, she's a member of our pigeon club and Stanley was in here yesterday with her. I don't think there is anything going on between them, but I think he's stopping round at her house. They are probably just good friends.'

'What's this Pat's address?' Raymond asked pleasantly.

Brian liked both Stanley and Pat and didn't want to get either of them into any trouble. 'I don't know,' he lied.

Raymond's pleasant persona changed instantly. He'd learned from Eddie that the quickest way to get information out of people was by putting the frighteners on them and it seemed to work every time. 'I said, what's the fucking address?' he spat, as he grabbed the collar of Brian's jacket and shoved him up against the wall.

Brian was petrified. 'It's Hemley Road, but I ain't sure of the number,' he stammered.

Raymond let go of Brian's jacket and politely smoothed the collar down. The number of the house didn't matter. As long as he knew the road, he would find the gaff easily enough, because his father's car would be parked outside. He smiled at Brian. 'Cheers, mate. Nice to meet ya.'

Pat the Pigeon was an expert when it came to cooking a decent roast dinner. Her husband Vic had been a massive fan and reckoned her crispy potatoes cooked in goose fat were the best he'd ever tasted.

Stanley smiled as Pat put his dinner down in front of him. Roast beef, potatoes, Yorkshire pudding, Brussels, carrots and peas – it was a meal fit for a king. 'Cor, this looks handsome,' Stanley said appreciating the presentation. They'd had a nice day today, he and Pat. They'd spent the morning out the back with the pigeons and had then had a game of cards. No more had been mentioned about the kiss they'd sort of shared and the only thing that Stanley wanted now was for Pat to stop wearing her low-cut tops. Her breasts were enormous and Stanley felt embarrassed every time Pat caught him looking at them. He tried not to, as he didn't want to give her the wrong impression, but they were so big, and when they were shoved in your face morning, noon and night, any man would have difficulty ignoring them.

'Have some horseradish, Stanley,' Pat said, as she sat down at the table. Seconds later, there was a knock at the door. 'Who the bleedin' hell's that?' Pat complained as she stood up again.

'Can I help you?' Pat asked politely, as she came face to face with Joyce and Raymond.

Joyce looked Pat up and down and was disgusted by what she saw. Unlike herself, the woman had no class. She was tarty, blonde and plump, with her Bristols hanging out for the whole world to see.

'I'm Joycie, Stanley's wife, and you must be Pat, the fucking old slapper.'

When his mother lunged at Pat, Raymond quickly stepped in. 'Fighting ain't gonna solve this, Mother,' he said.

Stanley was petrified when he heard Joycie's booming voice. Choking on his roast beef, he jumped up and hid behind the sofa.

'Where is he? Stanley! Stanley!' Joyce yelled.

Pat was shocked. Stanley had described Joyce as a person, but never her appearance, and she couldn't believe this brazen, tall woman was his wife. Stanley was such a kind, inoffensive man, yet his wife looked like a much uglier version of Yootha Joyce.

'He don't wanna see you. Get out of my house,' Pat shouted. Now she'd overcome her initial shock, she wasn't about to take shit from this woman. Pat was a true East Ender, and women from where she came from bowed down to no one.

Aware that his mother and Pat were about to start fighting, Raymond left them to it and went in search of his father. He really didn't need any of this shit. He had promised Polly he would get things sorted and return to her parents' to pick her up. 'Dad! Dad!' he yelled.

Stanley was sweating as he hid behind the sofa. He hated violence of any kind, it made his nerves bad.

Unable to find his father, Raymond ignored the hair-pulling that was going on in the hallway and ran up the stairs. Two women fighting was a sight for sore eyes and all he wanted to do was find his old man and get home to his wife.

'Look at ya, with all your lils hanging out. No wonder my Stanley can't keep away, revealing your body like that. It ain't right, you look like an Old Tom,' Joyce shouted as she tried to drag Pat down the hallway by her hair.

Raymond ran down the stairs and separated the brawling women once more. 'I've looked everywhere. Dad ain't here,' he told his mother.

Fiddling about with her messed-up bouffant, Joyce marched into the lounge. She knew what a coward her husband was and she knew a little weasel like him would find somewhere to hide. She saw the two dinner plates on the table and smirked. 'Stanley, I know you're in here,' she yelled.

As Pat tried to run into the lounge, Raymond restrained her.

'Get your hands off me else I'll call the Old Bill,' Pat screamed.

'Shut it you old trollop, you've already done enough damage,' Raymond spat.

Stanley started shaking as Joyce leaned over the sofa and spotted him.

'There you are. Now get your stuff, you're coming home with me,' she yelled.

Stanley stood up and, as he did, came face to face with Pat. She had just kneed Raymond in the nuts to come to his rescue.

'Stanley's going nowhere. He's told me all about you. You're always putting him down and making him feel small. He's a lovely man, is Stanley, and you don't bloody deserve him,' Pat informed Joyce.

About to start shouting and screaming once more, Joyce took in Pat's words and stopped herself. Over the years, she had always put Stanley down, but that was just their relationship. She didn't always mean what she said, it was just her way of speaking to him. Joyce turned to her husband. 'Please come home, Stanley. I need you there and I miss you.'

Raymond stood in the doorway holding his groin. Pat had really hurt him and he felt like smacking her one, but he didn't clump women. 'Dad, come home and we'll sort this out indoors,' Ray pleaded.

Stanley stared at all three of them. His villainous son, who was probably in a rush to get back to do some more dirty work for Eddie Mitchell. His gobby wife, who had encouraged his daughter to marry Eddie and spent the best part of her life mocking him and making him feel two feet tall. Then he turned to Pat. Nice, kind Pat, who treated him with respect, loved pigeons, and enjoyed his company. The decision wasn't difficult for him. 'I'm sorry, Joycie, but I'm not coming back home. I'm happy here and this is where I want to stay.'

As Joycie burst into tears and ran from the room, Raymond glared at his father before following his mother outside.

When the front door slammed, Stanley was grateful for the cuddle that Pat gave him. He smiled sadly and looked into her eyes. Seconds later, they shared their first proper kiss.

CHAPTER TWELVE

Georgie put down the spade and urged Harry to follow her over to the back door. They were both dressed in their little Puffa jackets and wellies and had spent the morning digging for worms. They now had loads wriggling around in a plastic bucket and Georgie wanted to ask her dad if they could keep them as pets.

'Stay outside, yous two, while I have a little chat with the lady. Go on, off you go,' Jed ordered, as Georgie opened the back door.

Georgie glanced at the nice social worker lady and then shut the door. Her dad had his angry voice on and even though he had been really kind to her and Harry lately, Georgie knew when not to push his patience.

'Is the lady taking us to see Mummy now?' Harry asked his sister.

Georgie put her forefinger over her lips to urge Harry to keep schtum. She then pressed her ear against the door to see if she could find out what was going on.

'The court hearing has been set for January the seventh,' Georgie heard the woman say.

'This is ridiculous, and I'm telling you now that I have found the best solicitor money can buy. That bitch who tried to kill me is not seeing them kids. Frankie's evil and I won't allow my chavvies to be dragged up to some poxy prison to see scum like her,' Jed shouted.

'The court will decide what is best for the children, Mr O'Hara. You will receive a letter in the post confirming the date and time. Now, if you'll excuse me, I must dash, as I'm running late for an appointment,' Carol said. She didn't like Jed O'Hara one little bit.

'What Daddy doin'?' Harry whispered to Georgie.

Georgie turned to him. 'I don't think Daddy wants us to see Mummy, but the lady will take us to see her.'

Eddie Mitchell smiled as Stuart sauntered towards him. He'd got to Ford Open Prison early and just staring at the building brought back awful memories of Wandsworth, which mainly involved Jessica.

'It's great to see you, boy,' Eddie said, as his old cellmate flung his arms around him. Stuart was like a son to Eddie and had been a wonderful comfort to him while he was inside, trying to come to terms with his fatal mistake.

'I hope no one's watching us. We must look like a right pair of soppy pricks,' Stuart joked as he pulled away.

Eddie sized his pal up. 'Christ, you look like a brick shit-house.'

'I took a leaf out of your book, Ed. I was bored shitless after you got released, and since I got moved, I've spent every spare minute training. I thought it would help with me new career.'

Eddie chuckled. 'Oh, it will, mate, I can assure you of that. I thought we'd stop for a beer then grab a bit of lunch on the way home. Gina's got all your room ready and she ain't expecting us back till teatime.'

'Sounds perfect! I could kill a nice juicy fillet steak.'

'Get in the motor and I'll fill you in on all the gossip. You won't believe the shit I've had with them O'Haras and rest assured, once my Frankie's out and gets them kids back, we'll have more than fucking fillet steak to kill.'

Frankie Mitchell sat opposite her solicitor and twiddled her thumbs nervously. Larry had just informed her that Jed was contesting the appeal for Frankie to have visiting rights with her children.

'So what happens now?' Frankie asked miserably. She had been so looking forward to seeing Georgie and Harry and she couldn't believe, after everything that had happened, Jed would have the balls to try and mess it up.

'Jed has appointed a solicitor by the name of Malcolm

Thompson. I don't know the man personally, but his reputation is of high quality. We still have a great chance of winning this case Frankie, especially with Carol Cullen on our side. Carol is very highly respected in her field and her evidence will be very much taken into consideration. Obviously, the end decision will be made by the judge or magistrate, but I'd say we have the edge with this one. As for your trial, I spoke to your QC over the weekend. He is positive that he can get you a not guilty, but he needs you to dish some more dirt on Jed. Both you and I know that you haven't yet told us why you did what you did, and the quicker you start spilling the beans, the better. The truth might hurt, but surely it's better than being stuck in prison and losing your children.'

Frankie's lip trembled, so she bit it to stop herself from crying. The truth did hurt, but if she admitted what had really happened, it would cause absolute bloody mayhem. 'I've told you the truth already. There is nothing else to add,' Frankie lied.

Disappointed at his client's lack of co-operation, Larry stood up. He was sick of trying to help people who had no intention of trying to help themselves. 'Goodbye Frankie, and if I were you, I'd think very deeply about admitting the truth. You can be your own worst enemy at times and in the end that could cost you severely.'

To lighten his mood, Jed O'Hara had taken the kids and his parents out for lunch to a boozer in Basildon that had a children's play area.

'So, tell me everything that old whore said again,' Alice asked as she sipped her Guinness. She and Jimmy had been out food shopping when Carol Cullen had dropped by, and Alice wished she had been at home, so she could have given the stuck-up tart a piece of her mind.

Jed repeated word for word what Carol had said. 'If Frankie gets visiting rights, I'm gonna fuck off somewhere and take Georgie girl and Harry with me. No court in the land is gonna tell me what's best for my chavvies and if they can't protect them from their shitcunt of a mother, then I will.'

Alice nudged Jimmy. 'If he goes, then we're going with him.'

Jimmy nodded, then smiled as he spotted Harry thump some little boy. He had been teaching Harry how to box earlier in the week and his efforts had obviously paid off. 'He's shaping up a bit, Harry boy, ain't he?' he stated.

Jed and Alice both chuckled as the little boy hit Harry back and Harry retaliated once more.

'Yeah, he's becoming a proper little bruiser now. He used to spend too much time with Frankie and she used to baby him. He would have turned out to be a right nancy boy if I hadn't split with her.'

'Harry, come over here,' Jed shouted.

Harry ran towards his father and was surprised to receive a cuddle. 'What happened with that boy?' Jed asked him.

'He hit Georgie, so I hit him,' Harry replied.

Jed smiled and kissed his son on the forehead. Since Lukey had died, Jed had grown fonder of Harry with every day that passed. 'For being such a good boy, Daddy will take you to the toy shop when we leave here and buy you whatever you want.'

'Can I have Mr Blobby?' Harry asked excitedly.

Jed laughed. He was desperate to turn Harry into a proper little travelling lad and the cost of that didn't matter. 'You can choose whatever you want, boy.'

Eddie treated Stuart to a nice slap-up meal in a steak-house in Canning Town, then drove towards the Flag. He had no intention of going in there. His pal, John, had retired years ago and the pub itself brought back so many memories of his dad, Harry, that any time Ed had been in there since his death, he'd felt like bloody well crying.

'See that boozer, Stu? That's the Flag where me, me dad and me brothers used to frequent. The old guvnor, John, ain't there no more, but we had some top nights in there years ago. It was sort of our headquarters in a way, I suppose.'

Stuart nodded. Eddie had mentioned the Flag a few times in prison and he remembered the name. 'Have you found out any more news about your dad, Ed?'

Eddie shook his head sadly. Even after six years, his dad's murderer still hadn't been found. 'No one knows fuck-all, mate.

I sent Gary and Ricky sniffing around again a few weeks back, but it's a stone-cold trail. As for the Old Bill, they won't admit it, but I'm sure they've closed the case. My old man was a thorn in the filth's side for years and I personally believe they were glad to see the back of him.'

Stuart put a comforting hand on Eddie's shoulder. Even in the nick, Ed had found talking about his dad's death difficult and Stu could see how upset he was now. 'Let's find a quiet pub and have a beer, eh, mate?'

Eddie took the handbrake off and pulled away. He shouldn't have come here, but he had wanted Stuart to see the gaff. 'There's a whore house down the road. Shall I take you there?'

Stuart looked at Eddie to see if he was serious or mucking about. He was serious. 'Fuck off, Ed. I could do with letting off a bit of steam, but I ain't that desperate. To be honest, I'm quite choosy when it comes to birds and I'd rather bide my time till I find one I like. Made a right ricket with the last one, didn't I? And I can't afford to do that again. I'd rather just concentrate on work from now on.'

Eddie glanced at Stuart and was glad to see him smiling. Stuie had done bird for killing a geezer who had raped his ex-girlfriend, Carly. The boy had expected to do his bit of bird then spend the rest of his life with Carly, until one day she'd sent him a 'Dear John' letter telling him she'd met someone else and was up the spout by her new beau. Stu had been devastated and it had taken him a while to snap out of his depression, but he seemed OK about it now, thank God.

'Do you know what, Ed, why don't we just head back to yours and have a beer indoors? That champagne at the restaurant has already made me feel a bit light-headed and I wanna enjoy my first day out. I like a beer and that, but I've never been one for getting shit-faced.'

Eddie grinned and headed towards home. Stuart was extremely sensible and with an attitude like that, he would definitely become a valuable asset to the firm.

Since her conversation with Larry, Frankie had felt as though she had the weight of the world on her shoulders. Babs was a great listener and Frankie had just explained to her what had happened earlier.

'So, what do you think I should do? I mean, if I had evidence, like the tape, I would have told the truth in the first place, but say they don't believe me? Also, even though me and my dad have fallen out again, I don't want anything bad to happen to him. If he finds out Jed killed my grandad, he will lose the plot, I know he will.'

Babs hugged her friend. 'If I was you, sweet child, I would get in touch with Jed and tell him to back off. You tell him if he stops Georgie and Harry from having contact with you, then you are gonna tell everyone, including your dad, what he did to your grandfather. Threatening him should do the trick, I reckon.'

'I can't ring him. My dad always told me never to talk about anything untoward on these prison phones and I can't write to him, 'cause he can barely read.'

'Well, you'll have to get a message to him via someone else,' Babs suggested.

'But who? I can't expect Kerry to go round there on her own and, apart from you, she's the only one that knows the truth.'

'You can get Kerry to ring him or, if you don't want to involve her at all, see if that travelling girl in here can get a message to the bastard. She didn't look like no monster and she was no fan of Jed's, was she?'

Frankie thought of her chat with Katie and shrugged. 'She sounded like she hated him, but how do I know I can trust her? I've never met a decent traveller yet.'

Babs smiled. 'You don't know if you can trust her, but that's the chance you take. Listen, lots of white people swear that all black people are bad, but not all of us are. The same probably goes for travellers or gypsies, whatever they're called. There is good and bad in every race, Frankie, and if I were you I would see if that Katie girl can get a message to Jed for you. I mean, if you can't ask your family or Kerry to do it, what choice do you have?'

Frankie nodded. 'OK, I'll ask her if she can do it.'

* * *

Jed dropped his parents back in Rainham, then took the kids to Lakeside to get them some toys. Both kids were currently obsessed with Mr Blobby, a character that had become famous on *Noel's House Party*, a Saturday-night variety show, and since Mr Blobby had released a song the previous week, both Georgie and Harry had done nothing but sing it constantly.

'Please can we have the record, Daddy?' Georgie begged.

Jed had already bought the kids three toys each in the first shop they'd been in, but he liked to see them happy, so agreed. Jed had a CD player over at his mobile home in Wickford, but since he'd been stabbed, he hadn't been back there. His cousin Sammy owned the trailer next door, they shared the piece of land, and Sammy was keeping an eye on things for him in his absence. One day Jed would return there, but at the moment he needed all the help with the kids that he could get, so staying with his parents suited him.

'Blobby, blobby, blobby,' Harry sang happily.

Crouching down, Jed smiled at both of his children. 'I'll make you a deal. Nanny has only got a cassette recorder, so I'll buy you a CD player that you can take up to the bedroom. But I don't wanna hear Mr Blobby, neither does your nan and grandad, so you only play it upstairs, OK?'

Georgie and Harry both nodded.

Hearing his mobile ring, Jed stood up and answered it. It was Sammy. 'What? Are you sure?' Jed asked in shock.

'Yeah, I had to take the boys back to Sally and she was proper going into one. Apparently, Sally got taken into hospital yesterday and she's definitely lost the baby. Her father's blaming you, apparently, so is Kerry, obviously.'

Jed ended the call and sat down on a nearby bench. Luke dying had broken his heart, but he felt nothing over this miscarriage. How can you be upset over something that wasn't even properly formed yet? he thought. It wasn't as though he could picture the kid's face or had memories of playing with it like he had of Luke.

'What a matter, Daddy?' Harry asked him. His dad had been nice to him recently and Harry decided he rather liked him now. When they'd lived with Mum, his dad used to ignore him a lot, but he didn't do that any more.

Jed ruffled Harry's hair. Sally losing the kid was a blessing in disguise, he decided. He could now concentrate on Georgie and Harry more. Just lately, Sally had felt like a fucking albatross hanging around his neck, anyway. Lukey's death had ruined any closeness between them and in Jed's opinion, it was definitely time to move on with his life and find himself another bird.

'Come on, let's go and find Mr Blobby,' Jed said, grinning.

Georgie and Harry held hands and skipped along. 'Blobby, blobby, blobby,' they chanted happily.

Gina hugged Stuart and told him to sit down, put his feet up and make himself at home. 'I'll crack open some champagne, shall I?' she said.

'I ain't much of a champagne drinker to be honest. Do you mind if I just have a lager?' Stuart asked. He loved the cottage. He had always lived with his mum in council accommodation in Hackney and he was already liking the serenity of Rettendon.

'Of course you can have a beer, love, but trust me, it won't be long before you get a taste for the bubbly stuff, especially if you're going to be working with Champagne Charlie over there,' Gina joked, pointing at Ed.

Eddie smiled. 'So, whaddya think of the place?'

'Oh, it's lovely, Ed. I've never been to this sort of area before.'

Eddie chuckled. Stuart was very blinkered, like Ed's Auntie Joan, and had rarely ever set foot outside London.

'Do you wanna see some photos, boy? I got the albums out ready for ya.'

Stuart thanked Gina for the lager and nodded. 'I can't wait to see the photos, but do you mind if I give my mum a quick ring first?'

'You take your time. There's a phone in the hallway and you can shut this door so you've got a bit of privacy.'

When Stuart left the room, Eddie turned to Gina. She'd seen Stu in the nick before when she'd visited Ed, but she'd never really had a chance to speak to him properly.

'Whaddya think? He's a nice kid, ain't he?'

'He seems lovely and he's so handsome, bless him. I bet he'll have girls falling at his feet in no time.'

Eddie grinned. Being a bloke, he'd never really taken much notice of Stuart's looks, but he had to admit that since he'd toned up, he looked like a man rather than a boy, which is what Ed had always classed him as.

'Well, he's tall, dark and muscly, so once I get him in a suit and show him a bit of the old Mitchell charm, I'm sure he'll do all right with the chicks,' Eddie said, laughing.

Stuart grinned as he came back into the room ten minutes later. 'My mum's fine and she's so relieved that I didn't go back to Hackney. She asked me would it be OK if she comes and visits me in a week or so?'

'Of course. She can stop over, there's enough room. You can even invite her over for Christmas, if you want. Now, you gonna look at these photos or what?'

Stuart sat down next to Eddie and listened as he explained who was who. 'Look at the size of your dad's cigar. He looks as though he were a real character, Ed. He reminds me of one of them old-style villains, a bit like the Krays or Freddie Foreman.'

Eddie chuckled. 'He was more than a match for any of them, boy.'

'Was he really that famous?' Stuart asked innocently.

'I should coco,' Eddie replied proudly.

'Who's that?' Stuart asked, pointing at a pretty girl with long dark hair.

'That's my Frankie. Get that other album out the drawer, Gina,' Ed urged.

Stuart was taken aback as Ed showed him lots more photos of Frankie and Joey. Stu had never seen Frankie before. She had visited Ed in prison a few times, but Stu had never had a visit himself on those particular occasions and Ed had always moaned how she'd put on weight and let herself go since she'd been with Jed. Studying a picture of Frankie standing next to her mother, Stuart smiled.

'They're both beautiful, aren't they? Is that Jessica?'

'Let me get yous boys another drink,' Gina said tactfully. She could tell that Eddie wanted to speak about Jessica and she didn't want to make him feel awkward.

Eddie stared wistfully at the photographs, then turned to Stuart. 'My Jessica was beautiful inside and out. She was a real head-turner and I felt like a king when she agreed to marry me. I loved her dearly and we were so happy together, but shit happens in life, don't it?'

Stuart put an arm around his pal's shoulder. 'It's time to move on now, mate.'

'I have and I love Gina very much. She's my life now,' Eddie replied, with tears glistening in his eyes.

Stuart turned the page and stared at another photo of Frankie.

'You like my daughter, don't ya, boy?' Eddie said knowingly.

'Don't be silly. She's very pretty, but I would never think of her anything other than your daughter, Ed. I'm not like that, you know I'm not.'

Gina walked back into the room and handed Ed and Stuart a beer each.

Eddie chuckled. 'Stuie's got the hots for my Frankie, Gina.'

'No I haven't,' Stuart said, blushing.

Eddie laughed and threw his arm playfully around his pal's neck. 'If my Frankie had ended up with a bloke like you, I'd have been truly fucking elated. Instead the silly little mare ended up with that pikey piece of shit, and with three kids by him, she'll be lucky if a decent geezer ever looks at her again.'

CHAPTER THIRTEEN

Eddie arranged a meeting at his Auntie Joanie's house the following weekend so that Gary, Ricky and Raymond could get to know Stuart properly. Ed could sense Gary and Ricky's reluctance at employing another pair of hands, and the situation reminded him of when Raymond had originally joined the fold many years ago. At the time, the firm had only consisted of Ed, his dad, Uncle Reg and his two brothers. It was Ronny and Paulie who had kicked up a stink over Raymond's arrival. They classed him as an outsider, but were soon proved wrong, and Ed had no doubt that Gary and Ricky would be, too.

'How long has your aunt lived here?' Stuart asked, as they pulled up outside Joanie's house.

'Donkey's years. I used to sort of live with her when I was a kid. After my mum died, Auntie Joan did everything for me and my brothers. A real fucking diamond she is and I love her dearly.'

'And how's my favourite nephew?' Joanie asked as she opened the front door.

'I'm fine, Auntie. This is Stuart, who I told you about. He's gonna be working with me and the boys from now on.'

Joanie smiled as Stuart kissed her politely on the cheek. Eddie had spoken fondly about the lad in his letters and when she'd visited him in prison. 'You go up. The others are already here and I'll bring yous some sandwiches up in a bit.'

Eddie introduced Stuart to everybody, then sat down at the head of the table. Gary had a face like a smacked arse and Ed had to restrain himself from clumping him one.

'You got a problem, boy?' he asked angrily.

'No, Dad,' Gary replied sensibly.

Eddie had warned Stuart on the way over that Gary and Ricky had doubts about him taking someone new on. 'We're a close-knit bunch and it's mainly always been family, but act keen, prove yourself and they'll change their tune in no time,' Eddie urged him.

Stuart listened intently as Eddie described the situation with Colin Griffiths and the outstanding loan.

'Stu needs to learn the ropes, so I suggest we all have a day trip to Milton Keynes tomorrow and show him how we work.'

'OK, but why don't you let Stuart confront Griffiths. I take it he's on trial until proven,' Ricky said sarcastically.

'No problem. I'm happy to do whatever it takes to prove myself,' Stuart said ambitiously. Prison had taught Stu not to be frightened of anyone, and the quicker he demonstrated his worth and got Eddie's sons off his back, the better.

Raymond grinned. He liked Stuart; he reminded him of himself when he'd first joined the firm. At twenty-six, Stu was older than he had been at the time, but he had the same glint in his eye, a look of steel and determination.

'Brings back memories of me and me butcher's knife, don't it?' he said, chuckling.

Remembering the demise of Mad Dave, Eddie laughed loudly. Raymond had only been a youngster, but he'd seen off Mad Dave all right.

'What's happening with the O'Haras? Any more news?' Gary asked his father.

'Not much, apart from Jed trying to stop the kids visiting Frankie. Once she's out and she's got them kids back, we're gonna shut that little fucker up for good. Until then, we can't do anything.'

'Is Ronny and Paulie OK?' Ricky asked.

'Yep, they got beaten up as planned and then they were moved. I think they've been shoved on a wing with all the nonces.'

'I bet they love that,' Raymond said jokingly.

Eddie chuckled. 'Like it or lump it, at least they're safe, and that's the main thing.'

Hearing Joanie's voice, Eddie jumped up and opened the door. Introductions over, it was time to eat.

Joycie Smith had never felt so lonely in all her living years. Even when she'd married Stanley, she'd been sure she never really loved him, but now he'd gone for good, she knew what love actually was. There was an old saying, 'you never know what you've got until it's gone' and Joycie couldn't stop thinking about him. She wasn't angry any more, just sad, tearful and full of self-loathing. Stanley leaving her for another woman was all her fault and she knew it. If only she had treated him better, spoken to him with respect and told him she loved him now and again.

Pouring herself another brandy and Baileys, Joyce stared forlornly at the photo album. In one of the photographs, Stanley was holding Raymond as a baby. He looked so happy, a real proud dad. It was just after Raymond was born when Joyce had stopped having sex with her husband. She'd only ever wanted a couple of kids and being lucky enough to have one of each spelled the end of her and Stanley's sex life. Determined that her husband wasn't going to have his wicked way with her ever again, Joycie had even stopped sleeping in the same bed as him. She'd forced Stanley to move into the spare room and he'd stayed there.

The shrill ring of the phone snapped Joyce out of her reminiscing.

'How are you, Mum?' Raymond asked. Since Joey had given him a talking-to, Ray was determined to be a better son.

'Not good, love. I miss your dad so much,' Joyce mumbled before bursting into tears once more.

Raymond sighed. He and Polly were meant to be visiting friends this afternoon, but he couldn't turn his back on his mum in her hour of need. It might help if he spoke to his dad, man to man. It might make the silly old sod see sense.

'I'm gonna go and see Dad right now and then I'll drive straight over to yours. Keep your chin up, Mum, the old man will come home at some point, I know he will.'

Over in Holloway, Frankie was having an interesting conversation with Katie Cooper. 'Freeflow', was the word the prison authorities used to describe the times where all prisoners on the wing were allowed to mix together, and Frankie had spent the last few days in this period getting to know Katie better. Frankie hadn't asked her to get a message to Jed yet, as she was still dubious as to whether Katie could be trusted or not.

'So, what happened with you and Jed? Do you wanna talk about it?' Katie asked kindly.

Frankie shook her head. She had no intention of spilling her guts to Katie.

Katie squeezed Frankie's hand. She knew what the poor girl had been through, as she and her sister had both suffered in the same way. 'Look, I know you don't trust me because I'm a traveller, but I ain't like Jed and his family. Some of us are decent people and my mum always brought me and my sisters up in the proper way. That's why what happened was so awful. My sister hasn't recovered from what Jed did to us, even to this day. Neither have I, to be honest, that's why I've ended up in here.'

Intrigued to know more, Frankie clasped Katie's arm. Instinct told her that this girl had something spicy to say and the more ammunition she had against Jed, the better. 'Do you wanna talk about it?' she asked.

Katie nodded and dragged Frankie towards her cell. Once inside, she urged the screw to leave them be and pushed the door to.

'I was fourteen and Debs, my sister, was fifteen when Jed moved onto our site in Basildon. It was only a small site and there were few lads our age there, so he was an instant hit with all us girls. Jed was only about thirteen then, but he was old for his age. He was good looking, a real charmer even then, and he had this old pick-up truck that he used to drive about in. He used to take me and me sister for rides up and down the lane outside, then try and snog us both before he took us back.'

Frankie nodded knowingly. Visions of her meeting Jed in the Berwick Manor flashed through her mind. 'He could charm the birds out of the trees when I first met him, so I know where you're coming from,' she said.

Katie had tears in her eyes as she carried on talking. Speaking about what had happened was extremely difficult for her, but she was determined to tell Frankie, she wanted her to know the truth. 'My sister started to date Jed properly when she was sixteen. My mum wasn't happy; she didn't trust Jed, and she hated his mum, Alice. My mum was a real lady compared to most travelling women. She never swore or drank and she kept herself to herself. Anyway, one night Jed and his cousin Sammy took me and my sister over to Tilbury in the truck. Jed's dad had a trailer there and he said we were going to a party. Me and my sister thought loads of other people would be there, but when we got there, it was just the four of us. The trailer was on an old scrapyard in the middle of nowhere, so there was no way we could escape.'

Frankie felt tears running down her own face as memories of her mum infiltrated her mind.

'Are you OK?' Katie asked, squeezing her hand.

'My mum died at that trailer,' Frankie whispered.

'I'm so sorry, perhaps I shouldn't tell you any more. I really didn't mean to upset you,' Katie said apologetically.

Frankie wiped her eyes with the cuff of her sweatshirt. 'I'm OK now. You carry on.'

'Me and my sister were both virgins. Outsiders always think that travelling girls are slags, but nothing could be further from the truth. We do tend to get married young, but that's because we are taught never to sleep with a boy until we have a ring on our finger. Travelling boys all sleep around, but that's why they go out with gorjer girls, 'cause they can't get what they want off us. Being a virgin on your wedding night is a must for a travelling girl.'

'Really?' Frankie asked, surprised. She'd always thought that travelling girls were tarts and was shocked by how little she really knew about them.

'Honest, it's classed as a sin to have sex before marriage in our community. Anyway, going back to that night, Jed and Sammy tried to get us drunk on vodka. Me and Debs weren't big drinkers, but we drank quite a bit just to be polite. We were quite enjoying ourselves until Jed dragged Debs into the bedroom and left me with Sammy.'

Frankie immediately knew the outcome of the story. 'You

don't have to tell me no more. I can guess the rest. Jed raped your sister, didn't he?'

Katie nodded tearfully. 'I remember my sister's screams as though it were yesterday. I begged Sammy to do something to stop Jed hurting her, but he laughed and then did the same to me.'

'What, Sammy raped you as well?' Frankie asked, horrified.

'Yeah, then they threatened us afterwards. Jed and Sammy told me and Debs if we ever breathed a word about what they'd done, they would kill our mum.'

'And did you tell anyone?'

'No, not for ages, but then my mum noticed me getting really fat and that was when I found out I was pregnant. Even then, I didn't tell her the truth. I was frightened of her getting killed, so I told her that I'd consented to sex with some boy I'd met in Pitsea market.'

'So, did you get rid of the baby?' Frankie asked her.

'Yeah, but not until after I'd given birth. His name is John and he lives with my aunt in Kent. I was too far gone to have an abortion, so we moved away and my aunt is now bringing him up as her own.'

'Do you still have any contact with him?' Frankie asked nosily. The story sounded a little far-fetched for her liking.

Katie burst into tears. 'No, when he was first born I couldn't even look at him, but then one day I went to see him and he was so gorgeous. He looked nothing like Sammy – he was as blonde as Sammy is dark. My mum went mental when she found out I'd turned up at my aunt's trailer. Our relationship has never been the same since she found out I was pregnant and she'd made me promise that I would never try to contact John. That's why I ended up in here. I so wanted him back that I kidnapped him and ran away to Scotland.'

'But how can they lock you up if John's really yours?' Frankie asked suspiciously.

'I never told the police that he was mine. My sister said she would never forgive me if I opened up a can of worms and I, stupidly, listened to her. I got two years for his kidnap and I've already done six months of that. When the solicitor told me that I was looking at a custodial sentence, I had a couple of flings, hoping that if I got pregnant they wouldn't put me away. That's how I ended up with this little one,' Katie said, patting her swollen belly.

'Can you do me a favour?' Frankie asked bluntly. She wasn't sure whether to believe Katie's yarn or not, but she had no other way of getting a message to Jed.

Katie shrugged. 'What?'

'Do you know anyone that can get a message to Jed for me? My kids ran away from him recently to find me, and my solicitor is taking the case to court so I can have visits with them. Jed, being Jed, is contesting it. He doesn't want them to see me ever again.'

'My cousin Danny still sees Jed. What is the message?'

'Tell your cousin to tell Jed that if he stops me seeing Georgie and Harry then I'm gonna tell the police the truth about everything.'

'And what is the truth?' Katie asked sympathetically.

Frankie was saved from answering by a screw opening the cell door.

'Come on, Mitchell, back to your own cell. Freeflow is over now.'

Squeezing Katie's hand, Frankie stood up and walked away. She glanced back at her. 'See what you can do for me, Katie.'

Katie nodded. 'I'll sort it, I promise.'

Raymond had little joy in tracking his father down, so he got up early and drove back to Orsett the following morning. Eddie had understood when he'd explained his predicament.

'Listen, I like Joycie, so you do what you can to make her happy again. Me and the lads can still go to Milton Keynes. It's silly five of us going, anyway,' Ed insisted.

Pulling up outside Pat the Pigeon's house, Raymond smirked. Unlike the previous day, his father's car was parked on the drive and he was pleased he hadn't had another wasted journey. Raymond knocked on the front door. His nickname for Pat was 'the Trollop' and it was the Trollop who answered it.

'Is me dad there?' he asked coldly.

'Wait there and I'll fetch him,' Pat replied, just as icily.

Stanley appeared a couple of minutes later and glared at his son. He'd never truly forgiven Raymond for his involvement on the night of Jessica's murder.

'I'm cleaning out the pigeons. What do you want?' he asked, clearly rattled.

'We need to talk, Dad. Not here, somewhere else.'

'There's nothing more to say, Raymond. I've said everything I wanted to your mother.'

'There's a boozer I know not ten minutes from here that opens early. Let's go there for a pint, Dad, so we can talk properly.'

'I don't want to drink at nine o'clock in the morning. Anyway I can't, Pat and I are racing the pigeons today.'

Getting annoyed by his father's shirty attitude, Raymond grabbed him by the neck of his jumper and dragged him out of the front door.

'What are you doing? Get off me, you fucking thug,' Stanley shouted loudly.

'I'm taking you back home where you belong. Mum is in bits because of you and I ain't having her heart broken. It's nearly Christmas, for fuck's sake. How's she meant to get through the festive period without you and Jessica, eh?'

Pat the Pigeon, who had had her nose pressed to the window, now flung it open. 'You OK, Stanley?' she yelled, as her fancy man was dragged down the path.

'Ring the police, Pat,' Stanley gasped.

Raymond glanced around and saw Pat with the phone pressed to her ear. Eddie liked his employees to keep their noses clean and he couldn't afford to get nicked for kidnapping his own father. Polly wouldn't be overly impressed, either.

As Raymond let go of him, Stanley fell backwards and landed on his backside. Ray stared at him with a look of pure hatred on his face. 'You're no father of mine any more. Mum can do better than you, anyway. You and that old trollop deserve one another.'

Eddie Mitchell got to Milton Keynes long before the Victoria Inn opened its doors. He checked out the park the dog-walker had told him about on his last visit and decided it was too open.

'What about over there, Dad? There's more woodland over that side,' Gary suggested.

Eddie shrugged. 'We'll have to see if we can park over that way somewhere. There's too many people over here and we'll stand out like sore thumbs dragging Colin across the park. We ain't even got a fucking dog to make it look kosher.'

'We can always put Colin on a lead,' Ricky joked.

Eddie chuckled, then turned to Stuart. 'We'll have a little drive around, there's bound to be somewhere more remote than this.'

The lads jumped back into the Range Rover and within ten minutes Eddie had found the exact kind of spot they were looking for. It was a dirt track over the other side of the park. There were no houses, no people and thick clumps of trees.

'Right, this will do nicely. Now, remember exactly where it is and we'll take a drive towards the pub. It will be open in half-hour and I wanna grab hold of the cunt before he goes in there,' Eddie said.

Fifteen minutes later, the Range Rover was parked in a turning between the pub and the road where Colin Griffiths lived.

'How do you know he walks there? He might take his motor,' Ricky said.

'Would you fucking drive if you lived less than a five-minute walk away?' Eddie replied sarcastically.

At five to twelve exactly, Ricky spotted Colin. 'That's him with the brown leather jacket on,' he told Stuart.

Stuart put on his baseball cap and got out of the Range Rover. He felt no nerves; the whole experience was exhilarating for him.

'All right, mate?' Stuart said as he crept up behind Colin and put a friendly arm around his neck.

'Get off me, you weirdo,' Colin said trying to push him away.

Stuart was tall and strong and Colin was no match for him. Stu glanced around and, positive that no one was watching him, flicked open the knife and held the blade against Colin's throat.

'Walk with me and you won't get hurt,' he said, as he led him towards the Range Rover.

'Who are you? What do you want from me?' Colin asked fearfully.

Eddie waved and Colin's face turned pure white as he spotted him.

Stuart shoved Colin in the back of the motor.

'I'm sorry about not paying you on time, Eddie. I weren't gonna knock you. I'll get you your money, I promise,' Colin stammered.

'Pass me the bat,' Ed ordered Gary.

Gary took the baseball bat out from under the seat and placed it on his father's lap. Eddie stopped at the red traffic light, turned around and clumped Colin over the head with it.

'Mr Mitchell to you. Only my friends call me Eddie, you cunt.'

Colin clutched his throbbing head. Whatever had possessed him to think he could stripe up Eddie Mitchell and get away with it? He must have been mad. 'I'm really sorry. I'll pay you interest and everything,' Colin begged as Eddie pulled up on the dirt track.

'Get him out and walk him through them trees,' Eddie ordered his sons.

'What exactly do you want me to do to him?' Stuart asked Eddie.

Eddie put on a pair of latex gloves, and took an axe out of the boot. 'He needs to be taught a lesson. One finger, perhaps two, I'll let you choose, boy.'

Gary stopped by a clump of trees, kneed Colin in the groin and sniggered as he rolled on the floor in agony.

Eddie walked over to their victim and crouched down beside him. 'I want twenty-five grand off you and I want it by the end of next week. Comprendes?'

'I'll get your money for you, I swear,' Colin promised.

'I'll be coming to your house at midday next Friday to pick it up and if you ain't got every last penny of it, you're a dead man.'

'I understand, Mr Mitchell.'

Gary glanced at Ricky as Eddie gave Stuart the nod. Now they would see what their father's golden boy was made of.

'Please God, no,' Colin screamed, as he spotted Stuart holding the axe.

Stuart knelt on Colin's left arm, then brought the axe down expertly just past his knuckles.

Colin's screams filled the cold December air as two of his fingers parted company with his hand.

Eddie found Colin's phone in his pocket. The prick looked as if he was losing consciousness and he needed to act fast. 'Can you hear me, Colin?'

Colin nodded.

'Right, I'm gonna dial nine, nine, nine, then you're gonna ask for an ambulance. Tell them that you're at the dirt track that leads to the back end of the park. When they turn up, you tell them you were chopping branches off the trees for a bonfire and you had a little accident, OK?'

'OK,' Colin croaked.

Eddie dialled the number and was relieved when Colin managed to tell the operator where he was.

'What they for?' Ricky asked, as his father threw a roll of dustbin liners on the ground.

'Well, he weren't gonna carry the fucking branches home in his hands, was he now?' Ed replied cuttingly.

'See you next Friday, Colin,' Ed said, prodding him. The two fingers were lying next to Colin's body, one with his wedding ring still attached.

Colin had his eyes shut now and Ed urged the lads to get back to the motor fast. 'We'd better wait nearby, make sure the ambulance finds him,' he said.

'Do you reckon they'll be able to sew his fingers back on?' Stuart asked seriously.

Gary, Ricky and Eddie all burst out laughing. Stuart had been a real dab hand with the axe and his cool persona had impressed all of them.

Hearing sirens, Eddie glanced in his interior mirror. The ambulance had slowed down and had turned into the road that led to the dirt track. 'I think we should stop for a beer when we get back near home. We can toast Stuart's success on passing his trial.'

Ricky held out his right hand. 'Well done, Stu. You were great.'

Stuart shook his hand and then grinned as Gary also offered him a handshake. 'You did good! Welcome to the firm, Stuie boy.'

CHAPTER FOURTEEN

The day prior to Christmas Eve, Jed and his cousin Sammy went out on one of their notorious all-day drinking sessions. Their pub crawl started with well-known travellers' haunts. They went to the Derby Digger in Wickford, the Bear in Noak Hill and had a skinful in the Farmhouse Tavern in Rush Green. They finally ended up in the Ship and Shovel in Barking, where they blagged two thirty-year-old birds and ended up back at their flat. At 6 a.m. Jed snorted his last line of cocaine, then wiped his finger over the wrap and rubbed the final grains around his gums.

'That's it, we've no more gear left,' he said to the none-too-pretty bird who had been sucking him off for the last fifteen minutes. The bird released Jed's penis from her mouth, moved up the bed and laid her head lovingly on his chest. Jed studied her as she tilted her head and smiled at him. He'd been well pissed when he'd met her last night, but in the cold light of day, she was not only fat, but also pig ugly. Jed pushed her off him, stood up and searched for his clothes.

'Shall I make you some breakfast?' the girl asked, completely smitten.

'No, I've gotta get home. Me chavvies will be wondering where I am.'

'What's a chavvie?'

Jed ignored her dumb question and went to find his cousin. He found him on the sofa, naked and snuggled up to the pig's mate. Jed punched Sammy on the arm.

'Come on, it's Christmas Eve. Let's gel.'

With only vague memories of the previous evening, Sammy

jumped up and quickly got dressed. He was now living with Julie, Sally's mate, but he had her well under the thumb and came and went as he pleased.

'You ain't going yet, are ya?' Sammy's conquest asked.

Jed and Sammy both stared at the girl. Her skin was pure white, and she had ginger hair, freckles and a wide nose that was far too big for her face.

'Fuck me and I thought mine was a moose,' Jed said, laughing.

'Come on, I feel ill looking at that,' Sammy said, dragging his cousin towards the front door. Neither Jed nor Sammy said goodbye to the girls; they didn't even know their names.

Unable to remember driving to the flat, Jed was relieved to see his Shogun parked across the road.

'You must have had a dig in this last night, Jed. Look at the bumper and your wheel arch,' Sammy said.

Jed glanced at the damage, then chuckled. 'If I were you I wouldn't worry about me having a dig in this – you wanna worry about what part of your anatomy you were digging into that monster you got hold of last night. I've shagged some rotters in my time, but ole ginger minge beats 'em all. You wanna get yourself down that clinic, Sammy boy.'

Playfully punching his cousin on the arm, Sammy got into the motor and was surprised to see a half-empty bottle of Jack Daniel's lying in the footwell. 'Where did we get this from? Did we drink all that?' he asked, picking the bottle up.

Jed shrugged. Neither he nor Sammy were usually whiskey drinkers, and Jed vaguely remembered a fellow traveller giving them the bottle in the Farmhouse Tavern.

Sammy unscrewed the lid, took a large gulp and handed the bottle to Jed, who did the same. 'Ain't there a boozer open now? I fancy carrying on for another few hours,' Sammy said.

Jed turned the ignition and grinned. 'I've got a better idea than going to some poxy boozer.'

'What?' Sammy asked.

'Harry Mitchell's buried not ten minutes from here. Let's go over the cemetery, drink the rest of our JD and trash his grave. I remember Frankie telling me that Eddie Mitchell goes over there on Christmas Eve, so we can give the cunt a nice surprise, can't we?'

Sammy roared with laughter. 'Come on, let's do it.'

Eddie Mitchell woke up early and arched his body into Gina's back. He was really looking forward to Christmas this year, having just spent the last four in Wandsworth nick. It would also be the first time he and Gina had celebrated the festivities together, which made it even more special.

'Stop it,' Gina giggled, as she felt his erection rubbing against her buttocks. Eddie chuckled and rubbed his hands against her pregnant stomach. She was only ten weeks gone and was hardly showing, but he liked to wind her up, as he knew she was paranoid about getting really fat and being unable to lose the weight after the baby was born.

'Fuckin' hell, girl. You ain't 'arf piling it on already,' he joked.

'Oh, don't say that,' Gina said turning towards him to see if he was serious.

'I'm only winding you up, there's fuck-all of ya,' Eddie said, laughing.

Gina playfully slapped his chest. 'What time is it?'

'Seven.'

'And why have you woken me at this unearthly hour? You'd better have a bloody good reason,' Gina said, pretending to be annoyed.

Eddie grabbed her hand and put it on his fully erect penis. 'That good enough for ya?'

Gina laughed. 'I suppose it'll have to be.'

Joycie Smith put the sausage rolls in the oven then sat down to drink her cup of tea. Everyone coming to her for Christmas Day had been a last-minute arrangement. Raymond had originally been spending the day with Polly and her parents in their new house in Loughton, but because of everything that had happened with Stanley, Raymond had insisted on coming to her instead.

'You can't rattle around on your own in this big house at Christmas, Mum. Why don't I invite Polly and her parents over here and we can all spend it together? There's plenty of room here and Polly, her parents and I can all stay the night.'

Joyce had reluctantly agreed. She hated Polly's parents, but was glad she was spending the day with her son. Since Jessica had died, Christmas had always been a difficult time for her and at least if she had a houseful she could keep herself busy with all the cooking and preparation that went with it. Joey and Dominic were coming for dinner and were also staying the night. Eddie had invited her over to his for dinner on Boxing Day, but Joyce had declined, as she was wary of meeting Gina. It would feel strange seeing another woman in Jessica's shoes, and Joyce was worried that she might find the experience too emotional, especially at this time of year.

Joyce hadn't heard a word from or about her philandering husband since the day Raymond had gone round to see him. She had been devastated when her son had returned home and told her that Stanley was staying with the old slapper, but her devastation had now turned to anger. She still had her off days where she would burst into tears but, overall, she was coping. Stanley had made her look a laughing stock and she would never forgive him for that as long as she lived. One day Stanley would come crawling back with his tail between his legs, and if Joyce allowed him to move back in, she would make his life hell.

Finishing her cuppa, Joyce stood up. She hated those shop-bought mince pies – her own were much better and she was determined to impress Polly's parents. The doorbell stopped her in her tracks. It was ever so early and she certainly wasn't expecting anyone. She had recently changed all the locks and briefly wondered if it was Stanley.

'Surprise!' two voices said in unison, as she opened the front door.

Joyce stood with her mouth open. Rita and Hilda were her oldest friends and had been brilliant since the Stanley episode.

'Ain't you gonna invite us in?' Hilda asked, waving a bottle of sherry in the air.

'Course I am. I'm just shocked to see ya both, especially this bleedin' early.'

Rita laughed and handed Joyce a big bouquet of flowers.

'My Albert has gone to see his witch of a sister in Ockendon, so he dropped us off on the way. Me and Hilda would like to come over Jessica's grave with ya. That's what the flowers are for.'

Smiling, Joyce led them into the lounge. She had a lovely family, wonderful friends and Stanley could go and fuck himself.

Half-an-hour later, the postman's arrival turned Joycie's new-found happiness into despair. 'Oh, my giddy aunt,' she cried.

'Whatever's the matter?' Rita asked, as Joyce sank to her knees.

Joyce waved the letter in the air. 'It's Stanley. He's filed for divorce.'

Over at East London Cemetery, Jed and Sammy sat down on a grave opposite Harry Mitchell's and admired their handiwork. Jed always kept a load of crap in the motor for when they did odd jobs for old people whom they later conned, and he had just decorated Harry's grave in red and blue paint. Sammy had joined in by smashing the headstone with a big hammer and Jed was now ready to put the icing on the cake.

'Why don't we trash his old woman's grave an' all?' Sammy suggested. Harry had bought his own plot years before his death so he could be laid to rest beside his beloved wife.

'Nah, we ain't got time,' Jed said, snatching the bottle from Sammy and downing the last of the Jack Daniel's. Smashing the empty bottle against Harry's headstone, Jed stood up, took some tissue out of his pocket and crouched down on Harry's grave.

'What the fuck you doing?' Sammy asked, confused.

'Having a shit – what does it look like?' Jed chuckled.

Sammy creased up laughing as Jed performed his dirty deed. 'Do you think we'll find a boozer open now?' he asked as Jed wiped his arse with a tissue.

Jed ignored his cousin's question and stared at the destroyed grave. Cocaine always gave him the shits and his diarrhoea was steaming in the cold December air. 'That's what you get for shooting my grandad, Mitchell. Happy Christmas, you old cunt.'

Laughing like hyenas, Jed and Sammy legged it from the scene of the crime.

Eddie was in a jovial mood as he picked Joey up and drove towards Upminster. Firstly they were visiting Jessica's grave, then his mum and dad's graves, where they were meeting his uncle Reg, and aunts Vi and Joanie. From there they were going to have a few drinks in Canning Town to toast Harry's memory.

'So, are Vi and Reg going to be there as well?' Joey asked warily.

'Yeah, why do you sound so worried?' Eddie asked.

'I just sense they aren't that comfortable with my sexuality, that's all.'

Eddie laughed. 'Fuck 'em, what do they know, eh?'

When they pulled up at the cemetery, Joey grabbed a bunch of flowers from the back seat and smiled. His dad's acceptance of him and Dominic as a couple meant the world to him.

'So where is lover boy today?' Ed asked.

'He's gone to visit his nan. Dom's parents forbade him to tell her about us in case it gave her a heart attack. She's got a dodgy ticker, apparently.'

Eddie chuckled, but as they reached Jessica's grave his mood turned sombre. 'Hello, my darling,' he said sadly.

Joey arranged the flowers and then placed the Christmas card he'd bought for his mum next to them. 'THE WORLD'S GREATEST MUM' was plastered across the front and as Joey began to read the inscription inside, Eddie crouched down and began to weep. 'I still love you, sweetheart, and I hope you don't think that because I'm now with Gina that I've forgotten about you. I'll never forget you, Jess, and there ain't a day goes by when I don't miss you, babe.'

Not used to seeing his dad cry, Joey bent down and put a comforting arm around his father's shoulder. He was crying himself now, but not to the same extent as his dad. 'Come on, let's go before we upset ourselves any further,' he said.

Eddie kissed the inside of his hand and placed it against Jessica's headstone. He'd been here a few times since he'd come out of prison, but he never stayed long, as it upset him

131

too much. As they walked back to the car park, Eddie dried his eyes on the cuff of his jumper.

'You must think I'm a right soppy prick,' he said to Joey.

Joey shook his head. 'Course I don't, but shall I tell you what I do think?'

'What?'

'I think me and you are far more alike than we ever gave ourselves credit for, apart from me being gay, of course.'

Eddie smiled. He loved Gary and Ricky dearly, but just lately he'd felt closer to Joey than he ever had to them. He put his arm around him.

'Like father, like son, eh?'

Joey laughed. 'Like father, like son.'

Back in Rainham, Rita and Hilda were caught in a bit of a quandary. The letter from Stanley's solicitor had tipped Joyce over the edge and, after crying and drinking herself senseless, she had now collapsed in a heap on the carpet.

'What are we gonna do? Try her Raymond again,' Rita ordered Hilda.

Rita had found Joycie's address book and had been ringing both numbers listed for Raymond. She tried them both again.

'Well?' Rita asked impatiently. Albert would be back to pick her up soon, but she couldn't leave Joyce on her own in this state.

'There's no answer on the home phone and on the other one some woman is saying, "We can't connect your call."'

'What woman? Ask her where Raymond is, then,' Rita yelled.

'Don't fucking shout: I can't ask her, it's one of them answerphone thingymebobs.'

'This is all your fault. What did you have to bring her that bloody sherry over for?' Rita said.

'Don't bleedin' well blame me. I didn't know she was gonna drink the whole bastard bottle, did I?' Hilda hollered.

Seeing the funny side of matters, Rita burst out laughing. 'There ain't never a dull moment with our Joycie, is there?'

Hilda creased up. 'You can fucking say that again.'

Another person currently drunk and lying on the carpet was Sally Baldwin.

'Terry, quick!' shouted Anne, Sally's stepmum.

Terry Baldwin ran up the stairs and stared at his comatose daughter in despair. Since having the miscarriage and coming out of hospital all Sally had done was sit in her room moping about and drinking herself senseless. Terry lifted his daughter's body up and lay her on the bed.

'I searched this room yesterday and couldn't find any booze. Have a butcher's around, Anne, see if you can find where she's fucking stashing it.'

Sick of the sight of Terry's daughter, Anne reluctantly did as she was told. She could understand that Sally had been through hell in the past few months, but even so, the girl wasn't helping herself and was causing marital misery between her and Terry. Wishing more than anything that Sally would sod off back to her own flat in Rush Green, Anne burst out crying.

'I can't stand this any more, Terry. The girl needs help and we're not doctors. She needs professional help, not ours.'

Terry held his unhappy wife in his arms. Anne did have a point, as Sally's behaviour was getting worse rather than better. 'We'll get Christmas over and I'll ring a doctor and sort it. I reckon they'll send her to rehab, but if they don't they'll probably section her.'

Anne hugged her husband and together they left Sally's bedroom. Terry glanced at his daughter to check she was still asleep before he closed the door. What he didn't realise at that point was that Sally was awake and had heard every word he'd said.

Eddie circled around like a vulture, looking for a parking space. Christmas Eve was always an extremely busy time at cemeteries and today was no different.

'Over there, Dad. Look, that geezer in the red car's pulling out.'

Eddie swooped for the spot and turned off the ignition.

'Where we meeting the others?' Joey asked.

'At the graveside. I knew there'd be nowhere to park, so I told Reg to pick Joanie and Vi up in a cab and I'll give him the dosh for it. None of 'em can walk far now, the poor bastards.'

Eddie and Joey were early, so took a slow stroll through the graveyard. The place was awash with people, flowers and cards. On some of the graves there were even presents and teddy bears that people had left for their loved ones.

As Eddie strolled past two elderly women who were talking loudly, he couldn't help but overhear their conversation.

'I think it's bloody disgusting. Go and find someone with one of them portable phones and get them to call the police,' the stout lady said.

'The bastards want locking up. How can they do something like that in a cemetery, of all places?' the other replied.

Forever the gentleman, Eddie turned around. It sounded to him as though one of the ladies had had their purse or bag snatched. 'Are you OK, ladies?' he enquired.

Both women shook their heads. 'You wanna see the state of one of the graves down there. It's been vandalised beyond recognition,' the stout woman replied.

'My sister's plot is only half a dozen away from it an' all,' said the other.

Eddie immediately felt his whole body stiffen. His inner sense told him that the grave that had been attacked was probably his father's. 'Whereabouts is the grave?' he asked, feeling queasy.

The smaller woman pointed her finger. 'Over the back there, on the right.'

Grabbing Joey's arm, Eddie broke into a run.

'You don't think its Grandad's, do you?' Joey asked worriedly.

As Eddie neared his father's grave the first thing he saw was the red and blue paint. 'The fucking bastards, I'll kill 'em,' he screamed.

When they reached the actual grave, Joey spotted the diarrhoea and grabbed his father's arm. 'Come on, let's go and find the others before they find us. You don't want Auntie Vi and Joanie to see this. Me and you can come back later and clean it up.'

Eddie stared at the expensive granite headstone, that was now smashed, and felt his eyes well up for the second time that day. 'I'll kill the fuckers when I get hold of 'em, Joey, I'll throttle the fucking life out of 'em.'

'Do you think Grandad's grave was picked on purposely? Or do you reckon it was just vandals?' Joey asked.

Eddie's eyes clouded over with anger. 'This was done on purpose all right, and whoever did it is the same cunt who murdered him.'

Oblivious to their father's gruesome discovery, Gary and Ricky were sitting in the Barge Aground in Barking having a few pints and debating what they should do next. Neither were particularly close to their mother. She was a drunk and an embarrassment, but they were still concerned for her well-being and had been unable to get in touch with her for the past week now.

'I think we should go back round there and break in,' Gary said. They'd already knocked at their mum's house twice this morning to give her her Christmas presents.

Ricky was concerned, but not as much as his brother. 'You know what muvver's like – she's probably on one of her benders and is dossing round some low-life's house.'

Gary sighed anxiously. When their mum had first met their dad she'd been absolutely stunning. Gary and Ricky would never have believed it if their dad hadn't shown him the photographs. Their mum's decline into alcohol addiction started the minute their dad walked out the door, and Gary and Ricky had had a crappy childhood living with her, even back then. The only thing that had got them through their younger years was spending the weekends with their father.

Ricky finished his beer and stood up. 'Come on then, if you're that worried let's go and break in.'

Beverley lived literally five minutes away from the Barge Aground. The house still belonged to Eddie, and because she was the mother of two of his children, he'd let Beverley live there rent-free for years.

'Shall we break a window or kick the door in?' Ricky asked, as he and Gary pulled up outside. Seeing the nosy old bat next door peering through the curtains, Gary stuck two fingers up at her. He'd knocked at a few of the neighbours', including her, earlier to ask if they'd seen his mum and they'd all been extremely unhelpful.

135

'Let's try and kick the door in; we can always put another lock on for her,' Gary said.

Kicking the door repeatedly with the sole of his shoe, Gary couldn't get it to budge. 'Let's walk back a few yards and when I count to three, boot it with me,' Gary ordered. 'One, two, three.'

As the door flew open, Ricky vomited and Gary staggered backwards overpowered by the rancid smell of death.

After explaining to Joanie, Vi and Reg that Harry's grave had been vandalised by mindless yobs, Eddie dropped Joey at his apparently pissed grandmother's house. Joycie's mates had rung Joey and, sitting at home now, being comforted by Gina, Ed wished he was as pissed as Joycie as well.

'Pour us another Scotch, babe,' he said to Gina.

As Gina stood up the phone rang.

'If that's for me, tell whoever it is I ain't in. I'm not in the mood for talking to no cunt today,' Eddie shouted out. He was stressed, angry and upset, and the more he thought about the state of his father's grave, the more he thought about the O'Haras. They had something to do with the vandalism and his father's death, he'd convinced himself of that.

Gina walked back into the room with her hand over the mouthpiece of the phone. 'It's Gary. He says it's urgent,' she whispered.

'I ain't in,' Eddie mouthed, waving his hands in annoyance.

'He's really upset, I think something has happened to him,' Gina whispered again.

Eddie snatched the phone angrily out of Gina's hands. 'Whatever it is, make it fucking quick,' he spat.

'It's Mum. She's dead.'

CHAPTER FIFTEEN

Jimmy O'Hara woke up in a foul mood on Christmas morning for two reasons. Firstly, his grandkids had woken him at 6 a.m. with that awful Mr Blobby record and, secondly, he'd had some news yesterday that had made his blood boil to an extremely high temperature.

Bobby Berkley had been avoiding Jimmy's calls, so Jimmy had spent the previous day tracking him down. He'd finally found him in a boozer in Crays Hill and had demanded to know what was going on.

'I'm sorry, Jimmy. I ain't been avoiding you, mush, I was just trying to get your wonga together before I contacted you. What's happened is that when you paid me that dosh up front for you know what, Pete told me to put it together with what I had stashed of his and purchase a bit of land with it. The land ain't far from here and was going for a song. Then a couple of days later, I visits Pete in Belmarsh and he informs me that Mr Mitchell's brothers have been shunted to a different wing. Apparently, they got beaten up and were moved for their own safety. Pete says he's still gonna try and get to 'em if he can, but I didn't wanna call you, Jimmy, not until I got ya five grand back. I was gonna return you your dough and if Pete does manage to catch up with 'em, you can give me the full whack all at once.'

Jimmy wasn't annoyed about the dosh. He'd known Bobby and Pete Berkley for years and he knew they wouldn't knock him. What he was annoyed about was Eddie Mitchell double-crossing him. He didn't believe for a minute that fate had played a hand in Paulie and Ronny being moved and Jimmy was determined to find out the truth and then make Eddie Mitchell pay the price.

'Nanny, Grandad, can we open our presents now?' Georgie asked, leaping on her grandparents' bed. Georgie had tried to wake her father, but he'd gone out last night with their Uncle Sammy and wouldn't get out of bed.

'Of course you can,' Alice said, hugging her granddaughter.

Jimmy pointed an angry finger at Georgie. 'That bastard record is driving me mad now. I don't wanna hear it no more today – got me?'

Seeing Georgie's lip wobble, Alice punched her miserable husband on the arm. 'I don't know what or who has rattled your cage, Jimmy O'Hara, but if you spoil mine and the chavvies' Christmas, I'm leaving you for good, understand?'

Wary of his wife's threat and temper, Jimmy immediately apologised.

Terry Baldwin bent down next to Sally's bed and gently shook his daughter. The money he'd shelled out to Jamie Carroll in the Thatched House car park in Barking had left him rather short of readies, but he'd still managed to push the boat out, present-wise, for Sally. He'd wanted to cheer her up a bit.

'Wakey, wakey, darling. Are you going to come downstairs and open up your presents?'

Sally ignored her father's question and pulled the quilt over her head.

'Sally, you can't carry on like this, love. I'm ever so worried about you. Please come downstairs.'

With memories of her son, Luke, flashing through her mind, Sally closed her eyes and wept.

Hearing his phone ringing in the other room, Terry shut Sally's bedroom door and went to answer it.

'It's done,' the caller said.

Terry smiled as the line went dead. That call was the best Christmas present he could have wished for.

Over in Rainham, Dominic had just turned up at Joycie's house with Madonna in his arms. He put the dog on the floor and hugged Joey.

'Did you bring all our presents with you?' Joey asked hopefully.

Dominic shook his head. 'I searched under the tree and found all the family presents. I thought what we'd do is pop home on the way to your dad's tomorrow and open ours then.'

Joey nodded. 'I'm gonna wake Nan up now. I think Raymond and the others are coming over at eleven, so she needs to get her skates on. I put the turkey in the oven at six o'clock this morning for her, but she'll have to do the rest herself.'

'How is she?' Dom asked concerned.

'She was in an awful state when I arrived last night and I'm really annoyed with my grandad. I can't believe that he sent her divorce papers through at Christmas; no wonder she got herself so drunk. I know my nan has been an old cow at times to Grandad over the years, but she doesn't deserve to be treated like this, it's so wrong.'

Dominic agreed. He liked Joycie; she was one of life's characters.

Upstairs, Joyce sat up with a dry mouth, vague memories, and a blinding headache. She stared at Joey. 'I don't remember coming to bed or anything,' she mumbled.

'Me and Rita had to half-carry you upstairs, Nan. I've never seen you that drunk before, you couldn't even stand. Grandad's bang out of order for what he did and I've decided I want no more to do with him.'

Joyce gave her loyal grandson a hug. 'What's the time?' she asked groggily.

'It's just gone nine.'

Horrified that she hadn't got up at six as she'd planned, Joyce jumped out of bed. 'The turkey!' she screamed.

'I put that on early this morning,' Joey told her.

Joyce thanked her grandson, then went for a shower. As the warm water cascaded over her body, Joyce vowed there and then that she would never be upset over, or mention her husband ever again. From today onwards, Stanley Smith was history.

Gina put a cup of coffee on the bedside cabinet, sat down on the edge of the bed and stared at her husband. He was so bloody handsome even when he was sleeping. Gina had been

139

up since the crack of dawn. The turkey she had cooked yesterday, but everything else she'd prepared this morning. Her friend Claire was coming over for Christmas and was staying for a couple of days. Claire was still single and it had been Eddie's idea to invite her.

'Stuart's mum is going to her sister's in Cornwall, so you'd best invite your mate, Gina, else you're gonna be surrounded by fucking geezers,' he'd insisted.

Gina smiled as Eddie opened his eyes. She lay on the bed next to him and gave him a big hug. Yesterday had been an awful day for him and he'd sat up until five o'clock in the morning drinking downstairs with his sons. Unlike Jessica, whom Eddie spoke about often, Gina had never heard him mention his first wife, Beverley. She'd once asked him about her and he'd given her a three-word answer.

'She's an alkie,' he'd said and immediately changed the subject.

Eddie sat himself up. He felt like shit and wanted Christmas to be over already.

Seeing the pain in his eyes, Gina kissed him tenderly on the lips. 'I know it's going to be crap Christmas now, but let's try and get through it the best we can. A couple of days and it will all be over,' she said understandingly.

Eddie put his arms around her. 'When you're struck with a double dose of bad luck there will always be a third, Gina. Mark my words, we'll have another fucking disaster – it's on the cards.'

Jed laughed at Harry's excitement as he sat in his toy car. The bloody thing had cost him a fortune, but it had a proper little engine in it that was recharged by a generator.

'How fast does it actually go?' Jimmy asked Jed. He'd cheered up a bit now and was determined not to let Eddie Mitchell's double-dealing spoil his Christmas.

'Ten mile an hour. Let's take him outside and teach him how to drive it properly.'

Georgie was on cloud nine. She had been given some fantastic presents, but her favourite was the Barbie doll and all the accessories. She had loads of clothes to dress Barbie

140

in and Barbie even had her own sports car and a horse. 'Do you think I look like Barbie, Nanny?' she asked.

Alice laughed and hugged her granddaughter. 'You're much prettier than Barbie, Georgie girl.'

'Am I?' Georgie asked surprised.

Smothering Georgie with kisses, Alice carried her into the kitchen. 'You gonna try one of Nanna's sausage rolls?'

Georgie nodded and greedily ate three. Alice grinned. Over the past month or so Georgie had stopped being finicky and was eating like a horse. She was still waif-like, but that was because she was tall for her age.

'Let's take some sausage rolls outside to Harry and Daddy, shall we?'

Georgie ran into the lounge, grabbed Barbie and followed her nan out of the back door.

Jed, Alice and Jimmy watched Harry with pride. 'Look at him; he's a natural in that motor,' Jimmy said, laughing.

'Drive down the end, then do a three-point turn like I showed you, Harry,' Jed shouted out.

Harry skilfully did as he was told and drove back towards his father. Jed clapped, lifted him out of the car and swung him around in the air. 'You're gonna be a great driver, just like your daddy, ain't ya, boy?'

As Grandad Jimmy fussed over him and Nanny Alice kissed him and handed him a sausage roll, Harry grinned. He rather liked his new family after all.

Over in Holloway, Frankie and Babs were on a bit of a downer. They'd spent the past hour talking about their children and the realisation that they were both about to spend their first Christmas without them had suddenly hit them like a ton of bricks.

'I bet my Georgie and Harry are so unhappy today. I used to make such a fuss of 'em on Christmas Day and I bet they will have the day from hell with Jed, Jimmy and Alice,' Frankie said sadly.

Babs' heart went out to Frankie. She had been allowed to phone Matilda and Jordan this morning and she'd spoken to them for a good ten minutes. Poor Frankie wasn't even allowed to speak to her children and Babs prayed that the civil court hearing would go in her friend's favour.

'Let's not talk about our kids no more today. I mean, it ain't every day Holloway throws a party for us, so let's just enjoy ourselves, eh?' Babs suggested.

'Yeah, sod it. We're stuck in 'ere, neither of us can change that, so we might as well make the most of Christmas.'

Babs put an arm around her friend's shoulder. 'Me and you are gonna groove to that music later. We gonna show 'em how it's done. I do a great impression of Gloria Gaynor, you know.'

Frankie laughed. Babs was one of the funniest, sweetest people she had ever met and she certainly didn't deserve to be cooped up in prison. 'I want you to promise me something,' Frankie said.

'What?'

'I want you to promise me that in the New Year you'll let me have a word with my dad to see if he can help you with your trial. You shouldn't be in here, Babs, and when I get out I want you to be out there with me. Who's gonna be my best friend if you're stuck in here for years, eh?'

Babs smiled at her friend. 'The only promise I can give you is that I'll think about what you're saying, sweet child. Now, no more sad talk, let's go party.'

Stanley Smith had had the best Christmas Day ever so far. It had been Pat's idea to buy the pigeons' Christmas presents and bring the birds indoors for the day. 'Look at my Mildred, she's gonna fall off the bloody thing if she swings any faster,' Pat said, laughing.

Stanley chuckled. The pigeons loved their swings and his three were fighting over the same one. 'No, Willie, that one's yours,' Stanley said, pointing to the empty swing.

As Pat approached him from behind and put her arms around his waist, Stanley flinched nervously. He adored everything about Pat, bar one thing. He loved her smile, her personality, her hearty chuckle, her adoration and knowledge of pigeons, but she was always trying to touch and kiss him, which made Stanley feel very awkward indeed.

'I'm busting for a wee, love,' he said, loosening her grip on him.

Once inside the lavatory, Stanley stood over the toilet and stared at his small, flaccid penis. He hadn't had an erection for years and didn't even know if he was capable of having them any more. He'd never been sex-mad, even as a young man, and the thought of having to poke his John Thomas in someone at his age filled him with dread. Shaking his little problem, Stanley zipped himself up, washed his hands and stared at himself in the mirror. He was divorcing Joycie, and if he was to have a happy future with Pat, then he had to try and give the woman what she wanted.

Terry Baldwin picked up the knife and began to carve the turkey. Originally, Anne's sister and her husband were meant to be coming over for Christmas and staying a couple of days, but because of Sally's recent behaviour, Anne had cancelled the arrangement.

'My sister and her husband absolutely adore the festive time of year and it's not fair on them or Sally if they come here. We are bound to have a morbid Christmas because of poor little Luke and we'd be better spending it alone,' Anne insisted.

Initially, Terry had been in a good mood earlier because of the phone call he'd received, but then memories of last Christmas, which he'd spent with Luke, had come back to haunt him and he'd broken down. Anne had held him in her arms until his tears subsided. Determined now to try and be as upbeat as he possibly could, Terry grinned at his wife as she brought the potatoes and parsnips in.

'Do us a favour, love, go and tell Sally that dinner's ready, will ya?'

Terry had been upstairs to see his daughter twice in the last three hours and, seeing as he was having no joy enticing her out of her bedroom, he hoped Anne might have more luck.

Anne walked up the stairs and as she opened Sally's bedroom door, let out the most awful blood-curdling scream.

'Whatever's wrong?' Terry said, running up the stairs.

In such awful shock that she couldn't even speak, Anne pointed towards the wooden beams in the ceiling.

'No, please God, no!' Terry yelled. He ran into his own

bedroom and grabbed his hunting knife. 'Wake up, sweetheart. Please wake up for your dad', he sobbed, as he loosened the towelling dressing gown belt from around Sally's neck. Receiving no response, Terry checked for a pulse. There was none. His beautiful daughter was already dead.

Back in Rainham, Joyce was a different person from the woman who had been in drunken hysterics the day before. She was cool, calm, and collected and so far had been the hostess of all hostesses.

'Let me pour you another glass of wine, Jenny,' Joyce uttered to Polly's borderline alcoholic mother. She topped Jenny's drink up and smiled. 'Who's ready for dessert yet?'

'Sit down Mum, for Christ's sake. You'll wear the bloody carpet out in a minute,' Raymond joked.

'You know me, like to keep myself busy,' Joyce said jovially.

Since her late twenties Jenny had struggled to control her drinking, and she had a terrible habit of saying the wrong thing once inebriated. She smiled at Joycie. 'So, do you miss Stanley, or not? Polly said he left you for another woman and, to be honest, I was shocked. I mean, he's no oil painting, is he?'

'Mum!' Polly exclaimed, horrified.

Joyce laughed. 'No, he isn't and no, I don't miss the old goat at all. The only thing I do miss about him is the lifts. I have to get cabs and bleedin' buses everywhere now.'

Raymond winked at his mother. Joey had rung him late last night and told him what an awful state Joyce had gotten herself into and Raymond had been fully expecting a repeat performance today. Instead, his mum had been the complete opposite and had done him proud.

When Joey said something funny and Dominic kissed him fondly on the forehead, Jenny turned her attention to them. She had never really been in the company of gay men before and she was curious to know certain things. 'So, what's it like, being gay?' she asked.

Dickie, Jenny's husband, roared with laughter. 'She isn't backward in coming forwards my wife, is she?' he said playfully, slapping Joyce on the bottom as she stood up.

Joey glanced at Dom. Neither of them were particulary taken with Polly's parents. They'd only met them once before, at Raymond's wedding, and on that particular occasion, Jenny had got herself so drunk that she'd pissed herself while jigging about on the dancefloor.

'It's the same as being straight I suppose, apart from being in love with somebody who's the same sex as yourself,' Joey replied.

Dickie, who sounded and laughed like Boycie out of *Only Fools and Horses*, egged his wife on. 'Go on, ask 'em more, you know you want to.'

Ignoring the warning looks from her daughter, Jenny continued to be nosy. 'But it's not the same, is it? I mean, I don't let my Dickie stick it up my dirt-box even though the crafty sod did try it in his younger years.'

Dickie was laughing uncontrollably and holding his sides. When he married his Jenny, he married the funniest woman ever to walk the earth.

'I'm gonna help Mum bring the dessert in,' Raymond said, embarrassed. He didn't want to stick up for Joey in case he upset Polly's parents and, unlike Eddie, he'd never really got his head around Joey being gay.

'I'll help you,' Polly offered, absolutely mortified.

Jenny topped her glass up again and smiled at Joey. 'Does it hurt?'

'Does what hurt?' Joey asked, getting more annoyed by the second.

'You know, when you shove it up one another's dirt-boxes?'

Dickie burst out laughing again.

Joey was furious. He stood up and urged Dominic to do the same. 'Come on, let's go. We don't have to sit here listening to homophobic imbeciles like these two. Let's go to my dad's house.'

Not used to seeing Joey lose his temper, Dominic glared at Jenny and Dickie and followed his partner out of the room.

Over in Holloway, Frankie and Babs were sitting at a big table with paper hats on their heads and had just finished their Christmas dinner.

'Weren't bad for prison food, was it?' Babs said enthusiastically.

Frankie turned her nose up. It was edible, but wasn't a patch on the Christmas dinners her mum used to cook.

'Your stalker's staring at you again,' Babs whispered in Frankie's ear.

Knowing where Katie was sitting, Frankie kept her eyes firmly averted. Ever since the day they'd had that heart-to-heart conversation Frankie had felt increasingly uncomfortable around Katie. In freeflow now, Katie always made a beeline for her, and the girl's desperation to be best pals with her made Frankie feel extremely awkward. Babs knew all about the conversation that had taken place between Frankie and Katie, as Frankie had told her, and Babs was fairly positive that Katie was telling the truth and was genuine. Frankie was still very unsure, though. Katie hadn't got the message to Jed via her cousin Danny yet and Frankie began to wonder more and more if Jed had employed Katie as a spy.

'She's coming over,' Bab's said, nudging Frankie.

Frankie looked up and smiled falsely. 'Hello, Katie. Merry Christmas.'

Katie crouched down next to Frankie. She didn't want the other girls to hear what she had to say. 'Jed will be getting your message tomorrow. Danny's going to a party and Jed will be there. Danny won't let you down, I promise.'

Eddie stood at the top of the table, carving the turkey and trying to be jovial. Gary and Ricky had been so distressed by discovering their mother's rotting corpse the previous day that they had gone home to spend Christmas together. With just Gina, Claire and Stuart for company, the day had been hard to get through for Ed, and he was pleased that Joey and Dom had turned up with Madonna, as their presence had lifted the atmosphere.

'So, why didn't you stay at your nan's? Don't get me wrong, I'm glad you're here, but weren't Joycie pissed off that you left? You were meant to be staying overnight, weren't you?'

Joey glanced at Dominic. He'd already warned his boyfriend not to tell Ed what had really happened. If Eddie found out

146

what Jenny and Dickie had been saying and how rude they had been, he would probably drive straight round to Joycie's and rip the pair of them to shreds. 'Nan seems fine now and Raymond and Polly are staying with her tonight. To be honest, we left early because Polly's parents are such a pair of prats. The old man is a proper know-it-all and the mother was pissed out of her brains and talking a load of old nonsense.'

'They didn't say anything to upset you, did they?' Eddie asked defensively.

'No, of course not,' Joey lied.

As Gina and Claire began bringing the potatoes, parsnips and dishes of vegetables into the room, Joey and Dominic chatted happily to Stuart. When Stuart excused himself to use the lavatory, Joey turned to his father.

'I like Stu, Dad. He seems like a real nice fella. Has he actually started working for you yet?'

Remembering Colin Griffiths' two dismembered fingers, Eddie prodded two sausages with a fork and put them on his plate. They'd got the money back from Griffiths the following week, so the episode was over now.

'Yes, son. Stuart has been working for me for a couple of weeks now and has already proved his worth. The boy's gonna be a real asset to me,' Eddie said, smiling at Stuart as he walked back into the room.

Gina and Claire sat down at the table and everybody began tucking into their dinners. Joey and Dom moved over to the sofa, as they had already eaten at Joycie's.

'Who the fucking hell is that?' Eddie said, as the doorbell rang.

Joey jumped up. 'You eat your dinner. I'll get it. It's probably Gary and Ricky.'

Seconds later, a worried-looking Joey walked back into the lounge. 'It's the police, Dad. They want to speak to you. They said it's urgent.'

Thinking this was probably to do with Beverley's death, Eddie put his knife and fork down and walked into the hallway.

'What's a matter?' he asked the taller copper out of the two.

'Are you Eddie Mitchell, the brother of Paul and Ronald Mitchell?' the policeman asked, knowing full well who Eddie was.

147

Eddie's heart lurched. 'Yes, I am.'

'I'm afraid I have some bad news for you, Mr Mitchell. There was an incident in Belmarsh this morning and both your brothers have unfortunately been found dead.'

Feeling the colour drain from his cheeks, Eddie clung to the banister for support. O'Hara must have got to them somehow, the fucking bastard. 'How did it happen? I need to know how they died,' he said, praying they hadn't been tortured.

The smaller of the two coppers glanced at his colleague and continued. 'The details we have been given are rather vague, but it seems they were found early this morning by a prison officer and both men had lacerations to the throat area.'

Eddie put his head in his trembling hands. He might not have seen eye to eye with his brothers over recent years, but they were still his flesh and blood and, in his heart, he had never stopped loving them. Now they were dead, some cunt had cut their throats and, the worst part of it was, by giving Jimmy O'Hara that money, Ed had effectively killed them himself. Overcome by guilt and grief, Eddie ordered the officers out and sank to his knees. Not only did he still bear the burden of having his wife's blood all over his hands, he now had his brothers' as well.

Over in Orsett, Stanley was extremely nervous as he changed into his striped pyjamas in the bathroom. He was reasonably drunk, had been supping bitter all day and it was that that had given him the courage to agree to sleep in Pat the Pigeon's bed with her.

'Stanley, where are you?' Pat asked in a singsong, seductive tone.

Stanley glanced at himself in the bathroom mirror. He was sweating like a pig, but it couldn't be helped, as he was petrified of what was to come. Scuttling into the bedroom like a naughty schoolboy, Stanley turned off the light, jumped under the quilt and lay frozen on the right-hand side of the bed, staring upwards.

Pat immediately leaned over towards him. She was very sexually frustrated. She fancied Stanley something rotten and had dreamed of this moment for months.

Feeling Pat's naked breasts against his chest, Stanley gasped in horror. Why didn't she have her nightdress on?

'Are you OK, Stanley?' Pat asked, as she began to undo the buttons on his pyjama top.

Stanley nodded dumbly. He tried to speak, but no words would come out. When Pat's hand travelled downwards to the opening of his pyjama bottoms, Stanley suddenly found his voice. 'Stop it! What are you doing, woman?' he shrieked.

Pat smiled as she clasped her right hand around Stanley's limp prized asset. 'Trust me, I'll be gentle with you, Stanley,' she promised. Pat was an expert with a penis, always had been.

Aware that his long-term-unemployed asset was not responding to Pat's gentle touch, Stanley shut his eyes. If only he could block out the embarrassment that he felt, it might just raise a slight gallop.

Harry O'Hara lay in bed, wide awake. He'd had the best Christmas presents ever and, even though it was ten o'clock, he couldn't sleep, as he was too excited about driving his new car again tomorrow. 'You awake, Georgie?' he asked his sister.

'Yeah,' Georgie replied.

'Can I get in your bed with you tonight?'

Georgie kissed Barbie goodnight then put her on the bedside cabinet to make room for Harry. As her brother got in, she snuggled up to him.

'I love my new car. I wanna be a racing driver when I grow up,' Harry told her in earnest.

'I love all my toys, especially Barbie and her horse. Daddy said he'll buy me a real horse so I can ride it like Barbie does,' Georgie replied excitedly.

Harry grinned. 'I like living here now with Daddy, Nanny Alice and Grandad Jimmy, do you?'

Georgie nodded.

'Do you think we will live with Mummy again?' Harry asked.

Georgie shrugged. 'Do you miss Mummy still?'

Harry thought carefully before answering. He knew that he used to love his mum very much, but due to his young age, his memories of being with her were fading rapidly. 'I miss Mummy a tiny bit. Do you still miss her?'

Georgie mused over her reply also. Being older than Harry, her memories of her mother were a lot clearer than her brother's, but she wasn't sure if she missed her any more or not. 'I think I still love Mummy and want to visit her, but I don't wanna live with her no more. I wanna stay with Daddy, Nanny Alice and Grandad Jimmy for ever and ever.'

Harry grinned. 'I wanna stay here for ever and ever too.'

CHAPTER SIXTEEN

1994

Beverley's funeral was arranged for the first week in January and on the morning in question, Eddie got ready early and sat downstairs flicking through some old photo albums.

Christmas and New Year had been a morbid affair and Eddie was as pleased as punch to see the back of 1993. What with his brothers being murdered, Beverley snuffing it, Frankie being banged up, and his grandkids being placed in the care of the O'Haras, it had been a poxy year overall.

Staring at the picture of his two brothers sitting in a restaurant with his father, Eddie slammed the album shut and picked up the other one. The police still had no idea who had killed Ronny and Paulie and, because of this, were refusing to release their bodies. Consumed by guilt because of his own involvement in their deaths, Eddie couldn't wait to get their funerals over and done with. The least he owed them was a lavish send-off, and once they were finally at peace, he would find out who had cut their throats and make sure the cunt who had done it had his cut, too.

'You all right, love?' Gina asked, as she sat next to Ed on the sofa and put her head on his shoulder.

Eddie nodded and pointed to a photograph of a pretty, dark-haired woman. 'That's Beverley not long after we got married. That's Gary she's holding; he was only about a month old there, I think.'

'She was very beautiful,' Gina replied honestly.

Remembering the state of his first wife the last time he had seen her, Ed shook his head sadly. 'You'd never have recognised her if you'd have seen her recently. When we split

151

up she turned to booze and binge-eating. I think she went up to about eighteen stone at one time. Gary and Ricky had a poxy childhood living with her. She used to let 'em run riot when they were nippers and play in the streets till all hours. I used to have 'em every weekend, but I'll never forgive her for being such an awful mother.'

'Perhaps she didn't mean it, Ed. If she had a bad drink problem she probably wasn't focusing properly,' Gina replied.

'Oh, she had a bad drink problem all right, and over the years it got worse. Last time I saw her was just before I went inside. She was about seven stone, had yellow teeth, greasy hair and looked a proper fucking low-life. It made me feel sick to think I'd once shagged her and married her.'

When Stuart walked into the room, Eddie threw the photo album to one side and stood up. He was dropping Stuart over at Raymond's and they were going to do the collections while he, Gary and Ricky went to the funeral. Gina walked to the front door with Eddie and gave him a big hug. Ed obviously hated Beverley and she could sense his bitterness.

'Whatever you thought of Beverley, Ed, remember if it wasn't for her you wouldn't have Gary and Ricky.'

Eddie kissed Gina and smirked. 'I'll try and be diplomatic, I promise.'

Jed jumped off the cart, tied the horse up to a post and followed Sammy into the boozer. What with Sally's suicide, Frankie's threat to spill the beans, and tomorrow's court case about the kids, he'd had a lot on his mind recently. Jed sat down opposite Sammy and slurped his lager.

'So, what did you wanna talk to me about that was so important?' Sammy asked.

Jed leaned across the table so no one could hear the conversation. 'I think things are getting a bit on top round 'ere. I think me and you should split.'

Sammy nearly chocked on his beer. 'What! Why? It ain't 'cause of that message you got from Danny Cooper, is it?'

Jed shrugged. 'It ain't just that, but if Frankie does spill her guts, me and you are both in shit street. Sally's old man is another worry. He's bound to blame me for Sally topping herself and I don't fancy another tear-up with him. I'm telling you now, Sammy, if I lose this court case tomorrow and they allow Frankie access to the chavvies, then I'm fucking off, whether you come with me or not.'

'Where you thinking of going then? You'll have to go miles away 'cause if the gavvers catch up with ya, they'll take Georgie and Harry away from you, ya know.'

'If they allow that slag access to 'em tomorrow, then I'm bound to lose 'em in the long run. You know what these do-gooding cunting judges are like. When Frankie gets out, they'll give her custody anyway, my brief told me that. He reckons they always side with the mother.'

'So, where you thinking of going?' Sammy asked shocked.

'Dunno, up north, I suppose. Come with me, Sammy boy, and bring your chavvies with you an' all. I mean how often do you get to see Sammy Junior and Freddy boy? Four times a fucking month is bollocks, mate. If you come with me, you can see 'em all the time.'

Sammy was dubious. 'What about Tommy and Julie? I can't just leave 'em. And what about your mum and dad? We can't just fuck off and not tell them, Jed.'

Jed smirked. 'If we go, you can guarantee me mum and dad will come an' all. As for Tommy boy – snatch him. Don't bring Julie though, it's too risky.'

Sammy shook his head. Usually he loved his cousin's bright ideas, but this one was bordering on ridiculous. 'You gotta be winding me up, Jed, and if you ain't, then you're a proper fucking dinlo.'

Beverley's funeral turned out exactly as Eddie has expected. Apart from himself, Gary, Ricky, Albert, Reg, Vi and Joanie, only ten other people turned up. One was Bev's sister, another her cousin and the other eight were drunken low-lifes.

Unable to set foot near the house where they had found their mother's rotting corpse, Gary and Ricky met their father at the City of London Crematorium. Beverley had developed a passion for marijuana as well as drink in the latter part of her life and had told Gary and Ricky of her wishes many times.

'When I go, I wanna be cremated so I can go up in a puff of smoke like one of these,' she would say, puffing furiously on a joint.

The service was short and sweet. Gary said a few words and Ed was glad when it was all over. He felt dreadfully sorry for his sons, but he had had no feelings for Beverley other than disgust for many years. The one tear Eddie did shed at the end was in memory of Jessica. Not being allowed to attend the funeral of the wife he had loved would leave an imprint on his heart for ever.

Jed sat on the sofa opposite his parents. The kids were in the garden playing, so he had their full attention for once.

'Don't be so fucking stupid!' Jimmy yelled, when Jed repeated what he'd told Sammy earlier.

'I dunno what you're worried about. There's no way them courts will ever let that old whore ever look after them chavvies again. She tried to murder you, the wicked bitch,' Alice said, her eyes brimming with tears at the thought of not seeing her grandchildren regularly.

'But I'd want you two to come with me. And what about Terry Baldwin? You know what a nutter he is, Mum. You saw him nearly batter me to death once and now Sally's dead, he's bound to come after me again,' Jed said, trying to make his parents see sense.

The truth was, it wasn't Terry Baldwin or Frankie getting her hands on the kids that Jed was worried about. It was the threat he'd received via Frankie and he hadn't had a decent night's kip since Danny Cooper had told him. Frankie knew everything bad about him and if she opened her big mouth, he could be looking at life in prison or, worse still, be chopped up in bits by Eddie fucking Mitchell. Jed didn't know which thought was worse, but he couldn't tell his parents the truth, as neither had a clue that it was he who was responsible for Harry Mitchell's death.

Alice walked over to the sofa, sat next to Jed and held her worried son in her arms. He was obviously anxious about tomorrow's court case, bless him. 'Georgie girl and Harry both know what they've got to say, me and your father went over it again with 'em this morning. All you've gotta do is keep calm and everything will work out fine.'

Jed sighed at the word 'fine'. He had an inkling that things were going to turn out anything but.

After leaving the cemetery, Albert, Reg, Vi and Joanie went straight home. None of them had been close to Beverley and they had only gone to the funeral to support Eddie and the boys. Eddie, Gary and Ricky went for a drink in the Barge Aground in Barking. Beverley had been more of an indoor's drinker, but when she had ventured out for an evening, the Barge was always her number-one choice. When Bev's low-life friends finally turned up, Ed smiled politely at them.

'You took your time, where yous lot been?' he asked. Ed had spoken to them after the funeral and told them to come to the Barge for the wake.

'We had to wait for a bus,' came the reply.

Generous by nature, Eddie walked up to the bar and handed £300 to the barman. 'I want to keep that mob over there in free drinks all day,' he said, pointing to Bev's eight friends.

The barman nodded.

'If any money's left over, give it to 'em to get some food or something with.'

The barman smirked and nodded. He could have a right little earner out of this mug.

Seeing the look on the barman's face, Eddie leaned across the bar and grabbed him by the neck of his scruffy t-shirt. 'Oh, and don't even think of pocketing any dosh, because I'll be back tomorrow to pick up the drink receipts and, believe me, if I find out you've fiddled me out of one penny, I will chop your fucking hands off, got it?'

The barman went deathly white and this time nodded with pure fright.

Eddie walked over to the table where Bev's pisshead friends had sat down. He told them the score, then walked back over to Gary and Ricky, who were standing in the corner looking melancholy. 'Come on, boys, let's get out of this dump and go and get pissed somewhere decent.'

*   *   *

155

The following morning, Alice dressed Harry in his new, smart suit, which Jed had purchased especially for the occasion, and Georgie in a pretty pink corduroy pinafore dress. The children hadn't been expected to attend the court hearing, but both Jed and his solicitor, Malcolm, thought it was a good idea that they went.

'It's important that these do-gooding cunts listen to what them chavvies have to say and Malcolm reckons that it will be good for the judge to see how happy and well-kept Georgie and Harry look. Remember, it won't be long till that slag gives birth to another one, and when she does, I want custody of it. No chavvie of mine is gonna be brought up by some psycho in prison,' Jed told his parents.

Alice was no Naomi Campbell in the fashion stakes and usually spent her days dressed in black leggings teamed with baggy t-shirts. Today however, Alice had made an effort and had chosen to wear a smart black suit that she usually only reserved for funerals. Her thick, dark, long hair she wore up in a bun and as she walked into the lounge, Jimmy wolf-whistled and Jed grinned.

'You really look the part, Mum,' Jed said, impressed.

'You look a million dollars, love,' Jimmy told her. He had also made an effort and both he and Jed were dressed in grey suits with shirts and ties.

Jed crouched down in front of Georgie and Harry, who were sitting quietly on the sofa. 'You're not nervous, are ya?' he asked them.

Both children shook their heads.

'Now, remember everything Daddy told you to say, won't you?'

'Yes, Daddy,' Georgie said grinning.

'You told us to say that we don't wanna visit Mummy in prison,' Harry said, proud that he'd remembered his father's exact words.

'And we gotta say it 'cause if we don't the nasty people will take us away from you, Nanny Alice and Grandad Jimmy and make us live somewhere else,' Georgie said, remembering the rest of her father's speech.

Jed ruffled his children's hair, stood up and smirked. He'd

brainwashed the little 'uns and now it was time to head to court and break Frankie's fucking heart in two.

Unaware of Jed's malicious plan, Frankie hugged her friend Kerry and sat down opposite her with a big smile on her face. Frankie had already told Kerry on the phone all about the civil court case and she could barely contain her excitement at the thought of seeing Georgie and Harry again soon.

'Today's the day and Larry reckons I'll definitely win. He says that social worker has got it all sewn up.'

Kerry was thrilled that Frankie looked so happy and enthusiastic. They had been through the mill together while living with Sammy and Jed, and Kerry couldn't imagine how awful it was for Frankie to have no contact with Georgie and Harry. Just knowing they were living with the O'Haras was awful in itself. However, Kerry was extremely aware of Jed's cunning nature and she didn't want Frankie to build her hopes up too much in case it all went wrong.

'I so hope the court lets you see Georgie and Harry, but you know what Jed's like. He's a born liar, Frankie, and he's bound to have made up some cock and bull story to tell the judge,' she warned her friend.

Frankie shook her head confidently and leaned across the table. 'I couldn't tell you this on the phone, but I sent a threat to him. I've warned him, if he fucks this up for me, I'm gonna tell the Old Bill everything.'

Kerry was stunned. 'How did you manage that?' she whispered.

Frankie explained how she had met Katie in prison and then befriended her so she could get the message to Jed. 'I bet the evil bastard is shitting himself as we speak,' Frankie said, grinning.

Kerry wasn't quite so convinced. Jed and Sammy were a law unto themselves, but, not wanting to burst Frankie's bubble, she smiled and nodded in agreement.

Over in Essex, Jed was anything but shitting himself as he spoke calmly and politely to the woman judge. His solicitor, Malcolm, had already said his piece, and Jed was pleased that he'd now been allowed to speak, too.

157

'That's why I brought my children here with me today, your honour. They might only be young in years, but Georgie and Harry are both very wise for their age and they certainly know what they want. Since living with myself and my parents, the children have flourished and I'm worried that seeing their mother in prison will upset them and disturb their young minds all over again. It was only recently that they witnessed the murder of their half-brother, Luke, and I don't think they could cope with any more upheaval.'

Larry, Frankie's solicitor and Carol Cullen, the social worker whom Larry had employed to take on this case, glanced at one another in disbelief. Scared of losing his rag, Eddie Mitchell had decided not to attend the court case, but, had warned them about Jed's cunning nature and had also said. 'He's a thick, uneducated pikey. He won't come across well in front of a judge.'

Larry stared at Jed as he continued his well-rehearsed speech. The little bastard seemed to have the woman judge eating out of his hand and, as for sounding uneducated, his use of the English language was top-drawer.

Jed had introduced his parents to the judge and then ordered them to wait outside the room. His mother had a habit of losing her rag and he didn't want her to balls things up for him. He smirked at Larry and Carol and then turned back to the judge. 'Shall I bring the children in now?'

The judge ignored Jed's question and turned to Carol and Larry. 'Would you like to speak on behalf of Francesca Mitchell now?'

Larry spoke first, then Carol did her very best to assure the judge that Georgie and Harry would benefit from contact with their mother. The judge listened intently about the evening the children ran away, until Carol brought the swear words that Alice had taught them into the equation.

'This is a court, not a playground, Mrs Cullen. Telling tales isn't going to sway my judgement,' she said sternly.

Carol felt deflated as she glanced at Larry. She had attended many of these civil court hearings and had had many success stories, but this particular judge, whom she had never dealt with before, seemed like a complete cow and Carol would put money on it that the old bat was childless herself.

The judge turned to Jed again. 'Could I speak to the children now?'

Georgie and Harry were waiting outside with Jimmy and Alice and, as Jed left the room to collect them, Larry turned to the judge. 'You do realise that the children are three and four years old, don't you? Whatever do you expect to gain by talking to them? Isn't it blatantly obvious that their father has probably taught them their answers? That's why he brought them here.'

'You have no right to say that about my client. His children have every right to air their views,' Jed's solicitor said angrily.

The judge ignored Larry's questions and, as Jed returned with Georgie and Harry, ordered Carol to wait outside. She had never been a fan of social workers and had taken an instant dislike to Carol Cullen.

Jed grinned cockily at Carol as she passed him. She might have passed a load of exams and all that palaver, but she was nowhere near as clued-up as he was.

Because of the children attending the case, the judge had chosen to hold the hearing in a room with a big round table, rather than a formal-looking courtroom. She always did this when young children were involved, as it was less daunting for them and they seemed to speak far more freely in pleasant surroundings.

The judge smiled as Georgie and Harry were helped onto two big chairs. She introduced herself and then asked them if they knew why they were at the court.

'We don't want to see Mummy in prison,' Georgie said immediately.

'And why do you not want to see your mother?' the judge asked.

''Cause we don't. We do love our mummy, but we don't want to go to prison,' Georgie said bluntly.

Larry shook his head in disbelief as the judge spoke to Harry and he virtually repeated word for word what his sister had said. It was obvious to any fool that these children had been brainwashed, so why couldn't the dopey tart who had been put in charge of the case see that?

The judge asked the children a couple more questions,

then told Jed to take them outside while she delivered her verdict.

Larry had extremely bad vibes about the verdict. He had told Eddie that this case was a foregone conclusion and had promised to ring him straight after the hearing.

Jed walked back into the room and sat down next to his solicitor. The judge cleared her throat to gain everybody's attention and spoke clearly and abruptly. 'I have decided that it is not in the best interests of the children to have contact with their mother while she is in prison. If and when Francesca Mitchell is released, we can review the situation once more.'

Jed wanted to laugh as Larry stormed out of the room with a face like thunder. Fuck Frankie and her idle threats, who did she think she was?

Jimmy and Alice were thrilled when Jed told them the verdict. They had sort of guessed what had happened when they'd seen Larry stomp past, but having confirmation that Georgie and Harry were all theirs was a fantastic feeling. Alice was overjoyed, as she loved looking after the kids, and Jimmy was as pleased as punch, knowing how annoyed Eddie Mitchell would be.

Jed thanked his solicitor once more, then smiled at his children.

'I'm hungry, Daddy,' Harry said, tugging his leg.

'Did we say the right thing, Daddy?' Georgie asked innocently.

Lifting up both of his children, one in either arm, Jed swung them around. 'You both did good and now no one is gonna take you away from me, ever.'

'We will see Mummy again one day though, won't we?' Georgie asked, remembering her father's promise. Her dad had told her and Harry that if they told the judge that they didn't want to visit their mother in prison, then he would let them visit her when she came out of prison, which would be very soon.

Jed ignored his daughter's awkward question. The kids had barely mentioned Frankie over the past few weeks and, give it another six months or so, their young minds would forget all about the evil bitch. He turned to his parents. 'Come on, let's go to a boozer and fucking celebrate.'

* * *

Eddie Mitchell was in total disbelief when Larry told him the grim news. 'So, you're telling me, after running away in search of their mother, Georgie and Harry both sat in that courtroom and said they didn't wanna see her?'

'That's correct and I'm positive that was what swung it, Ed. If the children had said differently, I'm sure they would have been allowed to visit Frankie. It looked to me like their father had preplanned their answers for them, but the judge was obviously fooled. As for Jed sounding uneducated and not coming across very well, he came across completely the opposite, I'm afraid.'

Eddie slammed the phone down and walked over to the drinks cabinet.

'Are you OK, love?' Gina asked, guessing full well that he wasn't, but not knowing what else to say.

Ed turned to her. He'd already had the day from hell: the Old Bill had rung him and said they were ready to release his brothers' bodies, so he'd spent the whole morning sorting out funeral arrangements, and now he had this shit to deal with on top of all that. Knocking back a large Scotch, Ed immediately poured himself another and turned to his fiancée. 'I wanna speak to Stuart alone and make some phone alls. Go and sit upstairs for a bit,' he ordered.

When Gina closed the living-room door, Ed turned to Stuart. 'That's it now: I've fucking had enough of them O'Haras. I'm gonna arrange a meet with the boys for tomorrow and end this once and for all.'

After leaving the court, Larry drove straight up to Holloway Prison as previously arranged. He was now sitting in a room waiting to speak to Frankie face to face. Telling Eddie hadn't been quite as bad as Larry had predicted. He had sort of expected Ed to blame him and Carol for failing to deliver, but he'd been relatively polite, considering what had happened.

Larry twiddled his thumbs as he waited for Frankie to appear. Telling her that she'd lost the case was going to be awful, and Ed had rung him back to tell him not to be too honest with his daughter.

'Whatever you say, do not tell Frankie that Georgie and

Harry told the judge they didn't want to visit her. Tell her any old bollocks, but not that, Lal, as that will fucking destroy her soul,' Ed insisted.

When Frankie was finally led into the room, Larry was expecting hysterics as he relayed the events of the hearing. Her reaction could not have surprised him more. Frankie did not cry, scream, shout or anything. All she did was sit opposite him with a look of hatred on her face and mutter two sentences.

'I want you to ring DI Blyth and tell her I want to see her. You tell her that I'm ready to tell the truth now, and don't you dare say nothing to my dad.'

Frankie then stood up and, leaving Larry open-mouthed, calmly walked out of the room.

CHAPTER SEVENTEEN

Sally's funeral was a tearful affair and, as his daughter's body was lowered into the ground, Terry Baldwin was positive that he felt his heart split in two. Sally was Terry's only child and he'd literally worshipped the ground she'd walked on. Finding her lifeless body swinging from the ceiling was a sight that would haunt Terry until his dying day. He'd tried everything to revive her, but he'd been too late and he'd never forgive himself for that. If only he'd kept popping upstairs every five or ten minutes; he'd known how depressed she was.

'Shall we make a move now, love? The funeral cars are waiting,' Anne asked her husband as he crouched down and stared at the flowers once more.

'I've checked every one of these cards twice and do you know what? That fucking piece of pikey shit didn't even bother to send my baby any flowers,' Terry said, referring to Jed. His daughter and grandson's demise were all down to Jed, and now Sally's funeral was over, Terry was determined to make things even.

Anne linked arms with her husband. Since Sally's death she'd become increasingly worried about Terry's rants about revenge and she was concerned that he might do something incredibly stupid.

'Promise me something, Tel,' she asked him.

'What?'

'Promise me that you won't take the law into your own hands.'

With sadness etched across his face and tears in his eyes, Terry turned to face Anne. 'I'm sorry, babe. I can't make that promise.'

* * *

Another person currently discussing the subject of retribution was Eddie Mitchell. He'd organised an emergency meeting at Auntie Joanie's house and was discussing how, when and where he and the boys were going to pounce.

'What about the mother, though? I mean, if we dispose of Jimmy and Jed, she'll have custody of the kids, won't she?' Raymond said sensibly.

'We're gonna have to do her in an' all. We can't take no chances,' Ed replied bluntly. He didn't usually like to involve women in any kind of violence, but in Alice's case he was willing to make an exception.

'But how we gonna kidnap Jimmy, Jed and Alice without the kids being around? Georgie and Harry are always gonna be in the company of one of them, ain't they?' Gary asked.

'We can't risk the kids seeing anything in case they say something. Fuck me, they're only nippers and if the Old Bill question 'em, they're bound to blab and stitch us up,' Ricky said worriedly.

Eddie turned to Stuart. He might be a relative newcomer and the youngest member of the firm, but he was as bright as a button and even in the nick, Ed had sought his advice over matters. 'You got any ideas?' he asked.

Deep in thought, Stuart rubbed the stubble on his chin. 'I think the only way to do this is to forget about kidnapping 'em. We're gonna have to break in their house while they're sleeping and do it there.'

Gary and Ricky glanced at one another and laughed sarcastically. Both lads had grown to like Stuart, but they were still slightly jealous of their father's close relationship with him. Therefore, if they could get a dig in against Stu, then they would.

'What a great idea! Let's blast 'em away in their beds while the kids are in the house as well,' Gary said mockingly.

Ed glared at Gary and mulled over Stuart's idea. It was dodgy and dangerous, but was there any other valid option? 'I think Stu has a point. I mean, some cunt broke into my father's house, murdered him in bed and got away with it, didn't they? It can be done, providing it's done properly.'

'Yeah, but Grandad lived alone. There's five living at the

O'Haras' if you include Georgie and Harry,' Ricky reminded his father.

'Does anyone know the layout of the house? If Jimmy and Alice sleep in a room that's nowhere near Jed's, we might just get away with it. If we break in in the middle of the night and use a silencer, I doubt the kids will wake up,' Stuart added.

Gary didn't like the sound of the idea at all. 'And what do we do when we've killed 'em all? Just fuck off and let the kids find their blood-soaked bodies in the morning?'

Eddie shrugged. 'Yeah, I suppose so.'

Raymond turned to Eddie. This was beginning to sound proper heavy now. Polly had their first child on the way and he didn't fancy spending the first twenty years or so of his kid's life stuck in some poxy prison cell. 'Ed, Georgie and Harry have already seen that Luke boy murdered. He was shot right in front of 'em, wasn't he? Can you imagine the trauma they're gonna endure if they find their dad and grandparents blasted to bits as well?'

Being the youngest son of a gangland boss, Eddie had been brought up around violence from a very young age and that had made him extremely thick-skinned. 'The kids are only young – they'll soon forget about it and get over it,' he said tactlessly.

Raymond, Ricky and Gary all glanced at one another. Once Eddie had made up his mind about something, there was usually no turning back.

'I still think the kidnapping idea sounded far more feasible,' Gary said, hoping his father would see sense.

Eddie drank the last of his Scotch and angrily slammed his glass against the table. 'I've spent years pussy-footing around the O'Haras and I've had a fucking gutful of it. I want 'em dead, all of 'em, and seeing as I run this firm, we'll do things my way – got it?'

Ed's eyes clouding over was always a bad sign, so Raymond, Gary and Ricky all did the sensible thing. One by one they nodded their heads in agreement.

Over in Holloway, Babs was becoming increasingly worried about Frankie's venomous behaviour. Usually kind and mild-mannered, Frankie had bitten everybody's head off that morning, including hers, and had just crowned it all by calling Linda, one of the nicest screws, 'a nosy, fat cow'.

As Linda walked off with a hurt expression on her face, Babs sat next to Frankie in the corridor. It was freeflow time and, with the mood Frankie was in, Babs wished they had stayed in their cell.

'Listen, sweet child, I know you're angry over the court case, but being vile to people ain't gonna help you get them wonderful babies of yours back. Linda is a lovely woman and she was only trying to be helpful. Where has my best mate gone, eh? The Frankie I know has a truly beautiful soul and I was thinking, is you her twin sister?' Babs asked jokingly.

About to crack a smile, Frankie spotted Katie, stood up, and ran towards her. 'Have you spoken to your cousin yet?' she asked. She'd managed to speak to Katie after she'd seen Larry the previous day.

Katie stared at Frankie for a few seconds, then nodded. Ever since she had got the original message to her cousin Danny, Frankie had avoided her like the plague. It was only now that she needed another favour that Frankie was being nice to her again.

'I told Danny last night and he promised to ring Jed today. I'll call Danny again later and see if he managed to get the message to him for you.'

'Thanks, Katie,' Frankie said, forcing herself to smile. She wouldn't rest until she knew that Jed had received her latest threat. She wanted the bastard to suffer just like he'd made her suffer.

When Katie walked away, Babs walked towards Frankie. 'You gotta start being nicer to that poor girl. She been good to you and you make it blatantly obvious that you don't like her.'

'I don't fucking like her. The way she speaks reminds me of Jed and I still reckon she's working for him as some sort of spy.'

Babs shook her head. 'I think Katie is genuine, and I'm sure you got her all wrong. Why would she help you by getting the messages to Jed if she were on his side?'

'I ain't got her wrong at all. Them travellers stick together like glue, mate, and do you know what? I bet that lying cow ain't even got a cousin called Danny. I bet she's ringing Jed up herself.'

Babs looked at Frankie with an incredulous expression plastered across her face. 'Really?'

Frankie nodded. She was Eddie Mitchell's daughter and had been bred by the finest when it came to being clued-up about people. She linked arms with Babs. 'I know exactly what's going on and, mark my words, I'm right.'

Jed and Sammy were sat in the White Hart in Rainham. After yesterday's court case, Jed had gone to a nearby boozer with his parents and children and had rung his cousin to urge him to celebrate with them. Sammy had turned up within the hour with two grams of coke in his pocket. Jed had got the flavour, sent the kids home with his parents, and then he and Sammy had gone off on one of their jaunts. They'd ended up in the Church Elm pub in Dagenham where they'd pulled two birds and stayed the night at theirs in some nearby flats called the Mall.

'So, what was your one like? Did you shag her?' Sammy asked his cousin.

'Nah, I'd had too much booze,' Jed lied. For once, the girl he'd pulled would not let him have his wicked way with her and Jed rather respected her for that. Her name was Amanda and the closest he'd got to the deed was a finger and a wank. 'I thought mine was quite pretty, as it goes. I took her number and I might ring her in a few days. What about yours? Did you give her one?' Jed asked.

Sammy grinned. 'She was a right goer. Stuck her finger up me arse and all sorts.'

Jed chuckled then quietly sipped his beer. On the journey to the pub, Sammy had informed him that Sally had been laid to rest that morning and even though towards the end of their relationship he had had few feelings for Sally, the news had sort of messed with his head.

'What's up? You thinking of Sally?' Sammy asked.

Jed's mood had been as bouncy as a trampoline until half

an hour ago when Sammy had mentioned her funeral. 'Nah, not really. I suppose it's just brought memories of Lukey boy back to me,' Jed said. He'd never been one to admit his feelings.

Sammy nodded understandingly. He would never forget the sight of that poor little boy with his brains hanging out as long as he lived. 'So, what are your plans now? You can't live with your parents for ever, so why don't you move back with me?' Sammy asked, cleverly changing the subject.

Jed shook his head. When he was with Frankie, he'd lived in a luxurious mobile home next to Sammy on a privately owned piece of land in Wickford. There were two reasons why Jed didn't want to move back there. The first was that Sammy was still shacked up with Sally's best mate, Julie, and the second was he had no intention of bringing up the kids alone.

'Nah, don't fancy going back there. There's too many memories and most of 'em are bad,' he replied.

'Well, what you gonna do then? You ain't still planning to do a runner, are ya?'

'No, that was a prickish idea. I think I'll just stay put at me mum and dad's for now. Me mum takes care of the chavvies for me and I don't want the hassle of it. I suppose I'll meet another bird I like soon and when I do, I'll move the trailer somewhere, and get her to look after the chavvies for me.'

'If it's Julie stopping you coming back to Wickford, just say and I'll get rid. To be honest, she bores the arse off me lately, so I might pack her off back to Rush Green anyway. She kept the flat on 'cause the social pay for it and she's renting it to a mate at the moment. I can always chuck the mate out and get her to move back in there. I won't split up with her because of Tommy boy, but I can just pretend we're working away and pop round there if and when I wanna see the boy or I fancy a bit,' Sammy offered.

'I'll be honest with you, Sammy, I don't fancy moving back to Wickford whether Julie's there or not. I wanna start afresh and I also think me and you should start grafting again soon. We ain't worked for months and I dunno about you, but I've spent thousands.'

Sammy smirked. Years ago he and Jed had earned a crust by getting some mug to steal motors, horse-boxes and caravans for them which they would then doctor and sell on again. More recently though, they'd learned the art of conning vulnerable old people. They referred to it as 'grunting', and would befriend their victims by doing odd jobs for them at first. In the past couple of years, they'd robbed some of them blind and, between the two of them, had had three properties left to them and a nice piece of land. Getting their victims to make out a will in their names was easy. They only targeted people who had no close family and lived alone and Sammy absolutely loved their new career.

'So, when we gonna crack on again, then?' he asked excitedly.

About to answer, Jed was disturbed by the sound of his mobile phone ringing. His face immediately drained of colour and he quickly ended the call without uttering a word.

'What's the matter now?' Sammy asked, concerned.

'I just got another message sent via Frankie. She says I fucked up big time and now she's gonna make me pay.'

'Don't take no notice of the silly whore. If she was gonna shop you or me, she wouldn't be telling us, would she?' Sammy said reassuringly.

'But, say she does?'

'She won't, you dinlo. All the fucking slag's doing is trying to put the fear of God into ya and it's worked. If she was gonna grass, she'd have done it yonks ago. Now chill out and go and get us another beer, you tight bastard.'

Jed stood up and walked towards the bar. Past experiences had taught him that people who placed threats of any kind rarely carried them out, so Sammy boy was probably right.

DI Blyth had had an extremely eventful day. From first thing this morning she had been run off her feet like a blue-arsed fly and it was only now, late afternoon, that she finally had a chance to sit at her desk, have a bite to eat and a coffee and, most importantly, check her answerphone messages. The first five messages were the usual run-of-the-mill rubbish that she encountered every day, but as she listened to the sixth, she spat a mouthful of prawn mayonnaise sandwich into her hand and immediately returned the call.

'Mr Peters, it's DI Blyth here. You left me a message saying that Francesca Mitchell has some vital information for me.'

When Larry relayed Frankie's exact words, DI Blyth felt the blood pumping faster through her veins. She had liked Frankie Mitchell and had always known when she'd interviewed her in relation to stabbing Jed that there was more to her predicament than met the eye.

'I'll speak to the prison now and will visit Frankie tomorrow, Mr Peters.'

Ending the call, Blyth picked up the rest of her sandwich and chomped away happily.

Terry Baldwin pulled up outside the iron fence with the red lettering where he'd been ordered to wait. He'd been instructed to drive to River Road in Barking, and, as he turned off his engine and headlights, the only sound was that of a ferocious-sounding guard dog barking its bonce off. Terry shivered. He didn't know whether it was because the area gave him the creeps or the temperature had fallen below zero. Tapping his fingers against the steering wheel to try and keep them warm, Terry thought of his Sally. He'd kept the wake small, just a few people back at the house. The thought of having a piss-up in the pub was unbearable and he couldn't have stomached it.

Terry nearly shat himself with fright as a light was flashed three times through the back window of his motor. He was expecting whoever he was meeting to arrive by car, not on a pushbike with a torch. He got out of the motor and walked towards the guy. He could barely see his face at all, as the bloke had a ski jacket on with a hood up and a scarf covering his mouth.

'Did Jamie send you?' Terry asked warily. There were no houses for miles and this weirdo could pull any kind of stroke if he wanted to.

Ignoring Terry's question, the man pulled a plastic bag from the inside of his jacket and handed it to Terry. Terry took the bag, looked inside to check the contents and handed the weirdo an envelope containing money.

170

Watching the delivery man cycle off into the night, Terry got back inside his car and started the engine. Hopefully, by this time next week, that vile little shit who had stolen his family from him would finally have paid for his sins.

CHAPTER EIGHTEEN

The following morning Eddie told Stuart and Raymond to go and do the collections alone. The loan-sharking business was booming and Ed had now split the collections into two separate areas. Gary and Ricky covered the East End, where the majority of their business was done, and Ed, Raymond and Stuart covered Essex and any other surrounding areas. Ed had always left south, west and north London alone. Each area had its own firm that carved a crust the same way that he did and stepping on someone else's toes just wasn't worth the agg.

When Gina walked into the lounge, freshly showered in a bathrobe, Ed pulled her towards him.

'So why have you taken today off?' Gina asked. Ed had been through a traumatic time recently and Gina just wished she could do more to help him.

'If I tell ya, I'll have to kill ya,' Ed said chuckling. Since Stuart had come out of the nick it was unusual for Ed and Gina to have the place to themselves.

'Is that a gun in your pocket, Mr Mitchell?' Gina said laughing, as he pushed his erection against her.

Eddie slipped off her bathrobe and made love to her on the shagpile carpet. He'd set the ball rolling late last night and, unbeknown to Gina, he'd taken the day off work to organise the surprise of her life.

'So, where are you going today? You're not normally this secretive,' Gina said, teasing him.

Eddie grinned. With everything that had happened recently, he'd needed to do something to cheer himself up and the idea had popped into his head as he'd driven away from Joanie's yesterday. He stood up, got dressed and winked at her. 'That's for me to know and you to find out, sweetheart.'

Larry Peters was sitting in Snaresbrook Crown Court. He was here to represent an accountant who had been charged with fraud, but he couldn't concentrate on the case, as he knew he had done something very wrong. Client confidentiality was everything in Larry's world, but not to tell Eddie what Frankie had told him was an extremely bad move. DI Blyth was visiting Frankie today in Holloway and if Eddie found out that Larry had known about the visit all along, Ed would probably string him up by the bollocks.

Sweating like a pig at the thought of Ed finding out about his misdemeanour, Larry stood up and turned to the judge. 'Could you please excuse me, your honour? I am in desperate need to use the lavatory.'

Outside the courtroom, Larry punched in Eddie's number. Unfortunately for him, Ed's phone was switched off.

Pat and Stanley were poring over the latest pigeon magazine. Spring would be approaching soon and they were looking for a top-class cock to breed with Mildred.

'It's a shame Georgie's squabs didn't turn out as expected,' Pat said remorsefully.

Stanley nodded. Pat had given him one of Georgie's offspring and he'd seen ducks fly faster than the bastard thing. Pat threw the magazine to one side and snuggled up to Stanley.

'I think we should pay that George Chalkley a visit. That cock he races is a bloody world-beater and I'm sure Mildred would produce fine squabs from him. What's the name of his cock, Stanley? It's on the tip of me tongue, but I can't remember it.'

When Pat's hand moved towards his cock, Stanley lost his memory also. He loved living with Pat, they had so much in common, but her sexual urges had started to drive him beserk. Since he'd been sharing the same bed as Pat, she'd tried to initiate sex with him virtually every night and the problem was that Stanley was unable to stand to attention. Nothing would happen whatsoever when she touched him in that area and the more she tried to fondle his John Thomas, the more embarrassed he became. Stanley grabbed Pat's hand, moved it away from his private parts and held it against his chest.

'I'm sorry love, but it won't work, you know it won't work.'

Pat chuckled naughtily. She had a special surprise planned for Stanley tonight and that, she was sure, would get his engine running again.

'Shall we have a can of bitter now, love?' Stanley asked chirpily.

Pat stood up. 'No, we're not drinking today, so I'll make us a nice pot of tea instead.'

'Why can't we have a proper drink?' Stanley asked, perplexed.

'Because that's what's causing your brewer's droop. I've got a nice surprise for you tonight and if you drink beer you're gonna spoil it.'

'For fuck's sake,' Stanley mumbled as Pat walked out of the room. He then thought of Joycie and, for the first time since he'd left his wife, wondered if he had made a terrible mistake.

Eddie felt strange as he sat down next to Joey on his old sofa in what used to be his and Jessica's living room. The photographs on the wall had changed and Joyce had added her own plants and ornaments, but other than that it was like going back in time.

Joyce was out in the kitchen making a brew and Joey, being perceptive, kind of guessed what his father was thinking. 'Are you OK, Dad?' he asked kindly.

Eddie nodded and, as Joyce walked back into the room with a tea tray, he forced himself to stop thinking about Jessica. Picturing her pretty face standing by the fireplace felt like a dagger piercing his heart.

'So, how's life without Stanley? Are you coping OK, Joycie?'

Joyce sat on the armchair opposite Eddie. 'I'd forgotten all about the old bastard, to be honest. It's a pain in the arse getting cabs and buses sometimes, but other than that I don't miss the old goat at all,' Joyce lied. Putting on a brave face was the only way she could cope with Stanley's departure. The winter nights were lonely and sometimes never ending, but Joyce would never admit that she missed Stanley, not even to herself.

'What about money? If you ever need any dosh, all you gotta do is ask, girl,' Eddie said genuinely. He'd always been generous to Joycie and, partly out of guilt, he'd even given her his house when Jessica had died.

'I'm fine for money, but thanks all the same, Ed. When we sold our old house in Upney I used to beg Stanley to buy a flash car and stuff, but you know what an old miser he was. We virtually lived off our pensions and when the old fucker left, he never took any of our money with him. It was always in my bank account, you see.'

Eddie chuckled. Joycie had never failed to make him laugh when he was married to Jessica and she hadn't changed one iota over the years.

'So where's Dominic today? Yous two ain't split up, have you?' Joyce asked her grandson suspiciously. Joey had rung her early this morning asking if he and Eddie could pop round, and she wasn't stupid – something smelled fishy.

'No, of course not. Dom's visiting his nan. She's very poorly and is in hospital at the moment with pneumonia. She has no idea Dom's gay and keeps asking him when he's gonna settle down with a nice girl and get married,' Joey replied.

Eddie chuckled. 'The poor old cow's got a long wait, bless her.'

'How's Frankie? I haven't heard a dickie from her since the children's court case. Terrible news about them little 'uns, weren't it? Why weren't they allowed to visit her in prison?' Joycie asked.

Joey glanced at his father. 'Go on, tell Nan the truth,' he urged. Joey had been furious when he'd heard the outcome of the court case. He'd wanted to attend, but hadn't been allowed to, as Jed's brief had stuck his oar in, saying it would upset the children to see him.

'The pikeys have brainwashed them kids, Joycie. Both Georgie and Harry sat in the court and told the judge they didn't want to see Frankie, apparently,' Eddie told her.

Joyce sat with her mouth open. 'No, I don't believe it! Christ, it was only just before Christmas that they turned up here in bits looking for her.'

'If you speak to Frankie, for Christ's sake don't tell her what

175

the kids said, will ya? Knowing that will break her fucking heart,' Eddie said.

Joyce nodded. 'So, how is Frankie doing in that prison? I'd like to visit her if that's OK. Have either of yous two been up there lately?'

'I'm seeing her tomorrow. Dom was coming with me but because of what happened with the court case, I'm gonna go in alone and he's gonna wait in a nearby pub,' Joey said.

'She ain't talking to me still, but I'm gonna have a word with Larry, see if he can sort out a visit for me. Then again, you know how stubborn our Frankie is, she's bound to tell me to take a running jump,' Eddie added.

Joyce chuckled. Frankie was her father's double, whereas Joey was much more like Jessica.

'You got your phone switched on, Dad? It ain't 'arf been quiet today,' Joey asked.

Eddie checked his mobile. It had rung while he was making love to Gina earlier and he'd switched it off and forgot to turn the bloody thing back on.

'So, is that the only reason you came to see me today to tell me what the children said at the court case?' Joyce asked sceptically.

'No, I've got something else to tell you,' Ed replied, looking a bit sheepish.

'I thought so. Come on, spill the beans,' Joyce exclaimed knowingly.

About to disclose the true nature of his visit, Eddie was disturbed by his phone ringing.

'Go on, you'd better answer that, it might be important,' Joyce said. She had a feeling she knew what Ed was going to tell her, and if he answered the phone it would give her an extra couple of minutes to get her head around it.

Eddie's face turned an angry shade of red as he listened to what the caller had to say. 'So why didn't you tell me all this fucking yesterday, then?' he screamed into the handset.

Joey glanced at his nan. So much crap had happened to their family recently, surely another disaster wasn't on the horizon.

*　*　*

DI Blyth sat in the visiting room waiting for Frankie to be brought in, and thought about the last conversation she had had with the girl. She could even remember Frankie's exact words at the end of it.

'The only thing I can tell you is Jed is a traitor. The rest is a secret and for my dad's and my children's sake, that's the way it will have to stay,' Frankie had stated.

Blyth would never forget the haunted look in Frankie's eyes that day. Alarm bells had rang in Blyth's mind and she knew whatever secret Frankie was carrying was enormous and would one day become a lead weight inside the girl's mind.

As the door opened, Blyth looked up and smiled. 'Hello Frankie. My, you look blooming. How many weeks until baby is born?'

Blyth had been prepared for Frankie to be agitated, nervous, perhaps even tearful; what she hadn't expected was for her to stroll into the room and sit opposite her full of anger and insolence.

'Cut the crap and let's just get on with it, shall we? I've asked you here to tell you the truth, but I'm not saying nothing in front of her,' Frankie spat, nodding in the direction of the screw standing by the door.

'Could you leave Miss Mitchell and myself alone, please?' Blyth asked the prison officer politely.

'I was told to stay inside the room,' the officer replied.

Blyth stood up. While Frankie was in this mood there was much more chance of getting the absolute truth out of her and she wasn't going to allow some jumped-up screw mess that up.

'Just get out! I'm a detective inspector and I need to speak to Miss Mitchell alone,' she screamed.

As the prison officer scuttled out of the room, Blyth turned to Frankie. Every police officer in the country had their own way of dealing with situations like this and Blyth had always found that if you behaved in the same manner as whoever you were dealing with, it worked wonders.

'I haven't got all day, so spit it out,' she said abruptly.

'Where do you want me to start?' Frankie asked.

'Why don't we start by you telling me why you kept calling

Jed a traitor when I last interviewed you and, while we're at it, what was the big secret that you couldn't disclose for the sake of your dad and children?' Blyth asked in a sharp tone.

Shocked by Blyth's manner, Frankie felt her lip begin to tremble. Perhaps the DI still had the hump with her because she hadn't grassed her father up in court when he was up for murdering her mother.

Noticing that Frankie's hands were shaking, Blyth leaned forward and clasped her own around them. 'Tell me Frankie, please tell me,' she pleaded in a much gentler tone.

Frankie looked up. The hard exterior she'd used as a front for the past few days suddenly evaporated into thin air. 'If I tell you, I want you to promise me that you'll never tell my dad.'

'I promise,' Blyth said sincerely. She suddenly had an awful feeling that Frankie was about to tell her that Jed had sexually abused Georgie. 'Is it Georgie? Did Jed touch her?' Blyth asked softly.

'No, it's my grandad.'

'What do you mean, Frankie? What has your grandad got to do with all this? You are talking about your grandad Harry, aren't you?'

With tears streaming down her face, Frankie nodded. 'It was Jed, he was the one that killed my grandad Harry.'

In all her years in the police force, Blyth had been the receiver of many a shock. She'd worked on the cases of the pleasant vicar who had committed bigamy ten times, the respected female school teacher who had been involved in a nationwide paedophile ring and also the sweet twelve-year-old girl who had knifed both her parents to death and had then blamed burglars, but never, ever had Blyth been more gobsmacked than hearing what Frankie had just said.

Pulling herself together, Blyth shut her open mouth, stood up and put her arms around the distraught girl who was now sobbing her heart out. 'Oh, you poor, poor thing. Everything will be OK now Frankie, I promise you that. Jed will pay for what he has done and I will personally make sure that he does.'

Terry Baldwin was frozen stiff. It was a bitterly cold January evening and the snow that had fallen earlier had now turned to ice. Once again, Terry was sitting outside the iron fence with the red lettering in River Road in Barking, but this time he was in a white transit van and was meeting Jamie Carroll, aka the fixer, in person.

Glancing at his watch, Terry clenched his hands together and blew into them to keep them warm. The heating in the van was broken and Jamie was over half-an-hour late. Wondering whether something had gone tits-up, Terry was relieved as he saw headlights approaching. As the blue Transit van pulled up behind him, Terry got out of his own van.

'Fucking taters, ain't it?' he said to Jamie.

Jamie ignored the comment and opened the back doors of his van. He was a man of very few words, especially when it came to discussing the weather. 'That's it. Untraceable, and goes like a fucking thunderbolt.'

Terry handed Jamie the envelope stuffed with cash and asked for a hand to get the motorbike into his own van.

'He was a bit weird, that geezer who met me last night. Are you sure he's kosher?' Terry asked, as he and Jamie pushed the bike up the wooden ramp he'd brought with him.

'Anyone I deal with is kosher,' Jamie replied, pissed off that Terry had questioned his work ethic.

'Well, thanks for everything and if I need anything else, I'll bell ya.'

Jamie nodded, jumped in his van and sped off.

Terry did the same and headed towards his lock-up. Jamie was an ignorant bastard and the other geezer he'd sent last night still sent shivers down his spine, but at least they had delivered the goods. Terry allowed himself a smirk. Now he had everything he needed, it was almost time for action.

Stanley was more anxious than usual as he got underneath the covers. Usually when he and Pat retired to bed for the evening he had plied himself with cans of bitter, but today Pat had insisted on a total booze ban and Stanley's nerves were beginning to jangle.

When Pat came in from the bathroom, took off her dressing gown and got into bed beside him, Stanley felt his legs start to tremble. Last week she'd grabbed his hand and rubbed it against her vagina and he just hoped that that wasn't part of her little surprise. In all the years Stanley had been with Joycie, he'd never had to touch her vagina, all they'd ever done was have missionary-position sex, and that was only to make babies.

'Now, take them pyjama bottoms off, Stanley,' Pat ordered him.

'Do I have to?' Stanley asked apprehensively.

'Yes, I can't give you your little surprise with them on, can I?'

Stanley took his bottoms off under the quilt and shut his eyes. Whatever Pat was going to do, he knew he wasn't going to like it and he just wanted to get it over with.

When Pat began kissing his chest, Stanley breathed a sigh of relief. It felt quite nice and relaxing. 'What you doing now?' he asked, as Pat's head moved down towards his belly button.

'Just relax and enjoy yourself,' Pat whispered seductively.

Stanley was anything but relaxed when a minute later Pat put his John Thomas in her mouth.

'What the fuck are you doing? There's something very wrong with you, woman,' he screamed as he jumped out of the bed and turned the light on. Heart beating like a drum, he quickly put on his pyjama bottoms.

'What have I done wrong? I only wanted you to have fun and enjoy yourself,' Pat said, bemused by Stanley's reaction.

'Have fun and enjoy myself? What, by indulging in utter filth? It's perverted, Pat, that ain't normal.'

'Well, my Vic used to like it,' Pat said, near to tears.

'Well, I ain't your Vic, am I?' Stanley yelled, as he slammed the bedroom door behind him. When he'd served in the army as a young man, he'd overheard men talking about vile sex acts like that, but he didn't think he'd ever be a victim of one, especially at his age. Didn't the stupid woman realise she had nearly given him a heart attack?

Walking into the spare room, Stanley sat down on the bed and put his head in his hands. He couldn't live with Pat any more, not after this, but he very much doubted Joycie would have him back, and he had little money and nowhere else to go.

Stanley felt like crying as he got into bed and pulled the quilt over his head. Tomorrow he would ring his grandson. If anyone could talk Joyce into taking him back, then that person was Joey.

CHAPTER NINETEEN

DI Blyth had been due to have the following day off. She had arranged to spend it with her husband and friends, but had now cancelled her plans to return to Holloway and take a proper statement from Frankie. The police had all but closed the case on Harry Mitchell's murder due to lack of evidence and Blyth was desperate to get Frankie's allegation written down in black and white so she could reopen the investigation.

'Are we ready?' Blyth asked Frankie.

When Frankie nodded, Blyth picked up her pen and paper. Frankie had insisted on giving a written statement, rather than a recorded one.

'It was my friend Kerry's idea to plant a cassette recorder in Jed's Shogun and press the "record" button just before him and his cousin Sammy went out. We knew that they were playing around with other girls and we also knew that they were earning a living by conning old people and we just wanted to get enough evidence on tape so that we could leave them. Jed had always threatened that he would never let me take the kids away from him and Sammy told Kerry the same, that's why we needed something on them, so we could blackmail them and threaten to give the tape to the police. That way they would have had to let us leave,' Frankie explained.

'So where is the tape now?' Blyth asked.

'Sammy got hold of it. I was so stupid, I left it in my handbag. If only I'd have hidden it somewhere else, we would have 'em bang to rights.'

Blyth was gutted. Without the tape, unless there was some evidence to link Jed to the scene of the crime, it was just

Frankie's word against his. 'So was it on this tape that you found out about your grandfather?'

Frankie nodded. 'They were laughing about his death and joking about how they had tortured him. What will happen now? Will you arrest Jed and Sammy?'

'Not yet. We need to reopen the case and find some evidence to link them to it first. What we musn't do is let Jed and Sammy know that we're on to them, so tell no one about this conversation, OK?'

Frankie had already told Babs, but she didn't tell Blyth this, as she knew her friend could be trusted. 'I did send a threat to Jed via a travelling girl in here,' Frankie admitted.

'What exactly did you say?'

'Just that I was going to tell you everything.'

'Well, don't send any more threats, for goodness' sake. We don't want to frighten them off,' Blyth said.

'What about my dad? Say Larry tells him that you've been to see me? What should I say?'

Like most police officers in the East of England, Blyth was only too aware what would occur if Eddie Mitchell got wind of Jed being responsible for his father's murder. There would be a massacre of some kind, that was for sure.

'You must say nothing to anyone about what happened to your grandfather, Frankie. If your father finds out that I've been to see you, you tell him that you gave me some information about Jed robbing old people, OK?'

Frankie nodded. 'What about Kerry? Will you speak to her as well? I told her I was going to tell you about the tape.'

'Yes, I will have to speak to Kerry to verify your story and obviously two witnesses who have heard what was on that tape are far better than one.'

'Now, can you remember Jed and Sammy's exact words when they were discussing your grandfather?'

Frankie's eyes filled up with tears. She would never forget that particular conversation until her dying day.

Seeing that Frankie was upset, Blyth put her pen down. 'Would you like to take a break and I'll ask if we can get a cup of tea or coffee brought in for us? I've got some chocolate biscuits in my bag.'

'Yes. Talking about what Jed did is making me wanna chuck up.'

Joey got to north London early. He wasn't due to visit Frankie until this afternoon and it had been his boyfriend's idea to make a day of it.

'Let's get a train and have lunch at the Angel before you see Frankie, then afterwards we can go up Covent Garden,' Dom suggested.

As soon as Joey stepped off the train his phone burst into life. It was his dad.

'Don't forget to tell Frankie what I told you last night and I need you to find out what's going on, Joey. If your sister's gonna tell anyone, it'll be you. Dig deep and make sure you find out why she spoke to the Old Bill. I'm relying on you to get the information, son.'

Joey promised his father that he would call him as soon as he left the prison. He ended the call and his phone rang again almost immediately. 'Oh, it's you,' Joey said when he heard his grandfather's voice. Stanley was the last person he'd expected to hear from, seeing as they weren't even talking at the moment.

'I was wondering if we could meet, Joey. I really need to speak to you about your nan.'

About to tell his grandad to get lost, Joey bit his tongue. He could tell by his grandad's grovelling tone that the silly old fool had probably come to his senses and, as much as his nan pretended she didn't miss his grandfather, Joey knew differently. He often caught her crying, and she'd never been quite the same woman since Stanley had left.

'I can't meet you today, I'm up town, but I can meet you for a drink tomorrow lunchtime, if that's any good. You'll have to come over my way, though.'

'That's fine. Where shall I meet you, Joey?'

'Say one o'clock in the Bell at Rettendon. Dom will be with me, as we were going there for a Sunday roast anyway,' Joey replied.

'Who was that?' Dom asked when his boyfriend ended the call.

184

'My grandad. He's meeting us down the Bell tomorrow. Sounds full of self-pity. I'd put money on it that he wants to move back in with my nan.'

Dominic shook his head in disbelief. Stanley running off with some tart had been a bolt out of the blue for all of them. 'Joycie won't take him back, will she?'

Joey chuckled. 'Dunno, but if she does, the one thing you can guarantee is that Nan will lead him a dog's life. If my grandad does move back to Rainham, I'm telling you now, the senile old philanderer will wish he'd never been born!'

Unaware that their mother had just given an in-depth statement to the police that, if proved, could put their father away for many years, Georgie and Harry were playing happily in the garden. Harry, who was now described to fellow travellers as an up-and-coming Stirling Moss, was now allowed to drive his Christmas present without any supervision.

'Get off!' he screamed at Georgie as she stood on the back of the car. She liked him to drive with her holding on to the back, but Harry hated it because her weight stopped the car from going as fast.

Georgie giggled at her brother's annoyance. She loved feeling the wind in her hair as Harry drove along – it made her feel as free as a bird.

Remembering the conversation he'd had with his father the previous evening, Harry put his foot on the brake. Jed had bought him a pair of boxing gloves recently and after last night's sparring session, his dad had sat him on his knee.

'When I was your age, your grandad Jimmy used to make me box in the ring against other boys. That's why I'm big and strong and no one messes with me now. You wanna be like your dad, don't you, Harry?'

Not really understanding the conversation, Harry decided it was best to nod.

'Well, you gotta promise me, then, that if anyone annoys you or won't do what you tell 'em to do, then you clump them. You got that?'

'What, punch them, Daddy?' Harry asked innocently.

'Yep, that's right, son. Whether it be a boy, girl, man, woman, or even a fucking animal, if it gets in your way, you crack it one.'

As Harry jumped out of the car, grabbed hold of her long dark hair and dragged her to the ground, Georgie stopped giggling. 'Stop it,' she screamed, as Harry started to punch her.

When Georgie clutched her face and began to cry, Harry immediately realised the error of his father's instructions. 'I'm sorry, Georgie,' he said as he kneeled down beside her and put his chubby arms around her. 'I love you, I didn't mean it. Daddy told me to do it.'

Frankie hugged her twin brother and then sat down opposite him with a false smile on her face. Reliving the memories of what Jed had done to her grandad had made her feel physically sick, but she knew she had to put on a brave face. Joey knew her better than anyone and she didn't want him clocking that anything was amiss.

'So, where's Dom? I thought he was coming with you,' she enquired brightly.

'He's waiting for me in the pub. I thought it was best I came alone, so we can talk, Frankie. There's stuff we need to discuss.'

'Talk about what?' Frankie asked, as innocently as she could.

Joey leaned across the table. 'Like why you wanted to speak to that DI Blyth woman. What's going on, sis?'

'Nothing! I just wanted to tell her some stuff about Jed, that's all.'

'Like what?' Joey asked suspiciously.

'Like that he used to fucking rob old people. You don't know the 'arf of it, Joey. Him and that Sammy used to get them to make wills out in their names and all sorts. They were pure evil, the pair of them.'

'Really! How did they do that, then?'

Frankie explained how Jed and Sammy earned a crust by conning pensioners who were living alone and was relieved when Joey seemed to relax.

'So that's the only reason why you wanted to speak to the Old Bill then, is it?' Joey asked her.

Frankie nodded. She really didn't need the Spanish Inquisition from Joey, not after the morning she'd had already. 'Who told you about the Old Bill coming to see me? I take it it was Dad, and Larry had told him?'

'Dad's just worried about you, that's all. I wish you'd make up with him, Frankie.'

Frankie chuckled sarcastically. 'So how is our wonderful father and the old tart doing? Painted the nursery yet, have they?'

Joey sighed inwardly. He had been closer to their mum than anybody, and if he could accept their dad building a new life for himself, then so should his sister. Remembering his father's orders, Joey took a deep breath.

'It'll be better coming from you and she's bound to hear it via the grapevine, so make sure you tell her tomorrow,' his dad had insisted.

'Look, Dad asked me to tell you something and I know you ain't gonna like it.'

Guessing what it was, Frankie stood up and angrily pushed her chair to one side. Joey was so far shoved up her father's arse these days that she doubted anyone would be able to fit a Rizla between the old man's cheeks.

'Frankie, where are you going?' Joey shouted, as she stomped off.

Ignoring her lap dog of a brother, Frankie approached the nearest screw. 'I feel really sick. Can you take me back to my cell now, please?'

Terry Baldwin couldn't believe how inconsiderate some people could be. Once, he'd met Anne's mother, bloody once, and she could have chosen any date on the calendar to pop her clogs, except now. Anne's mum had moved to Australia many moons ago to be near her beloved son and grandchildren. Anne had never been particularly close to her and, as far as Terry knew, they hadn't even spoken on the phone for months, which is why Terry couldn't understand his wife's overboard hysterics over her mother's sudden death.

'We need to book a flight today, Tel,' Anne stammered, between sobs.

'But it's the other side of the world, love. I've only met your mother once and you were hardly close to her, were you? You even told me you hated her guts once upon a time.'

'How could you say such a thing? I never said I hated her guts, all I said was that we clashed a bit. I loved my mum dearly,' Anne insisted.

'How about we go to a travel agent and I book you a flight. Your brother's out there with his kiddies and it'll be nice for you to spend some time alone with your family, won't it?' Terry suggested.

'You can be such an unfeeling bastard at times, Tel. I spent months caring for and putting up with your daughter and her problems, yet you can't come to my mother's funeral with me. I'm telling you something now, if you don't come to Australia with me, you and I are finished.'

'Whaddya mean, finished?'

'I mean I want a fucking divorce!' Anne screamed.

Terry had a difficult decision to make. He'd wanted to finish off Jed O'Hara as soon as possible, but if he refused to go to Australia, his marriage could be dead in the water. Cursing his luck, and Anne's mother's timing, Terry held his pretty wife in his arms. He couldn't lose her; she was all he had left in the world.

'Let's go and book our flights then,' he said softly.

'You definitely coming with me?' Anne asked, relieved.

Terry nodded. His plans to rid the earth of a vile piece of shit would just have to wait a little bit longer.

Over in Rettendon, Eddie Mitchell was busy making plans of his own.

'I want you to spy on the house for me, Stu. I've bought you a little black Fiat to use. Just clock their movements, see what time they go out, come home, go to bed, all that type of stuff. I think we're gonna have to strike on a week night. We can't risk Jed being out partying somewhere. If you sit outside the house on a Tuesday, Wednesday and Thursday, we'll get an idea of their movements and pick one of those three evenings. It's gonna be boring for you, mate, but I can't risk Gary and Ricky doing it, cause if the O'Haras spot them, we're fucked. You are the only one out of us all that ain't gonna be recognised.'

'So, what have I gotta do? Just sit outside their house in the motor?'

Eddie shook his head. 'That's far too risky. It's a proper remote road, so you'll have to park at Joycie's and spy on foot. There's plenty of trees and bushes on and near O'Hara's land, so you'll easily find somewhere to hide. O'Hara has security lights at the front and back of his gaff, though, so for fuck's sake keep away from them.'

Considering it was January and had been snowing on and off for the past week or so, Stuart didn't relish his task but, desperate to please Eddie, kept his thoughts to himself. 'When do ya want me to start?' he asked brightly.

'Next week. Hopefully, the snow'll be gone by then and there's no rush because we ain't gonna strike until after you know what.'

At the mention of, you know what, Stuart grinned. He was looking forward to the big day almost as much as his boss was.

Bobby Berkley was already in the Optimist pub when Jimmy and Jed walked in.

'Look at you, all spruced up. You got some old malt on the firm?' Jimmy asked jokingly.

'Nah, got a wedding reception to go to in Chelmsford. Old Sidney Hedge's grandson Toby got wed today.'

Jimmy grinned as Bobby handed him a padded brown envelope. It was the five grand deposit he'd put down to kill Paulie and Ronny Mitchell.

'I've gotta go now, Jim, my Mary's sitting outside in the motor waiting for me. Do you wanna check it's all there?'

'Nah, I trust ya, mush,' Jimmy said, shaking Bobby's hand.

When Bobby left the pub, Jimmy put his hand inside the envelope. The money was in bundles of a thousand and Jimmy handed Jed two. 'Treat yourself and them chavvies to something nice,' he said generously.

'You sure?'

Jimmy O'Hara nodded. That mug Eddie Mitchell had given him thirty grand to sanction the murders of his own brothers. Jimmy's contact hadn't been able to get near the bastards, but some other fucker had, and Jimmy was now thirty grand better off, thanks to steady Eddie.

'Thanks for that, Dad,' Jed said gratefully, pocketing the wonga.

Jimmy O'Hara burst out laughing. 'Don't thank me – thank that cunt, Mitchell.'

The following day a sheepish-looking Stanley sat down awkwardly opposite Joey and Dominic.

'Hello, little doggy,' Stanley said in a silly voice as he patted Madonna on the head.

Sensing Stanley's embarrassment, Dominic diplomatically stood up. 'I need to ring my mum and find out how my nan is, so I'll take Madonna for a little walk,' he said.

'So, what's the story then, Grandad? Sick of the old tart already, are you?' Joey asked in a brutal tone.

Stanley's eyes immediately welled up. 'I've made a terrible mistake, boy. I should never have left your nan. I miss her dreadfully.'

'Bit late for regrets now, isn't it? Joey replied bluntly. His grandad deserved to suffer for what he'd put his nan through and he was determined not to make this conversation easy for him, no matter how much he grovelled.

'Do you honestly think it's too late, Joey? Can't you have a word with your nan? Tell her how sorry I am. I was so annoyed with her for seeing your dad behind my back that I just sort of flipped. I would have stayed with Jock, but I fell out with him over it an' all, didn't I?'

'Don't blame Nan for seeing Dad behind your back. Until you've got all that anger and hatred about Dad out of your system, you're never gonna be close to any of us ever again, including me nan. My dad is a good bloke and everybody knows what happened to Mum was an accident, so why can't you see it? As for me speaking to Nan on your behalf, I'm not doing anything for you until you tell me the truth. What's happened? Something's gone pear-shaped with that old slapper you've been living with and I want to know what it is.'

Stanley stared at his grandson with displeasure. Joey used

to be such a big softie, and it was as if Stanley didn't recognise him any more. In fact, he sounded just like his bloody father.

'Well, you gonna tell me what happened, or what?' Joey demanded.

Feeling his cheeks start to redden, Stanley explained the situation in the best way that he could. 'I only wanted a friend, a shoulder to cry on, and I always got on with Pat because of the pigeons. But once I moved in with her, she made it clear she wanted more from me, if you know what I mean?'

Enjoying his grandad's discomfort, Joey shook his head. 'No, I don't know what you mean, actually. You need to explain it in more detail.'

'Well, she kept touching me, you know, down there,' Stanley choked, pointing towards his groin. He couldn't tell Joey that Pat had put his John Thomas in her mouth. He'd take that awful secret to his grave with him.

'So, you're telling me that you want to move back home to Nan because the old slapper has been trying to touch your cock?'

Feeling totally ashamed and also shocked by Joey's crudity, Stanley felt the tears start to roll down his cheeks. 'I want to move back to your nan because I truly love her. I even miss her moaning at me, Joey. Please help me. I'm nothing without her.'

Seeing the people at the bar clocking Stanley crying, Joey sat on a chair next to his grandfather and put a comforting arm around his shoulder. He couldn't be totally horrible to him, it wasn't in his nature.

'I can't stay at that awful woman's another night, Joey, I really can't,' Stanley wept, feeling dreadfully sorry for himself.

'You can stay with me and Dom for the time being and don't worry, I'll speak to Nan for you. She'll take you back, I know she will.'

'Do you really think so?' Stanley asked hopefully.

Joey hugged the silly old fool. 'I know so, Grandad.'

CHAPTER TWENTY

The night before his brothers' joint funeral, Eddie struggled to sleep a wink. Guilt, anger, regret: his brain whirled away like a tumble drier and, sick of tossing and turning, he finally got up at 5 a.m.

Ed made himself a coffee and, feeling nostalgic, began flicking through an old photo album that had once belonged to his father. Most of the pictures were old, some slightly creased, but he smiled as he clocked the one of Ronny dressed in a silver tonic suit with two-tone shoes. That had been taken in Ronny's mod days and at a guess, Ed reckoned it must have been the early to mid sixties.

'I heard you get up. Are you all right, love?' Gina asked, as she walked into the lounge.

'I'm OK. I couldn't sleep, though. Come and sit 'ere and I'll show you some old photos of the boys.'

Gina sat down next to Ed. She had only met Paulie and Ronny once and that had been the night in the restaurant, when Eddie had just come out of prison and introduced her to his entire family.

'Is that you?' Gina asked, nudging him.

Ed nodded. The photo had been taken at his Auntie Joanie's house. He was sitting on her gate in a pair of grey shorts and Ronny and Paulie were standing behind him, all suited and booted. 'I used to really look up to 'em when I was a kid, you know. I thought they were the bollocks,' Eddie said sadly.

Gina laid her head on his shoulder. She knew how difficult today was going to be for Ed, and for once she had no words of comfort for him. 'I'm gonna cook us a nice breakfast. I

192

think a fry-up's in order today, considering you're going to be boozing later. You can't drink on an empty stomach, you know.'

When Gina left the room, Ed continued flicking through the photo album. He had three trustworthy pals in Belmarsh, Ginger Mick, Lee Adams and Scouse Lenny, but so far none of them could find out who had murdered Ronny and Paulie.

'We're positive it was nought to do with any of O'Hara's cronies. We were watching 'em and none of them could have got near that nonces' wing, so chances are your brothers were killed by someone off our radar,' Ginger Mick relayed via messenger yesterday.

Eddie wasn't quite as convinced. As far as he knew, nobody else in Belmarsh had it in for Ronny and Paulie, therefore he still had to live with the thought that he had paid for his own brothers to be murdered. The guilt of that was overwhelming, but what was pissing Ed off more was he'd underestimated Jimmy O'Hara. To get to Ronny and Paulie in the nonces' wing meant the pikey piece of shit was a lot cleverer than Ed would ever have given him credit for.

Slamming the photo album shut, Eddie put his head in his hands. He'd already got a few outsiders on the case and he was determined to find out who his brothers' killer was. Looking up, he stared at the large photograph of his father on the wall and spoke in a whisper so Gina couldn't hear him.

'I'm sorry, Dad, I did the best I could and I really thought Ronny and Paulie would be safe. But don't you worry, I shall find out who did this and when I do, they're dead, I promise you that faithfully.'

Another person up with the larks was Frankie's cellmate, Babs. They had had a heart to heart the previous night and Frankie had begged her to see sense.

'Look, if I can tell the truth about what Jed did to my grandad, then you can do the same, Babs. Let me have a word with DI Blyth for you, she's a nice lady and I know she'll try and help you. My dad will get you a good brief. He'll be so glad to be back in my good books after what he's done, he'll do anything I ask him to. Do it for your children. Matilda will get over all that shit being brought up in court and I'm sure

193

she'd rather tell the truth than not be able to live with her mum for years to come. Also I'm a selfish cow and when I get out of this shit-hole, I need you to be out in the real world with me. We can even get a flat or house together if you want, mate?'

Babs had spent the whole night mulling Frankie's words over in her mind. She hated the thought of making Matilda relive what that paedophile Peter had done to her, but was that any worse than missing seeing her daughter growing up into a young woman? She missed her children dreadfully and every time Matty and Jordan visited her, it broke her heart when they left. Babs got up, walked over to Frankie's bed and shook her.

'What time is it?' Frankie asked dazed.

'It's time I told the truth, sweet child.'

Georgie O'Hara was having one of her little tantrums. Two things had already upset her this morning. Her dad hadn't come home last night and he had promised to take her and Harry out for the day, and now her nan had just informed her that she was starting a new school the following week.

'I hate school. Don't wanna go!' Georgie screamed. She had originally started school in September the previous year, when she had been living in Wickford with her mum and dad, and she had despised every minute of it. Georgie loved outdoor life and being stuck in a classroom day in, day out, did not suit her adventurous nature one little bit.

Alice put Georgie's breakfast in front of her and crouched down next to her granddaughter. 'You have to go, Georgie girl. Daddy's solicitor promised that judge you saw in court that you would go back to school. If you don't, Daddy will get into trouble and you and Harry might be taken away from us and forced to live elsewhere.'

'Can I go to school, Nanny?' Harry asked innocently.

'Yes, when you're older. Now eat your breakfast, Georgie,' Alice ordered, as she stood up.

Georgie stared at the sausage, chips and beans. The mention of school had made her appetite disappear, so she sulkily pushed her plate away with force.

'You naughty girl,' Alice yelled, as the plate smashed on the kitchen floor and the contents went everywhere. Alice yanked Georgie out of the chair by her arm and slapped her on the back of her bare legs. 'Now go to your bedroom.'

Georgie immediately started to cry. 'I want my Mummy!' she screamed.

DI Blyth thanked Kerry for her help and told her she would be in touch in due course.

'So what will happen now? Will you arrest Jed and Sammy?' Kerry asked hopefully. She hated her two sons spending time with their father. She didn't trust Sammy an inch and was frightened that one day he wouldn't bring them back at all.

'What happens now is I hand all the details I have over to the Met and then they see if they can find enough evidence to charge Sammy and Jed. I will be involved and notified of any happenings, but because Frankie's grandad was murdered in Canning Town, it's not my job to actually solve the crime. I work out in Essex, you see,' Blyth explained.

'So how will the Met solve it? Frankie said that her dad has since sold her grandad's house, so they won't find any clues there if new people have moved in, will they?' Kerry asked, perplexed.

'When a murder such as Harry Mitchell's has taken place, the Met would have taken scene exhibits at the time and they would have been stored for safe-keeping.'

'Like what?'

'Well, I'm not exactly sure because I haven't spoken to them yet, but say, for instance, the victim was wearing clothes, or in Mr Mitchell's case, probably pyjamas at the time he was murdered, they would have been stored in case they had the killer's DNA on them. From what I remember, the police had very few suspects, but now we've got names, we can match any DNA that is found.'

Kerry nodded. 'But say you don't find any DNA? You can't let Jed and Sammy get away with it; they definitely murdered Frankie's grandad, I heard the conversation with my own ears.'

'I shall get in touch with the Met tomorrow and they can do some tests. I would have contacted them earlier, but I needed to speak to you first to confirm Frankie's story. In the Met's eyes two statements are far better than one. If by any chance they can't match any DNA to Sammy and Jed, we will have to cross that bridge when we come to it, but the one thing I can promise you, Kerry, is even though I'm not allowed to work directly on the case, I will still do everything in my power to ensure a conviction.'

Blyth said her goodbyes and got into the car. She had never really doubted Frankie's statement, but the fact that Kerry had repeated what her friend had said virtually word for word convinced Blyth that both girls were telling the absolute truth. All she had to do now was help the Met prove it.

Eddie stood solemnly in his aunt's front garden. It had been his idea to use Joanie's abode, where he and his brothers had grown up, for the sad occasion. Paulie's wife had recently divorced him and wanted nothing to do with his funeral whatsoever. As for Ronny's long-suffering partner, Sharon, she now lived in a poky council flat in Beckton and there just wasn't room for the mourners or the flowers.

Spotting his uncles, Reg and Albert, Eddie walked over to them and shook their hands.

'Few blasts from the past 'ere today boy, ain't there?' Reg commented, referring to some well-known faces that belonged to the criminal fraternity.

Eddie nodded. Paulie and Ronny had never been particularly popular, especially towards the latter years of their lives, but the criminal world was a tight-knit community and on occasions like this people would come and pay their respects to the actual family rather than the dead themselves.

Seeing Sharon burst into tears, Ed went over and put a comforting arm around the poor woman's shoulder. Over the years, Sharon had stuck by his brother through thick and thin. Ronny had always been a bastard to her. He'd spoken to her like shit, had even knocked her about at times, and Ed had never understood Sharon's loyalty towards him. Even when Ronny was left paralysed after being shot in the spine, Sharon stayed put. They had no kids and Ed thought the poor cow deserved a medal for coping with a crippled, abusive alcoholic.

Eddie led Sharon over to where Gina was standing. 'Keep an eye on Shal for me, babe,' he whispered.

About to pop inside the house to check on Joanie and Vi, Ed heard the clip-clop of hooves and stopped dead in his tracks.

'Are you all right, Dad?' Gary asked him.

Ed felt his whole body stiffen as he clapped eyes on the two coffins. Picturing his brothers lying lifeless inside them, he felt anything but all right. In fact, he felt sick with guilt.

Over in Rainham, Joyce was sipping a large brandy, which she'd poured to calm her nerves. She still hadn't seen or spoken to Stanley since he'd moved in with Joey and Dominic but, at her grandson's insistence, she had agreed to meet her philandering husband for lunch today.

'Grandad said he'll pick you up at one,' Joey told her yesterday.

'You tell your grandfather that I shall get a cab and meet him at the carvery.'

'What's the point of you paying for a cab?' Joey asked, perplexed.

'If you think I'm getting into your grandfather's car after he's had that old tart sat in it, then you can bleedin' well think again,' Joyce replied stubbornly.

Hearing the cab toot up outside, Joyce knocked back the rest of her drink and checked her reflection in the hallway mirror. She knew she looked good, she'd made a special effort, and she could hardly wait to show that errant husband of hers exactly what he'd been missing. Smiling like the cat who had got the cream back again, Joyce picked up her handbag and slammed the front door.

Jed O'Hara got out of bed and quickly got dressed. He'd spent the night at Amanda's flat and, after three dates, had finally got his end away with her. Amanda woke up and smiled lovingly at Jed. Unlike her friend, who had slept with Sammy on the night that she'd met him, Amanda had morals and she never slept with a lad unless the relationship was destined to be long term. Last night, Jed had repeatedly told her he loved her and had also said that he wanted her to meet his children and his

197

parents. Knowing how serious Jed was about her, Amanda finally decided to drop her knickers, and now she was absolutely smitten with him.

'What time are we taking your children out, Jed? What should I wear? I want to look nice if I'm meeting your mum and dad.'

Remembering the lies he'd spun to have his wicked way with her, Jed shrugged. He'd actually thought he'd liked her over the past week or so, but now he'd had sex with her, he'd kind of lost interest. Unfortunately for Amanda, she wasn't very good at it.

'I've been thinking, I feel it's a bit early for you to meet me chavvies. The thing is, it ain't that long since I split up with their muvver and I don't wanna confuse 'em, do I?'

'Well, can't we still spend the day together like you promised?' Amanda asked in a clingy tone.

'I'd love to, babe, but I promised I'd take me chavvies out and I wouldn't be much of a dad if I let 'em down, would I? I'll give you a bell later, OK?'

Jed pecked Amanda on the cheek, walked out of her flat and immediately rang his cousin. 'What's occurring, Sammy boy?'

'I've been waiting for you to bell me. Bored shitless I am, and Julie's done my head in all fucking day. How'd it go with Randy Mandy?'

Jed chuckled. 'She finally let me give her one, but it weren't worth the wait. Frigid bitch in bed she was and I ain't gonna bother seeing her again. She was all lovestruck this morning, so I bet I have to change me mobile number yet again. So, what we gonna do? I dunno about you, but I fancy getting right on one.'

'I thought we were gonna take Georgie and Harry out,' Sammy replied.

'Nah, can't be arsed. Get your gladrags on and I'll meet you in the Derby Digger at half-two. I think me and you should pop over to Basildon and pay them two whores another visit.'

Sammy laughed. 'Half-two it is then.'

Stanley's heart filled with hope as Joyce strolled into the restaurant. She was twenty minutes late and he had thought that she had changed her mind about meeting him. His hands shook as he handed her the expensive bouquet he'd bought her.

'Thank you for agreeing to meet me, Joycie,' he said genuinely.

Joyce smiled inwardly as she put the flowers on the chair next to her. Stanley had his best suit on and, considering he was usually covered in pigeon shit, she was pleased he'd made the effort to look smart for once.

'I took the liberty of ordering you your favourite wine,' Stanley informed her, nodding towards the ice bucket.

'Best you pour me a glass and then tell me why you asked me to come here,' Joyce replied coldly.

Stanley did as he was told and then looked into Joyce's eyes with pure emotion in his own. 'I asked you here because I can't live without you, Joycie.'

'Pity you didn't think of that before you left me and moved in with that old slapper. It's a bit late for regrets, Stanley, our divorce is probably nearly finalised.'

'I don't want to divorce you, Joycie. Being apart from you made me realise just how much I love you. As for Pat, I only moved in with her because I had nowhere else to go. There was nothing between us, I swear there wasn't,' Stanley lied. Joey had promised he wouldn't tell his nan what Stanley had told him, and Stanley just hoped that his grandson would keep his word.

Joyce was in her element. The old goat grovelling was exactly what she had expected and wanted, and now she was going to milk it. 'So, what is it you're trying to say? Are you asking to move back into my house?'

'Yes, if that's OK with you, love.'

Joyce took her compact mirror out of her handbag. She applied some more plum lipstick and snapped the mirror shut. 'I shall need some time to think about things.'

'How long do you need? I can't stay with Joey and Dominic for much longer. I'm cramping their style as it is.'

Joyce smirked. 'A week, perhaps two. Now I'm starving, so let's eat, shall we?'

* * *

Eddie managed to hold himself together throughout the service and only shed a tear at the end when he heard Tom Jones singing 'Green, Green Grass of Home' . Ed had chosen the record to be played as everybody left the church. It had been Paulie's party piece and there had been many a boozer he'd crooned it in back in the good old days.

As his brothers' coffins were lowered into the ground, Ed walked away and lit up a cigar. The guilt he was feeling was awful and it was tearing him apart inside. 'All right, mate? I've organised the wake at the Flag. You're coming back for a bevvy, ain't ya?' Ed asked, as Flatnose Freddie approached him.

'Just walk with me, I've got some info for you,' Freddie replied in almost a whisper.

Eddie felt his heart start to pound instead of just beat. He'd gone to Flatnose Freddie a couple of weeks back and offered him ten grand to find out who had killed his brothers. 'You got a name for me?' he asked softly.

Freddie ignored Eddie's question. 'Not 'ere,' he mumbled.

Urging Eddie to follow him behind the wall that was the toilet block, Flatnose Freddie turned to face his pal. He and Mitchell went back years and although he'd often charged Ed to dispose of bodies for him, he had no intention of taking ten grand from him for the info he'd acquired about his brothers. Family was family and business was business in Freddie's eyes.

'Right, I don't know who actually murdered your brothers, but I do know who ordered the hit and I know who the middleman was.'

'O'Hara fucking ordered it, I know that already,' Eddie said angrily.

Flatnose Freddie shook his head. 'O'Hara's plant was Pete Berkley and when Ronny and Paulie got shoved into the nonces' wing, Berkley couldn't get to 'em.'

'So, who the fuck ordered it, then?' Ed asked, stunned.

'Terry Baldwin. He paid Jamie Carroll to sort it.'

Overcome by shock, Eddie's mind went completely blank. 'Do I know 'em?'

'Course you do. Carroll's out of Plaistow originally. Used to knock about with Dean Arnold. Everyone knows him as the

Fixer. As for Baldwin, he's the grandfather of the kid your brothers murdered, hence the hit, I suppose.'

Ed leaned against the wall to steady himself. He knew the Fixer – he was a slimy fucker and Ed had never liked him much. As for Baldwin, Ed knew him by sight, but had never really had many dealings with him. Ed had heard good things about Baldwin in the past, but he certainly wasn't in his league.

Shaking his head in utter disbelief, Eddie shook Freddie's hand. 'Thanks mate. I'll get Raymond to pop your dosh over to you later in the week.'

Flatnose Freddie shook his head. 'Call it a favour, pal.'

'There you are. What you doing, Dad? Me, Gary and Joey have been searching high and low for ya,' Ricky said, as he poked his head around the brick wall.

Pulling himself together, Eddie smiled falsely. With the wake being held in the Flag, he had to keep schtum about his discovery for now, because in the circles he mixed in, people had ears like little bats.

'You know me, boy, I hate that grave bit, it gives me the fucking heebies. Go and tell your brothers I'll be over in a sec.'

When Ricky walked away, Eddie turned back to Freddie. 'You'll be OK to get rid of any waste for me, won't ya, mate?'

Flatnose Freddie grinned. There were hundreds of missing persons propped up in flyovers all over the country and they were mostly down to him. He was an expert with a cement mixer. 'Does the Pope fucking pray?' he chuckled.

CHAPTER TWENTY-ONE

In the weeks following his brothers' funerals Eddie returned to his focused, jolly, businesslike self. Flatnose Freddie's revelation had left him thunderstruck at the time, but once the news had finally sunk in, Eddie had felt nothing but relief. Knowing that he'd had sod-all to do with murdering his own brothers was a wonderful feeling and, as the guilt ebbed away from his body, Ed felt his sanity return.

The next day was Gina's thirty-fifth birthday and Ed could barely wait to present her with the biggest surprise she'd ever had. She didn't have a clue what he'd planned, bless her, and Ed couldn't wait to see the shocked expression on her face when she found out.

Once tomorrow was over, it was going to be all guns blazing, literally. Jamie Carroll was the first on Eddie's hit list. Gary and Ricky had been clocking Carroll's movements for over three weeks now. He lived in Harold Hill and Ed planned to abduct him outside his local snooker hall, which he seemed to frequent as regular as clockwork on a Monday night.

Terry Baldwin had been pinpointed as victim number two. He'd recently returned from Australia alone; as word had it, his wife had decided to spend some extra time with her family, which suited Ed perfectly. Raymond had been clocking Baldwin and they'd decided to abduct him at his own house.

Last, but certainly not least on the hit list, were the O'Haras. Stuart had been watching their movements for over a fortnight now and it had been decided they would strike late on Wednesday night. Jimmy and Jed both went to Southall horse market very early every Wednesday morning and, apparently, arrived home as pissed as farts between nine and ten in the evening. This suited Eddie, as the more rat-arsed they were, the less alert they would be when he and the boys broke in and shot the bastards.

Eddie punched in Gary's number and smiled as he heard his son's hungover-sounding voice. It had been Gary's thirtieth birthday the previous day. They'd had a family lunch, then Gary, Ricky and Stuart had all gone clubbing up West.

'How'd it go, boy? I hope you looked after Stu. He never came home last night, so I take it he's with you still?'

'Him and Ricky copped off with a couple of birds, fucking models they were, the lucky bastards. Christ knows how I got home; I must have got a black cab. I feel like shit today, I can tell ya. I'm getting too old for all this partying lark.'

Eddie chuckled. 'Well, best you sort yourself out in time for tomorrow. Track down the other two for me. I expect all three of yous to be bright eyed and bushy tailed in the morning. I'm on me way to visit Frankie now. Fuck knows why she's asked to see me, but I expect I'll get an earful, I always do off her. I'll bell ya when I leave the prison and, in the meantime, sort yourself out, boy, OK?'

Gary sighed. The way he felt, another big celebration in the dysfunctional life of the Mitchells was the last thing he needed.

Joey and Dominic sat opposite Joyce in an Italian restaurant in Hornchurch. It had been Dom's idea to pick Joycie up, get her drunk, and then beg her to let her husband come back home.

'So, are you looking forward to tomorrow? Big day for you as well, isn't it?' Joyce asked her grandson.

Joey nodded. He was proud his dad had chosen him, very proud indeed. 'I wish you'd come, Nan. Dad was upset when I told him you wasn't coming. He thinks the world of you, you know.'

'I know he does, but I can't come, love, it don't feel right. Now, can we talk about something else?' Joyce asked, feeling herself becoming emotional.

Joey topped his nan's glass up with more wine. 'Let's talk

about Grandad. He's been as good as gold with us, Nan, but we can't have him stay there for ever. You know how old fashioned he is – me and Dom are too frightened to have sex in case he hears us.'

Dominic chuckled. 'I feel like a monk, Joycie. Please take him back. He loves you so much, he talks constantly about you to me and Joey every night of the week.'

Joyce smirked. She liked Stanley talking about her constantly, and she hoped he was hurting as much as he'd hurt her. She hadn't spoken to him since the day they'd met in the carvery. She had let him drop her home that day and had told him she would let him know in her own time if he could come back home.

'Well? What do you say, Nan?' Joey asked hopefully.

Joycie sank the rest of her wine and wiped her mouth with the napkin. 'OK, tell the old goat he can come home tomorrow. I'm only doing this for your sakes, mind. You can tell him that I shall be writing a list of house rules, which I expect him to abide by. If he doesn't, then the dirty old bastard is straight out the door again.'

When Joyce headed for the toilet, Joey laughed and turned to Dominic. 'Poor Grandad. I'd hate to be in his bloody shoes.'

DI Blyth was sitting opposite the superintendent in Arbour Square police station in East London. The superintendent had been on a skiing holiday for the past couple of weeks and Blyth had eagerly awaited his return before presenting her evidence. In Blyth's experience, you were always better to speak to the organ grinder rather than waste time talking to the monkeys.

The superintendent put the statements down on his desk and turned to Blyth. He knew the Mitchell family very well. Over the years they had become the bane of his life and not getting the murder conviction to stick against Eddie had been one of the worst moments of his career.

'This all looks very impressive on paper, but I wouldn't trust a Mitchell as far as I could throw them. This is the same girl that lied through her teeth at her father's trial, I take it?'

Without the superintendent's support, Blyth knew she was up the creek without a paddle, so she sold Frankie to him as a person as best as she could. 'Frankie had very little choice other than to defend Eddie Mitchell at his trial. What girl wouldn't speak up for their own father? And I'm positive that she was got at by her own brothers as well. As for Frankie's statement telling us that Jed O'Hara was responsible for murdering her grandfather, I am one hundred per cent sure that the girl is telling the truth. Kerry, her friend, backed up the story; her statement is virtually identical to Frankie's.'

The superintendent was still dubious. He had hated Harry Mitchell with a passion. For years, he'd known exactly what the head of the Mitchell clan was up to, but catching him and locking him up had proved an impossible task. Houdini, the superintendent had nicknamed Mitchell, the reason being that the bastard was the biggest escapologist he'd ever had the misfortune of dealing with. In fact, when Houdini had finally met his maker, the superintendent had breathed a massive sigh of relief that he couldn't be tormented by the man any longer.

'I can see what you're saying, Blyth, but I would really like to speak to the Mitchell girl myself or send one of my own team to speak to her before I reopen this case.'

'Both Frankie and Kerry have flatly refused to speak to any officer other than myself, nor will they do a taped interview. Like it or not, sir, if this investigation does go any further, then I will have to be involved. The girls trust me, you see,' Blyth explained.

The superintendent rubbed his fingers around his moustache. He'd overslept this morning and hadn't had time to trim the bloody thing. 'OK, on your insistence, I'll reopen the case. We'll start by getting some DNA tests done on the crime exhibits, see if we can get a match to the suspects. I'll also send some men round to speak to Mitchell's neighbours again. But if these girls are lying, be it on your head, and I truly mean that, Blyth.'

Filled with relief, Blyth smiled and shook the SI's hand. 'Thank you so much for taking me seriously, sir.'

Eddie Mitchell didn't know whether to hug, kiss, or just curtly say hello to his only daughter. Frankie was an unpredictable character at the best of times and, as alike as they were, he would never understand her way of thinking as long as he lived. As he walked towards her, he opted to give her a quick peck on the cheek.

'You all right, girl? Christ, you ain't 'arf showing now,' Ed said, stating the obvious.

'You wanna see my mate, Babs. She's only got a couple of weeks to go and she's twice the size of me,' Frankie replied.

'So, how long exactly you got to go now?'

'Six weeks. I can't wait now, I'm so excited.'

Eddie grinned. Frankie was acting much warmer towards him than he'd expected her to be. Not one to brush things under the carpet, Ed leaned towards her. 'I know you've been pissed off with me, sweetheart, and I do understand how you feel, but I ain't 'arf missed ya and I really want us to be friends again. Can we put all that crap behind us now?'

Frankie could be just as blunt as her father at times. 'It all depends if you help me or not. I need a big favour, Dad.'

Eddie smirked. He'd thought his daughter had asked him to visit her because she had missed him, but in true Frankie style, the only reason she'd requested his presence was because she wanted something in return. 'Go on, hit me with it.'

Eddie was appalled as Frankie explained the true horror of what had happened to her cellmate, Babs. He hated nonces, fucking despised them, and he admired Babs for killing the bastard in the way that she had. Seeing Frankie's eyes well up, Eddie held his daughter's hand.

'It's OK, you don't have to tell me no more. I'll sort your mate out with a brief, babe, and I'll cover all the costs for her, OK?'

Frankie squeezed her father's hand. 'Thanks, Dad, I knew I could rely on you.'

Alice O'Hara was a bundle of nerves as she walked through the corridor of Georgie's infant school. Dealing with people in authority wasn't Alice's cup of tea and she was dreading facing her granddaughter's headmaster.

'So, what's she done now?' Alice coldly asked the secretary. Since starting her new school Georgie had been off her food again, and Alice was becoming increasingly worried about her granddaughter's weightloss and quietness indoors. In the last couple of weeks she'd become very sullen and introverted, and trying to get her to school in the mornings was an absolute nightmare.

'The headmaster will explain all to you. Take a seat and I'll let him know you are here,' the secretary informed her.

Alice sat down on the chair and twiddled her thumbs anxiously. The school head had rung up just over an hour ago. Jed was up in Cambridgeshire grafting with Sammy, and Jimmy hated authority as much as Alice did, so had opted to wait outside in the motor.

'The headmaster will see you now,' the secretary said, smiling.

Alice walked into the small room.

'Please sit down, Mrs O'Hara,' the headmaster instructed.

'So, what's she done?' Alice asked him. He was an ugly man, with silly glasses perched on the end of his nose.

'Georgina ran away from the playground earlier and if it wasn't for one of the other children telling the teacher on duty, we wouldn't have known until playtime was over.'

'Surely the gates are locked, though? Where is she now?' Alice asked worriedly.

'Georgina is in her classroom. She's fine, and of course the gates are locked. We take every precaution possible to ensure the safety of our children. Georgina is the first child who has ever managed to climb over the railings. Mrs Morris, who was on playground duty, informed me and we immediately sent out a search party. We finally found Georgina walking along the main road. I know she has had problems in the past, but Georgina doesn't seem to be settling in very well here. She really doesn't seem happy and that worries me greatly. I don't want to worry you, Mrs O'Hara, but anyone could have snatched her along that main road today. There are some very dangerous people out there, as I am sure you are only too aware of. Georgina is a very bright girl for her age. She is behind the other children with her reading and writing, but other than that, she is years ahead of them in her speech and her ways. I propose we send her to a special unit where the classrooms are smaller and she can get one-to-one tuition. They can help her overcome her emotional difficulties, and then you can find a more suitable school for her. I really do think this would benefit Georgina in the long run.'

Alice was furious. In her eyes, a special unit was for either difficult or backward kids, and there was no way her precious Georgie was going to one of those. 'No granddaughter of mine is going anywhere with a load of loonies and divs. Where is she now?' Alice screeched.

The headmaster was horrified by Alice's shouting. 'As I said earlier, Georgina's back in her classroom. I really think you should think about what I . . .'

Alice stopped him mid-sentence. She jumped off her seat and pointed her chubby finger into his face. 'Now, you listen to me, you ugly, four-eyed old shitcunt. I am taking my grand-daughter out of this crappy school this very minute and I shall find her somewhere decent to attend. And while I'm at it, I might report you to the gavvers for putting her poor little life in danger.'

'Is there really any need to use such language?' the head-master asked, shell-shocked by Alice's use of appalling vocabulary.

Alice opened the door and glared at him. 'Go fuck your grandmother.'

After agreeing to help Babs, Frankie and Eddie enjoyed a pleasant visit. Gina wasn't mentioned by either of them; instead they discussed the rest of the family in detail.

'I really can't believe that Nan's letting Grandad move back in with her. I know I forgave Jed when he messed about with that Sally bird, but I would never do it again with any other bloke. Don't get me wrong, I'm glad Nan and Grandad have sorted out their differences, but knowing Nan as well as I do, I'm just shocked that she's taken him back. She always came across to me as someone who would never forgive that type of thing.'

Eddie chuckled. It had been wonderful spending time with his daughter today and he didn't want visiting time to end. 'Your grandmother will give that poor old sod a dog's life, trust me on that one.'

Frankie laughed. She, too, had enjoyed the visit, so much so that she realised exactly how much she'd missed having her dad in her life. 'Is that boy still living with you, Dad? You know, the one you were in Wandsworth with?'

'Yeah, he ain't a boy no more, though. Stuart's a man now and he liked you when I showed him your photos, reckoned you were beautiful, he did.'

'Don't be showing photos of me to strangers, Dad. You know how I hate having my photo taken; I look awful in 'em,' Frankie said, embarrassed.

'No, you don't! That's just you being paranoid. He'd make a nice boyfriend for you when you get out of here. Stu's the same age as Ricky and, unlike your ex, he's a true gentleman. He'll make a fucking great husband for some lucky girl one day, I know that much.'

'Well, it won't be me! Jed has put me off men for life and when I finally get out of here, all I wanna do is get Georgie and Harry back and concentrate on them and my new baby. Please don't start trying to fix me up with blokes when I get out, Dad, it's really humiliating.'

'I'm not trying to fix you up, I was just saying I thought you'd be well suited, that's all. Now, tell me more about this little chat you had with that DI Blyth. Joey said that Jed was conning old people or something.'

Frankie began to explain about Jed's business dealings and was relieved when the bell rang for the end of visiting time. She had been enjoying herself until her dad had mentioned DI Blyth. As soon as he'd said her name, it reminded her of the awful secret she was keeping from him.

'I'd best go now,' she said, hugging her father tightly.

'Don't go yet, no other bastard has jumped out their seat,' Ed replied.

Frankie took in the scent of her father's aftershave. The smell of him always reminded her of when she was a child. She pulled away from him. 'So, when will you sort out the Babs situation for me?'

'I'll speak to Larry tomorrow. He'll have a chat with her and then we'll see if we can get her that good QC that's representing you.'

'Thanks, Dad,' Frankie said gratefully.

When Eddie walked away, he heard Frankie shout his name. He turned around again.

'Oh, and good luck for tomorrow. I hope you have a good day.'

Surprised by his daughter's sudden change of heart, Eddie winked at her. Grinning like a Cheshire cat, he walked out of the room with a gigantic spring in his step.

CHAPTER TWENTY-TWO

Eddie Mitchell was as happy as a pig in shit the following morning. Planning Gina's surprise was the lift he had needed after his awful Christmas, and being on good terms with Frankie again had only heightened his good mood. Next week would be very different, as that was when the shit would start to hit the fan, but for now, all Ed wanted to do was concentrate on the day ahead.

'Wakey, wakey,' Eddie said, as he snuggled up to Gina's back.

Gina turned around and grinned. Ed had been banging on about her birthday surprise for the past few weeks and the suspense was doing her head in. 'Please tell me what it is now,' she pleaded. All Ed had told her is that they were attending a friend's wedding this morning, then later this afternoon she would receive her actual present.

Eddie pushed his groin playfully against Gina. 'You're not having your wicked way with me unless you put me out of my misery,' Gina joked.

Eddie chuckled. 'If I tell ya, I'll have to kill ya, babe.'

Stanley Smith had never been the bravest of men, so instead of collecting his beloved pigeons from Pat's house himself, he'd sent his friend Brian to do his dirty work. His clothes he had taken on the day he had moved in with Joey and Dom. Pat the Pigeon had been very tearful that day and had practically got on her hands and knees begging him to stay, but there was no changing Stanley's mind. The vile sex act she had attempted to perform on him had put him off Pat for life, so much so that he couldn't even look her in the eye any more.

211

Stanley stood at the window as though he was dancing on hot coals. He knew Pat would have taken good care of his beloved pigeons for him, but he couldn't wait to see them again. Pat had given him one that he'd named after her, and he'd have to change that now. Joycie would be furious if he didn't. Not only that, he wanted no reminder of Pat in his life ever again.

Seeing Brian's car pull up outside, Stanley ran out to greet him. 'Hello, my little cherubs. Have you missed me?' he crooned, as he opened the back doors of Brian's van.

'Pat was very upset that you didn't pick them up yourself, Stanley. She started crying as I left and she told me to tell you that she's sorry for what she did and she hopes that you and her can still be friends. Whatever happened between yous two, mate?'

Feeling himself blush, Stanley busied himself by transferring the pigeon basket over to his own car. He'd already packed his clothes earlier, so once he got rid of Brian, he was ready to go home to Joyce.

'Nothing bad happened, we just had a silly row that's all. Anyway, I wanted to go back home to my Joycie, so I think it's best I don't come to the Orsett Cock any more. Also, if you can inform me which race meetings Pat will be attending, I would appreciate that as well. Me and her can't be friends 'cause it ain't fair on Joycie, so I'd just rather avoid Pat altogether in future, to be honest.'

Brian nodded. He knew there was more to Stanley's story than he was letting on, and he'd already made up his mind to ply Pat with a few G&Ts at the weekend to see if he could loosen her tongue a bit. 'Well, good luck with Joycie, mate, and I'll catch up with you at one of the race meetings. You'll be coming to Peterboro', won't you?'

'If Pat ain't going, I will. Listen, I'd best make a move now, Joycie was expecting me home by eleven. Thanks again for today, Bri, I owe you a pint or two, pal.'

As soon as Brian drove off, Stanley got into his own car and turned the ignition on. Then with a big smile on his face, he drove towards Rainham. Joycie would treat him like a doormat when he got home, he had no doubt about that, but he didn't care because he loved her. However badly she treated him, he knew that living with Joyce was where he belonged and he never wanted to spend a day apart from her again.

Jed and Sammy were in a jolly mood as they drove back towards Essex. They'd just returned to work and had had quite a successful day yesterday. They had made friends with three old people who all lived alone and seemed potentially easy to con. Jed was the one who had decided to move their business activities away from the Essex area. Their last victim, Mr Franks, had been just about to leave Jed and Sammy everything in his will, when his nosy next-door neighbour had got involved and threatened to call the police. As luck would have it, Mr Franks had no idea of Jed or Sammy's surnames or where they came from. If the will had already been made, Jed and Sammy could have been caught red-handed, and they'd had a lucky escape in the end. Cambridgeshire was a perfect area for them to now start all over again. There were lots of old people living there and they were far less clued-up than most of the old people who lived in London or Essex.

'I reckon that fucking old grunter, Mrs Marsh, is loaded, ya know. Out the three of 'em, I reckon we should sting her first. Them antiques and paintings she was showing us must be worth an arm and a leg alone,' Sammy said excitedly.

Jed agreed. Mrs Marsh had said she had no family whatso-ever and she lived in a cottage and owned a couple of acres of land. There were no neighbours to poke their trunks in, which was a plus point for Jed after what had happened with Mr Franks. 'We'll go back on Saturday and mend that leak in her roof she was telling us about. Then we can paint the room she said the damp's got into,' Jed suggested.

'What shall we charge her? We've gotta hit her for, say, five grand just for the roof and we won't have to do ought, we'll just patch it up as best we can,' Sammy said, chuckling.

'Let's not hit her for too much wonga to start with. We'll charge her two or three grand for the roof and see how she reacts to that before we sting her good and proper,' Jed said cautiously. Some of these old people were slightly less senile than they seemed and he didn't want any alarm bells to start ringing in that wrinkled old head of Mrs Marsh's.

Pulling up outside his parents' house, Jed was greeted by his mother running towards him. The battery on his mobile had died a death yesterday afternoon and he'd forgotten to take his spare with him.

'Whose truck is this? And why are you both wearing overalls and baseball hats?' Alice asked suspiciously.

'The truck belongs to Sammy and me and we're dressed like this 'cause we've been grafting,' Jed explained. The truck was actually a ringer that couldn't be traced to either him or Sammy. Neither lad had wanted to use their own motor this time, in case there was a repeat of the Mr Franks fiasco.

'Now, don't have a go at me, but I've taken Georgie out of that school, boy.'

'You've done what?' Jed spat angrily. Part of his custody conditions was that Georgie returned to school and then Harry would also go as soon as he was old enough.

'Daddy!' Harry screamed, as he got out of his little car and ran towards him.

Jed picked his son up and turned back to his mother. 'So, what happened, then?'

'The headmaster rang me up and asked me to go up and see him. He reckons that Georgie ain't settling in and needs to go to one of them special units. I was fucking livid, Jed, so I told him where to go, and brought Georgie girl home with me. I ain't having her go to one of them divvy places! Bright as a button she is and I ain't having her mix with a load of dinlos.'

Jed sighed. He needed to find Georgie another school double quick, or else Frankie's solicitor would start creating havoc for him again. 'You should have left this for me to deal with, Mum. I'll shoot up and have a chat with the headmaster, see if I can sort it out. What exactly did you say to him?'

'I told the four-eyed old shitcunt to go fuck his grandmother.'

Jed felt his face redden with fury. 'You stupid woman! If Frankie gets visiting rights because of this, I will never forgive you, Mum, and I truly fucking mean that.'

* * *

Eddie Mitchell asked the taxi driver to drop him and Gina off at the entrance of Brentwood Registry Office. Years ago, his pal Dougie had surprised his wife Vicki in exactly the same manner and Ed had admired his cavalier style.

'I didn't realise all your family were going to be here today as well. How did you say you know these people that are getting married?' Gina asked innocently.

Eddie paid the driver, got out the car and opened the door for Gina. She looked an absolute picture in the cream pencil skirt suit she had bought especially for the occasion. She'd moaned like hell because she'd had to buy a size twelve instead of a ten, but considering she was now fifteen weeks pregnant, she still looked amazing in it.

'The groom's dad was one of my dad's best pals. That's why all my mob are 'ere. Now, I need to have a quick chat with the boys. You'll be OK with Joanie and Vi for five minutes, won't ya?'

'Well, yeah, but don't forget to introduce me to the bride and groom before they get married, Ed,' Gina said haughtily. She guessed that the people getting wed must have known Jessica, which made her feel a bit awkward. Not only that, she also felt a complete tit attending the wedding of two faceless strangers without as much as a formal introduction beforehand.

'Don't she look beautiful?' Vi commented, nudging Joanie.

Ed winked at his aunts and kissed Gina on the cheek. 'I promise you faithfully I will introduce you to the bride and groom before the ceremony, OK?'

'OK.'

Eddie walked over to Joey. He was feeling a bit edgy now and was desperate for the day to go without any hitches. 'Is everything on cue? Has everyone turned up?'

'Yep. Uncle Albert and Uncle Reg have gone to the toilet. Your mates are all standing around the back and the only person I ain't seen yet is Flatnose Freddie. Oh, and Raymond and Polly are on their way; Ray just rang and said he'd be here in five minutes.'

'What about Stuart?' Eddie asked.

Joey nodded and, ignoring the bored expressions on Gary and Ricky's faces, led his father inside the building.

'Dominic and Stuart have been entertaining Gina's family and friends and I checked with Claire that everybody on Gina's side had arrived. Her brother's a nice guy, so are her mum and dad, but they're proper Irish and I can't really understand what they're saying, to be honest.'

Eddie chuckled. Apart from Claire, he had never met any of Gina's family or friends and he just hoped that they liked him and vice versa.

'Do you wanna go and meet them now, Dad?' Joey asked.

'No, I think I'll let Gina introduce me. I'm sure she'd prefer it that way.'

'Well, you wait here and I'll go and round everyone up, including Gina. Has she still not got a clue?'

Eddie shook his head and grinned. 'She might have been a private detective once upon a time, but she ain't as clever as me, boy.'

Joey smiled. 'Good luck, Dad. I really like Gina and I'm so happy for you both.'

Eddie looked at his son and felt his eyes well up. Gary and Ricky had been extremely pissed off when he'd asked Joey to be his best man, but he was so glad that he had gone with his heart. Years ago, when Joey was growing up, Eddie had never understood his son. He had been desperate for him to be more like his Gary and Ricky, but Joey was his own person, and once Ed had got down off his high horse and accepted his son for what he was, he'd realised for the first time just how much he adored the boy.

Eddie pulled his son into his arms and slapped him on the back. 'I love you, boy, now jog on outside and get the others before I make a complete fucking prick of meself.'

Joyce was on tenterhooks as she peeped through the corner of the curtain, waiting for Stanley to arrive. He was fifteen minutes late and she prayed to God that he hadn't had a last-minute change of heart. Finally, his car pulled onto the drive and Joyce jumped away from the curtain, ran into the kitchen and began sweeping the floor with her broom.

'One minute,' she shouted as Stanley rang the doorbell.

Stanley stood patiently on the doorstep. He hadn't asked Joyce if it was all right to bring his pigeons back home and he hoped she wasn't annoyed that he had just presumed it would be OK. His pigeon shed was still in one piece in the back garden, thank God. Once, years ago when he'd walked out briefly, Joycie had smashed his old shed to smithereens with a massive bloody hammer.

'Oh, it's you, Stanley,' Joyce said with a surprised expression on her face.

'Are you expecting somebody else?' Stanley asked politely. Surely she hadn't forgotten he was coming home today.

'No, I just didn't remember what time you said you'd be back,' Joyce lied.

'I hope you don't mind, love, but I brought me babies home with me. Is that OK?' Stanley asked cautiously.

'Yes, I suppose so. Walk them around the back, though, I don't want them coming through the house any more.'

Stanley obediently did as he was told, then returned to the car to unload his clothes and other bits and bobs. 'Shall I take these straight upstairs to my old room, love?'

'Yes, in a minute. Come and sit down first. I've made us a pot of tea and I want to go through my list of house rules with you.'

Stanley felt like a naughty schoolboy as he sat on the sofa opposite his wife.

Joyce cleared her throat. 'Rule number one. I am not getting in that stinking, pigeon-shit-infested car of yours any more. Keep it to use for carting your pigeons about by all means, but I am going to choose a car out of the money we have in my bank account and I expect you to take me anywhere I wish to go in it, any time I ask.'

'Yes, dear,' Stanley replied immediately.

'Number two. I don't mind cooking for us on weekdays, but unless we're having guests over, I expect to be taken out for meals at weekends in future and I expect you to pay.'

'Yes, dear.'

'Number three. I want you to apologise to Jock for what you did to him. You were bang out of order blaming that man, he's been a good friend to you, Stanley.'

'OK, I'll call him first thing tomorrow,' Stanley said sheepishly.

'Number four. I want you to help me with the garden and the housework from now on. I don't see why it should all be left to me.'

'But I ain't no good at gardening, Joycie, you know that,' Stanley said, alarmed.

'Well, like it or not, these are my rules and you either abide by them or piss off back to your old tart's house.'

Stanley flinched at the mention of his old tart. Praying that Joycie didn't have many more rules, he nodded his head.

'My fifth rule is, you must never utter another bad word about Eddie Mitchell in this house ever again. That man's been bloody good to me since you did your vanishing act and I am determined that he's going to be part of my life from now on and I'd like him to visit this house whenever he wishes.'

'But he's getting hitched again today. I hope you ain't gonna invite that new wife of his around here. It ain't right – this was our Jessica's house,' Stanley complained.

'I'll decide what's right and wrong. This house belongs to me and, like it or not, you're just the lodger here now, OK?' Joyce said adamantly.

'OK. I suppose if Eddie's been good to you, then it's only right that you keep in touch with him,' Stanley replied reluctantly.

'Number six is –'

'How many more are there, Joycie?' Stanley asked, dismayed. He was thrilled she'd allowed him to come back home, but this rule lark was getting beyond a joke now.

'Shut up. Don't you dare interrupt me. Rule number six is my last. I want you to call your solicitor and cancel that divorce. Even though you and I know you're only the lodger, Stanley, I will not have our friends and family under the impression that we are living in sin. It's not morally acceptable.'

Stanley smirked at this rule. 'Yes, dear.'

Proud of her set of ground rules, Joyce put her pen and paper on the glass table and smiled at her husband. 'Right, hurry up and finish your tea. I need you to cut the grass in the back garden for me.'

'But it's freezing out there, Joycie. The ground will be bleedin' rock hard.'

218

'I'll decide whether the ground's rock hard or not. Now drink that tea, come on, chop chop.'

Stanley gulped the rest of his tea down and bolted outside to get the lawnmower out of the shed. His life would be hell from now on, he was well aware of that, but he also knew that deep down, his Joycie still loved him. Why else would she stop their divorce?

When Eddie opened the registry office door, Gina stood open mouthed as she spotted all her family and friends. 'Oh my God!' she exclaimed as the realisation of what was happening finally hit home.

Forever the charmer, Eddie took Gina by the hand and led her to the two front rows where her family and friends were sitting. He stopped right in front of her parents and dropped to one knee.

'Soppy cunt,' Gary whispered to Ricky.

Raymond squeezed Polly's hand and Stuart grinned. In prison Ed had been such a hard nut and it was nice to see a softer side to him.

'Ahh, bless him,' Joanie said, wiping her eyes.

Reg and Albert glanced at one another in amazement. Had Ed lost his marbles? they both thought silently.

Eddie cleared his throat. 'Gina, I love you so much, darling, that I couldn't wait any longer for you to become my wife, so would you do me the great honour of marrying me right now?'

Overcome by a mixture of shock and emotion, Gina burst into uncontrollable tears. 'Yes. Oh Ed, this is the best birthday present I've ever had,' she sobbed.

Ricky nudged Gary. 'Fuck this for a game of soldiers – let's go outside and have a fag.'

Joey glared at his half-brothers as they stood up and left the room.

'Ignore them. They're just playing up because your dad chose you to be his best man,' Dominic whispered in his boyfriend's ear.

The registrar allowed the introductions to take place, then asked Eddie and Gina if they were ready for the service to begin. Aware that Gary and Ricky were still absent, Joanie stomped outside to find them. When she did, she found them both in hysterical laughter.

'What's so fucking funny? Ain't you coming back inside?' she asked angrily.

Gary was laughing so much that he was almost bent double. Unable to speak, he pointed at the horse and carriage that had just trotted into the car park. Neither Gary nor Ricky had had any idea that their father had booked this monstrosity to take him and Gina to the reception.

Vi appeared by Joanie's side. 'What the hell's goin' on? The service has already started.'

Ricky nodded towards the horse and carriage. 'We were just laughing at that. Who do they think they are, Charles and Diana? Look at its poncy roof.'

'The old man is such a soppy prick at times. Can you imagine if Jimmy O'Hara or some other face he knows drives past him in that? They'll think he's lost the fucking plot,' Gary chuckled.

Joanie was furious. 'Yous two will never understand a bit of old-fashioned romance while you've got holes in your arses. Now get inside before I brain the fucking pair of ya.'

The boys ignored their aunt's stern warning and carried on taking the piss. 'Let's take some photos of him sitting on it and send it to the East London rag. Can you imagine what a laugh that will create in Canning Town?' Ricky chortled, nudging his brother.

Joanie moved closer to the boys and, unable to control her temper any longer, slapped both of them around their smarmy faces. 'If you send anything to the papers, you'll have me and Vi to deal with. And shall I tell you something: if anyone needs laughing at, it is yous two pair of weirdos. I've never known two men at the ages of twenty-seven and thirty that have never had a serious girlfriend before. It ain't fucking normal, and I've started to wonder if yous two bat for the other side like our Joey does. Now, do yourselves a favour and get your arses inside that building before I really lose my rag.'

With the smiles now wiped off their faces, Gary and Ricky did exactly as they were told.

The short service was nearly over by the time Vi, Joanie, Gary and Ricky returned to their seats. Joey stood up, handed the rings over and shared a poignant look with his father that nobody else in the room would understand. A particular woman was on both of their minds, and Joey knew, from the glimpse of sadness he'd spotted in his father's eyes, that no matter how much his dad thought of Gina, in his heart she would always play second fiddle to his beautiful mum, Jessica.

CHAPTER TWENTY-THREE

Eddie and Gina's honeymoon consisted of a long weekend away in London. Being a man of extravagance and class, Ed booked them into the Savoy Hotel and they then spent a wonderful weekend taking in the sights and sounds of the best city in the world. Eddie had never been a lover of foreign holidays. The last time he'd been abroad, his brother Ronny had gone missing, so he'd had to cut his holiday short and fly back home. Ronny had been found barely alive – he had been shot in the spine and paralysed – and that had put Ed off foreign holidays for life. Having said that, Gina was a big lover of New York and Ed had promised to treat her to a proper honeymoon in the Big Apple once she had had the baby.

Gina was giggling to herself as she started to pack their clothes into the case. She had made Eddie take her to see a musical the previous night and he had hated every single moment of it.

'What you laughing at?' Ed said, pinching her bum.

'You! Them poor people sitting behind us last night were really pissed off with your comments. That woman's son was in the bloody show and she was ever so posh as well.'

'Bollocks to 'em. Fucking load of pansies prancing around a stage. I can't believe people pay good money to watch that shit. I'm just gonna pop outside to make a couple of phone calls. You all right packing everything? Don't forget me razor, will ya, it's still in the bathroom.'

'I'm fine. Go on, you sod off, I can pack quicker without you,' Gina said cheerfully. They'd had a wonderful few days and she would never forget her birthday surprise if she lived to be a hundred.

Eddie walked out of the room, shut the door and punched in Raymond's number. 'Well, is it all systems go?'

'It sure is, pal. I've spoken to the boys and everybody knows the cue.'

Eddie ended the call and smirked. Now he'd got the wedding over and done with, the killing spree was about to begin.

Alice O'Hara was having a nightmare of a morning. Firstly, the washing machine had broken mid-cycle. Then, when she had forced open the door, the water had pissed out and she had slipped on the kitchen floor and hurt her back and, last but not least, her daughter-in-law, Shannon, had asked her to look after her son for the day and he, Georgie and Harry hadn't stopped arguing and fighting since he'd arrived.

'Will yous three fucking stop it now? Nanny's had enough,' Alice screamed, as she heard a commotion in the lounge again.

Harry, Georgie and Billy Junior, who everyone called 'Mush', took no notice of their nan's orders.

Mush was older than Georgie and Harry. He was eight, and Harry was furious when he saw him slap Georgie around the face and pin her to the floor. Remembering his dad's words to always stick up for himself and his sister, Harry picked the glass ashtray up off the table and, just as the doorbell rang, clumped Mush over the head with it.

Ignoring her grandmother's shouts not to answer the door, Georgie jumped up and did the exact opposite. Mush's head was bleeding and she was worried that the police had come to take her little brother away. It wasn't Harry's fault; Mush had started the fight and Georgie was determined to tell them the truth, so they could take Mush away instead.

'Is your Dad there, Georgie?' the caller asked.

Georgie recognised the lady immediately. She was the nice social worker lady who had come round to speak to her and Harry in the past. She had also been at the court when they had been taken there that day.

'Nan, the nice lady wants to see Daddy,' Georgie shouted out.

Alice got up off her hands and knees. She'd been mopping

the floor for the past two hours now and there was still water everywhere. 'What do you want? If it's about Georgie not going to school, we took her out of there because the headmaster virtually called her a dinlo. Her father is in the process of finding her a new school,' Alice said defensively.

When Harry ran into the hallway with a glass ashtray in his hand, followed by an older boy who was screaming, with blood running down his forehead, Carol Cullen looked at the scene before her in horror.

'Are you the gavvers? I hit him 'cause he hit my sister,' Harry said, not recognising Carol at all.

Alice was mortified as she saw the state of Mush's head. The inch-long gash looked deep and was bleeding profusely.

'Can you come back another time? I'd better get him to the hospital. I always keep me eye on 'em usually, but Jed and Jimmy are both out and me washing machine's flooded the kitchen. You know what kids are like: they were playing nicely and then they have a little barney, and all hell breaks loose,' Alice said, embarrassed by the situation.

'That definitely looks like it needs stitching, so yes, you'd best go straight to the hospital, Mrs O'Hara. I will pop back tomorrow at twelve noon, so can you make sure that you are here, please? It would also be helpful if Jed was present.'

Alice nodded and, as Carol Cullen turned away, she slammed the front door and clumped Georgie around the head in temper.

'Now look what you've done. I told you not to open the bloody door, didn't I? We'll have gavvers and social workers all over the poxy place now, you dinlo.'

When Georgie held her head and started to cry, Harry dropped the bloodied ashtray onto the floor. His dad had had a right go at him when he'd found out he'd had a scrap with Georgie a couple of weeks back.

'You never, ever hit your own sister, Harry, but if anyone else touches her, no matter who they are, then you fucking clump 'em one, boy,' his dad had told him.

Glaring at his nan, Harry ran towards Alice and punched her repeatedly as hard as his little fists would allow him to. 'You leave my sister alone!' he screamed.

*　*　*

DI Blyth felt the adrenalin pulsate through her veins as she took the call and recognised the superintendent's voice from Arbour Square. She hadn't heard a word from him since their meeting in his office last week, but he had promised to contact her personally if and when he had news of any substance.

'I thought I'd best give you a brief update. We've no good news on the witness front so far, I'm afraid. My officers have drawn a complete blank in Harry Mitchell's old neighbourhood. Two of the witnesses that gave us a description of the suspects and statements at the time are no longer able to help us. The elderly chap, Cyril Miller, who lived opposite Mitchell, passed away last year, and Iris Jones, Mitchell's next-door neighbour, now has Alzheimer's and is residing in a rather luxurious care home, all courtesy of the generous Eddie Mitchell, apparently. There were two other neighbours who also gave us statements, but one has since moved to Spain and the other moved to an address in Canvey Island that no longer seems to exist.'

'Any news on the DNA yet?' Blyth asked in a slightly deflated voice.

'The results should be back in the next few days, so fingers crossed on that one. As soon as I hear anything, I will let you know immediately.'

Blyth thanked the superintendent for the information and ended the call. Frankie was going to be devastated if there was insufficient DNA evidence to arrest Sammy and Jed, and the thought of having to break the bad news to the poor girl filled Blyth with dread.

Eddie Mitchell was surprised to arrive home to an empty cottage. Stuart rarely went anywhere without him, so much so that Ed had had to virtually blackmail him to have a night out with the lads for Gary's thirtieth birthday last week.

'I wonder where Stu is? I'd better ring him to make sure he's all right,' Eddie said to Gina.

Gina put her arms around her husband's neck. So many people were frightened of Eddie because of his reputation, but deep down he was such a big softie and Gina was honoured to finally become the new Mrs Mitchell. 'You worry too much. Stuart's a grown man, Ed. What's the betting he's out with that girl you said he met up town at Gary's birthday bash. Either that or he's out with the boys.'

'I just worry about him, that's all. He did a long stretch for a young 'un and to have to move away from all his family and friends in Hackney must be difficult for him an' all. I'm gonna give him a quick bell, just in case something's wrong.'

Ed walked out of the room and returned five minutes later with a big grin on his face. 'You were right, the crafty little sod is out with that bird he met the other night. Her name's Emma and he's taken her for lunch in Brentwood. That's where she lives, apparently.'

'See, I know these things. That's why I was such a good private detective once upon a time.'

Eddie put his arms around Gina and squeezed her fit body. He'd felt terribly guilty at his wedding when all he could think about was Jessica.

'I hope Stuart strikes lucky like I did when I met you. I had a word with him the other day, and he knows once the baby is born we're gonna need the place to ourselves. With a bit of luck, he might make a go of it with this bird. I mentioned to him about moving in with Gary and Ricky, but I don't think he was that keen. He ain't as wild as them pair of fuckers, is he?'

'Stuart will be just fine, Ed, so for Christ's sake stop worrying about him. Right, I need to go shopping, so what do you fancy for dinner tonight?'

'Something light, babe. I've gotta shoot out the next couple of nights. Sorry, I forgot to tell ya.'

Gina stared at his rugged, handsome face. He had that faraway look in his eye and that always worried her. 'Where you going then?'

'Nowhere. Just got a bit of business that needs sorting.'

Gina clutched his hands. 'Promise me you won't do anything stupid, Ed.'

Ed laughed and kissed her lightly on the nose. 'And you call me a worrier. I ain't gonna do nothing stupid, you have my word on that, babe.'

Frankie felt like a cat on a hot tin roof as she waited for Babs to return to the cell. Her dad had been true to his word and

Larry had come to visit Babs to sort out the awful predicament she found herself in. Every minute seemed like an hour to Frankie, but finally the cell door opened and an upset-looking Babs returned.

'Are you OK? What did he say?' Frankie asked as Babs fell into her arms.

'Larry was really nice, but it was so awful having to relive it all. I thought I was gonna give birth in there at one point. I had a feeling me waters were gonna break.'

Frankie stroked her friend's frizzy afro. Babs' baby was due in a week's time, a month before her own, and she wondered if the anguish of discussing her paedophile ex might bring on an early labour.

'Let's sit you down, you need to rest,' Frankie said, leading her over to her bed. 'Listen to me – the worst is over now, Babs, apart from the actual court case, obviously. You did tell Larry everything like I told you to, didn't you?' Frankie asked.

Babs nodded her head and forced herself to smile. 'Larry reckons he can definitely get me out of here, and that's all thanks to you, sweet child.'

'Well, that's brilliant news,' Frankie exclaimed excitedly. She and Babs had spoken many times about renting a little house on their release and living there with their children like one big happy family. Now their dream could finally become a reality.

Babs held Frankie's hands. 'I want you to thank your dad for me, Frankie. He must be a very lovely man to do all this for someone he's never even set eyes on.'

Frankie grinned. 'I wouldn't go as far as calling him lovely, but he's a proper character, Babs. As you know, me and my dad clash something rotten, but I can honestly say I wouldn't swap him for the world.'

Over in Rainham, Terry Baldwin had just pulled up on his motorbike. He'd found the perfect place to hide himself and the bike and had his escape route well planned. The one big problem he did have was that Jed never seemed to be alone. For the past five nights, Terry had frozen his bollocks off in the cold February air waiting to shoot the little bastard that had destroyed his, his daughter's, and his grandson's lives, but Jed was either always with that cousin of his, or if he wasn't, he was with his bloody father.

Crawling behind the hedges, Terry sat down and prepared himself for another long wait. Jed's motor was currently on the drive, and Terry hoped he'd go out again this evening, which seemed to be his usual routine. Thinking of the predicament he found himself in, Terry sighed. Anne had rung him from Australia today to inform him that she was flying home the next week and he desperately needed to finish the job before she got back. Anne could be a suspicious cow at the best of times and there was no way he could disappear every night when she returned. Terry made a decision there and then. He couldn't arse about much more; he had neither the time nor the patience. Three more days he would give it and if he couldn't get to Jed alone, then he would have to shoot whoever was with him as well.

Less than ten miles away, Eddie, Gary, Ricky, Raymond and Stuart were all sitting in the back of an inconspicuous-looking white Renault van. Eddie had bought the van off an old pal of his father's and, like most things he got his grubby paws on, it was clean but untraceable. Ed had added some easily removable stickers down the side of it that read 'Beryl's Flowers' and showed a false address and phone number underneath. The windows in the back were blacked out, but only from the outside, so the lads could easily see Jamie Carroll if and when he left the snooker hall.

Seeing as they had arrived early, Eddie designated Ricky to keep lookout and then decided to run over their other plans again. He turned to Raymond. 'Right, tell me about Baldwin now. I couldn't speak properly when you rang earlier, Gina was in the room. Where did you say he was going of a night?'

'He's been leaving the house between seven and half past every evening. I've followed him a few times and he headed towards a real quiet road, so I had to stop tailing him. I was worried he might clock me because there was no other bastard about. I went back to the same road to have a nose in daylight and all there is is a load of garages down the bottom of it.

Maybe he's dealing in stolen goods and has a lock-up down there or something.'

Eddie paused for a minute. He needed to think things through before he made a decision. 'Any idea what time he gets back indoors?'

'I've checked three times and he definitely don't get back before midnight,' Raymond replied.

'Well, we can't ambush him at seven in the evening, so we're gonna have to park outside his gaff and wait for him to come back. We'll strike tomorrow, as planned. His old woman might be back any day now and we don't wanna have to top her an' all,' Eddie said thoughtfully.

'What about the O'Haras? Is that still on for Wednesday night?' Gary asked his father.

'Yeah, of course it's still on. I just wanna get all this shit over and done with as quickly as possible. Flatnose Freddie knows the score and he wants to sort the bodies his end ASAP. I've changed me mind about us breaking into the house, though. I've had a long, hard think about it since we had our original meeting, and I've come to the conclusion that it's far too risky. We're better off ambushing Jed and Jimmy alone as they near the house.'

Gary, Ricky and Raymond all breathed an enormous sigh of relief. They'd all thought that breaking into the O'Haras' was an extremely stupid idea. If Georgie or Harry woke up, they'd all be in shit street.

'What about Alice, though? I thought you wanted her out of the picture as well,' Stuart asked, bemused. It was only because Ed had insisted that Alice must also be killed that he had suggested breaking into the O'Haras' gaff in the first place.

'Larry rang me today. Alice has already created havoc up at Georgie's new school and Georgie has now been asked to leave. Apparently that social worker bird popped round the O'Haras' earlier to inform them that Georgie has to attend school to comply with the custody agreement and she told Larry it was mayhem round there. She's written another report and Larry's gonna appeal against them pikey shitbags getting custody. Once Jed and Jimmy are propping up the A13 in one of Freddie's newly built flyovers, Alice ain't got a cat in hell's chance of getting her hands on them kids.'

'So, what's the plan now? How and when exactly are we gonna strike?' Raymond asked.

'Stu's clocked the route Jed and Jimmy use on the way back from Southall. They drive past my old house, so the plan is that two of us wait in a motor a mile or two down the lane.'

'Me and Ricky can do that. We know what their horse-box looks like,' Gary said immediately.

'OK, then as soon as you spot 'em, follow 'em, but keep way back, and ring us when they're a couple of minutes away. We're gonna be parked up in that layby between my old gaff and Jimmy's. Me and Raymondo will hide in the back of the van and Stu can be in the driver's seat. Jimmy and Jed have no idea what Stu looks like, and I'm gonna put some butcher stickers down the side of the van and dress Stu up to look like a fucking mobile butcher. If he pretends the van's broken down, them drunken pricks will have no option but to get out and give him a push. They won't be able to get the horse-box past, so they're gonna have to help out. When they do, we'll bundle 'em in the back of the van and take 'em to meet their maker.'

All five men fell silent as they thought over the plan. Ridding the earth of four men in the space of three days was a big risk and they all knew that. Ten minutes later, Ricky muttered the words that everybody had been waiting for.

'He's just walked out the club.'

Eddie Mitchell pushed Ricky out of the way and stared at the thin, dark-haired geezer who was standing at the entrance with a snooker-cue case in his hand. He was laughing and chatting to two older blokes.

'You sure he'll walk home alone?' Eddie asked anxiously.

'Yep. He stands at the door talking to them geezers every week. They walk the opposite way to him and Carroll gets a takeaway from that Chinese I pointed out to you earlier.'

'Well, let's hope the cunt's hungry tonight, 'cause if he ain't, and walks along with them two, we're fucked,' Eddie said frankly.

'He won't, Dad. He lives in the complete opposite direction,' Gary said assuringly.

Eddie smirked as he saw Jamie Carroll say his goodbyes and walk towards the van. 'Right, wait till he gets to that corner, then you jump in the front, Stu. Just pull up beside him and we'll drag him in the back. If you see anybody or there are any motors coming along, drive past, give it a minute and turn around. The coast must be clear, OK?'

'No probs, boss,' Stuart said confidently.

Eddie felt hatred flow through his veins as Carroll strolled past the van. He left it five seconds, then clapped his hands. 'Come on, let's do this.'

Jamie Carroll was in an unusually good mood as he ambled down the street. Keithy Evans was one of the best players at the snooker club and tonight Jamie had kicked his arse. Looking forward to his usual Monday-night feast of spare ribs and special chow mein, Jamie clocked the van, then took little notice of it as he spotted the words 'Beryl's Flowers' written down the side. Seconds later, he wished he'd been more observant.

'Who the fuck are you? Get off me, you cunts,' he screamed, as he was grabbed from behind by three men.

'Get that case,' Gary ordered, as he realised Carroll had dropped his snooker cue on the pavement.

Raymond grabbed Carroll's hair, kneed him in the nuts, then threw him down against the metal floor of the van.

Lying spread-eagled, Jamie Carroll began to panic like he had never panicked before. 'Where you taking me? Tell me what you want and I'll do whatever,' he pleaded.

Eddie crouched down, lifted Carroll's head up by his hair and smiled at the fright on his face as Jamie registered exactly who he was dealing with.

Jamie Carroll started to shake. 'I don't know nothing, I swear I don't,' he whimpered. He was going to die, he knew that, and the thought of never seeing his four-year-old son again was the worst feeling he'd ever experienced in the whole of his colourful lifetime.

CHAPTER TWENTY-FOUR

Alice was furious that Jed's phone was still switched off. He'd promised her that he'd be here to speak to the social worker himself, but the little shit still hadn't come home from the night before. All of a fluster, Alice rang her husband.

'I'm gonna kill that son of ours when I get me hands on him, Jimmy. He still ain't home and I don't know what to say to this woman. Where are you? Can't you come home and speak to her for me?'

When Jimmy informed her that he was attending to a bit of business up in Colchester, Alice ended the call in a huff. As much as she loved having Georgie and Harry living with her, nobody else lifted a finger to help out.

'Nanny, can me and Harry have Angel Delight?' Georgie asked, tugging Alice's apron. Since she'd stopped being forced to attend that awful school, Georgie's appetite had returned with a vengeance.

'I'll make you some after the lady's been. She'll be here in a minute and I need you and Harry to be on your best behaviour while she's here. Can you do that for Nanny?'

Georgie put her hands on her little hips. 'Not goin' a school. Don't like it,' she said sullenly.

'You musn't say that in front of the lady, Georgie. If you do you ain't having no Angel Delight,' Alice said as the doorbell rang.

Carol Cullen politely refused Alice's offer of tea or coffee. She always felt uncomfortable at the O'Haras' house, was always wary of things kicking off. 'Is Jed not here?' she asked Alice. It was important she spoke to the children's father rather than their grandparents.

'He was on his way back from work and his motor broke down. He's stuck on the bleedin' A13 somewhere,' Alice lied.

Carol explained to Alice how important it was for Georgie to be properly educated. 'The court will take a very dim view of the custodial rules being broken, Mrs O'Hara,' she warned.

Harry didn't really understand the conversation, but Georgie did. She threw herself on the carpet and, screaming blue murder, pummelled her little fists against it. 'I hate school! Not goin',' she sobbed.

Alice shouted at Georgie to behave herself and was relieved when she heard her son's Shogun pull up outside. 'Jed must have got his motor fixed. He'll talk some sense into this little madam,' she said, smiling falsely at Carol Cullen. Seconds later Alice's smile was completely wiped off her face as a blotto Jed and Sammy staggered into the lounge.

'We're fuckin' starvin', Mum. Do us a bit a grub,' Jed said. He and Sammy had pulled a couple of birds and had been drinking, snorting and shagging all night, which was why Jed had completely forgotten about the social worker's visit. Spotting her sitting in the armchair, he smirked at his cousin.

'I ain't goin' a school, Daddy,' Georgie said, tugging at his ankle.

'You ain't gotta do nothing you don't wanna do, sweetheart,' Jed said, picking his daughter up.

Alice glared at her son. 'You and Sammy have obviously been working all night; you look knackered. Go upstairs and clean yourselves up and when Mrs Cullen has gone, I'll do yous some lunch.'

Due to the narcotics and alcohol that were still in his system, Jed was in an obstinate mood. 'Ooh, Mrs Cullen now, is it?' Jed mocked, grinning at the po-faced social worker.

'Just go upstairs, Jed,' Alice ordered.

Jed put Georgie on the sofa, flopped down next to her and lifted Harry onto his lap. 'As you can see, my kids love me very much, darlin', so what's your problem? Why do you keep coming round 'ere and sticking your trunk in where it ain't wanted?' Jed jeered in an arrogant tone.

'Yeah, Jed's a blinding dad, so why don't you go and nuisance someone else?' Sammy said, backing his cousin up as per usual.

'I've no doubt that you love your children and they love you, Mr O'Hara, but if you don't comply with the court's ruling over their schooling, then I'm afraid you could cause yourself problems,' Carol said, wording the sentence as nicely as she could. Jed's eyes were glazed, his pupils were enormous and he was obviously high, drunk, or both. How he had driven home in that state she didn't know, and as he stared at her, she decided there and then that if she had to return to the O'Haras' again, she would bring a colleague with her for safety purposes.

'Now, you listen to me, sweetheart. I never went to school, neither did my mother, father, my brothers or Sammy boy over there. It ain't affected our ability to get on in the world and it won't affect my chavvies either. These schools teach a load of old bollocks that kids never get to use in life anyway. I can teach 'em how to be streetwise and how to earn a crust. Before my brother Marky got murdered, he'd just bought five acres of land over in Kent, and look at this gaff my dad owns. Our family are no dinlos and if Georgie girl don't wanna go a school, then she'll be taught all she needs to know by me and her grandparents.'

'But the courts won't –'

Jed stopped Carol Cullen mid-sentence. 'Fuck you and the courts! What yous people don't seem to understand is a traveller's way of life is totally different to the shallow little existences that yous gorjers lead. I bet I can guess what you've got, a three- or four-bedroomed house, a husband you're bored with, a couple of kids, a dog and a fucking cat. And I bet the highlight of your whole year is the one or two foreign holidays that you go on. Am I right or am I wrong?'

Carol Cullen was shaken by Jed's perception of her life. Apart from the fact that she didn't have a dog, he was virtually right about everything else. 'You're very wrong, actually,' Carol lied. She hated this flash little shit with a passion and would never admit that his portrayal of her existence was almost spot on.

'Jed, you've said enough now. Go upstairs or you'll have me to deal with,' Alice shouted.

'No, why should I? I'm sick of this shit and I'm only telling the truth. What Mrs Cuntsmouth here don't realise is

by the time Georgie girl is eighteen, she will be married to
a nice travelling lad that has my stamp of approval. All Georgie
needs to learn is how to cook, clean, produce chavvies and
be a good wife and mother, so why should she be forced to
sit in some poxy classroom until she's sixteen years of age?
I ain't gonna let her settle down with a mush that don't come
from a wealthy family and ain't clued up, so she ain't gonna
want for fuck-all, is she?'

'I love babies, Daddy. When can I have one?' Georgie asked
excitedly.

'When you're sixteen,' Jed said, stroking his daughter's long
dark hair.

Carol Cullen took in the situation before her. In some ways
the travelling culture reminded her of the Indian way of life.
The fathers married their daughters off young to chaps chosen
by them and who came from families they approved of.

'I'd best make a move now. Thank you for your time,' Carol
said, standing up. Trying to get through to Jed was like talking
to a brick wall and she was just wasting her breath.

Alice followed Carol into the hallway and slammed the
living-room door shut. 'I'm really sorry about Jed. He's obviously had a few beers and you know what rubbish men spout
when they've been out boozing. He'll think differently tomorrow
and Georgie will go back to school, I promise you that.'

When Carol nodded curtly, Alice shut the front door and
stormed back into the lounge. She then slapped her drunken
son as hard as she could around his silly, smirking face. 'If
them chavvies are taken away from us, I will personally fucking
kill you. Now get out my sight, you dinlo.'

Over in Holloway, Frankie was not in the best of moods. DI
Blyth had just informed her that unless they had sufficient
DNA evidence to link Jed and Sammy to Harry Mitchell's
murder, then they would not be able to arrest them just yet.

'Well, when can you arrest 'em? Don't the police believe
me?' Frankie asked in a dismayed tone.

'As soon as we have some kind of evidence, Frankie, they
will arrest them and bring them in for questioning. Until then,
the last thing we want to do is alert Jed and Sammy that we

are on to them. Everybody believes your story; that's not the problem, I promise you that. The problem is that without proof we haven't got a leg to stand on. There is no point in us taking this case to court when it's just your and Kerry's word against Jed and Sammy's. We need more than that to secure a conviction.'

'So when will the DNA results be back? Surely if they beat my grandad like they boasted about on the tape, then something must show up?'

'I've spoken to the superintendent and the results could be back as early as tomorrow. If they aren't, we should definitely have them by the end of the week. As I said earlier, Frankie, it is imperative that Jed and Sammy do not get wind of this, so please make sure that anything I tell you is kept solely to yourself. You haven't told anybody else about this, have you?'

Frankie shook her head. Apart from Kerry, Babs was the only one who knew what was going on, but there was no point telling Blyth that. Babs was as dependable as they come, and Frankie didn't want the DI to think she was a blabbermouth who couldn't be trusted. 'I would never tell anyone because I'd be too frightened of my dad finding out. What about Larry? Does he know you've come here today?' Frankie asked worriedly.

'I haven't informed Larry about this visit, but if anything is mentioned, just stick to the original story that we are trying to get enough evidence to arrest Jed for conning old people, OK? I must go now. I have an important meeting at two o'clock and if I don't dash, I'll be late for it. As soon as we have the DNA back, I will let you know, but whatever the result, good or bad, I promise I won't let this rest, Frankie. I know you're telling me the truth and I want Jed and Sammy behind bars just as much as you do.'

Frankie said goodbye to Blyth and walked dejectedly back towards her cell. On the way she bumped into Katie, the travelling girl who knew Jed and who, in Frankie's opinion, was her ex's little spy.

'I'm way over me due date. If me contractions ain't started by Friday, they're gonna induce me,' Katie said brightly.

Frankie stared at Katie. Her accent made Frankie feel sick because she sounded so much like Jed and his family. In fact, everything about Katie and travellers in general made Frankie feel nauseous. Untrustworthy bastards, the lot of 'em, she thought.

Seeing the look of hatred on Frankie's face, Katie took a step backwards. 'Are you OK, Frankie? Have I done something to upset you?' she asked, with a hurt expression.

Frankie laughed nastily. 'Look Katie, I don't like you, I don't trust you, and I only spoke to you in the first place because I needed to get a message to Jed, so do yourself a favour – stop trying to be my friend and fucking leave me alone.'

As Frankie stomped off, Katie stood gawping with shock.

Stanley Smith felt absolutely knackered as he flopped onto the armchair. When Joycie had said she wanted him to help out indoors more, he had thought she'd meant a bit of vaccing and polishing. Unfortunately for him, she hadn't, and he'd spent the last couple of days painting one of the bedrooms, tiling one of the bathrooms, and putting up new curtain rails all over the poxy house.

Ten minutes later, Joyce was horrified when she walked into the lounge and saw her sleeping husband snoring his head off. She crept over to the armchair, bent down and clapped her hands as hard as she could next to his left ear.

'What the fuck!' Stanley yelled, as he jumped up like a kangaroo.

'What are you doing lazing about down 'ere? You took that bedroom carpet up yet? I want the new one put down by tomorrow.'

'I can't move the bed and furniture on me own, Joycie. I'll break me bleedin' back.'

'Well, best you ring Jock, then, and ask him to come round and help you.'

Stanley sighed. He'd obeyed Joyce's rules and gone round to see Jock at the weekend to apologise for their fall-out. Under the circumstances, Jock had been extremely gracious, but Stanley didn't want to take the piss by asking him to do bloody odd jobs. They hadn't even been out for a pint together yet.

'I don't wanna ask Jock. Can't you ring Joey and Dom? I'm sure they'll come round and give me a hand.'

'We're not asking them!' Joyce exclaimed.

'Why not? They're a damn sight younger and fitter than me and Jock are.'

'Because they're gay! In that programme I watched recently, it said that homosexual men liked dancing and shopping; these gays ain't into physical heavy lifting, Stanley,' Joyce said seriously.

Stanley knew there was no point in arguing with her. 'OK, I'll ring Jock, then,' he said.

Joyce smirked. Not only did she love getting her own way, she also loved having Stanley back home with her. She would never tell him that, though. She would keep the old bastard in the doghouse for the rest of his life and, after what he'd done, that's where he deserved to be.

'Come on then, chop chop, ring Jock,' Joyce demanded.

'Fucking old witch,' Stanley mumbled, as soon as his wife was out of earshot.

Joycie went into the kitchen and put the kettle on. She'd worked him so hard that Stanley had been as stiff as a board as he'd stood up and limped towards the phone. 'Serves you right, you philandering old goat,' she chuckled.

Terry Baldwin was not having the best of spying missions. Jed's Shogun had not been on the drive when he'd arrived earlier and there'd been no sign of the pikey little shit since. To make matters worse, Terry had an upset stomach and had twice had to crap in a nearby bush. Feeling pains shooting through his stomach again, Terry crawled out of his hidey hole. This evening had doom written all over it, so the best thing he could do was go home get an early night, then come back tomorrow nice and refreshed.

Still on a high from torturing the name of his brothers' killer out of Jamie Carroll then blowing his brains out, Eddie Mitchell was in a rather buoyant mood as he climbed into the back of the white Renault van. The removable number plates had been changed and the stickers had now been replaced: instead of reading 'Beryl's Flowers', the side of the van was now advertising 'Suzie's Blinds and Curtains'.

'Everthing pan out all right? Have you spoken to Flatnose Freddie today?' Gary asked his father.

Eddie nodded and told Raymond to start driving. 'I met Freddie at lunchtime, the body's already gone and the warehouse has been spring-cleaned.'

'How much extra is he charging us for the use of that warehouse, Dad?' Ricky asked. Usually Flatnose Freddie just disposed of the bodies, but this time round he'd sorted out a disused warehouse in Aveley for the killings to take place in.

'Five grand per head, on top of the ten to get rid of the carcasses; it works out sixty, all told.'

When Eddie had killed geezers in the past, he'd do it anywhere that took his fancy, but to top four men in three nights was adventurous, even by his standards and he'd decided to leave the dirty work to Freddie. Old Flatnose was the best clean-up merchant in the business.

To take everybody's mind off what was about to take place, Ed decided to rib Stuart over his love life. 'So when you seeing this Emma bird again, Stu? You've had that look of love in your eyes since you took her out for lunch. Gina spotted it; she's going out shopping for a hat tomorrow.'

'Fuck off. Best you tell Gina to keep the receipt, 'cause no way am I ever getting married,' Stuart said laughing.

'Credit where it's due, Emma's a right sort,' Gary added. He'd been with Stuart the night he'd met her.

'You shagged it yet?' Ricky asked bluntly.

Stuart smirked. 'A decent bloke never kisses and tells, lads.'

The banter continued for another few minutes, until Raymond said something that killed the humorous conversation stone dead. 'That's Baldwin's Land Cruiser, boys. He's a couple of motors in front of us.'

'It's only eleven o'clock. I thought you said he didn't get home till after midnight? You sure it's his?' Eddie asked.

'Of course I'm fucking sure. I've been stalking the cunt for days,' Raymond replied sarcastically.

'Raymondo, overtake him so we get to his house before he does,' Ricky ordered.

239

Eddie disagreed. 'We're in a poxy old Renault van, not a fucking Porsche! Just keep him in sight, Ray, follow him home, then we'll leap out and 'ave him as he pulls up.'

Terry Baldwin's stomach was still giving him terrible gyp. He'd dropped the motorbike off back at the garage, but had had to stop twice on the journey to squat behind a tree. Feeling the griping pains shoot through his stomach once more, Terry knew he was going to have to stop again before he got home. It was either that or shit himself. Seconds later, he spotted some trees: he pulled over and clenched the cheeks of his arse together as he waddled towards them. He spotted the white van slow down, but after glancing at the writing on the side, thought nothing of it.

Feeling nothing but relief as his bowels opened for the fifth time that evening, Terry pulled his trousers up. Seconds later he was approached by two angry-looking men in black hooded jackets.

'Move now,' one hissed at him.

'Bollocks. Don't fucking start with me, I ain't no mug, you know,' Terry replied angrily. He didn't recognise the blokes, so just assumed they were going to mug him or nick his motor. Wishing he now hadn't hidden the gun at the garage, Terry froze as he clocked Eddie Mitchell appear from the shadows. 'Shit,' he mumbled.

'Me and you need to have a little chat, Baldwin. Now, you have two options, number one is follow me and get in the van nicely, or number two, I'll blow your brains out here and you die in your own shit.'

Terry Baldwin immediately chose option number one.

Over in Rainham, Joycie Smith's conscience had begun to prick her. Jock hadn't been able to help Stanley move the bedroom furniture today and had offered to do so on Thursday but, determined to make her husband pay for his recent sins, Joyce had insisted that she couldn't wait that long and Stanley must move the furniture and take the old carpet up alone, which somehow he'd managed.

Seeing Stanley's legs buckle for the second time, Joycie stood over him. 'You'd better not be putting all this on to get out of laying the new carpet tomorrow,' she said suspiciously.

'I'm not, Joycie, I swear. It's me knees, they're seized up. I don't think I can get up the stairs, I reckon I'm gonna have to sleep down 'ere tonight.'

Feeling more than a tad guilty now, Joycie went out of the room and returned five minutes later with a piece of fruit cake, a mug of Horlicks, a bottle of horse liniment and two paracetamol tablets. 'Take your trousers off and I'll sort you out while you eat your cake and drink your Horlicks.'

'What! Why have I got to take me trousers off?' Stanley asked in horror. The awful experience Pat the Pigeon had put him through had left him scarred for life.

'Because I'm gonna rub this on your knees, you silly old git,' Joyce said waving the glass bottle that contained the white liquid at him.

'Oh, right,' Stanley said, relieved.

'What did you think I was gonna bloody do? I ain't been near your little maggot for years and I certainly wouldn't wanna touch it now, in case it's been up that old slapper you were living with.'

'Don't be so bloody stupid, Pat was just a friend,' Stanley said red-faced, as he undid the button and zip of his trousers and let Joyce tug them off.

Joyce rubbed the horse liniment into Stanley's knees, made him take the paracetamol, then went upstairs to get him his pyjamas, a quilt and a pillow. 'I think you should leave that new carpet, Stanley. I'll speak to Eddie, let him sort it, he's bound to know someone who lays carpets. If not, he'll send one of the boys round to do it.'

'Thanks for looking after me, love,' Stanley said, as Joyce helped him put on his pyjama bottoms and tucked him in.

'Goodnight, then. As soon as them legs are better, we'll go and buy ourselves that new car, Stanley. I'm choosing it, though; my taste is classier than yours.'

Stanley grinned as his wife turned off the light and left the room. He might be in terrible pain, but as long as his Joycie was warming to him, nothing else mattered.

*　　*　　*

241

Another person currently suffering from a rare twinge of guilt was Eddie Mitchell. Unlike the spineless Jamie Carroll, whom Ed hated and had had great pleasure in killing, Baldwin seemed a decent geezer and was actually talking a lot of sense. Usually, when Ed confronted his victims, they turned into shivering wrecks begging and pleading for forgiveness, but not Baldwin, he had stood his ground and Ed had to admit the geezer had bottle. He even had the front to look Ed straight in the eye without as much as a flinch as he said his piece.

'You can do what you like to me, Eddie. After what I've been through, nothing or no one can hurt me any more. I've lost my grandson, my daughter – my life's all but over, anyway. One thing I will say, though, is you would have done the same thing as I did. I had no choice as a proud man other than to get your brothers killed. They blew my grandson's brains out and what would you have done if that had happened to one of your grandkids, eh?'

'I'd have probably done exactly the same,' Ed replied honestly, admiring the man more and more as each minute ticked past.

'As for my Sally, my only regret about you getting to me is that I ain't got revenge for her yet. That's what I've been doing for the past week, stalking that cunt Jed. I was gonna shoot him, blow the pikey bastard's brains out, and if I'm gonna die tonight, I hope you can at least do that for both of us. I mean, he fucked your daughter's life up an' all, didn't he? Do what you want to me, Eddie, but man to man, swear to me you'll get revenge for both of our daughters by killing Jed. Can you promise me that? I'll never rest in peace if you don't.'

Stuart was at the wheel, driving towards the warehouse. Gary, Ricky and Raymond were sitting in the back and were virtually struck dumb, not only by Baldwin's honesty, but also the balls the man had.

'So if you were gonna kill Jed, where's your gun?' Gary asked, breaking the silence.

'In a garage over in Dagenham. I bought a motorbike, and rented a lock-up where I've been stashing both. My wife Anne's due home from Australia next week, she's been over there 'cause her mother died recently. I was gonna kill Jed in the next couple of days before my Anne came home. If she'd have clocked what I was up to, she would have killed me more violently than yous lot probably will.'

Eddie looked into Terry Baldwin's eyes. He was sure the man was genuine and, even though he was responsible for Paulie and Ronny's deaths, Ed couldn't hate him. Paulie and Ronny had dug their own graves because of their own stupidity, in a strange sort of way. 'Pull over,' Ed ordered Stuart.

'What you doin', Dad?' Ricky asked, perplexed.

Eddie ignored his son's question. 'You got the keys on you to this garage of yours?' he asked Terry.

Terry nodded and gave Eddie the address.

'Best I drive; I know where it is,' Raymond said, winking at Ed. It was the same road in Dagenham to which he'd followed Baldwin recently.

Raymond swapped places with Stuart and five minutes later pulled up outside the garages. Eddie got out of the van, ordered Baldwin to follow him and told the others to stay where they were.

'I'm coming with ya; you ain't goin' in alone if that cunt's got a gun in there,' Gary said, wondering if his father had lost his senses.

'You do as I say,' Ed replied, glaring at his eldest son.

As Terry Baldwin opened up the garage door, Eddie immediately spotted the motorbike. 'So, where's the gun? And don't you move, just tell me where it is,' Ed said. He was already gloved up.

Terry Baldwin pointed to a stack of boxes in the left-hand corner of the garage. 'If you move them boxes, there's a loose slab of concrete underneath. The gun's under there, wrapped in a shammy leather.'

Eddie had no doubt that Baldwin was telling the truth, but checked anyway, and then turned to him again. 'I'll do a deal with ya. You kill Jed successfully, then in return you get to keep your own life and you also owe me a favour or two.'

'What?' Baldwin asked. He felt as though his hearing was deceiving him.

'You heard.'

'But what about me ordering the hit on your brothers? I

243

know you ain't the type to sweep something like that under the carpet, so how do I know I can trust you not to kill me once I've killed Jed? It ain't me I'm worried about, but my Anne's been through enough already, if you know what I mean.'

Eddie stared Baldwin in the eyes, took his gloves off and held out his right hand. 'My word is my bond. I'm Eddie Mitchell, for fuck's sake. Anyway, what choice have you got other than to believe me?'

'None,' Terry Baldwin replied as he gripped Ed's right hand.

Eddie let go of his hand and smirked. 'Right, let's get back to the van and we'll drop you back at your motor. It's getting late now, so let's meet again in the morning to discuss the finer points. Oh, and by the way, Baldwin, if you cross me or balls things up in any way, shape or form, I will personally make sure that you die in the worst fucking way possible to mankind.'

CHAPTER TWENTY-FIVE

Refusing to discuss his apparent change of heart until the following day, Ed arranged an early-morning meet at Auntie Joanie's gaff. Gary, Ricky and Raymond arrived before Ed and were still all dumbfounded by the events of the previous evening.

'I reckon the old man's going soft in his old age. I mean, how can he not kill that cunt after he had Ronny and Paulie's throats cut?' Gary said angrily.

Ricky agreed with his brother. 'I've noticed a change in him ever since he's been with that Gina. Look at what a prick he made of himself at his wedding, getting down on one knee, declaring his undying love in front of every bastard and then trotting off like some bell-end on that stupid horse and carriage,' he added.

'Don't ever underestimate your father. He's no mug, and if he's changed his mind about killing Baldwin, then you can guarantee that he'll benefit from it in some way, shape or form. Ed ain't gone soft; he might have perhaps mellowed a bit, but that's probably 'cause he's got another nipper on the way. I've mellowed since Polly got pregnant and one day, when yous boys have pregnant wives or girlfriends, you'll understand what I mean,' Raymond explained.

'I ain't fucking getting married or tied down with kids. Too much grief, mate,' Gary said immediately.

'Me neither. I'm staying footloose and fancy free an' all,' Ricky added.

Seconds later, the door opened and Eddie walked in, followed by Stuart, who had travelled with him.

'Why is it you always arrange these early meets and you're the one that's always late?' Gary asked his father in a sarcastic tone.

'Because it's my fucking prerogative to be late. I run this firm, remember?' Ed replied, as he took his seat at the head of the table.

Ricky got straight down to business. 'So what's going on, Dad? Why did we capture Baldwin and then let him go again?'

'Cooey!' a voice shouted out.

Eddie jumped up and answered the door to Auntie Joanie. 'Cor, they look 'andsome. You cooked them bleedin' quick, didn't ya?' he said, taking the tray off her.

'I'd put the bacon on and buttered the baps before you bloody got 'ere. I know what yous boys are like, always starving. I've made you a brew an' all and some homemade shortbread. Shall I bring 'em up now?'

'Stuart will get 'em. You rest your legs, Auntie, and thanks, sweetheart, you're a diamond.'

'Let's eat, and talk after,' Eddie said. Nobody made a bacon bap like Auntie Joanie. She used thick butter and put four slices of quality bacon in each one.

Gary was the first to push his plate away. 'Look, I didn't drag meself out of bed at seven this morning just to indulge in a monkey's tea party, so do you think we can get this meeting started?'

Ed glared at Gary, then wiped his mouth with a serviette. 'Right, there are three reasons why I decided not to kill Baldwin last night. Number one, I admired the geezer's balls and honesty. Number two, what he did to Ronny and Paulie was an act of revenge for his grandson and any proud man would have done the same thing – I definitely would. And number three, he's gonna kill Jed, which'll save us doin' it.'

'You've gotta be kidding us! What about our plans for tonight? You can't trust some nomark you barely fucking know to do a job like that properly,' Gary shouted.

Ricky stared at his father in total disbelief. 'Gal's right, you've lost the fucking plot, Dad. How do you know that Baldwin can be trusted? He might be a grass and get us all banged up, for all you know.'

246

'I personally don't think it's a bad idea, as long as he's gonna do Jed alone. At least we can make sure we're seen somewhere, then we've all got an alibi,' Raymond responded sensibly.

The only person who didn't chip in with a comment was Stuart. Being the newest member of the firm, he tended not to get too involved in any disagreements and instead just went with the flow.

Eddie walked over to the drinks cabinet, poured himself a Scotch, then walked back to the table and slammed the bottle down in front of his two sons. 'I haven't even told you the plan yet and if you stopped putting your two penn'orth in and listened for five minutes, you'd realise it makes fucking sense.'

Furious that the night's ambush of Jed and Jimmy was now off the radar, Gary grabbed the bottle of Scotch and poured himself a large one. Gulping it back, he grimaced at the taste, slammed the glass on the table and stared at his father defiantly. 'Come on, then. What's the plan? I'm all ears.'

'I had a meet with Baldwin while you were still lying in your pit this morning. He's gonna shoot Jed tonight and I've told him, if he fucks up, he's a dead man walking.'

'What about Jimmy, though? Why don't you get him to kill him an' all?' Ricky demanded.

Eddie fingered the scar down the left-hand side of his face that Jimmy gave him in 1970. 'That cunt, I'm absolutely determined to do meself and I will, but first I really want to see him suffer. That little fucker Jed has always been the apple of Jimmy's eye, so can you imagine how he's gonna feel when his favourite son gets his brains blown out in front of him? To do it this way is the biggest torture we can put old wonky-nose through, trust me on that one.'

'But why the change of plan?' Gary asked suspiciously.

'The more I thought about us killing Jed, the more I had a bad vibe about it. I mean, people don't just disappear off the face of the earth, do they? I just had a feeling that if we'd have done what we planned to, the filth might have started sniffing around us and we can do without that. Jamie Carroll don't matter, as we have no history with him. Seriously, I think Baldwin falling into our laps like he did is a fucking act of God.'

'What about Flatnose Freddie? Is he still gonna dispose of Jed?' Ricky asked.

Eddie smirked. 'No need, is there? Baldwin can just shoot him and leave him on the driveway. We ain't involved, are we? We're all going to a nice restaurant tonight, so we'll have our alibi.'

'What if Baldwin bottles it, though?' Gary questioned. He had to admit his dad's plan sounded half sensible, but he still had reservations about trusting a man they barely knew.

'Look how composed Baldwin was last night and he thought we were gonna kill him. You gotta give credit where it's due – the geezer's got nerves of steel. Plus, he has more motive than anyone to want Jed six feet under; he's lost his daughter and grandson and he blames it all on that pikey lump of shit.'

'Have you told Baldwin that Jed and Jimmy are in Southall today? He knows they'll be in the horse-box, don't he?' Stuart asked.

'Of course I've told him and I told him they're bound to be pissed. He's gonna get there just after seven on that motorbike of his. He said he wants to be in place well before they get back. You gotta remember, this geezer ain't no mug, he's been holed up at the O'Haras, waiting for an opportunity to kill Jed for the past four or five days. Tonight he'll have that opportunity, won't he?'

'Don't forget Georgie and Harry will be at home. Let's hope they're in bed, eh?' Raymond said, reminding Eddie of the possibility of his grandkids witnessing their father's death.

Eddie shrugged. 'Obviously I'd rather the little 'uns not witness it, but if they do, then it can't be helped. Even though they act older than their years, they're only nippers and they'll soon forget about that wanker of a father of theirs as soon as our Frankie gets out of the nick.'

Gary and Ricky smirked at one another. So their father hadn't gone soft after all, they both thought silently.

'So, what restaurant we goin' to?' Gary asked chirpily.

'I think it's gonna look a bit phoney if we all sit together in a restaurant like the fuckin' Waltons. I mean, we ain't even got a birthday to celebrate unless we say it's a belated bash for you, Gal. What I suggest is me, Gina, Raymondo and Polly eat in the Bell in Rettendon, and you, Ricky and Stu have a bite in Nico's gaff in Canning Town. If you get bored, you can go and have a beer in the Flag afterwards. All three places are perfect for an alibi. The Bell is always fairly busy and full of nosy old cunts, plus the landlord knows me and Gina. As for Nico's and the Flag, everyone knows you and Ricky there, even if they don't know Stu, so just make sure you introduce him to anyone you speak to.'

'I must admit, I didn't think I'd like the new plan, but I do. Having said that, there's one more question I need to ask you, Dad, and please don't think I'm trying to be funny, 'cause I ain't,' Gary said.

'Go on, ask away.'

'Paulie and Ronny. Surely you ain't gonna let Baldwin get away with what he did to 'em?'

Eddie hated having to answer this question. Images of his father's face entered his brain and he quickly banished them away. 'Listen, Paulie and Ronny chose their own paths in life and, unfortunately for them, they chose the wrong ones. That ain't my problem and it shouldn't be yours, either. Yes, they were my brothers, and yes, in my own way I loved 'em, but I know and you know they were mugs and their downfall was all their own doing. I shook hands with Baldwin last night and, providing he don't fuck up, I'll let him live. Ronny and Paulie dug their own graves, and that ain't our fucking fault, or Baldwin's.'

Seeing his father's eyes cloud over, Gary said no more. He knew when it was safe to push his father that extra inch, but he was also aware of when it wasn't. 'So, are we done, then?' he asked chirpily.

'Yep. Now, as per usual, no phone calls tonight. I've already arranged a time and a place to speak to Baldwin in the morning, so what I suggest is we meet here again tomorrow about two-ish. I'll have all the info by then.'

'Do you fancy a quick pint in Stratford, Dad? Me and Gal are gonna pop down the Railway for a couple, we've gotta see a couple of geezers in there,' Ricky said.

Eddie stood up and nodded at Stuart to do the same. 'Nah, Stu's taking his little bird out for lunch and I'm gonna go and settle up with Flatnose Freddie for the other night. Stu will meet you in Nico's at seven, OK? And Ray, you and Polly meet me and Gina in the Bell at the same time. You know where it is, don't ya?'

Raymond nodded. 'I dunno if Polly will wanna go out at short notice, though. She's been a bit of a home-bird since she's been pregnant.'

Eddie sighed. He'd never been the biggest fan of Raymond's old woman. 'Fuck her, then. Just come on your own if you have to, but make sure you're there by seven. Right, laters all, and keep smiling, 'cause this time tomorrow that little fucker Jed will be brown bread. Rhymes that, don't it?'

Laughing at his own wit, Eddie sauntered out of the room.

Unaware that if things went to plan, today would be the last day of his life, Jed was over in Southall horse market debating whether to buy a rather frisky-looking black stallion. Paddy Brady was Irish, and a rather notorious ex-prize-fighting champion. He had a reputation for being flash, and apart from knocking fifty pounds off as luck money, would not be bated down any more.

'Gissa minute. Me and my cousin are business partners and I just wanna have a quick word with him,' Jed said, walking over to where Sammy was chatting to three geezers.

'What's up?' Sammy asked, as Jed rudely dragged him away.

'We've gotta have the gry, but that Paddy Brady's a proper cunt to deal with. It's a shame me old mush ain't 'ere, 'cause I know Brady's only mugging me off 'cause he thinks I'm wet behind the ears. Talking to me like I talk to me chavvies, he was, the cheeky Irish bastard.'

Usually Jed's dad always accompanied him on their regular trips to Southall, but hadn't been able to make it today because one of his brothers was at death's door.

'Whaddya think?' Jed asked, as Sammy studied the stallion.

'He's a bit lively, but they're always the best ones. I'm sure we can sort him with a lot of hard work and a few cracks of the whip.'

Feeling brazen, Sammy decided to try his luck with Paddy

himself. 'Knock another fifty off and we'll take him,' he said, confidently holding out his right hand.

Paddy Brady laughed, grabbed Sammy's hand and in a flash, twisted it behind his back. 'I've already told your so-called business partner, pay the wonga, or fuck off.'

Jed was fuming. Irish and English travellers clashed at the best of times, but this bastard was taking the real piss out of him and Sammy.

Paddy released Sammy from his grip. 'We got a deal then, boy?' he asked Jed.

Jed grinned. He'd never been one to sense fear, and wasn't about to start now. He also hated being called 'boy'. 'No, we ain't got a deal. As for you, you inbred, lowlife tinker, go fuck your grandmother.'

As Paddy Brady lunged at him, Jed ducked, grabbed Sammy's arm and, laughing, the pair ran from the market as fast as their legs would take them.

Terry Baldwin was in pole position by seven-thirty. Eddie had told him which way the horse-box would be coming from and he'd also informed him that Jed and Jimmy were usually so inebriated it seemed to take them for ever to unload any of the horses they'd bought, which gave Terry the perfect opportunity to strike.

Aware that Jimmy O'Hara was no mug, Terry decided to hole up in the middle of some bushes on the right-hand side of O'Hara's driveway, which enabled him to see the horse-box approaching. His previous hideout had been on the left. Knowing that he probably had a good couple of hours' wait, Terry chopped some leaves off the bush with a Stanley knife he'd brought with him, to give himself more room to manoeuvre and a better view. He'd decided to shoot Jed as he pulled onto the drive, rather than when he got out of the horse-box. That way, Jimmy had less chance of guessing where the bullets had come from and he could be on his bike and away in sixty seconds flat.

Having made enough room to now sit down, Terry gave his legs a rest and thought about his strange encounter with Eddie Mitchell the previous evening. Like the majority of London's

East End, Terry Baldwin had always known who Eddie Mitchell was. Over the years, Terry had attended a couple of functions where Eddie had also been present, but he had never been properly introduced to him before. Having now met Eddie in person, Terry understood the aura that surrounded the man. From his looks to his mannerisms, Mitchell had that something special, but the thing that had surprised Terry the most was Ed's fairness and integrity. Terry had honestly thought he was a dead man last night, but Eddie had listened to what he had to say and had now given him a chance to save his own bacon.

Staring at the gun that lay beside him on the ground, Terry smirked. He was no mug himself and he couldn't wait to show Eddie Mitchell his capabilities and prove to him that he had made the right decision by letting him live.

In a boozer over in Southall, Jed O'Hara was extremely drunk and was giving it the large. 'My old mush will kill that shitcunt Brady when I tell him what's happened today. Who do these two-bob Irish tinkers think they are, eh? They ain't fit to clean the boots of us O'Haras.'

Aware that there was a crowd of Irish travellers standing no more than two feet away, Sammy grabbed his cousin's arm. 'Come on, Jed. We're both pissed and we've gotta get this horse-box home. We don't wanna smash the fuckin' thing up, do we? Your old man will kill us.'

Aware of the Irish travellers glaring at him, Jed pushed Sammy away and marched over to them.

'When you see your old mucker Paddy Brady next, you tell him from me that Jed O'Hara ain't finished with him yet. Ex-prize-fighter, my arse, the cunt looks more like a bus driver to me.'

'I'm a good pal of Paddy's. Now fuck off, you little shit, before you get badly hurt,' one of the older Irishmen in the crowd warned Jed.

Jed, being Jed, decided to try and punch the fella. He missed and was quickly escorted away and marched out of the pub by some English travellers who were pals of Jimmy's.

'I think I'd better drive,' Sammy said as Jed got shoved in the driver's seat.

'Shut up, I'm fine,' Jed insisted, turning the ignition.

As Jed pulled out in front of a car without checking his wing mirror and very nearly wrote the motor off, Sammy sighed. It was a long old trip around that A406 and in the state Jed was in, he just hoped that they made it home in once piece.

Alice O'Hara smiled at Georgie's excited face as she took the iced fairy cakes out of the oven. Georgie would be five in a couple of weeks' time and today Alice had decided that if Georgie was one day going to secure a sought-after husband, then it was high time her granddaughter learned how to bloody well cook.

'Hurry, the cakes are ready, boy!' Alice shouted. Her grandson had had the hump earlier on and had stomped out of the kitchen because Alice wouldn't let him help ice the cakes. 'Cooking's for girls, Harry. Your dad will kill me if he finds out I've been teaching you to bake cakes, boy,' she'd told him.

Leaving her grandchildren in the kitchen stuffing their faces, Alice went into the lounge to make some phone calls. Jimmy's eldest brother was seriously ill in hospital, Jed and Sammy had gone to Southall and, seeing as none of them had bothered to call her all day, she didn't know whether they wanted any dinner when they got in or not. She rang Jimmy first. His phone was still switched off, so she then rang Jed.

'What can I do for you, Mummy dearest?' her son slurred.

'How many drinks you had? Who's driving your father's new horse-box?' Alice asked, annoyed.

'I am! Sammy's a dinlo when it comes to driving a beast the size of this,' Jed said, chuckling.

'I'd do a better job than him. Nearly wrote off a motor and hit the kerb twice already,' Alice heard Sammy shout out in the background.

'Just be careful, Jed. Now do you and Sammy want me to cook you any dinner tonight?'

'Yeah, we're fucking starving. We'll probably be about half-hour or so.'

As Alice replaced the receiver, she was hit like a thunderbolt by one of her feelings of doom. Alice believed herself to be a true psychic. She'd been born with the gift, and years ago she'd have travellers visit her from all over the country for advice and readings.

'Oh my gawd,' Alice said as she put her hands on her forehead. This was a similar feeling of foreboding to the one she'd had on the day that her Lukey boy had been murdered. She immediately picked up the phone and rang Jed back again. 'Boy, I've got one of me premonitions. Park that horse-box up somewhere and get yourselves a cab home. I ain't mucking about; I think you're gonna have a bad accident.'

Jed burst out laughing. 'We're gonna die, Sammy boy, we're gonna die,' he joked in a silly tone.

'Please Jed, I know you're drunk, but please listen to me. Park that horse-box up. Your dad can pick it up tomorrow, OK?'

Aware that his mum had now started crying, Jed decided to humour her to stop her worrying. 'OK, I'll park it up and we'll get a cab back, all right?'

When Jed ended the call, Sammy turned to him. 'Your mother ain't no fool when she has one of her funny turns, you know. Perhaps we should get a cab back. I mean, we ain't got an 'orse in the back or nothing.'

Jed burst out laughing. 'Are we fuck! I only said that to shut her up. You see, you Sammy boy, you're a first-class dinlo.'

Terry Baldwin was feeling masses of adrenlin but no nerves whatsoever as he waited for the horse-box to appear. He'd loved his daughter Sally, idolised his grandson Luke, and he could almost taste revenge on the end of his tongue. The O'Haras' gaff was in a country lane with no street lighting, which meant every motor that came along this time of night usually had its full beam on. Seeing another beam of light heading his way, Terry picked the gun up. As the motor drove past, he put it back down again. Taking his lighter out of his pocket, Terry flicked it so he could check his watch. It was just gone ten, so surely the little bastard wouldn't be that much longer.

God must have been looking down on Terry, as seconds later he saw another beam heading his way but, more importantly, this time he could hear the sound of a large diesel engine.

Feeling his heart pounding, Terry picked up the gun and

stood up. He was clad in black leathers and had a black crash helmet on to match. He was so ready for this and he instantly decided to take a gamble and shoot Jed up close instead of from a distance. If he fucked up, Eddie Mitchell would kill him anway, so what did he have to lose?

Jed and Sammy were both taking the piss out of Alice as the horse-box approached the entrance of the driveway.

'I'm gonna tell Mystic Meg to hang up her fucking crystal ball when I get in,' Jed joked.

'Well, I always believed in your old lady and her bad vibes, but she was definitely wrong this time. 'Ere, considering she thought we were both gonna die in a bad road accident, I hope she's bothered to cook us some grub. Fucking starving, I am,' Sammy replied.

Jed laughed. 'The devil looks after his own, Sammy boy, and with all the conning and thieving me and you have done in our lifetime, we're definitely immortal.'

Terry Baldwin felt like a starving tiger ready to pounce on its prey as he waited for the precise moment to make his move. The security lights had just come on as the horse-box had pulled onto the drive and Terry had known immediately that it was Jed and not Jimmy driving. Jimmy was thickset and the person driving was thin-faced with a baseball cap on his head. As the horse-box drove past him, Terry stepped out of the shadows. This was it. The moment he'd been waiting for had finally arrived.

Hearing the horse-box pull up outside, Alice O'Hara darted out to the kitchen to dish the boys' dinners up. Pork chops, Yorkshire puddings, roast potatoes, greens and carrots she'd cooked them and even though she was thrilled Jed was home safely, she hoped the little sod choked on his, as that would teach him not to lie to his mother again.

'Daddy, Daddy, Daddy!' Harry shouted, jumping up and down excitedly.

'Can I go and see Daddy, Nanny?' Georgie asked.

'No, stay 'ere, 'cause he's parking the horse-box up and he might run you over. He'll be in in a tick.'

255

Seconds later, Alice screamed as she heard the unmissable sound of gunshots. 'Jed, please God, no. Not my Jed,' she cried as she dropped the tray of roast potatoes and ran to the front door.

Sensing their nan's fear, Georgie and Harry both began to sob as they chased after her. 'Daddy!' they both yelled.

Alice ran towards the horse-box. The security lights were on and, as she got closer, all she could see was the blood and gore splattered against the windscreen on the driver's side.

'Jed! Not my baby, not my beautiful baby boy,' she shrieked.

Overcome by shock, Alice sank to her knees, vomited and then promptly passed out.

'Nanny, Nanny!' Georgie and Harry shouted as they prodded and poked her. Realising that Nanny was fast asleep, Georgie decided to take the matter into her own hands.

'Stay with Nanny while I get Daddy,' she ordered Harry.

Climbing up on the metal step that led to the driver's-side door of the horse-box, Georgie tugged it and tugged it until it flew open. As the bloodied body fell on top of her and sent her sprawling to the ground, poor little Georgie screamed louder than she had ever screamed before.

CHAPTER TWENTY-SIX

Ed got up at the crack of dawn the following morning. He'd had a crap night's sleep and was desperate to know if Baldwin had succeeded in his attempt to kill Jed. Such was Ed's impatience, he'd even debated whether to ask Joey to visit Joycie late the previous night, so he could have a butcher's and see if there were any Old Bill lurking about. In the end, though, he'd decided against it. Joey didn't drive, so Dom would have to be involved as well and as much as Ed liked Dom, he thought it was too risky to involve him.

'You're up early. Couldn't you sleep?' Gina asked, rubbing her tired eyes.

Eddie sat on the bed next to his pregnant wife, pulled back the quilt cover and laid his head on her stomach. Gina was four months gone now and Ed could hardly wait to become a father again. Having a newborn at his age might seem like madness to some people, but he looked and acted more like a forty-year-old, instead of his true age of fifty-three.

'I've got an early morning meeting, babe. In fact, I've got a few meetings today, so I probably won't be back until teatime. What about you? You going out, or staying in all day?'

'I might go for a mooch round Lakeside. Most of my clothes don't fit me any more, so I'm gonna have to get some bigger sizes. I hope I don't get enormous and then struggle to lose the weight after the baby's born.'

Eddie chuckled. He'd never met a woman as paranoid about her weight as Gina. 'It'll all be worth it when you give birth to a little Mitchell. You should think yourself extremely lucky, you know. There ain't many women in the world that wouldn't

257

give their right arm to breed with an 'andsome bastard like me.'

Gina punched him playfully on the arm. 'Has anyone ever told you that you're so full of shit, Eddie Mitchell?'

Ed kissed her gently on the forehead and stood up. 'You wouldn't have me any other way, sweetheart.'

An hour later, Ed was sitting in the office of his salvage yard in Dagenham. He had very little to do with the business any more. He'd had a guy called Big Pete running it for him for years, but he liked to keep hold of it in case the Old Bill ever came sniffing around. In Ed's eyes, every wise man should have at least one legal business to cover their arse.

Eddie had told Terry Baldwin to meet him at the salvage yard at half-seven.

'Take an hour off, Pete. Go and grab yourself a bit of scran down the café,' he told his employee.

When Pete left the yard, Ed put his feet up on the desk in the Portakabin and as he often did when he was deep in thought, rubbed the stubble on his chin. At his end, everything had gone to plan the previous night. He and Raymond had stayed in the Bell and had had afters with the landlord and four other geezers, and he knew everything had gone OK with the others, as Stuart had got home at half-two and said both the restaurant and pub were full of people who knew both Gary and Ricky.

Eddie glanced at his watch. It was nearly half-past and there was no sign of Baldwin yet. Wondering if he'd ballsed up and the O'Haras had ended up killing him instead, Ed smirked seconds later as he saw Terry's Land Cruiser pull into the yard. Ed opened the Portakabin door.

'Well?' he asked as Baldwin approached him.

'Done and dusted,' Terry replied, grinning.

Ed led him inside and urged him to sit down. 'Start from the beginning.'

Terry explained exactly what had happened the previous evening.

'Are you one hundred per cent sure he was dead?' Eddie asked.

'Of course I am. I was only about two feet away from him

and I blasted him three times in the bonce. I saw his brains splatter all over the windscreen before I ran off. No one can survive that.'

'What about Jimmy? Did you see him?'

'No, I ran like a fucking greyhound, but it was definitely Jed and not Jimmy driving. Jimmy must have been with him, as I saw someone in the passenger seat – I saw the silhouette as the horse-box pulled in. You never know, one of my bullets might have gone astray and Jimmy might be dead an' all.'

'What about the motorbike you used?'

'Already ceased to exist. The helmet, leathers, everything's been torched,' Terry replied.

'Good stuff.'

'So, are we OK now? I'm really sorry about your brothers, Ed, but Luke was my grandson, and I loved him dearly. I know me and you are never gonna be best pals, but I do hope you understand why I had to do what I did.'

Eddie Mitchell ran a hand over his stubble once more. He'd heard of Baldwin in the past. He wasn't major league like himself, but the more Ed spoke to him, the more taken he was with the guy. Terry Baldwin was fearless, composed and incredibly honest, and in this day and age they were rare qualities to have.

'Did anybody else, other than Jamie Carroll, know you'd ordered the hit on my brothers?'

'What do you think? I knew they were your brothers, so I was hardly gonna advertise it, was I?'

Eddie stayed silent for a minute or two. He knew what he wanted to ask Terry, but he also knew if he did, Gary and Ricky would blow a fuse. Deciding to go with his gut instinct, Ed looked Baldwin in the eye.

'How are you fixed for work at the moment? I reckon I could do with an extra pair of hands working for me.'

Terry stared at Eddie in complete and utter disbelief. For a second he wondered if his hearing had deceived him. Then he wondered if Ed was taking the piss. 'Is this some kind of joke?' he asked bluntly.

'Do I look like a fucking comedian?' Eddie replied sarcastically.

'I'd fucking love to work for you, Ed, and I truly mean that. Things have been tough workwise for me the past year or so and I ain't exactly rolling in it at the moment.'

Eddie leaned across the desk and held out his right hand. 'We'll have to make sure the filth don't come sniffing around ya first over Jed's murder. As soon as we know everything's kosher, you can start. It won't be nothing iffy, you'll just be collecting dosh and threatening or roughing up any one who don't pay on time.'

'If I ask you a question, will you be honest with me?' Terry asked.

'Go on.'

'Why are you doing this for me after what I did to your brothers?'

'Because I know what it's like to have your daughter's life ruined by some little cunt like Jed. I also know what it's like to have somebody you love brutally murdered. I will never rest until I find out who killed my old man. I want revenge for that so much, I can almost fucking taste it.'

'Thanks ever so much, Ed. I dunno what else to say to you, mate.'

'Don't say nothing then. Go on, you can fuck off now. I'll be in touch as soon as we're sure the coast is clear. Until then, don't contact me, OK? And if I need to speak to you at all, I'll get Stu to call you with a time, then we'll meet at the Leonard Arms in Rainham.'

Terry Baldwin smiled gratefully and as he walked away, Eddie felt a slight twinge of guilt run through his veins. He just hoped all that life after death shit was a load of old cobblers, because if it wasn't, his father would currently be turning in his fucking grave.

'Morning everybody,' DI Blyth shouted to her colleagues as she walked into her office.

'The superintendent from Arbour Square rang up about half-an-hour ago. He wants you to call him back,' said Julie, her young assistant.

Blyth shut the office door, put her takeaway coffee on the table and immediately picked up the phone. 'Good morning, sir. DI Blyth here.'

Blyth listened intently as the superintendent told her the results of the DNA test. He then explained to Blyth what would happen next. Blyth thanked him, ended the call, then immediately rang up Holloway Prison. She would need to speak to Frankie face to face, and the sooner she got it over with, the better.

Eddie Mitchell arrived at Joanie's house at quarter to two. He was early for once, and had purposely got there before Gary and Ricky did.

'Happy birthday for tomorrow, Auntie,' Ed said, handing her a card and a separate envelope with five-hundred quid stuffed inside. Ed knew Joanie like the back of his hand and she was bound to argue with him for five minutes, telling him she didn't want his money, but in the end she would take it. He'd already told Stuart the score on the journey to Whitechapel and Ed winked at him as Joanie opened the envelope.

'I'm not taking that, Eddie. You can take it all back,' she demanded, shoving the envelope back into his hands.

Stuart tried not to laugh as Ed argued with her. 'They reckon we're in for another cold spell next week. Get yourself a new winter coat,' Ed urged her.

'It's nearly March. I'm no spring chicken you know, and the way this arthritis keeps playing me up, I'll probably be bleedin' housebound or even dead by next winter, so what do I want a new coat for?'

'Do you always have to be so fucking cheerful?' Ed asked her in a sarcastic tone. The thought of losing his favourite aunt just didn't bear thinking about. He'd been a young boy when his mum had died of TB and Joanie had always been a mother and aunt rolled into one.

The argument over the money continued until Joanie finally gave in. 'Oh, if you're gonna drive me mad, give us the bleedin' envelope back, then. I suppose I can help out some of me friends with their winter fuel bills or something.'

As Joanie walked out into the kitchen to hide it in her special tin, Eddie nudged Stuart. 'That won't go towards anyone's fuel bills. She'll spend the whole lot down the fucking bingo,' he said, chuckling.

'Oi, I heard that. I might have dodgy legs, but there's sod-all wrong with me ears, you know,' Joan shouted out.

Laughing, Eddie opened the door to Gary, Ricky and Raymond. 'So, who's late today, then?' he asked sarcastically.

'Talk about the pot calling the kettle black,' Ricky replied, laughing.

'Take these trays up with you. Me plates of meat are giving me gyp today and I can't be doing with going up and down them bleedin' stairs,' Joanie shouted out.

Eddie smiled as he and Stuart took the trays of hot boiled-bacon sandwiches off the kitchen top.

'Shall I make yous a brew?' Joanie asked. She knew the boys sometimes preferred to have a little tipple when they were discussing business.

'No, we're gonna have something a wee bit stronger today, Auntie. We've got something to celebrate,' Ed replied smirking.

As the apple of her eye walked out the room, Joan made a mental note to watch the main and local news later. She would guess which bulletin was down to her nephew and the boys; she always did.

Frankie said a silent prayer as the screw led her towards the room where DI Blyth was waiting for her. Surely if there was a God, he would ensure Jed got punished for what he had done to her grandfather, she thought to herself.

As soon as Frankie saw Blyth, she knew whatever news she had was not good. 'Well?' she asked impatiently as she sat down opposite the DI.

Blyth took Frankie's hands in her own. She had grown to like the young girl sitting in front of her very much, but there was no point in dressing up the awful truth. Frankie was far too clued-up to believe any bullshit.

'The results are back and there is insufficient DNA on the samples we tested to give a positive identification to anybody. I'm so sorry, Frankie, I really am.'

Wanting to cry, Frankie chose not to and decided to be stroppy instead. She snatched her hands away from Blyth's. 'Can you repeat that in English now?' she asked sarcastically.

Blyth explained the situation in simplified terms. 'Look, I know this is a setback, but I can assure you that nobody is giving up on this case. The superintendent in charge is doing his utmost, I promise you that. He was only saying this morning that he is going to try to get a reconstruction of your grandad's murder on that TV programme, *Crimewatch UK*. Have you ever watched it, Frankie? It's presented by Nick Ross and Sue Cook and it's really good at jogging people's memories and subsequently getting convictions.'

Frankie was far too disappointed and inwardly upset to discuss some poxy TV programme. She stood up. 'I like you, so please don't take this personally, but my dad has always said that the police were useless and the only thing they could catch was a cold and do you know what, I make him fucking right.'

Turning on her heel, Frankie stormed out of the room.

Gary, Ricky and Raymond were all elated to hear that Jed had now met his maker. Even though Stuart had never met Jed, he was also thrilled because he knew how the bloke had torn Eddie's family apart.

'So Baldwin was absolutely sure he was dead?' Raymond asked.

'Yep, he was positive. He blasted him three times in the head, apparently at close range and he even said he was sure he saw his brains splatter against the windscreen.'

'What brains?' Gary exclaimed, laughing.

'Let's have a drink to celebrate, eh?' Ricky said, grabbing a bottle of Scotch from the cabinet.

'We had the local news on the radio on the way up 'ere. There's nothing on there yet,' Gary said.

'Me and Stu did an' all. I reckon it's a bit early for anything to be announced. They've probably still got the forensics round there fuck-arsing about,' Eddie replied.

'Why don't you ring your mum, Raymondo? She only lives a spit's throw away and you know how nosy she is,' Ricky suggested.

Raymond shook his head. 'Me dad's moved back there now and I don't want him getting wind that we knew anything about this. You know how righteous he is.'

'What about Pat Murphy? He's virtually O'Hara's neighbour, ain't he? Can't you pretend you're ringing him about something else and see if he says anything?' Gary asked his father.

'No, that's way too risky. Murphy's a pal of Jimmy's and he's bound to smell a rat if I ring him up. We're just gonna have to wait until some bastard rings us and tells us what's happened. Then we act shocked.'

'So what did Baldwin say about Jimmy? Didn't he chase after him or anything?' Ricky asked.

'He didn't really see Jimmy, but he said he was in the passenger seat. Be funny if he's killed him an' all, won't it? Actually, I'll take that back, because I'm determined to have that bastard for meself and I intend to torture him for hours before I end his useless fucking life.'

Gary chuckled. 'What about that old pal of yours, Doug? Can't you ring him, he lives near O'Hara, don't he?'

'Dougie recently moved to Hutton Mount. I barely hear from him these days, to be honest. Vicki was Jessica's pal, weren't she? And when Jess died, Dougie seemed to give me a wide berth afterwards. Never mind, who needs friends like him when I've got my ole mucker, Stu?' Ed chuckled, playfully punching his lodger on the arm.

'So, how did you leave it with Baldwin? I take it you ain't having no more contact with him now, are ya?' Raymond enquired.

Eddie took a gulp of his drink and prepared himself for the torrent of abuse that was bound to fly his way. 'Actually, I offered him a job. He won't be starting yet like, we'll let all this die down first.'

Gary and Ricky looked at their father in astonishment. 'Ha, ha, very funny. You're winding us up, right?' Gary jeered.

'No, I ain't, actually. Listen, if we take on another pair of hands we can cover more ground. Not only that, when Gina has the baby, I don't wanna be working me nuts off, day in, day out. I was hardly ever at home when yous two were little or when Frankie and Joey were young and I ain't making the same mistake again. Don't worry, I'm not gonna retire, I just wanna ease off a bit, if you know what I mean?'

'Well, surely there's someone else you can take on? How can you even consider employing some cunt that got your brothers murdered? It's like Ricky getting topped and me befriending whoever killed him. It ain't fucking ethical, Dad,' Gary shouted.

Eddie stood up and slammed his glass against the table. 'I decide what's fucking ethical and what isn't. This is my firm and until I hang me boots up, I make all the decisions. Paulie and Ronny might have been my brothers, but Baldwin had every right to do what he did. Any man with a bit of spunk would have done the same, so like it or not, he will be coming to work for us. He's big, strong and brave and I'm positive he'll be a great acquisition to the firm. Now, I've said all I'm gonna say on the subject and I don't wanna hear another word about it, all right?'

Gary and Ricky glanced at one another. They were anything but all right, but as usual, there was sod-all they could do about it.

'What about Frankie? Who's gonna tell her that Jed's been murdered?' Stuart asked.

'I haven't really thought about that yet, to be honest. I reckon it's better coming from Joey than anyone else, though,' Ed replied.

'She's bound to think it had something to do with us. Do you think she'll be all right about it?' Raymond asked.

'Course she will. She wanted him dead more than any of us, so I shouldn't think she'll care who's done it. I spoke to Larry again yesterday and he reckons that once Jed's out the picture, we should have the kids back within a month. Joycie's offered to have 'em live with her until Frankie gets out. She said she'll get a better conversation out of them than she does Stanley,' Eddie said, chuckling.

Ricky smiled. 'I bet Frankie can't wait to see 'em again. They must be getting big now.'

Gary lifted his glass up. 'To Frankie, Georgie and Harry being reunited.'

As everybody raised their glasses, Eddie stood up and beamed. 'And to Jeddy boy. May you rot in hell, you little cunt.'

CHAPTER TWENTY-SEVEN

Three days later, Eddie was beginning to get more anxious as every second passed. There had been no mention of Jed's murder on the TV or radio and there'd been nothing written in the newspapers about it, either. Even more worryingly, Ed had not heard a dickie bird from Joycie, Pat Murphy or any other bastard that lived near Jimmy O'Hara, and Ed now had a gut instinct that something had gone very wrong indeed.

'Are you OK, love? You've not been yourself the last few days, you've been ever so quiet,' Gina said, putting her arms around her husband's toned waist.

'I'm fine, babe. Just ain't been sleeping that well and it's making me agitated,' Eddie replied.

Gina laid her head on his shoulder. She knew something had happened that Ed didn't want to tell her about and she just hoped he wasn't in any kind of trouble.

Feeling like a cat on a hot tin roof, Eddie knew he had to do something. 'I need to pop out for a bit, babe. Dunno how long I'll be, but I doubt I'll be back before late afternoon.'

Gina stared into his worried eyes. Usually on a Sunday they ate out and spent the whole day together but, not wanting to kick up a fuss, she smiled and nodded. 'No probs. I'll pop across to Asda and make sure there's a nice roast dinner on the table for you when you get back. Give me a ring when you're ten minutes away.'

Eddie kissed her goodbye, got into his Range Rover and immediately rang Raymond. 'Get your arse in gear and meet me at the Leonard Arms in an hour,' he ordered.

'Ed, I can't. I'm going out for a meal with Polly and her parents and I've booked the restaurant for twelve.'

'Well, best you fucking unbook it then, or let Polly do lunch with 'em on her own. This is important, Raymond, comprendes?'

Ending the phone call before Raymond had a chance to argue, Eddie rang his two eldest sons and told them to head to Rainham as well. Stuart hadn't come home all night and Ed knew that he'd taken his new bird out.

'Where are ya?' he asked, as Stuart groggily answered the phone.

'I'm round Emma's flat.'

'Yes, I know that, but what's her address?' Ed asked. Stu gave it to him and he wrote it down on the back of his hand. 'Get your skates on and I'll pick you up in twenty minutes.'

Joycie Smith opened the front door with a silly big grin on her face. It had been Dominic's birthday the previous day and she was so pleased when he and Joey had agreed to spend today with her and Stanley. It would be the first time they'd been over for a meal since her wanderer of a husband had returned.

'Mmm, the meat smells nice. What are we having for dinner?' Dominic asked.

'I've cooked roast beef, leg of lamb and all the trimmings, and for dessert we've got homemade apple crumble or sticky toffee pudding.'

Joey handed his nan a gift bag that contained a bottle of Baileys and a box of Thornton's chocolates. 'Dom bought you these,' he said.

'Oh, you are silly. You don't have to buy me bleedin' presents. I'll put the Baileys away for my birthday,' Joycie said gratefully.

'That'll be gone by tomorrow,' Joey whispered to Dom as his nan turned her back.

'Now what do you want? Beer, wine, coffee or tea?'

'Just a coffee for now, Nan. Where's Grandad, by the way?' Joey replied.

'Where do you think? Out in the garden fiddling about with his cock, as per usual. I'll give him a shout in a minute and let him know you're here. Now, when do you want to open your present, Dominic? Now, or after dinner?'

Remembering the 'Gay and Proud' t-shirt his nan had bought him a while back, Joey couldn't help but burst out laughing. 'He'll have it later. He needs a couple of glasses of wine first, Nan.'

'What are you both laughing at?' Joyce asked in a displeased tone.

Joycie's annoyance only made Joey and Dominic laugh all the more. 'You ain't bought him a t-shirt, Nan, have ya?' Joey asked, holding his sides.

'Gertcha, you ungrateful little bastards,' Joyce replied. Pretending to be furious, she stomped out of the room, shut the door, and then burst out laughing herself.

Eddie Mitchell had chosen the Leonard Arms for a reason. Big Pete who ran his salvage yard drank in there, and over the years Ed had often popped in for a bevvy or two, so his face was known. Also, if they were going to investigate for themselves, they needed to be somewhere near where O'Hara lived.

'Did you get hold of him?' Eddie asked hopefully as Stu got back in the motor.

'Yep. I said exactly what you asked me to and he just said, "OK." Fucking hell, Ed, that phone box has really turned my stomach. It reeked of piss and sick.'

Eddie chuckled, then drove towards the pub. 'How'd it go with the bird last night? Do you like her?'

Last night was the first time Stuart had had sex since he'd got out of prison, and the thought of it made him break into a smile. 'Yeah, Emma's a very pretty girl.'

Eddie glanced at his sidekick and smirked. 'I can see by the look on your face you got your nuts in, boy.'

Stuart laughed. 'You've a charming way with words, Ed.'

Five minutes later, Eddie pulled up in the car park of the Leonard Arms. 'Right, come in for a beer with me, then at quarter to one, go outside and sit in the motor. As soon as Baldwin turns up, ring me and I'll come outside. If we're standing in company, say you're goin' outside to ring your bird, OK?'

Gary and Ricky had already bagged a table in the corner of the pub. Apart from them, there were only four other punters in there and no sign of Big Pete.

'Get a round in, Stu, and get one for Raymondo an' all,' Ed said, handing Stuart a twenty-pound note.

Raymond walked in five minutes later with a face like thunder. 'This better be fuckin' important, as it's probably just cost me me marriage,' he groaned, plonking himself on a chair.

'Of course it's fucking important, and you really need to tell that old woman of yours that it's what we do for a living that keeps her in designer shoes and handbags,' Ed replied cynically.

'Spit it out, then. What's happened?' Gary asked his father.

Glancing around to make sure there were no unwanted ears listening in, Eddie leaned forward. 'Nothing's happened, that's the problem. Something's gone tits-up, I can feel it in me bones. There ain't been a mention of it anywhere and nobody could have kept it this quiet.'

'I don't wanna say I told you so, but you should never have trusted Baldwin in the first place. You don't even really know the geezer and we should have just gone ahead with our original plan,' Gary said knowingly.

'Baldwin's meeting us 'ere at one. Stu's gonna wait outside for him. I'm positive he never fucked up, he was too certain that Jed was a goner. We'll take him for a drive and go over it again with him. He can explain what happened, and you see what you and Rick think. I can't believe Pat Murphy or Joycie ain't rang me. I know I said none of us should go anywhere near O'Hara's gaff, but I want you to pop in and see your mother, Raymondo. Just say you was passing or something and stay for a quick cuppa. Stu can go with ya and he can have a butcher's at O'Hara's gaff as you drive past it.'

'I'd better go outside. It's quarter to,' Stuart said, standing up.

Gary and Ricky spent the next five minutes trying to convince their father that Terry Baldwin had messed up, big style. 'He probably shot the horse in the back of the poxy box,' Ricky said, sniggering at his own wit.

'He's 'ere,' Eddie said as his mobile rang. 'You and Stu pop round to Joycie now, Ray, while me and the boys take Baldwin for a little drive.'

Terry Baldwin was already sitting in the passenger seat of his Range Rover, so Ed walked over to the driver's side. 'You're goin' with Raymondo, Stu. I'll meet yous back at the Albion. We can't come back 'ere, it'll look fishy.'

'Have you heard something?' Terry asked, as Gary and Ricky got in the back and Ed zoomed out of the car park.

'Not a fucking dickie. Now, Tel, I'm only gonna ask you this once and I expect you to be truthful with me. Are you sure that you never dropped a bollock?'

'May my Sally and Lukey rot in hell if I'm lying; I swear I killed Jed O'Hara. He had a baseball cap on and as I aimed the gun at it, I saw half his skull splatter everywhere. No one can survive that, Ed, and I shot him twice more after that.'

'Well, how comes there's been nothing on the news or in the papers then? We ain't even had a phone call from anyone who lives nearby,' Gary said accusingly.

'I dunno why you ain't heard nothing, all I know is that I killed him. I ain't gonna lie to you, am I? And if I had cocked up, don't you think I'd be lying on a beach in Spain somewhere by now? You made the consequences clear what would happen if I messed up and that's why I made sure I did the job properly. I ain't bloody stupid.'

Eddie went past the Circus Tavern, turned the Range Rover around and headed back towards Rainham. He could spot a liar a mile off and he was absolutely positive that Baldwin was telling the truth.

'I'll be in touch,' he said as he dropped Baldwin off at the road next to the Leonard Arms.

As soon as Baldwin walked off, Eddie turned around to face his sons. 'He ain't lying,' he said bluntly.

Gary and Ricky both shrugged. Neither knew what to say any more – the whole episode was a complete and utter mystery.

Joey pushed his dish away and undid the button on his jeans. His nan's dinners were always delicious, but he should never have had the sticky toffee pudding as well as a slice of apple crumble.

'Who fancies a Baileys?' Joycie asked.

'I'll have one, love,' Stanley replied.

'I wasn't asking you, I was talking to the boys. You can have another bitter, Stanley, a classy drink like Baileys is wasted on a man of your ilk.'

Joey and Dominic both wanted to laugh but didn't. 'So how have you and Nan been getting on Grandad?' Joey asked, when Joycie left the room.

'How do you think? Been leading me a bleedin' dog's life she has. I'm surprised she ain't built a kennel and made me sleep in the poxy garden.'

'I'm sure she'll mellow in time,' Dominic said, kindly.

'You're having a laugh, ain't ya? The old witch ain't mellowed since the day I bleedin' well married her,' Stanley said, chuckling.

'You're not talking about me in there, are you, Stanley?' Joycie shouted out.

'No, dear,' Stanley shouted back, winking at the boys.

Joyce put the flowers in a vase that Raymond had brought round, then giggled as she lit the candles on the cake. Her mate Rita's sister baked them to order and Joycie had ordered a very special one indeed.

'Happy birthday to you, Happy birthday to you, Happy birthday dear Dominic, Happy birthday to you,' she sang as she placed the cake on the table in front of Dom. Joey took one look at the cake and burst into hysterical laughter. Dom didn't know whether to laugh or cry as he saw Stanley's confused face.

'What's that on the front, then?' Stanley asked innocently, twisting his head one way then the other.

The cake was facing Dominic and Joey and Stanley couldn't make head nor tail of what it was meant to be.

'It's a willy, Stanley,' Joyce replied proudly.

Stanley looked at his wife. 'What, Free Willy?' he asked, referring to the whale in the film he and Joycie had taken Georgie and Harry to see last year.

'No, a willy, as in a penis. Well, there was no point me getting boobies or naked women iced on the front, was there? Dominic's a gay man and he likes a willy, especially our Joey's.'

'That's disgusting! It's immoral! And do you have to spout filth like that? The shop that sold that cake to you wants bloody reporting to the police. As for you buying the bleeding thing in the first place, there must be something wrong with you, woman.'

'Oh shut up, you miserable old goat. I bet that old slapper Pat weren't complaining when you was waving your willy at her, eh Stanley? That's what you call bloody immoral, especially when you're married to somebody else.'

Feeling his cheeks turn beetroot red, Stanley stood up. 'I'm busting for a wee, it must be all that bitter,' he said, as he bolted from the room.

Joycie looked at Joey and Dom and all three of them burst out laughing.

'You shouldn't wind him up like that, Nan. You'll give him a heart attack one of these days,' Joey said seriously.

'Good! Serves the philandering homophobic old bastard right,' Joyce cackled.

'Well?' Eddie asked, as Raymond and Stuart sat down at the table opposite him.

'Swarming with Old Bill,' Stuart said, grinning.

'We came back a different way. We didn't wanna drive past there again,' Raymond added.

Eddie felt a sense of relief rush through his veins. 'The Old Bill didn't clock ya, did they?'

'Nah, they were all inside the driveway,' Stu replied.

'Well, thank fuck for that. I told you Baldwin weren't lying, didn't I?' Eddie said, beaming from ear to ear.

'I'm gonna get us all a large Scotch to celebrate, then I'm gonna have to gel, Ed,' Raymond said.

As Raymond walked up to the bar, Eddie's phone burst into life.

'All right, Mr Murphy? What you up to, mate?' Ed asked grinning. He put his forefinger to his lips to warn the others to keep schtum. Within seconds, Ed's grin had disappeared and his healthy-looking complexion had turned a deathly shade of white. 'You what? They can't have. Are you fucking sure?'

Gary and Ricky glanced anxiously at each other. Whatever

news Pat Murphy had was obviously not good. Stuart ran up to the bar to tell Raymond. 'Pat Murphy's on the phone to Ed. Something's gone wrong, I think,' he whispered, grabbing two of the drinks.

Gary, Ricky, Stuart and Raymond all stared at Eddie as he continued and then ended the conversation. 'Whatever's wrong?' Gary asked his father.

Overcome by shock, Eddie felt physically sick as he gulped back his Scotch in one. He slammed the glass on the table. 'The O'Haras have gone. They've done a runner and they've taken Georgie and Harry with 'em.'

'What about Jed? Did Murphy say he was dead?' Ricky asked.

'He didn't say. All the Old Bill would tell him was there'd been an incident, the family had disappeared and he said the police seemed to be swarming around the horse-box like flies. They wouldn't let him inside the gates, obviously.'

Eddie put his head in his hands. He looked up seconds later, his eyes brimming with tears. 'How the fuck am I gonna tell Frankie?'

CHAPTER TWENTY-EIGHT

Unaware that her children had all but disappeared off the face of the earth, Frankie had spent the night dreaming about them. They'd all been at the zoo together and Georgie and Harry's presence had been so real that when Frankie was awoken by a piercing scream, she thought one of the children had fallen over and hurt themselves. Sitting bolt upright, Frankie immediately realised that it was Babs in pain.

'What's a matter? Is the baby on its way?' Frankie asked, dashing over to her bedside.

'I don't know, it don't feel like contractions,' Babs mumbled fearfully.

When she let out another tortured cry, Frankie immediately ran to the cell door and pummelled her fists against it. 'Help! Quick, we need help!' she shouted at the top of her voice.

Seconds later, two screws ran in and, seeing Babs, face covered in sweat and contorted with pain, they immediately called for medical assistance.

'I think my baby's dying. It's in trouble, I just know it is,' Babs sobbed.

Frankie mopped her friend's forehead with a wet flannel. 'Sssh, your baby is gonna be just fine, Babs, I know it is.'

When the prison doctor finally appeared, Babs was swiftly whisked away and Frankie begged to be allowed to go to the hospital with her.

'No, Mitchell, you know the rules,' one of the newer screws barked, slamming the cell door in Frankie's face.

Exasperated by the woman's callousness, Frankie kicked the cell door. 'Bitch!' she screamed as she sank to her knees.

Frankie clasped her hands together, looked up at the ceiling and prayed. 'Please God make my friend Babs and her baby both be OK. And also God, give Jed his comeuppance for what he did to my grandad. Amen.'

Over in Rettendon, Eddie Mitchell was sitting at the kitchen table gingerly sipping a strong black coffee. His initial reaction to Pat Murphy's phone call the previous day had been one of pure shock, but within minutes, the shock had turned to anger. He'd wanted to drive round to the O'Haras' himself to stick a bullet up the Old Bill's arses to find his grandkids, but Raymond had managed to stop him.

'Don't do anything stupid, Ed. Ring Larry and ask his advice before you go charging round there like a bull in a china shop.'

Larry was kept in the loop about most things that went on in Eddie's world and he immediately warned him that under no circumstances should he go anywhere near the O'Haras' house.

'Just leave it with me to deal with, Eddie. I'll make some phone calls and find out exactly what's going on. If I get no joy over the phone, I'll drive straight down to Rainham first thing in the morning. You do not go anywhere near that house, OK?' he had insisted.

'Why didn't you come up to bed last night?' Gina asked, as she sat down at the table opposite her husband.

The news of Georgie and Harry's disappearance had literally knocked Ed for six and he'd spent the whole of last night knocking back the Scotch and planning how he was going to break the news to Frankie. Finally, he'd passed out on the sofa.

'I was drunk. I didn't wanna disturb ya,' Ed replied.

Gina leaned across the table and held his hands. 'Please let me cook you a decent breakfast, Ed. You didn't touch your dinner yesterday and you've got to eat something.'

'This must be Larry. Cook some bacon sandwiches or something and bring 'em into the lounge,' Ed replied when the doorbell rang.

Larry followed Eddie into the lounge and sat down in one of the armchairs. He'd got up at four o'clock that morning and had been in Rainham by daybreak. Still, he couldn't complain as, like his father before him, Eddie paid him a handsome yearly wage, which over the years had kept him in the life of luxury he was now so very used to.

'What's the score, then?' Eddie asked.

'I couldn't find out a great deal at first, to be honest. All the police would tell me was there had been an incident at the house and nobody was aware of the current whereabouts of the family. I then got on to an old pal of mine who's as bent as a nine-bob note to make a couple of phone calls. He called me back and reckons, due to the amount of blood found in the horse-box and on the driveway, the police are positive they are dealing with a murder inquiry, although they are yet to find a body.'

'Yet to find a body! That's fucking insane! Surely the O'Haras ain't driven off with their dead son's body in the boot? No one could do that, could they?'

Larry shrugged. 'Your guess is as good as mine, Eddie. The local hospitals have all been checked and apparently nobody's been admitted in the past few days with gunshot wounds. Perhaps they've buried Jed themselves or something. I personally don't know a great deal about the travelling community, but from what you've told me, I wouldn't put anything past them.'

The men stopped their conversation as Gina walked into the room with a tray of bacon sandwiches and two mugs of coffee. 'If you need anything else, just shout,' she said, as she diplomatically closed the door behind her.

'So, have the Old Bill said if anything's missing inside the house?' Ed asked, wondering if they'd taken any of the kids' clothes and toys.

'I don't think there is. It just sounds like they left in a real hurry. Both Jed's and Jimmy's motors are gone and obviously the police have put a trace out on the registration numbers.'

Eddie was bemused. 'They ain't gonna do a runner and not change their fucking number plates, are they? In fact, they're probably driving about in new motors as we speak. What I can't understand, though, is that house is worth a fortune and is in Jimmy's name, or I think it is. Surely he ain't just gonna wipe his mouth of that, is he?'

'I can't understand their way of thinking either, I really can't. Why wouldn't they have reported their own son's murder? It really doesn't make sense,' Larry replied.

'They're brainless cunts, that's why. Anyway, getting the kids back is all I'm bothered about at this moment in time, so what we gonna do to find 'em?'

'I'm picking Carol Cullen up at eleven o'clock and she is coming to the police station with me. She is going to tell the police that she feels the children's lives are in danger, so they'll have to get their backsides into gear then. I'll also get Carol to contact the authorities to let them know that the custodial rules have been broken. We need a warrant put out for the O'Haras' arrest immediately.'

Eddie put his head in his hands. He had a feeling that finding the O'Haras was going to be anything but easy.

'Do you know if the children had passports, Eddie? I'm sure that's one of the first questions the police are likely to ask me.'

'I dunno. The only one that might know that is Frankie. Pikeys don't really go abroad much, so I doubt Jed would have got 'em one,' Eddie answered.

'You're going to have to tell Frankie what's happened today, Eddie. I'll call the prison, inform them what's occurred and we'll both go up there this afternoon. The police are bound to need to speak to her at some point very soon. They'll want to know if she has any idea where the family might have run off to.'

'Oh, Jesus. What am I meant to say to her, Lal?'

'I don't know, mate, but you're going to have to explain things to her as best as you can. Whatever you say, do not mention that Jed is dead. We can't chance Frankie knowing that, in case she puts her foot in it when she speaks to the police. They'll be bang on your case if that were to happen.'

Eddie nodded. 'Don't you think the Old Bill will wanna question me anyway?'

'I really don't know, but I should imagine so. If there has been an incident around there, unfortunately for you, you will almost certainly be a suspect.'

Eddie put his head in his hands once more. 'Me and the

lads have all got alibis for Wednesday night, but say the Old Bill ain't got a clue when it happened? We'll all be in shit street then, won't we?'

'You'll be OK,' Larry said, in the most confident tone he could muster. He stood up. 'I'd better dash and pick Carol up now. I need to run a few things past her before we go to the station. I'll call Holloway and arrange a time on the way. I can meet you in the Albion car park and we can travel up together if you like?'

Eddie nodded, saw Larry out and shut the front door.

'Are you OK? What did Larry say?' Gina asked, putting her arms around her husband's fit body.

Eddie held Gina tight and stroked her long, dark hair. He knew she was worried about him and he couldn't allow that, especially with the baby on the way. He forced a big grin and pulled away from her.

'Larry said we'll get a warrant out for the O'Haras' arrest and we should have the kids back in no time. And don't you worry about me – I'm Eddie Mitchell, sweetheart.'

Frankie lay on her bed and stared at the ceiling. She'd felt very tearful since Babs had been taken away that morning and she still hadn't heard any news about her friend.

Shutting her eyes, Jed's smarmy face popped into Frankie's mind. To say she hated her ex now was an understatement and she often beat herself up for stupidly getting involved with him in the first place. The only thing that stopped her truly hating herself and blaming herself for her mother's death was that if she hadn't fallen pregnant by Jed, then she wouldn't have her wonderful Georgie and Harry. Also, her unborn baby was one of the only other things, bar Babs, that had kept her going through the long, dark days she'd spent imprisoned.

As she heard the key go in the door, Frankie sat up. 'Have you got some news on Babs?' she asked the screw.

'Yep, she had an emergency C-section and now she's got a little boy. They're both fine, apparently.'

'That's fantastic news,' Frankie said, elated.

'And you have visitors, my dear,' the screw announced.

'Who? I'm not expecting anyone today,' Frankie asked,

intrigued. She wondered if it was DI Blyth with some good news for once.

'I've no idea, Frankie. I'm just the messenger,' the screw replied brightly.

Frankie followed her along the corridors. She was led into the same room she'd spoken to Blyth in, but was shocked to see her father and Larry sitting inside. She knew by the looks on their faces that this was no routine visit and she wondered if they had found out she'd told Blyth that Jed had killed her grandfather. Her heart was pounding with pure fear as she sat down.

'Would it be possible if we could have some privacy, please? We need to discuss a rather delicate subject,' Larry told the screw.

Frankie felt griping pains in her stomach as the screw left the room. She felt as if she was desperate to use the toilet, but was too nervous to ask. She stared at her dad. He knew, she was positive he knew. 'What's going on?' she asked anxiously.

Eddie nudged Larry. He was no good at explaining stuff like this.

'The O'Haras have left Rainham, Frankie, and have taken Georgie and Harry with them. I've been to the police station this morning and insisted they put a warrant out for their arrest, as they have broken the custodial agreement,' Larry explained.

'Whaddya mean, left Rainham? Where have they gone, then?' Frankie asked dumbly.

'We don't know, sweetheart, but we'll find 'em and get the kids back, I promise you that,' Eddie assured her.

Frankie couldn't quite believe what she was hearing. There had to be some mistake. Why would Jed run off with the kids when he'd already been given custody of them? 'It doesn't make sense to me. How do you know the O'Haras haven't taken Georgie and Harry on holiday or something? Jed wouldn't do a runner with them, he's too clever for that. Who told you they were actually missing?'

Eddie nudged Larry again to prompt him to tell Frankie the rest of the story. 'It was Julie, Sammy's girlfriend, who reported their disappearance. She'd been unable to contact Sammy, so she called the police. There was some kind of incident at the house, apparently, but the police don't know exactly what happened yet. Their theory is that the O'Haras left quickly because of this particular incident.'

Frankie had been reasonably calm, but the word 'incident' filled her not just with dread but also with anger. 'Spit it out, then. What really fucking happened? I ain't a child any more, you know,' she shouted.

'The police believe that somebody was shot in Jimmy's horse-box. They found a bullet and blood by all accounts,' Larry said bluntly.

'What if it was one of my babies? Say it was Georgie or Harry that got shot!' Frankie screamed.

Eddie jumped out of his seat, crouched down and held his daughter's shaking body in his arms. He had to put her mind at rest. She looked ill and he couldn't leave her in this state. 'It definitely ain't one of the kids, babe. The Old Bill told Larry that, didn't they, Lal?'

'Yes, they seemed sure it was one of the adults,' Larry assured Frankie.

'But how do they know that? The same might have happened to Georgie or Harry what happened to Luke,' Frankie sobbed.

Eddie gripped his daughter's slouched shoulders. 'Listen, it ain't the kids, it's either Jed or Jimmy, OK? And you mustn't tell anyone we've told you that, because Lal got that piece of information on the sly and you'll get him into trouble, all right?'

Frankie stopped crying and stared her father in the eye. She was suddenly sure he knew more than he was letting on. She turned to Larry. 'Can I speak to my father alone for a minute, please?' she asked coldly.

Within seconds of Larry leaving the room, Frankie gave her father what for. 'This is all your doing, ain't it? What did you do? Go round there yourself and shoot the wrong person like you did with my mother? Or send someone else to do your dirty work instead?'

'What the fuck you on about? Whatever happened round the O'Haras' is sod-all to do with me. I swear on my life, I've been nowhere near their poxy house.'

'Well, I don't believe you,' Frankie spat.

'You can believe what you want, but don't be blaming me. Do you think if I was gonna hit on Jed or Jimmy that I'd be stupid enough to do it at their house in front of my own grandchildren? And as for bringing your mother into this conversation, that's well below the fucking belt, Frankie.'

The fire left Frankie's eyes and she immediately burst into tears again. 'I'm sorry, Dad. I'm just so worried about my children, I don't know what to say or think.'

Eddie held her in his arms again. 'I need you to be strong for me, Frankie, 'cause if you ain't, then I ain't gonna be able to cope either. I love you so much, girl, and I know you'll be OK because you're a chip off the old block, ain't ya?' Eddie remarked, drying her eyes with his handkerchief.

'Larry's gonna need to ask you some questions. We need to give the Old Bill as much information as we can to help 'em find Georgie and Harry, OK?'

Frankie nodded. 'OK.'

'Have the kids got passports?' Eddie asked.

'No, but Jed can get hold of anything like that. He used to get dodgy insurance certificates, tax discs, MOTs, even driving licences.'

Eddie stood up. He would have liked to have told his daughter that he knew Jed was dead, just to ease her worry, but he daren't in case the police questioned her and she put her bloody foot in it. 'I'll go and get Larry,' he said.

'Dad, can you ask the screw if I can have some painkillers and a glass of water? I really don't feel well,' Frankie said.

Eddie stood up. He hadn't even reached the door when Frankie let out a painful yelp. 'Whatever's wrong?' he asked, running to her aid.

Frankie was holding her stomach, her face contorted with pain. 'Get the screw, quick. My waters have broken.'

Over in Essex, Joyce and Stanley were car hunting and hadn't stopped arguing for the past couple of hours. Joycie was insisting that they purchase a brand, spanking-new motor and Stanley was trying to make his obstinate wife see sense.

'I ain't being mean, love, but we'll lose thousands off the bloody thing as soon as we drive it off the forecourt. If we get something a couple of years old, it's not only more practical, but financially sensible,' Stanley said.

'Nope, they've all been a load of old shit we've seen and my mind's made up now. I've decided I want a new Jaguar. In all the years I've been married to you, Stanley, we've never had a decent motor. Do you really begrudge me this one small pleasure after everything you've put me through recently? Well, do you?'

'No, dear,' Stanley replied miserably.

Ten minutes later, Stanley pulled up outside Grange Motors in Brentwood and nearly jumped out of his skin as Joycie firstly shrieked, then began clapping her hands with glee.

'That's the one I want. Look, that one over there.'

Stanley got out of the car and stared in horror at the brand-new, white Jaguar XJ6 that Joycie was pointing at. 'It looks like a wedding car. People will think I'm a bleedin' chauffeur or something if they see me driving about in that, Joycie.'

'Well, you are one. You're my bloody chauffeur. I'll have to get you one of them peak caps that they wear, so you really look the part,' Joyce cackled as she ran over to the gleaming XJ6.

'Oh, Stanley, I love it. I'll look the bee's knees in this. You'll have to drive me over to Rita and Hilda's straight away, so I can show it off.'

Seeing the price of the car, Stanley had one of his little coughing fits. Their old house in Upney had cost them less.

'Can I be of any assistance to you?' asked a well-spoken young man in a pinstriped suit. He had clocked the old banger the couple had pulled up in, so knew he had no chance of clinching a sale.

'Yes, we want to buy this car,' Joyce said proudly in her poshest tone.

The man smiled politely. He was used to dealing with messers; it was, unfortunately, all part of his job. 'This car is brand new. Would you like me to see if I can find you something second-hand?' he asked, with more than a hint of sarcasm in his voice.

Joycie stared at the spotty-faced little shit. He wasn't much older than her Joey. Who did he think he was talking to? 'Do we look like vagrants or paupers?' she snapped.

'No, of course not. It's just that this is the most expensive of our current range. It has all the extras on it, you see,' the man said, horrified.

'And that's why we want to buy it. Now are you going to sell it to us, or not?' Joyce asked, enjoying his obvious discomfort.

'We haven't even test-driven it yet, Joycie,' Stanley mumbled.

'Don't you bloody well start an' all. I've got enough on me plate with this jumped-up little shit. I want this car whether you like it or not, and if you don't like it, Stanley, I suggest you pack your bags and sod off back to that old slapper with the big tits. Now, what's it to be?'

Both red faced, Stanley and the young salesman looked at one another.

'We'll take it,' Stanley mumbled.

Frankie's baby entered the world just over an hour later. Considering he was a month early, he was a hefty little lump and weighed six pounds seven ounces. After initially being whisked away to be fully checked over, Frankie had just been reunited with him and was thrilled to hear he'd been given a clean bill of health.

'Are you sure everything's OK with him?' she asked anxiously, as the nurse handed him to her.

'He's absolutely fine and ever so big, considering the circumstances. I delivered a full-term baby yesterday and that only weighed six pound,' the nurse said reassuringly.

Frankie stared at her son and smiled. He looked nothing like Harry when he was born; he looked more like Georgie with his tuft of dark hair and long, dark eyelashes. 'Is my dad still outside?' Frankie asked Mandy, the prison officer who had travelled in the ambulance with her.

'Yep, he and your solicitor are both still outside.'

'Is it OK if I spend some time alone with my dad and the baby?'

Mandy nodded. Unlike some of the other prisoners she dealt with, she had always found Frankie to be a decent, good-natured girl with impeccable manners. 'While your dad pops in, I'll go and find Babs, see how she's doing. I'll tell her your news, but don't you dare tell anyone back at the prison that I left you alone, else you'll get me into trouble. You've got ten minutes, OK?'

'Thank you and I promise my lips are sealed,' Frankie said gratefully. Some of the screws were right bitches, but Mandy was one of the nicest ones Frankie had met in Holloway.

Seconds later, Eddie Mitchell walked into the ward, kissed his daughter on the cheek and stared at the new addition that she was cradling in her arms.

'Can I hold him?' he asked, his voice full of warmth.

When Frankie handed the baby over, she felt a pang of guilt. Everything had happened so quickly and she'd been so thrilled to give birth to a healthy son that she'd barely given Georgie and Harry a thought since her waters had broken.

Eddie kissed his grandson on the forehead. 'Hello, mate. I'm your grandad,' he said, gently stroking the child's cheek.

'What you gonna call him?' he asked Frankie.

'I quite like Justin or Brett. I suppose that's one good thing about Jed disappearing. He can now be a Mitchell, not a bloody O'Hara.'

'Brett Mitchell sounds all right. I ain't too sure about Justin though, it sounds a bit poncy,' Eddie chuckled.

Without warning, Frankie suddenly burst into tears. 'Brett it is then, but he ain't gonna get to meet his brother and sister, is he, Dad?'

Eddie laid his grandson in the little cot next to Frankie, sat on the edge of the bed, and hugged her. 'Look, I know the O'Haras doing a runner ain't ideal, but it does have its plus points – for now, anyway. Larry reckons the case will be laughed out of court if Jed can't be found and he also reckons he can now get you bail. He's making some more phone calls as we speak.'

'Really? You're not just saying that to cheer me up, are you?'

'No, I wouldn't do that, babe. Seriously, Larry spoke to James Fitzgerald Smythe earlier and he reckons we can get you bail as early as next week. Just be strong and hold on in there until then, OK?'

Mandy's return immediately changed the subject.

'How's Babs? Did you see her?' Frankie enquired.

'Yep, she's a bit sore, but doing just fine. Kelvin, she's called her son, and he weighs ten pound. No wonder she was so big and in so much pain. She couldn't believe that you had a little boy today as well. She said it's a crazy coincidence and reckons it's a sign that your babies will be just like you and her, best friends for life.'

Happy that Frankie was now laughing rather than crying, Eddie stood up. 'I'd better make a move now, darling. Poor Larry is shattered, he's been up since four dealing with our latest drama and he's gonna stay at mine tonight. I'll come back and visit you tomorrow and bring Joey with me. And don't forget what I told you, so keep your chin up, eh?'

Frankie smiled. 'I will, Dad, and thanks for everything. I know I don't say this a lot, but I do love you, you know.'

Feeling his eyes well up, Eddie walked towards the door before anybody noticed. His voice was gruff with emotion as he replied. 'And I love you too, sweetheart.'

CHAPTER TWENTY-NINE

The following week was full of highs and lows for Frankie. The highs included the first days with her son, Babs returning to the prison with Kelvin and the date for her new bail hearing. The lows were the constant worry over Georgie and Harry's whereabouts, the thought of life outside prison without Babs and the uncertainty over whether Jed was alive or dead.

On the morning of her court case, Frankie was up with the larks, and started packing her worldly goods together. Part of her wondered if she was tempting fate by doing this, but Larry seemed so certain that she would get bail this time, that it seemed extremely lazy to leave the job for somebody else to do.

Babs sat up, picked up her son and smiled as he clamped his mouth around her large, swollen breast. Kelvin's father was the pervert who had raped her beautiful daughter, Matilda, and Babs had been worried that she wouldn't bond with her son for that very reason. She couldn't have been more wrong though, as the moment Kelvin had been placed in her arms, she had felt nothing but unconditional love for her child. He looked nothing like the dead monster that had helped create him, and Babs thanked God for that small mercy. Kelvin was very dark, considering his dad had been white. He was almost as black as she was.

'Good morning, sweet child. I hope you gonna spare a thought for poor old Babs when you wake up in a nice cosy bed in some warm house tomorrow morning.'

Checking that Brett was breathing OK while he was sleeping,

Frankie sat on the edge of Babs' bed. 'If I do get out today, I ain't 'arf gonna miss you, mate. I'm so glad you got your trial date through and I promise if I'm still on the outside, I will attend the court every day to support you.'

Babs smiled. The thought of life inside prison without Frankie didn't bear thinking of, but she didn't want to dampen her friend's spirits by telling her that. She was truly thrilled that her pal was more than likely going home and, hopefully, in four months' time Babs would join her on the outside.

'Why the ifs, Frankie? You goin' home today and that's where you deserve to be. As for me, don't you dare worry that pretty head of yours. I'll call you every day and that nice solicitor man, Larry, swears blind that now I've told the truth I will walk free. In four months' time, sweet child, me and you can share that house with our children like we always dreamed about,' Babs said brightly.

'I am worried about going home though. Say Jed tries to kidnap Brett as well? I just wish I knew if the bastard was alive or dead. I'll never be able to sleep at night until I have proof that he's six feet under.'

'I know that feeling. Even though I'm stuck in here, I can still smile 'cause I know Peter is dead and he can never hurt me and my children again. I'm really glad I killed him and even if I end up doin' life, I'll never regret what I did. A mother's duty is to protect her children and that's what I'll tell the jury at my trial.'

Frankie sat in silence as Babs winded her son and gently laid him in his cot. Something Larry had said to her was playing on her mind and when Babs hugged her, Frankie couldn't stop herself from crying.

'What's the matter? You should be happy you finally goin' home.'

'I am, but Larry said that it's better for my actual court case if we don't find the O'Haras beforehand. How can I not look for my children, eh, Babs? I think about them every minute of every day. I wonder if they remember me and miss me. Do you think they're being looked after OK?'

As the sobs racked through Frankie's body, Babs held her friend tightly. She wished she could promise Frankie that her children were OK, but she couldn't make promises she didn't know the answer to herself. It wasn't right.

Over in Essex, Stanley Smith was cursing under his breath as Joycie barked out yet another order. Not only had the idiotic woman dragged him out of bed at 6 a.m., but now she was giving him directions to a house he used to live in and was also telling him how he should drive.

'Go a bit faster then, Stanley. We haven't bought a top-of-the-range Jaguar XJ6 for you to pootle along as though you're driving some poxy old Skoda.'

'I've got a van in front of me, Joycie. I can't bleedin' overtake it; I can't see what's coming the other way.'

Joycie tutted and glanced at her watch. Four times she'd made Stanley drive over to Rita and Hilda's since they'd brought their new car home and four times her friends had been out, or pretended to be.

'I bet they're hiding behind the bastard curtains. They've always been jealous of me, Stanley,' Joycie said suspiciously on their last visit.

'Don't be so bleedin' daft. Rita and Hilda ain't got a jealous bone in their bodies. They're obviously just out, Joycie. People's lives don't revolve around you, you know,' Stanley reassured her.

Joyce smirked as Stanley turned into the road she and he had once lived in. It was only ten past seven and if Rita and Hilda had been avoiding her, then she would have the last laugh this morning.

'You wait here, Stanley, while I go and fetch them. Then you can take us all for a nice drive somewhere pleasant.'

About to say that seeing as they were in Upney, there was nowhere pleasant to drive to, Stanley clamped his mouth shut again. What Joycie wanted, Joycie got, so there was little point arguing with the deranged woman.

Joyce strolled up Rita's path first, banged on the door and, without waiting for an answer, did the same at Hilda's.

'Whatever's the matter, Joycie?' Rita shouted, looking out of her bedroom window. She had her hair in rollers and, even from a distance, Joyce could see she had a discoloured white dressing gown on.

288

'What the hell's going on?' Hilda screeched, answering the front door in a pink nightdress and fluffy slippers.

As proud as a peacock, Joycie pointed to her new car. 'I've come to take you both for a ride in my new top-of-the-range Jaguar XJ6,' she announced boastfully.

'But you've just woken me up. What time is it?' Hilda asked, bemused.

'Just gone quarter-past seven, now, come on get yourselves ready. Stanley's our chauffeur for the morning and he'll drive us wherever we want to go,' Joyce replied.

'It's gonna take me a good hour or so to get bathed and dressed. Do you want to come in and wait?' Hilda asked dismally.

'Nope. Stanley and I will wait in our new car. It smells lovely and fresh and the leather seats are just so comfortable,' Joyce said, smiling.

Hilda shut the front door, picked up her phone and dialled Rita's number. 'What a fucking liberty, waking us up this time in the morning just so she can show off a poxy new car. She's off her head, that one.'

Rita agreed. 'She's a bleedin' nuisance, Hild. No wonder poor Stanley pissed off and left her that time, and why he would want to go back, I'll never know.'

Thanks to James Fitzgerald Smythe's insistence, Frankie's bail hearing was to take place at ten o'clock at Snaresbrook Crown Court instead of Chelmsford. Eddie had chosen to travel to Snaresbrook alone with Larry so they could have a good old natter about stuff in private. Stuart had last week treated himself to a BMW and had offered to pick up Joey. Raymond, Gary and Ricky were travelling together and had arranged to collect Carol Cullen on the way.

'I can't believe the Old Bill haven't released any more details. I mean, there should be something in the papers or on the news about the O'Haras' disappearance now, surely,' said Eddie.

Larry shrugged. 'All the police seem bothered about is finding out whose blood it was they found. Oh, that was one other thing I did find out. Somebody had thrown bleach all over the inside of the horse-box and the driveway to try and wash the blood away, apparently. Bar that, they don't seem that bothered, Ed. In their eyes, Jed's the kids' father. It isn't like they've been abducted by a stranger. You have to remember, they don't know that it's Jed that is no longer with us, do they?'

'I think it's fucking bollocks. I bet if it was someone else's grandkids they'd get off their fat arses and find 'em. It's because they're mine they don't wanna know, I'm telling ya. The filth have always hated me, Lal, you know that. They hated me father an' all. I bet the bastards see this as some kind of payback for all the years me and the old man led 'em a merry dance, don't you?'

'I spoke to Fitzgerald Smythe again the other day. He has no doubt he will get Frankie off, whether the O'Haras are traced or not, but he did say it will make his job ten times easier if they aren't found until after her trial. Perhaps this is something you should bear in mind if you are thinking of tracking them down. Frankie's trial is looking likely to be in August, which is only five months away, isn't it?'

Eddie stared out of the window and took in the murky weather. How could he choose between his daughter and grand-children's well-being? It was a nigh-on impossible choice, but he knew that if he was forced to, he would put his daughter's liberty above anyone else in the world.

Frankie was barely listening as her legal team pleaded for her release. All she could think about was Brett being back at the prison without her and she just hoped that the staff were looking after him properly. Frankie had begged them to let Babs look after her son in her absence, but the prison staff said that it was against the rules.

Wrapped up in her own little cocoon of worries, Frankie never heard the judge say the words, 'Application for bail granted,' and it wasn't until her dad leaped out of his seat and punched the air that she realised that she was a free woman. Well, until her trial at least.

Rita and Hilda were sitting side by side in the back of Joycie and Stanley's new car. Both women were used to a bit of tedi-ousness in their everyday lives, but as Joyce rambled on about the car's fixtures and fittings yet again, Hilda and Rita glanced at one another in pure boredom.

'We're gonna have to be getting back now, Joycie. I've gotta take the cat to the vet at eleven and I've got tons of washing and ironing to do first,' Rita said politely.

'And I ain't even had a chance to wash me bleedin' fanny yet,' Hilda whispered in Rita's ear.

'What's so funny?' Joyce asked in annoyance as both her friends burst out laughing.

Joycie's angry tone only made Rita and Hilda laugh all the more. Both suddenly saw the funny side of being woken at some unearthly hour, being forced to go for a drive, then having private lessons on the workings of a Jaguar XJ6.

'I said, what are you bloody laughing at?' Joycie asked, this time turning around in her seat.

'We're laughing at you, Joycie. I don't think you realise how funny you are at times,' Rita commented, holding her sides.

'You've explained every detail of the car to us three times over and we still don't know what the fuck you're talking about,' Hilda added, crippled with laughter.

Furious that her friends were amused rather than impressed by her new car, Joyce punched her husband on the arm.

'Ouch, that bleedin' hurt. What was that for?' Stanley asked, bewildered.

'Turn the car around now, Stanley, and drive back to Upney. I refuse to be mocked by jealous, classless fools.'

The words 'jealous' and 'classless' made Rita and Hilda both laugh all the more. The reason being, if they had to pick one woman in the world that those words summed up, then that woman would be Joycie.

Thrilled to have now collected her baby from prison, Frankie was in reasonably good spirits on the journey back to Essex. Her dad had wanted her and Brett to stay at his cottage but, not ready to make friends with Gina just yet, Frankie had flatly refused and had opted to stay with Joey and Dominic instead.

Eddie was on cloud nine as he sat in the back of Larry's motor. He had one arm around Frankie and was stroking his grandson's cheek with the other. 'I wish you'd change your mind about staying with me, babe. You really will like Gina if you give her a chance and you won't be bored with us oldies, 'cause Stuart's still living with us an' all.'

'Thanks, Dad, but no thanks. I'd much rather stay with Joey for now, if you don't mind. Perhaps when I get settled, we can go out for a meal or something and I can meet Gina properly. I feel so comfortable with Joey and Dom and I don't fancy sharing your cottage with people I don't even know.'

'You'll love Stuart. He's a great lad and a real gentleman. He's the sort of geezer you should have ended up with. He's coming back to Joey's for some grub, so I can introduce you to him properly.'

Frankie looked at her father in horror. 'Don't you dare start all that! I've had enough of blokes to last me a lifetime, and all I'm bothered about from now on is my children. If you want to help me, then concentrate on finding Georgie and Harry for me, rather than finding me a husband.'

Eddie chuckled. Frankie might have lost her liberty for a while and had temporarily lost her kids, but she hadn't lost her spirit, bless her.

'So who else is gonna be at this meal at Joey's? You haven't invited all and sundry, have you?'

'Nope. There's just me, you, Lal, Dom, Joey and Stuart. Gary, Ricky and Raymond ain't coming back. The boys said they'll take you out for lunch once you're acclimatised to the outside world once again.'

'What about Nan and Grandad?' Frankie asked.

'Joey didn't want to tell them about your bail hearing just in case it all went tits-up. They don't even know that Georgie and Harry are missing yet. Joyce rang me up to tell me she'd seen the Old Bill at the O'Haras' house, but I played it down 'cause I didn't wanna upset her. Joey thought it best to wait until you got out and then tell 'em. At least then he'd have some good news to tell 'em as well.'

'I wish I knew if Jed was dead or not, Dad. I wouldn't worry quite so much if I knew Alice was looking after the kids. Jed's pure evil, no one knows that more than me and that's why I'm so concerned for their safety,' Frankie said, her eyes brimming with tears.

Larry glanced at Eddie in his interior mirror. They locked eyes and Larry nodded his approval.

Eddie moved his daughter's hair out of her eyes. Now he had the OK from Larry, he could sort of tell her the truth. 'Don't cry, angel. I'm gonna tell you something now, but you mustn't tell anyone, OK? Can you promise me that?'

Frankie nodded.

'Now I swear on my life this has nothing to do with me, but Larry heard through the grapevine that it was Jed that got killed and that's why the O'Haras have bolted.'

'How do you know?' Frankie asked in shock.

'A little birdie told Larry, but if you tell anyone, Frankie, you'll get us all banged up, because Lal got the info off an insider, if you know what I mean?' Eddie lied.

Frankie sat in stunned silence. Images of Jed flashed through her mind. His piercing green eyes, the night they'd first made love, his proposal when he'd asked her to marry him.

'Are you OK? You ain't upset, are ya?' Eddie asked her gently.

Banishing the good memories from her mind, Frankie pictured her grandad Harry's face. What goes around comes around, she thought silently. 'I'm not upset. I hope Jed rots in hell,' she replied bluntly.

Larry and Eddie both breathed a sigh of relief. They'd been a bit worried as to how she might take the news. 'We will find Georige and Harry very soon, Frankie,' Larry promised.

Frankie looked at her father for reassurance. 'Do you honestly think we will, Dad?'

'Has your old man ever promised you something and not delivered?'

Frankie shook her head.

'And has Larry ever broken his promises to ya? He promised you'd be coming home today, didn't he?'

When Frankie's face suddenly lit up with a big grin, Eddie and Larry both chuckled.

What neither man realised, as they jovially continued the rest of their journey, was that for the first time in their lives, they had both made a promise that neither would be able to keep.

CHAPTER THIRTY

2001 – seven years later

'Georgie, stop, no!' Frankie cried, thrashing about under her quilt. Seconds later, she woke up crying.

Desperate not to return to her nightmare, Frankie switched on the bedside lamp. Today would be Georgie's thirteenth birthday and Frankie hadn't been able to think of anything else all week. Was her daughter happy? What did she look like now? And, most importantly, where the bloody hell was she?

It had been over seven years since Frankie had last seen either of her children. November 1993 to be exact. Harry would be eleven now, Georgie a teenager, and not knowing their whereabouts or being part of their lives had literally broken Frankie's heart. Everybody had tried to find them for her. The police, the authorities, her solicitor, her dad, but to no avail. When the O'Haras had done a runner from Rainham, it was as though they had disappeared into thin air, and even a private detective her father had hired had drawn nothing but a blank.

Jed not being found had allowed Frankie to walk free at her trial. She had gone down the self-defence route, saying that her ex regularly battered her. Kerry, her friend, had backed up her story and the jury had, thankfully, believed every word of it. Obviously, they had no idea that Jed was dead. No body had ever been found and Frankie often had nightmares about him as well. She often dreamed that the bastard was still alive, and even though she knew her dad and Larry would never lie to her about such a thing, she would never truly rest until Jed's corpse was found.

Desperate to take her mind off her daughter, Frankie tried to concentrate on the day ahead. Her dad knew how badly her children's birthdays affected her every year and he was coming round to spend the day with her. He'd wanted to take her out for a meal, but knowing how upset she would be, Frankie insisted on staying indoors. How could she sit in a restaurant enjoying herself on a day like today? It was totally impossible.

'You OK, sweet child? I woke up wanting a wee-wee and saw your light on,' Babs said as she opened Frankie's bedroom door.

Frankie lifted her quilt up and gesticulated to her friend to get in bed next to her. Babs had got out of prison two months before Frankie's trial. Babs' trial had been heartbreaking. The jury had been in tears when Matilda had given her evidence via video link. Matty had spoken bravely and candidly about Peter, Babs' paedophile ex who had raped her, and Babs had been stunned to learn that he had been grooming and sexually abusing Matilda for months before she had caught him in the act. This knowledge had sent Babs spiralling into the depths of depression. She had questioned her qualities as a mother and it was only Frankie's kind and constant support that had got Babs through it.

When they first moved in together, Frankie and Babs had lived in Upney. The house belonged to Eddie. It was the same one that Gary and Ricky's mum, Beverley, had lived in until she died. The girls had been happy living there with their children, but as Brett and Kelvin neared school age, Eddie had insisted they move to a nicer area with better schools and had bought a house in Brentwood, which they now shared. Matilda no longer lived with them. She was twenty now, and a couple of years ago had succumbed to the drugs scene. Once again, Babs had blamed herself for her daughter's troubles, but Matilda was, thankfully, clean now, working as a trainee hairdresser and was living with her grandma in West London.

'So, what are our plans for today?' Babs asked brightly. She knew how difficult today was bound to be for her friend and she was determined to try and keep Frankie's spirits up in any way she could.

'Dad, Joey and Dom are coming round about one. Dad's bringing the kids with him as well, so we'll have a bloody houseful. I'm not cooking; we'll order a takeaway later.'

'Ain't Gina coming?' Babs asked. She really liked Eddie's wife, but knew Frankie had never truly accepted her as part of the family.

'No, her mum's broken her leg, so she's gone to Ireland to visit her for a few days.'

'I bet you are glad about that, ain't you?'

Frankie shrugged. Gina was so nice and had always been so warm towards her that it was impossible to actually dislike her. Frankie was always polite towards her whenever their paths crossed, but Gina wasn't her mum and, no matter how hard she tried, she never bloody would be.

'And what about Stuie-wooie, is he coming over?' Babs said, tickling her friend's neck.

'Stop it,' Frankie said giggling. The Stuart situation was a standing joke between her and Babs. He was always popping round to the house and, over the years, he and Frankie had become really good friends. Stuart was handsome, funny, kind, and offered a great shoulder to cry on when she needed one, but Frankie had never looked at him in a romantic way. Jed had put her off romance for life.

'Well, is he coming?' Babs asked again.

'I dunno. I suppose he might.'

Babs chuckled. Stuart owned a flat that was only five minutes from their house. He'd lived there with his girlfriend, Emma, for years, but had split up with her last year, just before they'd been due to get married. The relationship had run its course. 'I'll always love Em, but we were more like brother and sister in the end,' was all Stu had said when Emma had moved back to her parents' house.

'Stuie-wooie wanna get in them panties of yours,' Babs teased her friend.

'Well, he's got more chance of getting in yours than mine. Now drop it, will ya?' Frankie said getting annoyed.

'Sorry. I was only trying to cheer you up,' Babs replied apologetically.

Frankie turned to her best friend and hugged her. 'I know you were, mate, but there ain't gonna be nothing that cheers me up today, I'm afraid.'

Babs had left the bedroom door open and as Brett and Kelvin ran in and both leaped onto the bed, Frankie managed a smile. Brett had just turned seven. He was such a happy child, with dark brown hair, eyes to match and a loving nature. Not only was he the light of Frankie's life, but he was also her saviour. If it wasn't for Brett, Frankie would never have coped at all with losing her other children. She would have given up if it hadn't been for the strength of her feelings for her son. Brett was literally her life now, and she hated letting him out of her sight. Even when he went to school, she fretted, in case the O'Haras turned up there and kidnapped him.

'Can we go to the park, Mummy?' Kelvin asked Babs. He and Brett were like brothers. They were inseparable and loved sharing their bedroom and toys with each other.

'Why don't we go to the park, Frankie? We'll only be moping around in here until your family arrive. It'll do us and the boys good to get a bit of fresh air.'

'Please, Mum, I wanna feed the ducks,' Brett said, looking at her with his big, brown, soulful eyes.

Frankie got out of bed and put her dressing gown on. 'Bath first, then we'll go to the park.'

As Brett and Kelvin jumped up and down on the bed with excitement, Babs grinned. She loved living with Frankie and the kids. They really were just like one big, happy family.

Over in Rettendon, Eddie Mitchell was on the verge of having a nervous breakdown. Since Aaron and Rosie had been born, he'd always considered himself to be a hands-on dad, but Gina's absence from home had proved he was anything but.

'What has Mummy told you about making your own breakfast, eh?' Eddie said as he mopped up the milk and soggy Frosties that were scattered all over the kitchen floor.

'Well, you weren't up,' Aaron replied cheekily.

Eddie stared at his son, who was standing two feet away with his hands on his hips. At six years old, Aaron really was a chip off the old block. He was a ringer for Ed at the same age. He had dark hair, the same-shaped eyes and had also inherited Eddie's temper and cockiness.

'Get your arse upstairs now, and choose what you're gonna wear today,' Ed ordered him. That was another thing they had in common, style. Aaron refused to wear anything Gina bought him that he didn't like and demanded to wear what he wanted.

'Make me,' Aaron replied, grinning.

As Ed raised his hand and moved towards him, Aaron laughed, ran out of the kitchen and up the stairs.

Sitting at the kitchen table, Rosie was happily munching on her breakfast. Most of the Frosties and milk were down her pyjamas, as she had a terrible habit of completely missing her mouth. 'Finish,' she said proudly, pushing her dish away.

Smiling at his daughter's beauty, Eddie lifted her into his arms. Unlike his and Gina's, Rosie's hair was as blonde as blonde could be. Joey was blonde, like Jessica had been, and his grandson Harry had been blonde, but nobody else in his family had blonde hair, other than his dear old mum, whom he barely remembered. That's why they'd named her Rosie. His mum's name had been Rose, but everyone had called her Rosie because of her beautifully coloured complexion, his dad had told him.

'You're all stinky. Pooh,' Eddie said, rubbing noses with his daughter.

Rosie giggled and Ed laughed with her. Her hair was curly and her beauty was topped off with long blonde eyelashes, big blue eyes, and an infectious smile that made everybody she came into contact with melt.

'Chocolate, Daddy,' Rosie said, pointing towards the fridge.

'Nope, bathtime, missy, and if you're a good girl for Daddy, you can have some chocolate later.'

'Humpty Dumpty, Daddy.'

Singing his own version of 'Humpty Dumpty', which included Rosie's name in it, Eddie carried his little angel up the stairs.

Over in Rainham, Stanley was sitting in his pigeon shed talking to his beloved birds. Bertha and Sid were the only two he had left now. The others had all flown the nest and, at seventy-two years old, Stanley thought he was a bit too old to invest in any more. The thought of croaking it before his birds filled Stanley with dread, and he'd made Jock promise to take good care of Bertha and Sid if they were still alive when he was gone.

'I'll always look after your Joycie for you an' all, make sure she's OK, like,' Jock had said sensitively.

'Sod that wicked old witch, she can look after her bleedin' self. You just make sure you look after me babies for me,' Stanley replied truthfully.

Seeing his wife putting the washing out on the line, Stanley lifted Bertha up in his hands. 'Who's that 'orrible woman out there, eh? It's Joycie, isn't it?' he said in a silly, childlike voice.

Spotting his wife glance over at the shed, Stanley ducked down quickly. They'd barely said a word to one another for the past two weeks, since the unfortunate incident with the car. Stanley hadn't felt comfortable driving for the past couple of years, his eyes weren't what they used to be and he was a bit doddery with his pedal reactions. On the particular day in question, he and Joycie had been on their way to Tesco in Rainham when he'd accidentally hit the accelerator rather than the brake and had ploughed into the back of a 103 bus. The Jaguar was a write-off. Joycie had gone totally ballistic. She'd called him every name under the sun and used every swear word that had ever been invented. They'd both been taken to hospital in an ambulance to be checked over and Joycie had even continued her assault in the back of that.

'Gertcha, you brainless, bald-headed old bastard. Thinking of that fucking Pat with the big tits instead of concentrating on the road, were ya? You dirty, disgusting old pervert,' she'd screamed at him in front of the paramedics.

Unbeknown to Joycie, Pat the Pigeon had passed away last summer. Brian from the pigeon club had told him the news. Pat had been living with a chap fifteen years her junior and had died of a heart attack, apparently. Stanley had never laid eyes on the woman since the day he'd moved out of her house. He'd avoided every pigeon race he knew she'd be at. He would never get over the vulgar ordeal that she'd put him through, and he often wondered if it was her appetite for nookie that had finally killed her. Thoughts of Pat were erased from Stanley's mind as the shed door flew open.

'Get your arse upstairs and get washed and changed. Joey and Dominic are picking us up. We're going over Frankie's for the day, to help cheer her up.'

Stanley immediately put Bertha away. 'Yes, dear,' he said, almost methodically.

'And put something decent on. Wear your grey slacks and that nice blue shirt I bought you last Christmas.'

'Yes, dear,' Stanley said again. He shut the shed door, locked it and smiled. After fourteen unbearable days, Joycie had finally forgiven him.

After a pleasant stroll around the local country park with Babs and the boys, Frankie returned home to find Kerry sitting on the doorstep. Once upon a time Frankie and Kerry had been inseparable, but since she had come out of prison, Frankie made excuses whenever Kerry asked to meet up. Being with her old pal brought back too many bad memories and hearing Kerry drone on endlessly about her two sons, Freddy and Sammy Junior, depressed Frankie no end.

'All right, what you doin' here?' Frankie asked, forcing a smile. Kerry had been brilliant at her trial, which made Frankie feel all the more guilty for blanking her invitations.

'If Mohammed won't come to the mountain, or whatever the saying is,' Kerry said, giving Frankie a hug.

'Sit in the lounge with Babs while I make us a cuppa.' Frankie told her.

Kerry did no such thing and instead followed Frankie into the kitchen. 'I brought you a bottle of wine. I know what day it is today, so I thought you could probably do with some cheering up. Ain't Brett got big? Christ, I could have walked past him in the street and not even recognised him. Why don't we ever see each other any more, Frankie? You ain't seen Sammy Junior or Freddy for yonks and I'd love you to be part of their lives. I was gonna bring them with me today, but I didn't want to upset you. I know how hard it must be for you still not knowing where Georgie and Harry are, but we shouldn't lose contact, mate, not after everything we went through together.'

Not in the best of moods anyway, Frankie decided to be brutally honest for once. 'I'm really sorry, Kerry, but everytime I see you it just brings all the bad stuff back to me. Don't get me wrong, I'm thrilled that you still have your boys, but seeing them upsets me too much. It reminds me of Georgie and Harry, and whenever I see you, I think of Jed and Sammy as well. I wish I didn't, but I do, mate.'

Kerry put the bottle of wine on the side and stared at Frankie. The hurt expression in her eyes was clear to see and Frankie felt awful when tears started to stream down Kerry's face. 'I'm really sorry you feel that way, Frankie, and to say you've hurt me is an understatement. I shall leave you in peace now, and I won't contact you any more. If we can't be friends that see one another, there's no point in us staying in touch at all.'

'I don't want us to lose touch completely. You'll always be my friend and I can never thank you enough for all the stuff you said at my trial. Please let's not fall out over this,' Frankie begged.

Kerry picked up her car keys and walked towards the front door. She had come here today to find out what the hell was going on and now she had, it was time to leave.

'Good luck with the rest of your life, Frankie. With an attitude like yours, you're gonna need it.'

'Are you OK, sweet child?' Babs asked as the front door slammed. She had been in the living room and had heard every word of the conversation.

Frankie shrugged. 'I'm a bit sad, but I'll be OK. I hate being reminded of Jed and Sammy, so a clean break is best all round, I suppose.'

Babs had always liked Kerry and didn't agree at all with the way Frankie had just treated the poor girl. Deciding to keep her thoughts to herself for now, she smiled. 'Shall we have a glass of wine and cheer ourselves up?'

Frankie grinned. 'Yeah, sod it. Why not?'

Knowing that Georgie and Harry's birthdays usually turned into a melancholy piss-up, Eddie got Stuart to pick him and the kids up in his motor.

301

'Why you not drive, Dad? You gonna get drunk?' Aaron asked bluntly.

'I can't get drunk while I'm looking after yous two, but I shall have a few, boy,' Eddie replied. Since Georgie and Harry had been abducted, he and Frankie had always spent their birthdays together and got rat-arsed. Christmas Day was the same; without the alcohol they just couldn't cope on these sad occasions.

'What's in the bag?' Eddie asked, pointing at the pink gift bag that was sitting in the footwell next to his legs.

'A gift for Frankie,' Stuart replied.

'What is it, then?'

'A pair of cowboy boots. She spotted 'em in Brentwood town centre last week when we were walking past a shop, so I went back the next day and bought them for her. I thought it might cheer her up, especially on a day like today.'

'You're a star, Stu, and I wish you and her would stop arsing about and get it together,' Eddie replied.

'She don't look at me in that way, Ed. Jed put her off geezers for life, I think, and I don't wanna spoil our friendship by complicating things.'

Eddie raised his eyebrows. He was well aware that Stuart was in love with his elder daughter, even though he would never openly admit it. 'If you don't make a move, you'll never know how Frankie feels about you, will ya? Think about it, Stu, she's a pretty girl and if you don't snap her up, somebody else will.'

By the time her dad arrived, Frankie was on a proper downer. Gary and Ricky had unexpectedly turned up with their dimwit, silly-voiced wives and everytime either of the girls opened their very Essex-sounding mouths, Frankie felt like clumping them one.

Gary and Ricky had been destined to be playboy bachelors for the rest of their lives until they'd met identical twenty-one-year-old twin sisters, Nicole and Amy, in a London nightclub in the summer of 1999. At the time the girls had both been working as successful models, but since marrying Gary and Ricky in a joint wedding in the Bahamas last year, both Nicole and Amy had jacked in their careers at the insistence of their respective husbands. They now spent their days shopping, lunching and pampering themselves at health farms and beauty parlours.

Frankie had hated her brother's wives on sight. They were incredibly thick, had skinny-minnie figures, long blonde hair, false boobs and the most stupid laughs and voices that Frankie had ever heard. In fact, they really put a capital D into the expression 'dumb blonde'.

'You all right, babe?' Eddie asked when Frankie opened the door with a face like thunder.

'No I ain't. Gary and Ricky have bought them two silly tarts with them, and Nanny's half-pissed already and keeps having a go at grandad. I only wanted a quiet day and every bastard's turned up. There ain't even enough chairs for people to sit on.'

Eddie wasn't the biggest fan of Gary and Ricky's wives either. He liked a woman with a brain, and Nicole and Amy unfortunately didn't own one between them. Still, they made his sons happy, so they couldn't be all bad.

'Calm yourself down, they won't stop long,' Eddie responded, hugging his daughter to his chest.

'Frankie, look at my wabbit,' Rosie said, waving a bright pink fluffy toy.

Frankie bent down, picked up her little sister and smothered her in kisses. Rosie was absolutely adorable and her presence never failed to cheer Frankie up, however bad her mood. Aaron was cute as well, but he could be a boisterous little sod at times and was forever breaking Brett's toys, which pissed Frankie off no end.

'Brett and Kelvin are in the garden if you wanna go and play with them,' she said, ruffling her little brother's hair.

As Aaron ran off, Eddie nudged Stuart. 'Where's the bag?'

'I'll get it out the car later,' Stuart said. He didn't want to make himself look like a knob by giving Frankie her present in front of the whole of her family. He'd rather do it later when most of them had gone home.

Babs helped Frankie pour everybody a drink. 'Have you got to pick Jordan up later?' Frankie asked her friend as she clocked her pour herself another one.

Babs smiled and shook her head. Her elder son, Jordan, was fourteen now and football-mad. He played for a local team on a Saturday and today his friend's mum was dropping him home for her.

Joey thanked Babs for his drink, then turned to his father. 'The O'Haras' house looks well posh now. Me and Dom had a good nose at it as we drove past earlier. It's all been painted and they've laid new grass all around the front. Whoever bought it is obviously a keen gardener, as they've planted trees and all sorts. Did you ever find out who the bloke was that supposedly sold it, Dad?'

Eddie glanced at Gary and Ricky. The O'Haras' gaff had been sold about a year after their disappearance, and finding out that it wasn't in Jimmy's name and instead was in the name of a traveller from Birmingham called Johnny Bullock was a real kick in the teeth for Ed and the police. It was Larry who had got hold of the inside information on Bullock, and Ed and the lads had gone to Birmingham to pay him a little visit. Neither they nor the police had had any luck finding him, though, as he'd also done a disappearing act.

'No. We're still looking for him, though, and I'm sure if we find him, he'll lead us to Jimmy. I've got loads of people on the lookout. In fact, I had a phone call from an old pal who has links to Wolverhampton yesterday. He gave me the address of a remote site there where a geezer called Bullock lives. Ray and Terry are gonna check it out on Monday for me.'

'You should have seen Baldwin clump that flash bastard that cut us up the other day, Dad. The geezer flew about four feet in the air; he was a big old lump an' all,' Ricky said, laughing.

Eddie grinned. Gary and Ricky had been extremely dubious when he'd first taken Baldwin on, but Terry was loyal, hard working and over the years had become a great addition to the firm. In fact, he had one of the best right-handers on him that Eddie had ever seen in his life.

'Did I hear my Raymond mentioned?' Joycie asked, walking into the lounge with yet another brandy and Baileys in her hand.

'Yeah, I was just saying Ray is shooting up to the Midlands for me on Monday,' Eddie replied.

'What a terrible son that boy's turned out to be, ain't he, Stanley?' Joyce shouted out.

'Did you call me, dear?' Stanley asked, running into the lounge like a naughty schoolboy. Even after all these years he still never felt comfortable sitting in the same room as Eddie. He was always polite to him for Joycie's sake, but he would much rather play with the children in the garden than breathe the same air as the man who had brutally murdered his daughter.

'Yes, I did. I was just telling Eddie and the boys what a terrible son our Raymond is. Never visits us, does he? And even if he does pop in, he's always got that monster of a child with him. What a spoilt little bastard that is.'

Eddie burst out laughing. As per usual, after a few bevvies Joycie was as blunt as blunt could be. In this case she was right, though. Chelsea was now six years old and was Polly and Raymond's only child. She'd been totally mollycoddled since she was a baby and was given everything she wanted. Raymond and Polly had recently had three attempts at IVF and Ed just hoped that one day it would work, because if it didn't there was little hope for Chelsea's future.

'I don't think it's Raymondo, it's the bloody mother. Ray was telling me Polly even bought Chelsea a designer handbag recently. I mean, what the fuck does a six-year-old want a designer handbag for?' Eddie said, sticking up for his pal.

'Who you talking about?' Frankie asked as she walked into the room with Babs.

'Chelsea. Do you wanna sit down?' Stuart asked, standing up, and offering Frankie his chair.

About to sit down, Frankie saw Nicole stick her tongue in Gary's ear and at the same time put her hand on his groin. 'Excuse me. We're meant to be having a family get-together to mark Georgie's thirteenth birthday, not a fucking orgy,' she said.

Joey, Dom, Stu, Babs and Eddie all laughed. Stanley and Joycie looked at one another in disgust. Slobbering all over one another in public was something they'd never done, even when they were courting.

'Can we go now, babes?' Nicole whined at Gary. What Frankie had said had gone in one ear and straight out the other. She couldn't help it if she had a high sex drive, could she?

'Yeah, we need to make a move, guys. We've got to get our

nails done and have a sunbed before we start getting ready for the party tonight,' Amy added.

Gary and Ricky stood up and both gave their sister an awkward hug. 'Keep your chin up today. I know it's difficult, girl, but we'll never give up looking for Georgie and Harry for you. One day we'll find 'em, I know we will,' Gary promised her.

Frankie saw her brothers out and went to check on the kids in the garden. The house her dad had bought for her and Babs to live in had five bedrooms and a massive garden, so there was plenty of room for the kids to play happily in.

'Sing to me, Frankie,' Rosie shrieked, running towards her. She was a sturdy little girl with chubby little legs to match and as she neared Frankie she held her arms out to her. Taking hold of Rosie's hands, Frankie had tears in her eyes as she remembered singing the same song to Georgie when she was her sister's age.

'Ring a ring o'roses, a pocket full of posies, atishoo, atishoo, we all fall down,' Frankie sang.

Rosie giggled as she fell onto the grass. 'What a matter?' she asked, realising her big sister was crying.

'Nothing. I'm just being silly because I love you so much,' Frankie replied, scooping Rosie into her arms.

The rest of the day was full of laughter and tears. Most of the laughter came via Joyce, especially when Eddie said he was sorry to hear the Jaguar had been written off and asked Joyce if they were going to buy another car.

'Not on your nelly. That dirty old pervert nearly killed me! He can't drive no more, he's bleedin' senile,' came Joycie's humorous reply.

The sadness was all centred over conversations about Georgie and Harry, and there wasn't a dry eye in the room when Frankie asked, 'Do you think when she's sixteen, Georgie will try and track me down? Or do you think she's totally forgotten who I am?'

At nine o'clock everybody bar Stuart and Dominic were quite inebriated. The Chinese takeaway had been greedily eaten by all and Jordan had just taken Brett and Kelvin up to bed.

'Oh dear, I feel ever so giddy, Stanley,' Joycie said, laying her head on her husband's lap.

Stanley immediately jumped up. Joyce had laid her head right near his crotch area and any woman's head that came within a foot of his John Thomas would always dredge up terrible memories of what Pat the Pigeon had done to him that time.

'I'll drop you and Joycie home, Stanley. Come on, Joey, time to go,' Dominic said, shaking his boyfriend's shoulder.

'Where's Madonna?' Joey asked, half asleep.

'We left her with our neighbour, you pillock. Now stand up will you?' Dominic said sternly.

'I'd better make a move now an' all. You all right to drop me off home, Stu?' Eddie asked.

Stuart nodded.

'You carry Aaron and I'll take Rosie,' Eddie said, nodding towards his kids, who were both sound asleep on one of the armchairs.

'How's Auntie Joan now, Dad? She weren't well last time I saw you and I meant to ask after her earlier,' Frankie enquired, as she followed her father towards the front door.

Eddie grinned at the mention of his favourite aunt. His dad's brother Albert had died a couple of years back, but even though they were now all in their eighties, Joanie, Vi and Reg were all still going strong. 'She's fine, babe. She'll outlive all of us, will Joanie,' Ed replied, chuckling.

As Stuart unlocked his BMW, he immediately spotted Frankie's present. He put Aaron in the back and grabbed the bag. 'Get in the car, Ed. I just wanna give this to Frankie,' he said, running back towards the house.

Frankie was still standing at the front door. 'What's that?' she asked.

'Have a look inside and you'll find out.'

Frankie looked inside the gift bag. 'Ahh, Stu, you shouldn't have done that, you silly sod. Why did you buy them for me?'

'Because you liked 'em, you doughnut. I also thought you might need a bit of cheering up today.'

Frankie put the bag down and flung her arms around Stuart's neck. 'Thanks ever so much, mate, that's really thoughtful of ya.'

'I'd better go, else your dad'll be cursing,' Stuart said. He was enjoying the feel of her body against his a bit too much.

307

'You popping round again tomorrow?' Frankie asked him.

'Why don't me, you, Babs and the kids all go for a Sunday roast tomorrow? My treat.'

'We'll come with you, but you ain't paying for us all. Me and Babs can pay half towards it.'

'Whatever. I'll pick you up at one,' Stuart said, walking away. Frankie rarely let him pay for anything for her and he knew deep down it was because she didn't feel romantically about him. There was little point in arguing with her, because if he did, she wouldn't go for the bloody meal.

Babs giggled as Frankie shut the front door. 'You and that man gonna get married one day. You a match made in heaven, sweet child.'

Frankie glared at her friend. Babs hadn't changed since they'd first met in prison. Her mass of afro hair was exactly the same, her smile could still light up a room, and she was, unfortunately, still a bloody wind-up merchant.

'Don't start all that bollocks, 'cause I'm telling you now – see me? I'm never gonna marry anyone. All men are wankers, Babs. I hate 'em.'

CHAPTER THIRTY-ONE

Georgie O'Hara put on her red low-cut top, wiggled her voluptuous hips and smiled at her reflection in the mirror. Her ripped jeans clung to her buttocks and legs like they were moulded to her skin and the new top she had bought yesterday showed off her fantastic cleavage, just as she'd known it would.

Most girls her age were still in bunches, playing with their dolls, but not Georgie. She was extremely aware of her sex appeal and, with her pretty face, long legs, mass of dark wavy hair and ample breasts, she looked more like an eighteen-year-old, rather than a young girl who had just entered her teenage years.

'What you doin' in there? I hope you're not putting that crap on your face again,' Alice shouted, banging on her granddaughter's bedroom door.

Georgie quickly put on her black Puffa jacket and zipped it up to the neck. She checked that she had her make-up and compact mirror in her pocket, then flung open her bedroom door. 'I told you, I threw the make-up away. If you don't believe me, search my bloody room,' she replied, her voice full of attitude.

Alice stared into her granddaughter's fiery green eyes. When Georgie was angry, beauty shone from her like a beacon and her stunning looks worried Alice immensely. She was already a hit with the boys, especially that Ryan Maloney, who was always sniffing around.

'You're not too old for a cuddle, are you?' Alice said, smiling. She hated rowing with Georgie, liked to keep the peace.

Georgie obediently put her arms around her nan's plump

body and hugged her lovingly. Unlike most of her friends' nans who were ugly old bats, Alice was still quite attractive. She had stunning green eyes, which were enhanced by her jet-black, thick hair and Georgie was actually quite proud of her. The only thing that grated on her was that her nan still treated her like a little girl, and she was anything but.

'What you up to today? Not going out with that boy again, are you?' Alice asked worriedly.

Desperate to avoid the usual long-winded interrogation, Georgie decided to lie. 'No, Nan. I'm goin' pictures with Josie, and then I'm gonna go shopping with my birthday money.'

'Enjoy yourself, then, and make sure you're back by nine,' Alice shouted as Georgie shut the trailer door. She liked it when Georgie went shopping and to the pictures with young Josie. It was what little girls should be doing at her age, not knocking about with boys all the time. Feeling happy, Alice picked up her duster. She was proud of her luxurious five-bedroom mobile home, especially when it was gleaming, and she had two women coming over later for a reading.

When Alice dusted the photo frames, she took extra care of the ones that held pictures of the deceased. There was a beauty of Jimmy holding her grandson, Lukey boy, and a lovely one of her son, Mark, on his wedding day. Alice picked up the photo of Jed and Sammy sitting side by side on their horse and cart. Jed and Sammy had been more than just cousins, they'd been best pals, business partners and had spent their whole lives together as if they'd been joined at the hip, bless them.

'God rest your soul, boy,' Alice said as she put the photograph back on the cabinet.

Feeling mournful all of a sudden, Alice made herself a brew and took it outside to drink. It was a warm day for March, the birds were singing and the sun was shining brightly. Sitting on the step, Alice tilted her head towards the sun's rays. She loved living in Scotland, preferred it a thousand times more than living in that doomed house in Essex.

Alice shut her eyes and allowed her mind to drift back to all those years ago when Jimmy had first bought their house in Rainham. It was certainly lavish and very posh, but Alice had had bad vibes about it from the moment she had first stepped over the threshold to view it. 'I don't like it, Jimmy. We'll have no happiness living here. Please don't buy it, let's stay where we are,' Alice had pleaded.

Desperate to get one up on Eddie bloody Mitchell, who he knew had enquired about the property, Jimmy had ignored her advice and bought the poxy place. Alice shook her head. If only Jimmy had listened to her warnings, their lives would have been so very different. The house had been cursed from the word go. So much badness had happened while they'd lived there, it was beyond belief. Jimmy having an affair had set the ball rolling. Alice had left him for years, but when she finally forgave him and moved back home, everything else started to go wrong. Jed got involved with Eddie Mitchell's slut of a daughter, Frankie. Marky boy was killed by Eddie's brothers, and just when Alice thought things could get no worse, her grandson Luke had had his brains blown out at poor Marky's funeral. Then there was the last murder, the final nail in the coffin that had forced them to do a moonlight flit to Jimmy's pal's plot of land in Scotland.

'Why fucking Scotland?' Alice had screamed at her husband at the time.

'Glasgow is the perfect place for us to hide out with the chavvies. It has such a small travelling community, it'll be the last place anyone comes looking for us and even if they do, they'll never find us on Mickey Maloney's land,' Jimmy had reassured her.

For once, her husband had been right. Mickey Maloney owned five acres of land situated off the southbound carriageway of the A80. Mickey's family also lived on the land, along with four other travelling families. They were a happy, tight-knit little community that trusted one another implicitly and Alice had become especially friendly with Sarah, who lived in the mobile home opposite her.

Hearing the sound of her son's cumbersome tipper truck approaching, Alice snapped out of her daydream and opened her eyes. When she and Jimmy had first moved to Scotland, they'd refused to tell their son Billy their whereabouts, because they didn't trust his big-mouthed wife, Shannon. Billy had left Shannon just over a year ago and had since moved to Glasgow with his eighteen-year-old son, Mush. Alice loved having her son and grandson living next door to her. After losing so many important people in her life, the family she had left meant the world to her.

'You seen or heard from your father on your travels?' Alice asked, with a hint of annoyance in her voice. She'd been trying to get hold of Jimmy earlier, but he wasn't answering his bloody phone.

'Yeah, I spoke to him earlier. He was dropping a horse off in Stirling, then he was going for a game of cards with the lads.'

Knowing full well that whenever her husband played cards, he rolled up home pissed, Alice batted her eyes in pretend annoyance. She wasn't really angry, though. As the old saying goes, boys will be boys.

Harry O'Hara ducked behind a tree as he saw the farmer's Land Rover heading towards him and urged his pal Sonny to do the same. 'Right, let's do this quick while the coast is clear,' Harry said, with a mischievous glint in his eye.

At eleven years old, Harry was virtually unrecognisable as the timid little boy he'd once been. His once almost white hair had now darkened and was more of a messy strawberry blonde. He had a front tooth missing, which had recently been knocked out in a fight with some older boys and, worse still, he'd picked up every bad trait he had ever heard his father talk about.

''Ere cacker, you chase the kanny towards me and I'll catch it,' Harry ordered Sonny. Kanny was the Romany word for chicken.

The bird clucked and darted about for a good five minutes before Sonny and Harry managed to corner it.

'Gertcha, ya shitcunt,' Harry shrieked, grabbing the chicken by its scrawny neck.

Knowing it was about to die, the bird let out one more tired cluck. Seconds later it went to chicken heaven.

Jimmy O'Hara was with Mickey Maloney and four other travelling lads in a pub called the Babbity Bowster in Glasgow town centre. Rumour had it the boozer was named after a Scottish country dance, but Jimmy didn't know if there was any truth in the fable or not. Jimmy sorted through his cards and confidently smirked. There was over three-hundred quid in the kitty and if he didn't win this game of nine-card brag, he'd eat his fucking hat.

'Come to Daddy,' he said, as he laid his four sevens onto the sticky table.

'You're a jammy cunt, O'Hara,' Mickey Maloney said, laughing.

'Same again?' Jimmy asked, standing up.

'One for the road and then we'd better get home to them women of ours,' Mickey replied.

Jimmy was in a jolly mood as he strolled up to the bar. Life in Glasgow was wonderful, and since moving from Rainham, apart from selling a few motors and horses, Jimmy spent his days in the boozer and his evenings with his family. He had no need to work any more. He'd sold the house in Rainham for nearly two million quid, and could quite easily manage on the proceeds if he lived to be a hundred. Jimmy smirked as he thought about how clever he'd been about that house. He'd originally bought it in 1978 and, because he was dodgy-dealing at the time, had put the deeds in Johnny Bullock's name. Johnny Bullock was the closet friend that Jimmy had ever had. They were brought up together as kids and were more like brothers than mates. At the time Johnny had owned an incredibly successful building empire, therefore trust wasn't an issue. Jimmy had obviously treated Johnny for his massive favour. He'd given him ten grand back in the day and another fifty when he'd sold the gaff in 1995. Johnny had now moved to the Costa Blanca. He'd always been a fucker for the young birds and had recently married a twenty-year-old Spanish tart called Adriana. Johnny's address was still registered to the authorities as Birmingham and this thought always made Jimmy chuckle because it was another master stroke he'd managed to pull off against Eddie Mitchell. Jimmy rarely thought about Mitchell any more these days. He still wished him dead, but he could no longer be bothered to kill the man himself. Jimmy was fifty-eight now, age had mellowed him to some extent and he just wanted to live the rest of his life in peace. Too many of his family had already lost their lives because of his feud with Mitchell, and Jimmy couldn't bear the thought of losing any more.

'Three times I've just asked you – what you want to drink? Are you OK, pal?' the young barman asked, waving his hand in front of Jimmy's weatherworn face.

Jimmy automatically snapped out of his trance. 'Yes, mush, I'll have the same round again. Sorry about that, I was miles away, boy.'

Ryan Maloney groaned with pleasure as he ran his hands over Georgie O'Hara's perfect breasts. He knew she was young, very young, but she looked so much older than thirteen and he couldn't help the way he felt about her. Lunging his tongue inside Georgie's mouth, Ryan put her hand on the zip of his jeans.

'Wank me off, babe. Please just do it the once,' he begged.

Georgie immediately snatched her hand away. She knew the effect she had on Ryan Maloney and she thoroughly enjoyed tantalising him.

'Stop it, Ryan. You know I'm not gonna do it,' Georgie said, flicking her hair seductively over her naked shoulder.

'But I love you Georgie, you know I wanna marry you when you're sixteen.'

Spotting Ryan's hardness clearly showing through his jeans, Georgie purposely brushed her hand against his penis as she lent on his leg to stand up. 'Where's this special birthday present you keep banging on about, then?' she asked. He'd already given her three presents yesterday, but had held one back for today.

'Touch me cory for ten seconds and you can have it,' Ryan replied cheekily.

'I'll touch it for five, but only if you keep it inside your jeans.'

'Deal,' Ryan replied, grinning.

Georgie did as she'd promised and smiled as Ryan caught his breath, shut his eyes and shuddered. At fifteen years old, Ryan was the youngest son of Mickey Maloney. Like Georgie,

Ryan didn't go to school, but his arms and legs were full of muscle where he'd always worked for his dad. He only did odd jobs and stuff, but they had given him a physique of a twenty-one-year old. Ryan had short, dark brown hair, bright blue eyes, a cheeky smile and had been the heart-throb of all the travelling girls until about six months ago. It was then that Georgie had sprouted enormous breasts, grown a few inches and had virtually changed from a child into a woman overnight. Ryan had become besotted with her, and they'd been a couple ever since.

'Never give yourself to a mush before he marries you, Georgie. Once men get their wicked way with you they lose interest almost immediately and you don't want people to think you're a slag like your mother was, do you now?' her nan had said in one of her many birds and bees talks.

Georgie inwardly laughed at her nan's words of advice. She had been streetwise from a very young age and, apart from letting Ryan Maloney fondle her naked breasts, had no intention of doing anything overly sexual with him until he married her. Ryan's father was extremely wealthy and Georgie knew full well that once she and Ryan were wed she would live a charmed life and want for nothing.

Ryan stood up and grinned as he pushed his groin against Georgie. He put his hands on her juicy buttocks and kissed her passionately.

Georgie touched tongues with Ryan, then immediately pushed him away. 'Er, present,' she said stroppily, holding out her right hand.

'Shut your eyes, then,' Ryan urged her.

When Georgie did as he asked, Ryan put his hand inside the pocket of his jacket and placed a small, red velvet box in her hand. 'You can open 'em now,' he told her.

Georgie opened the box and squealed with delight as she clocked the ring. It was a round gold band with what looked like diamonds in the centre of it. 'Give us it 'ere. I wanna put it on for ya,' Ryan said, placing it on her wedding finger. 'You know what this ring means, don't you, Georgie?'

'No.'

'It's an eternity ring,' Ryan told her.

315

'What's that mean, then?' Georgie asked, showing her young innocence for once.

Ryan lifted up her left hand and gently kissed the ring. 'Eternity means that me and you are gonna be together for ever.'

Georgie grinned. She'd captured her man, got a ring to prove it, and couldn't wait to tell all the other girls on the site. They would be so bloody jealous.

Alice O'Hara was just dishing up her homemade shepherd's pie when Jimmy walked through the door, looking slightly worse for wear.

'You must smell me dishing up, Jimmy O'Hara. Nose like an elephant's trunk you've got. Where ya been? I've been trying to ring ya all day.'

'Pub,' Jimmy replied curtly, as he drunkenly sparred up to Harry.

'What pub? You ain't been to that one with the funny name that's miles away again, have ya? I wish you wouldn't drink and drive like that. Say the gavvers catch ya? Can't you drink somewhere nearer home?'

'I like the Babbity Bowster and I'm fine driving back from there. Anyway, even if the gavvers do catch me, I've got me licence in the name of Jones, ain't I? You worry too much, woman.'

Alice sighed. Apart from their old friends and fellow travellers, who knew who they were, they introduced themselves by the surname of Jones to anybody else they came into contact with now. You could never be too careful, especially when you were on the bloody run.

'Gotcha, Grandad,' Harry yelled, as he landed a right hook on Jimmy's chin.

'That hurt, you little fucker,' Jimmy chuckled, as he wrestled his grandson to the floor.

'He is a little fucker an' all. Bought home another dead chicken that he'd nicked off the farmers again today. I wish you'd have a man-to-man chat with him, Jimmy. If he gets caught and the gavvers nick him, it might blow our cover.'

'Of course it won't. I've told you a thousand times, woman,

316

all our documents are cushti and they're all in our new name. We ain't Alice and Jimmy O'Hara no more, we are Alice and Jimmy Jones, so for fuck's sake stop worrying about it.'

'Your dinner's getting cold. You gonna stop arsing about and eat it? I don't slave over a hot stove all day for the fun of it, you know.'

Jimmy playfully slapped his grandson around the head, sat at the kitchen table and greedily began shoving the food into his mouth. 'Where's Georgie girl?' he asked, showing Alice a large mouthful of shepherd's pie as he spoke.

'Supposedly went shopping and to the pictures with Josie, but I saw Josie come home with her parents earlier, so I know Georgie's with that bloody boy again. I wish you'd have a word with Micky Maloney, Jimmy. Ryan might be a nice enough lad, but our Georgie's too young to be courting a mush of that age. There's no point me asking silly bollocks to talk to him, 'cause that dinlo's all for their relationship. He won't be saying that when she comes home pregnant though, will he?'

Jimmy roared with laughter. He had every faith in Georgie girl. She might only be young, but she was clever, not stupid. He also liked Ryan Maloney. The boy's father, Mickey, was cakeo and his granddaughter would never want for anything if she married his son.

'Whatever's wrong with you today, Alice? Did you get out of the bed the wrong side this morning, my sweet?'

Harry smirked. He loved winding his nan up by being crude. 'Georgie knows what she's doin', Nan. She says she only lets Ryan touch her titties and she's not gonna touch his cory until he marries her.'

Picking up the tea towel, Alice walloped her foul-mouthed grandson straight around the head with it.

Georgie and Ryan's love-nest was an old barn that belonged to Ryan's father. It was where all the groping, kissing and cuddling took place and they'd even put two pillows and an old quilt in there, so they could lie side by side in the warmth if the weather was cold.

Ryan held Georgie's hand as they took the short walk back to their respective mobile homes. 'I've got to go to Fife with my dad tomorrow to look at a gry, but I'll be back late afternoon. I'll get us some cider and I'll meet you in the barn about six,' Ryan said.

'You can ring me again now. I got another phone for my birthday and I got the number written down for you.'

'Thank fuck for that. I hated it when I didn't know where you were. You're my woman now, Georgie. That's what that ring says and don't you ever forget it.'

Georgie dragged Ryan round the back of her neighbour's mobile home and began snogging him again. She put his hands on her breasts and smiled teasingly.

'You'd better stop that or you'll get me shot,' Ryan said, as he heard the familiar sound of the Mitsubishi Shogun's engine pulling in.

'The old man ain't gonna shoot you. He knows we're a couple and he likes you. Come and say hello to Shelby with me,' Georgie said.

'You all right, Georgie girl?' Lola asked, spotting her stepdaughter appear from the shadows. Lola was only seven years older than Georgie, so they were more like sisters than stepmother and daughter.

'Is Shelby awake?' Georgie asked hopefully. She loved her little sister dearly.

'No, she's soundo,' Lola answered, lowering the sleeping child in her arms to prove it.

'You all right, darling? Been looking after her for me again, have you, Ryan?'

Ryan grinned. 'Of course! Your daughter won't come to no harm while she's with me, so you've got no worries on that score.'

Bursting with pride, Georgie couldn't help showing off the ring that Ryan had given her. 'This was my surprise birthday present from Ryan. It's an eternity ring. Do you like it, Dad?'

CHAPTER THIRTY-TWO

Frankie felt bright and breezy when she arose the following morning. The migraine she'd had the previous day had now cleared and she felt ready to face the world again.

'You look nice. Are you looking forward to seeing Matty?' Frankie asked her friend as she ventured into the kitchen.

When Matilda had briefly dabbled with heroin, Babs had been devastated and so disappointed with her, but since her daughter had got herself clean their relationship had got back on track again.

'Yeah, I am. Kelvin's coming with me and I'm gonna take both of them to Oxford Street. Then later, my mum's gonna cook us all chicken, rice and peas for dinner. I'm gonna stay at my mum's tonight. Jordan's gonna stay at his mate's house. Will you be OK on your own, Frankie?'

'I'll be fine. I'm gonna let Brett have a day off school and Stuart's gonna take us both for lunch.'

'Is that the same Stuie-wooie who wants to get into those panties of yours?' Babs asked teasingly.

'No, it's the same Stuie-wooie that we were meant to go out with yesterday, but couldn't 'cause I was ill. I only said I'd go today 'cause I felt horrible about letting him down.'

'Pull the other one, it's got bells on,' Babs said, laughing.

At the other end of Great Britain, Georgie O'Hara was sitting in Josie's trailer and was desperately trying to comfort her friend, who had just been told that her mother's cancer had returned. Georgie wasn't very good with situations such as these and as Josie started to cry, she desperately searched for the right words to say to her.

'I know it's awful, but if your mum did die, you would get over it you know. I ain't seen my mum since I was four and as far as I know, she could be dead an' all,' she said tactlessly.

'Do you ever think about your mum?' Josie asked, genuinely interested. It was the first time she had ever heard Georgie actually mention her mother.

'Not really, but I still sort of remember her. I sometimes wonder if I look like her or if we're alike in our ways, but other than that, I don't think about her much at all.'

'What was she like? What do you remember about her? Was she pretty?'

'I think so. I know she had long dark hair and she used to give me lots of cuddles, but I don't remember much else. I never talk about her indoors 'cause everybody hates her. My Nan calls her "the old shitcunt" because she tried to murder my dad once.'

'Really?' Josie asked in amazement.

'Yep, she went to prison and everything,' Georgie replied.

'Is she still in prison now?'

Georgie shrugged. 'Dunno and I don't really give a shit, to be honest.'

'So, where we going then? Aren't we just going to Brentwood town centre?' Frankie asked, as Stuart took a turn in the opposite direction.

'Nope. I thought Brett would get bored there, so we're goin' somewhere he'll like for a change.'

'Where, Stuie? Where?' Brett asked excitedly.

'Southend, boy.'

'What's there, then?' Brett asked, bemused.

'There's a fairground, amusement arcades and proper fish and chip shops,' Stuart explained.

'Yes!' Brett shouted, bouncing up and down excitedly.

Frankie did not share her son's enthusiasm. Her last trip to Southend had been with Jed in the early stages of their relationship. They'd gone to a hotel by the seafront and it was there that Frankie had lost her virginity to him.

'Are you OK? You're all right with Southend, ain't ya?' Stuart asked, aware of Frankie's sudden silence.

'Yeah, course,' Frankie lied. She stared out of the window as all the memories came flooding back. That was the day Jed had bought an old tape recorder for fifty quid off a girl in the reception. He'd then got his cassettes out of his motor and they'd danced to Tammy Wynette's 'Stand By Your Man' before they'd finally fallen onto the bed and made love for the very first time. Oh, how stupid and naïve I must have been, Frankie thought silently.

'You ain't 'arf gone quiet, girl. What you thinking about?' Stuart asked her a couple of minutes later.

Determined not to spoil a day out that she knew her son would enjoy, Frankie turned to Stuart and smiled. 'I'm just thinking how thoughtful and kind you are. You'll make a lovely husband to some lucky girl one day, you know.'

Stuart raised his eyebrows. He wanted to tell Frankie that he would like her to be that lucky girl, but as usual, he didn't have the guts to say anything.

Eddie Mitchell was relieved as he heard Gina's car pull up outside. Looking after the kids on his own had done his head in and he now realised just how hard women worked when men were out grafting.

'Mummy!' Rosie and Aaron screamed excitedly as they ran to greet Gina.

'Why aren't you at school?' Gina asked her son.

'Had a sore throat,' Aaron lied.

Gina grinned as Eddie put his arms around her. 'How's your mum?' he asked.

'Fine. She's driving me dad mad again, so she must be on the mend. What about you? Did you cope all right with the kids?'

'Piece of piss. I dunno what yous women moan about,' Eddie replied untruthfully. Admitting he'd struggled to cope with anything just wasn't part of Ed's make-up.

'Your phone's ringing, babe,' Gina told him, hearing his familiar ringtone.

Eddie ran indoors. Raymond and Terry had driven up to Wolverhampton early that morning to check out a gypsy site where Johnny Bullock might be hiding out, and as Eddie saw Raymond's number flashing up, he hoped the news was good for once. 'Well?' he asked expectantly.

'No joy, Ed. There is a Johnny Barrett living there and also a Robbie Bullock, but neither are our man, mate.'

'Are you absolutely sure?'

'Positive. We did some snooping around with the locals before we went there and both families come from Liverpool. We then checked the site out and they all have Scouse accents, unlike our man, who supposedly comes from O'Hara's neck of the woods.'

'Fuck,' Eddie mumbled as he ended the call.

'What's up?' Gina asked, walking into the lounge with her daughter in her arms.

'Just another lead we had to the O'Haras that's gone by the wayside.'

'Oh, I'm sorry, Ed. Shall we go out for lunch? I can't be bothered cooking today?'

'McDonald's!' Aaron shouted.

Eddie picked his urchin of a son up and dangled him over his right shoulder. 'Little boys with sore throats shouldn't eat McDonald's, so we'll have to go to a boozer instead.'

'Says who?' Aaron asked cockily.

Eddie looked at Gina and laughed. 'Says me, you cheeky little shit.'

Surprisingly for Frankie, once she got over the initial shock of returning to Southend, she found she actually enjoyed herself. Peter Pan's was like a proper fairground and watching Brett's excitement reminded her of when she and Joey were young.

'Me mum and dad took me and Joey to the fairground once. I think it was the Dagenham Town Show, actually. Oh, it was hilarious, Stu. Joey was a right wimp when he was a kid. He was travel sick and would spew up at the drop of a hat. Anyway, he didn't like the rides and 'cause my dad was always trying to toughen him up a bit, he forced Joey to go on a scary one with him. I can't remember what ride it was, but within seconds of them getting on it, Joey sicked up all over my dad's expensive clothes. You can imagine the old man – he went mental and we were dragged straight home after that,' Frankie recalled, laughing.

Stuart chuckled and decided to drop one of his regular hints. 'Your dad's a top geezer, you know. I would never have got

322

through my sentence if I hadn't been sharing a cell with him. That's what you should look for in a geezer, Frankie, someone who has your father's manner and qualities.'

Frankie linked arms with Stuart. 'Sod off. Men are off the menu for me, and as long as I've got you as a mate, I'm happy.'

Alice O'Hara was not having the best of days. Georgie's eternity ring had worried the life out of her when she'd set eyes on it this morning. Then she'd done a reading for her neighbour, Mary, and had seen the woman's husband, Bill, being terribly injured in some sort of accident and, to top it all, Harry had just been driving Jimmy's truck up and down the road and had accidentally run over Mary's lurcher dog and killed it stone dead.

'Get in 'ere now, you little fucker,' Alice screamed, as Harry studied the dead dog that was lying, mouth open, in the middle of the site.

'I didn't mean it – it run out in front of me, Nan,' Harry said, defending himself.

'What have I told you about nicking the keys to your grandfather's truck? You're too short to see over that steering wheel, you dinlo.'

'No I ain't and anyway, it's only a bloody dog,' Harry snapped.

'But it ain't no stray, is it? It's Mary's dog. I wouldn't mind, I looked into me crystal ball not two hours ago and saw her poor husband having a bad accident.'

'Well, perhaps you got Bill mixed up with the dog, then,' Harry said, giggling.

'Don't push me, Harry, 'cause I'll give you such a good hiding you won't know what day it is. Now, where's your sister? I ain't seen her since this morning.'

'Probably playing with Ryan's cory,' Harry replied cheekily.

As Alice lunged towards him, Harry ducked her swipe and ran outside laughing.

Frankie was now sitting in a fish restaurant under the arches in Southend thoroughly enjoying the taste of freshly caught cod and chips. Then, without warning, Brett piped up with the question she'd always dreaded him asking.

'Mummy, I know Stuart is my pretend daddy, but who is my real daddy? Why don't I see him?'

Frankie's hunger immediately vanished and she put her knife and fork down. 'Why are you asking, darling? Did somebody tell you to ask?'

Brett nodded. 'Josh, my best friend at school.'

Stuart squeezed Frankie's hand under the table. 'Do you want me to help out?' he whispered in her ear.

Frankie shook her head. Jed was her mistake; therefore it was her duty to explain so to her son. 'Mummy was very young when she met your daddy, Brett. I was only sixteen when I fell pregnant with your older sister, Georgie, and then eighteen months later I was pregnant with Harry, your brother. As time went on it turned out your dad wasn't a very nice person, sweetheart, that's why we split up and that's why you don't see him.'

'Why ain't he nice?' Brett asked confused.

'He used to hit Mummy. He did lots of other stuff as well, which I'll tell you about when you're a bit older.'

'Will I ever meet him?' Brett asked, picking a chip up with his fork.

'I don't think so, love.'

'What about Georgie and Harry? Can I meet them?'

Seeing Frankie's eyes well up with tears, Stuart automatically stepped in. 'One day you will, Brett, but not just yet. Now, no more questions, eat them fish fingers before they get cold, boy.'

After recovering from his earlier annoyance over Raymond and Terry hitting yet another brick wall, Eddie Mitchell had had a rather jolly day. They'd taken the kids to a boozer with a playground and he, Gina and the children had all enjoyed themselves immensely. Gina had offered to drive home so that Ed could have a good drink and as he glanced in the back at his zonked-out children, he had a naughty urge come over him.

'Stop it, Ed,' Gina said giggling, as he put his hand up her skirt and moved it towards her thigh.

Ed stared at her excited expression as he ignored her request. 'Pull over somewhere where there's no houses,' he ordered.

'No, and please stop doing what you're doing, in case I crash the bloody car.'

Ed found her clitoris with his middle finger and smirked as Gina gasped with pleasure. 'I said, pull over,' he said, putting her left hand on his swollen penis.

A mile down the road, Gina was so turned on that she had no choice other than to comply with her husband's orders. 'We're only a short distance from home. I'm not doing anything in the car in case the kids wake up,' she said maternally.

'Turn the engine off, lock the doors, and you see that tree over there? I'm gonna fuck your brains out against it.'

'We can't leave the kids in the car on their own,' Gina said anxiously.

'We're only ten yards away from 'em, babe and they're soundo.'

About to argue, Gina smiled as Ed unleashed his rock-hard manhood from his trousers. 'Come on, then, let's be quick though.'

On the journey back from Southend, Stuart did his best to cheer Frankie up by chatting away endlessly and telling silly jokes. As she laughed at his latest quip, he glanced at her and could see that her laughter wasn't quite reaching her eyes.

'We're nearly home now. Shall I come in for a nightcap or not?' he asked her hopefully.

'Not tonight, eh? That fairground's worn me out,' Frankie replied, falsely yawning.

Stuart drove the last few minutes of the journey in silence and only spoke again when he spotted a car parked outside Frankie's drive, blocking it. 'Who the fucking hell's this piss-taking bastard?' he mumbled in annoyance.

Frankie stared at the black Golf and gasped as she recognised the girl that got out of it.

'What's a matter? Do you know her or something?' Stuart asked, concerned.

'She's a pikey. I was inside with her. What the fuck does she want? Why has she turned up here?'

'Stay in the car, I'll sort it,' Stuart said gruffly.

'Please get rid of her. I hate her,' Frankie begged him.

'What do you want?' Stuart asked, as he slammed the door of his BMW. The girl had long brown hair and looked as rough as old boots, so he could understand why Frankie didn't like her very much.

'I need to speak to Frankie. It's really important,' the girl replied in a strange kind of accent.

'You talk to me, then,' Stuart said angrily.

The girl ignored Stuart, ducked past him and ran over to the car.

Frankie was frightened now and quickly locked her door. She'd always thought that Katie was one of Jed's spies and wondered if Jed had sent her to snatch Brett. 'Go away, leave me alone!' she screamed tearfully.

'Please listen to me, Frankie. I'm trying to help you,' Katie pleaded with her.

'Right, that's enough, get in your car and fuck off,' Stuart warned, grabbing Katie by the shoulders.

'Frankie, I know where Georige and Harry are,' Katie screamed as she was dragged away.

'Get in the car and lock the doors, Stuart. I'll speak to her,' Frankie shouted out.

'Don't get out, she might be a fucking loony,' Stuart said apprehensively.

Frankie ignored his advice and, as he got back in the car, she got out and nervously faced Katie.

'What's a matter? Is Mummy OK?' Brett asked, crying. All the shouting had woken him up.

'Your mother's fine. She'll be back in a minute,' Stuart reassured him.

'What do you mean, you know where my kids are?' Frankie spat, as she walked towards Katie.

'They're in Scotland. They're living on a private site in Glasgow with Jed, Jimmy and Alice.'

'You fucking liar. Jed's dead,' Frankie screamed.

Katie glared at the angry girl she was so desperately trying to help. 'No he ain't. Jed's alive and if you'd just trust me for once, I can prove it to ya.'

CHAPTER THIRTY-THREE

Frankie was shell-shocked as she stared at Katie in a gobsmacked silence.

'I ain't lying. I swear on my chavvies' lives, I ain't lying,' Katie said.

Stuart lifted Brett out of the back of the car and walked towards where Frankie and Katie were standing. 'What's goin' on?'

'She reckons Jed's still alive and is living in Glasgow with Georgie and Harry,' Frankie replied. She felt sick and her legs and hands were shaking uncontrollably.

Stuart glared at Katie. If she was building Frankie's hopes up and playing some sick joke, he would personally kill the fucking girl himself. 'Let's go inside. We can't talk properly out here,' he commented sensibly.

'So, what's the address? Have you seen my kids? What do they look like?' Frankie rambled. She had so many questions, she didn't know where to start.

'What's a matter, Mummy?' Brett asked, tugging Frankie's arm.

'Can you put him to bed for me and then pour us all a large brandy or something?' Frankie asked Stuart.

As Stu left the room, Katie answered some of Frankie's questions. 'I went to a family funeral a few weeks back and my cousin Danny was there with his wife, Trisha. When Trish's pissed, she's a bit of a blabbermouth and she was the one that told me about Jed. They'd been loads of rumours flying about over the years as to why the O'Haras had disappeared. Some people thought Jed had been murdered, but Trish reckons his cousin Sammy was killed, not him. That's why the O'Haras left, apparently, 'cause they knew the bullets were meant for Jed.'

'Have you got an actual address for him?' Frankie asked. She was still very sceptical.

'No, I couldn't ask too much, 'cause I didn't want people to get suspicious, but I wrote down all the info I managed to get out of Trish for yer. I was worried I'd forget it if I didn't.'

As Stuart walked back in the room, Frankie told Katie to repeat what she'd just said. Stuart felt his hand tremble slightly as he poured out the brandies. If what Katie was saying was true, and Terry Baldwin had shot the wrong person, Eddie would go fucking apeshit.

Frankie studied the piece of paper that Katie had given her. 'Who's Babby Bower?' she asked, confused.

'It's the pub in Glasgow Jimmy O'Hara drinks in. I dunno if I got the name exactly right, I ain't much good at spelling, but that's what it sounded like.'

Stuart handed the girls their drinks and snatched the piece of paper from Frankie. 'Who's Mickey Maloney?' he asked Katie.

'He's the bloke that owns the land where Jed and the kids are meant to be living. Jimmy and Alice live there as well, so Trish reckons.'

'So, why did this Trish tell you all this?' Stuart asked suspicously.

'Because she knows that Sammy raped me and I had his kid. She wanted me to know that I ain't ever got to worry about him turning up again. It was my cousin Danny that told her Sammy was the one that got murdered and Jed is still alive. Trish might have been drunk when she told me, but I know she weren't lying. The truth comes out in drink, don't it?'

'Where you going?' Frankie asked, as Stuart got up.

'To get me phone out the car. We need to tell your Dad all this, Frankie.'

'No, you can't tell him. He'll go mental; he'll do something stupid and get himself locked up again. Ring DI Blyth instead, I've got her number in the address book, she'll know what to do,' Frankie insisted.

Usually Stuart allowed Frankie to get her own way with things, but on this occasion he couldn't. Ignoring her advice, Stuart picked up his car keys and walked out of the room.

Over in Rettendon, Eddie Mitchell was winding up his wife. When they'd stopped the motor earlier, she'd thoroughly enjoyed their spur-of-the-moment liaison, but since returning home she'd had her appalled head on instead.

'Don't you ever do that to me again, Eddie Mitchell. It wasn't even that dark. Say the police would have pulled up or something? They'd have definitely reported us to social services for leaving the kids unattended.'

Eddie laughed out loud. 'A bit of spontaneity never hurt anyone, and you certainly weren't complaining earlier.'

'I'll answer that while you pour me another glass of wine,' Gina said haughtily as the phone rang.

Ed took a bottle of Pinot Grigio out of the fridge and was about to open it when Gina dashed into the kitchen. 'It's Stuart. He said it's really urgent.'

Eddie snatched the phone off her. 'What's up?' he asked. When Stuart answered his question, Ed's face paled within seconds.

'I'm coming over right now. Keep the girl there,' he insisted.

'Whatever's the matter?' Gina asked him.

Eddie picked up his bunch of keys and ran to the front door. 'I'll explain later.'

Frankie spent the next twenty minutes firing question after question at Katie. She was now ninety-nine per cent sure that the girl was telling the truth, but she would never be totally convinced until she saw her children with her own eyes. Over the years, because she had thought Jed was dead, Frankie had tried to erase what he had done to her grandfather from her mind. Apart from Babs and DI Blyth, she had never told another living soul about her and Kerry's discovery, but if Jed was still alive, perhaps she should have told her dad. If he ever found out that she knew, her dad would disown her, Frankie was sure of that.

'Explain to my dad outside what's happened, so I can talk

to Katie alone for a minute,' Frankie said, as she heard Ed's car pull up outside.

'I'd better go soon. I left the kids with my sister and she'll be wondering where I've got to.'

'You'd better leave your address and phone number, in case I need to contact you again. I'll give you my number an' all. How did you find out where I live, by the way?'

'I've known roughly where you lived for a while. I only live in Basildon meself and I have a lot of mates round this way. One of my mates, Dawn, her son David goes to the same school as your Brett. Dawn don't live anywhere posh like you, though. She lives in a tower block near the town centre. Anyway, I asked her to follow you home from the school so I could come and see you myself.'

Frankie had heard Aaron mention a boy called David. 'So is David's mum a traveller?' she asked, paranoid. Her dad had moved her from Upney and bought the house in Brentwood just so Brett could go to a better school and mix with a better class of kid. Also, if this David's mother was a traveller and Jed was still alive, she might tell him which school Brett attended and he might try and abduct him as well.

'No, Dawn ain't a traveller. Apart from my own family, I don't mix with many travellers. Most of my mates are gorjer girls.'

Suddenly the lounge door flung open and Eddie flew into the room like a man possessed. 'This best not be some kind of a sick fucking wind-up, 'cause if it is and my daughter gets her heart broken once again, I'll break more than your heart and I mean that,' he snarled at Katie.

'Dad, stop it. See, this is why I didn't want him involved – I knew he'd lose the plot,' Frankie screamed. Katie looked petrified and if Eddie continued shooting his mouth off and making dumbass threats, then he would lose them the only bloody lead to her kids that they had. 'Katie's not lying. I know her well enough to know that much. She hates the O'Haras just as much as we do,' Frankie said, glaring at her father.

'I'd better go now. Do you wanna meet up again tomorrow?' Katie asked, standing up.

'Oh no you don't,' Eddie spat, standing in front of the girl so she couldn't leave.

Frankie stood up and with fire in her eyes, ordered her father to sit down and calm down. 'I've got Katie's address, home number and her mobile number,' she told him.

'And have you checked out the address and tried ringing the fucking number?' Eddie asked cockily. He hated pikeys so much that he found it hard to believe that there was a decent one among their breed.

'Ring my mobile now if you like, and my landline. My sister will answer 'cause she's looking after the kids for me at my house,' Katie said worriedly.

Frankie did what Katie had suggested and was relieved as her mobile rang. She then tried her landline and handed the phone to Katie as a woman answered. 'Tell my mate how we're related, and also tell her whose house you're at now and the address,' Katie asked.

Frankie put the phone to her father's ear as Katie's sister confirmed what they had already been told. She gave the phone back to Katie, waited until she'd ended the call and took her by the arm. 'Right, you get home to your kids now, mate, and I'll call as soon as I have some news. If the news is good, I'll take you out for a nice meal to say thank you.'

'Follow her,' Ed ordered Stuart as Frankie showed the girl out. Anyone could change their phone number, but it was more difficult to change their bloody abode.

'Where you goin'?' Frankie asked, as Stuart walked towards the front door.

'I've just gotta pop out for a bit, I'll be back soon.'

Frankie poured herself a vodka and her dad a Scotch. 'So, what's the plan? Can we go to Scotland tomorrow? If I ring DI Blyth, I reckon she'll come with us. If we turn up with the Old Bill in tow, the O'Haras will have to give me my kids back.'

'No, we ain't involving no Old Bill, so you can get that silly idea out your head.'

'Why not? Blyth's always been good to me and I know she'll help me get Georgie and Harry back.'

'Because if the O'Haras get one whiff of the filth, they'll gallop off faster than Red Rum once could. Seriously, Frankie, the Old Bill are fuck-up merchants, most of 'em couldn't catch a cold, love. I'll get ya your kids back and as soon as I bring 'em home, you can ring that Blyth bird and tell her what's happened. Until then, you don't tell a fuckin' soul, OK?'

Frankie nodded.

'Right, I'm gonna make some phone calls. I ain't schlepping all the way up to Joanie's gaff at this time of night, so I'll get all the lads over here.'

Eddie rang Larry first to tell him the score, then he called Gary, Ricky and Raymond and ordered them to meet him at Frankie's. He took deep breaths before he rang Terry Baldwin. If what Katie had said about Jed being alive turned out to be true, he would not be a happy man. With a plan forming in his mind, he punched in Baldwin's number. 'Meet me at Frankie's, mate. It's urgent,' he said politely. He ended the call and stared at the phone. 'Cunt,' he mumbled.

Stuart was back within half an hour. Ed ran to greet him and put his finger to his lips to warn him to keep schtum about where he had been. 'Where did she go?' he whispered. Stu repeated the address he had seen on the piece of paper and Eddie breathed a massive sigh of relief. Surely that Katie bird wouldn't give both her phone numbers and her home address if she was lying. Then again, knowing travellers as well as he did, the whole thing could be a set-up and the O'Haras could be waiting to blow his brains out when he got to Glasgow.

Frankie was looking out of the window.

'What you doing?' Eddie asked, as she ran to the front door.

'Letting Joey and Dom in. I rang Joey while you were on the phone, told him what had happened and asked him to come over. Don't worry, we can sit upstairs and have a drink if you need privacy,' Frankie replied sarcastically.

Joey held his twin sister in a tight embrace. 'Don't build your hopes up too much, Frankie, in case it's another wild goose chase,' he warned her.

'I think Katie's telling the truth, I really do, Joey,' Frankie told him.

'But I remember you talking about her when you were in prison, sis. You hated her and was positive that she was working as Jed's spy.'

'Oh, that's fucking great, that is. We'll probably drive up to

Glasgow and all be bastard-well shot at. Why didn't you tell me all this earlier?' Eddie shouted at his daughter.

'I thought Katie was a wrong 'un in prison, but I don't think she is now,' Frankie replied tearfully.

'Don't have a go at her, Dad, she's upset,' Joey said angrily.

'And you'll all be fucking upset if I schlep all the way to poxy Glasgow and get me brains blown out,' Ed replied unfeelingly.

'I'm gonna take Frankie upstairs. Pour us some drinks, Dom, and we can talk in her bedroom,' Joey said. He could tell his dad was in a real shitty mood and when he was like that there was no reasoning with him.

Gary and Ricky were the next to arrive and were shocked to be told what had happened. 'What you gonna do about Baldwin if he has fucked up? You gonna keep him on?' Gary asked.

Ed shrugged. 'Can't sack him, can I? He knows too much. I've only got two choices, forgive him or kill him.'

'You can't kill him Dad, Terry's a good geezer,' Ricky said, sticking up for the man.

'No point worrying about it now. For all we know, this pikey bird might be fucking lying,' Ed replied.

Raymond was the next to turn up. 'Jesus Christ,' he said, as Eddie explained the story to him.

Hearing another car engine, Gary looked out of the window. 'Baldwin's just pulled up. Now, let's not get on his case, let's just worry about getting the kids back for now, eh?'

Everybody agreed, bar Eddie. He didn't reply.

'I can't believe it. I'm positive it was Jed that I killed,' Terry said, as Gary explained what had happened to him.

'But how positive? I asked you before if you'd seen the cunt's face and you said no,' Eddie yelled, inches away from Terry's face.

'Listen, you told me that Jed would be with Jimmy that night, and I know it weren't him I killed. He had a youngster's baseball cap on, for fuck's sake. If what this girl is saying is true, then it ain't my fault. If I'd have known that his cousin was gonna be with him, I'd have made sure I clocked Jed's face when I shot him. All I know is that I killed the driver and he was a young 'un. It most certainly wasn't Jimmy O'Hara.'

'Terry's right, Ed. If we gave him the wrong information, then it ain't his fault,' Raymond said, bravely defending his colleague.

Stuart, who was usually the one to sit back and let all the others do the talking, was getting angrier by the second. 'This is fucking ridiculous. Poor Frankie is sat upstairs in bits wondering if her kids are coming home and all we've done so far is sit here blaming each other. Why don't we just concentrate on bringing Georgie and Harry home, eh? Surely that's the most important thing, isn't it?'

Eddie felt a bit guilty as he ran his hands through his hair. Stuart was right, and had made him feel like a complete moron. 'I'm sorry, Stu's right, so let's get cracking. This is the plan.'

Everybody listened intently as Eddie began to explain. 'I suggest we use two untraceable vans with stickers down the side again. I'll ring Flatnose in the morning to sort those out. Once we've got the motors, we drive straight up to Scotland. I've already found out the proper name of the boozer that Jimmy O'Hara supposedly drinks in. It's called the Babbity Bowster and the tart on directory enquiries said there's nothing of a similar name, so that's got to be kosher. What we do then is follow Jimmy back from the boozer – he's bound to be half-pissed, so won't be that vigilant. We can take it in turns to tail him, and I'll make sure Freddie gets us two completely different vans, that way Jimmy won't notice anything following him. Once we find out where the cunt's living, we keep watch on his gaff. We wait for Jimmy and Jed to both go out, snatch the kids and bring 'em home. Job done!'

Gary and Ricky glanced at one another. Their father made everything sound so easy, but in their minds his plan was full of pitfalls.

'How we gonna know what the kids look like now? There could be hundreds of kids living there, for all we know. You know what these pikeys are like, they bang 'em out one after the other,' Ricky said.

'We'll know. I'm gonna go out tomorrow and purchase the most expensive binoculars money can buy. Georgie and Harry have gotta be living with Jimmy and Alice, Jed, or both. They're my flesh and blood, I'll fucking know 'em when I see 'em, don't you worry about that,' Ed snapped.

Gary picked up the bottle of Scotch and topped everyone's glasses up. 'If Jed is still alive, he'll be down 'ere like a rocket trying to snatch the kids back. Even if he ain't, Jimmy will. We need to kill 'em, Dad. It's the only way to end it once and for all,' he said.

'Don't you think I know that? We are gonna kill 'em once the dust settles. Remember, we're gonna have to inform the authorities that the kids are back home, and if Jed and Jimmy disappear at the same time Georgie and Harry are snatched, the Old Bill will be all over us like a swarm of bees. I know pikeys don't usually deal with the filth, but that fat slag Alice will be on the phone to 'em as quick as you can say Bob's your uncle if her whole family vanish. What we've got to do is bide our time just for a couple of weeks, sort ourselves out with strong alibis, and then deal with Jed and Jimmy.'

'I doubt they'll stay on the same site or wherever it is they're living, Ed. Not if they know you know where they are,' Terry added.

'I know that. That's why you'll be staying up in Scotland watching their every movement, Tel,' Ed replied, enjoying the look of shock on the man's face.

'I can't do that, Ed. I can take it in turns with someone else if you like. My Anne will go apeshit if I fuck off for weeks on end. She moans that I'm always working all the time as it is.'

'She won't go as apeshit as I will when I find out for definite that you've shot the wrong bloke, so I'd button it if I were you and do as you're told. Anyway, if you ain't made a cock-up, then you won't need to stay up there, will ya? And if you have, you wanna think yourself lucky I don't blow your kneecaps off.'

Recognising the look of fire in Eddie Mitchell's eyes, Terry Baldwin didn't argue. 'OK, mate, I'll do it,' he replied wisely.

'Anyway, you won't be on your own, Stu's gonna be with you,' Ed informed him.

'Why me?' Stuart asked. The thought of not seeing Frankie for weeks made him feel instantly depressed.

'Because you're single. I can't let Tel do this on his own. Say the O'Haras spot him following 'em, and he goes missing or something? We never work alone, you know that, boy.'

'OK,' Stuart said, knowing he had no choice but to agree.

'How we gonna grab the kids? I mean, they ain't toddlers no more, are they?' Raymond asked.

'The same way you grabbed Frankie that night in Tilbury. We bundle 'em in the van and, if necessary, tie 'em up, Raymondo. We'll go well prepared; we might need to use duct tape on 'em or something to stop 'em screaming. They're bound to be frightened and kick up a fuss, ain't they?'

'You can't tie 'em up like hostages. They're only young and they're your grandchildren,' Ricky piped up, horrified.

Eddie smirked and shook his head in amused disbelief. He knew exactly what type of children he'd be bringing home with him, but nobody else seemed to have a clue.

'I don't care if we have to drive the whole journey with canvas sacks over the kids' heads, as long as we get them home. They ain't gonna be normal children, you know. How can they be when they've been dragged up by them scumbag cunts? They'll be loud, wild and probably fucking violent. You won't recognise their nature, and neither will I. They'll be out-and-out gypsy kids. Getting 'em home is the easy part; getting them to adjust to living a normal life will be far more difficult. You mark my words on that one.'

CHAPTER THIRTY-FOUR

Forty-eight hours later, Eddie and the boys set off for bonny Scotland. Stuart drove the blue van, accompanied by Terry Baldwin and Raymond. Ed drove the white one and was joined by Gary and Ricky.

'So did you book us somewhere to stay in the end?' Ricky asked his father.

'Yeah, I booked us three rooms in a B&B in the town centre. I rang up a few and this one was a bit dearer than the others, so it should be OK. It's only five minutes from the boozer that Jimmy supposedly drinks in.'

'Why don't we ring up the pub later and ask if Jimmy's in there? Or do you think that's a bit dodgy?' Gary asked.

'It's way too dodgy, and for all we know he might be using a different surname now. Jimmy's a slippery cunt and the last thing we wanna do is alert him that someone's looking for him. If he does another runner, we're fucked.'

'Have you let Larry know what's going on?' Ricky asked.

'Yep. Providing things go to plan, I'll bell him as soon as we've got the kids and are on the way home. He's gonna get Carol Cullen involved again, and he'll notify the Old Bill. I got that Blyth bird's number off Frankie, so he can ring her directly.'

'Just think, this time in twenty-four hours, Frankie might be reunited with her kids,' Gary said in an upbeat manner.

'Let's hope so, boy, but let's not build our hopes up too much, 'cause nothing's ever fucking straightforward when it involves Jed and Jimmy O'Hara.'

* * *

Frankie put the quilt over her head to shut out the light that was peeping through the gap in the curtains. She'd had an awful night's sleep, and every time she dozed off she'd dreamed about her kids returning home, which had then woken her up again.

'You awake, sweet child?' Babs asked, opening the bedroom door with a tray in her hand.

'You ain't cooked me breakfast, have you?' Frankie asked, sitting up.

'Two boiled eggs and two slices of toast. You have to eat something, Frankie, or you'll make yourself ill.'

'I can't face food until I hear some news. I've got butterflies in my stomach and I keep feeling sick.'

Babs sat down on the edge of the bed and handed Frankie a slice of toast. 'Please, just eat that for me,' she urged.

'I spent the whole night wondering what they might look like now. When they were kids, Georgie was the extrovert out of the two. Harry was quite timid. Do you think they'll recognise me? Say they're happy living with Jed and they don't like me or something?' Frankie said anxiously.

Babs put the tray on the floor and hugged her worried friend. She had been astounded when she'd returned from her mum's house and heard Frankie's news, and she just hoped that at long last there would be a happy ending for Frankie. 'Obviously it's gonna be a little strange for Georgie and Harry at first, but they'll soon adapt, kids always do. I'm sure they'll remember you, mate, and I bet they've wondered how you are millions of times over the years. They are gonna love you, Frankie, everybody does, so stop worrying that pretty head of yours. Now, shall we go out and do something today to take our minds off things? How about going to the pictures or having a browse around the shops?'

Frankie shook her head. 'I can't concentrate on watching a film and I couldn't face going shopping. I think I'll ring Joey, get him to come over. He's a great comfort to me when the going gets tough, he always has been.'

The journey up to Glasgow took Eddie and the boys seven-and-a-half hours. They'd spent over an hour stuck in rush-hour traffic, and had also stopped at a service station for some much-needed breakfast.

Ed wasn't overawed by the vans that they'd acquired. Flatnose Freddie knew that Eddie didn't like using big beasts for anything undercover, but because the vans had to be got at short notice, a Mercedes-Benz Sprinter and a Renault Trafic was all Flatnose could come up with. 'They're both newish, clean and untraceable, so stop worrying, they'll be fine,' Freddie had assured him.

The B&B was clean, tidy, but also very basic.

'Hardly the fucking Ritz, is it?' Raymond complained to Eddie.

'It'll do us. Hopefully, we'll only be here a couple of days – if all goes well, that is.'

Eddie unpacked his bag and hung his clothes up in the musty, old-fashioned-looking wardrobe. 'Smells fucking rotten, that does. I'm glad I never brought any good clobber with me,' he moaned.

Raymond laughed. 'Come on, let's go and meet the others.'

Gary, Ricky, Stuart and Terry were already waiting in reception. Seeing Terry in deep conversation with the owner of the B&B, Ed strolled over.

'So you're property developers, are you? Your friend was just telling me about your plans to build flats,' the woman commented.

Eddie smiled politely. He could tell the woman was a nosy old cow and made a mental note to find somewhere else for Stuart and Terry to stay when he and the others went home. 'We have to go now. We musn't be late for our meeting,' he replied, dragging Terry away.

'Don't forget, breakfast is served at eight,' the woman shouted out.

Eddie ignored her, and half-shoved the lads out the door. 'I don't like her one little bit. If we don't get no joy in a day or two, I'll check us into a hotel somewhere.'

'She was all right. She was only trying to be friendly, I think,' Terry said.

'Nah, she was a complete wrong 'un. I can sense 'em a mile off, mate,' Ed replied knowingly.

'So, what's occurring now? I dunno about yous lot, but I could kill a quick pint. My mouth feels like a nun's fucking crotch,' Ricky said blatantly.

'We ain't 'ere to party. We'll pick the vans up and plot ourselves somewhere near that boozer. The quicker we find O'Hara, the quicker we get home,' Ed snapped.

'But it's only one o'clock. Jimmy ain't gonna go for a lunchtime pint and leave this early, is he?' Ricky replied.

Ed glared at his son. 'I don't care if we stake out that boozer until ten o'clock tonight. We've come 'ere for one reason only – to get them kids back – and the quicker we achieve it, the better.'

Unaware that Eddie Mitchell was on his tail, Jed O'Hara was in an extremely buoyant mood. Marrying Lola had been the best decision he'd ever made and, for the first time ever, Jed was loyal to his woman, and felt no urge to play around with others. 'I always told you you'd be happy with a nice travelling girl, didn't I? We need to stick with our own kind, not them gorjer shit-bags,' his mum told him on a regular basis. Jed had to admit that for once she was right.

Sammy's murder had knocked the stuffing out of Jed for a very long time. The bullets were meant for him, he knew that, and if it wasn't for his psychic mother having one of her premonitions, he would now be six feet under. His mum's tearful phone call was the only reason Jed had swapped seats with Sammy on that fateful night. He had been driving the horse-box in a very drunken state, and after he'd spoken to his mum, he'd allowed Sammy to take the wheel to ensure they got home safely. Picturing his cousin's smiling face, Jed sighed. He would never forget all the blood and gore, and the look of death on Sammy's face. The images of those particular things would live with him for ever.

Sammy's father had been the one to collect his son's body and Sammy was given a private send-off less than twenty-four hours after his death. Jimmy had known the bullets were meant for Jed and had begged his brother not to involve the police. 'If you involve the gavvers, all our lives will be in danger. We'll sort things in our own time and in our own way,' Jimmy had promised, before heading up to Scotland.

'You've been quiet today, Jed. Are you OK?' Lola asked, walking into the bedroom.

'I was just thinking about life, but I'm OK. I'm not working today, so shall we do something? We can take Shelby out somewhere if you want.' Since moving to Scotland, Jed had given up his previous career of conning old people. Without Sammy by his side, it just wasn't the same and he was also afraid of getting his collar felt and blowing his cover. These days he earned his dosh buying and selling horses and motors and he also did a bit of roofing here and there. He was by no means rich, but was reasonably well off, and was happy enough with his lot. Jed stood up, put his arms around his wife and smiled.

'Well, whaddya think?'

'I think it would do you good to go out for a drink with your dad and the boys. I might take Georgie shopping. Your mum can look after Shelby for us, can't she?'

Jed looked into his wife's beautiful face and, not for the first time, thought how lucky he was. At twenty years old, Lola was seven years younger than him. She had naturally curly, long dark hair, pale blue sparkling eyes and a sunny, upbeat nature.

'I really do love you, girl. I'll go and give the old man a knock now. I fancy a pint or six.'

Lola grinned. 'You just make sure you have fun.'

Back in Essex, Frankie sat staring at the phone, willing it to ring. Her dad had told her not to call him, but had promised to call her if and when he had anything important to disclose.

'Will you stop it, Brett? You're getting on Mummy's nerves today,' Frankie shouted, as her son strummed his toy guitar and sang a silly song at the top of his voice.

'Why can't I go to school with Kelvin?' Brett asked sulkily.

'Why don't I take him to McDonald's? It'll give you and Joey a chance to have a good natter,' Babs offered.

'I dunno. My dad said not to let him out of my sight until all this is over,' Frankie replied anxiously.

'Yeah, McDonald's!' Brett shouted, jumping up and down excitedly.

'I know he said don't send him to school, Frankie, but the

341

boy needs a bit of fresh air. Anyway, nothing will have happened just yet, your dad would have called you if it had.'

Frankie shrugged. 'Go on then, but don't be too long.'

As the front door closed, Frankie's eyes welled up and she fell into her brother's arms. 'What if Katie was lying to me, or say Dad gets killed or something. And what about Stuart? He might get murdered as well, or Gary and Ricky,' she said.

'You're thinking silly now. Jed might be an arsehole, but he's hardly a mass murderer,' Joey replied, stroking his sister's hair.

'He is. You don't know him like I do.'

'What you talking about, Frankie? Who has he meant to have killed, then?' Joey asked concerned.

Knowing she had already said too much, Frankie shook her head and wiped her eyes. Her family would never forgive her for keeping her grandfather's death to herself, so what was the point of upsetting everybody? 'No one. I'm sorry, I'm just being over-dramatic.'

Eddie Mitchell was becoming extremely impatient, but more excited by the minute. He'd recognised Jimmy O'Hara as soon as he'd got out of a grey Shogun and strolled into the pub, but he hadn't recognised Jed. Raymond had, though, he'd sworn blind it was the little shit, and Ed could barely wait to follow them home.

'Over four hours they've been in there now. Surely they can't be much longer if Jimmy's driving?' he said to the lads, who were all sitting in the back of the van. It had been decided that Stuart would drive the Renault with Baldwin in the back, and Ricky would drive the Merc with the rest of them in the back.

'One good thing about 'em taking so fucking long is they're bound to be pissed and less alert,' Gary replied.

'The door's just opened again,' Ricky said excitedly.

They could clearly see the pub from where they were parked, but were far enough away to avoid suspicion. Having said that, a few locals had given them the odd glance earlier.

Eddie looked through his binoculars. 'Nah, that's some old boy. Hang on a minute, this might be Jimmy following him out, I think. Yep, he's walked over to the Shogun. Right, lads, get in the other van and you pull away before us.'

'Is Jed with him?' Raymond asked Eddie.

'Not sure, someone's just followed him out, but I can't see who, he's got his back to me now.'

When Jimmy switched the lights of the Shogun on, Eddie jumped in the back and waited for Stuart to drive past. 'Go, Ricky, and whatever you do, don't lose the cunt.'

Oblivious to the fact they were being followed, Jimmy and Jed were in an inebriated, jolly frame of mind.

'I love my Lola, you know. Never messed her about, Dad, not once since the day I met the girl,' Jed slurred.

Jimmy chuckled. He was glad Jed had found happiness, but he'd only been with Lola for three years, and he doubted his son's abstinence from other women would last for ever. 'The thing with us travelling men, Jed, is poking the same hole for years on end gets boring, boy. I mean, good luck to ya if you can do it, but if you can you're a better man than most.'

'I wanna be a good role model to my chavvies and their partners. Georgie's found herself a good 'un with that Ryan Maloney, and I'm gonna have a man-to-man chat with him now they've got serious. I won't let him mess her around, Dad. If he does, I'll beat the granny out of him.'

'You can't be beating the granny out of Ryan, Jed. He's Mickey's boy and we don't wanna upset him, do we now? Anyway, our Georgie's too young to be getting overly serious with lads. Your mother nearly had a cardiac when she spotted that ring on her finger.'

'My Georgie's mature for her age. She knows what she wants and she won't open her legs to get it. I bet her and Ryan get hitched as soon as she's sixteen. I don't worry about Georgie at all, Harry worries me more. Proper little fucker he is lately, he'll chore anything that ain't nailed down. I don't mind him choring, but I don't wanna see him getting nicked.'

'With me and you as role models, what do you expect?' Jimmy said seriously.

Seeing the funny side of Jimmy's comment, both men laughed.

* * *

343

Eddie Mitchell was anything but happy as he clambered into the front seat. 'You fucking idiot,' he said, clouting Ricky around the side of his head.

'It weren't my fault. O'Hara shot through the lights, so did Stuart, and the motor in front of me stopped dead. What was I meant to do? Shunt him off the road?'

'Just put your fucking foot down and drive. He can't have got far,' Eddie shouted.

'There's a sign saying Moodiesburn. Shall I go that way?' Ricky asked.

'I don't care which way you go, just find the pikey cunts,' Eddie yelled.

'I'll ring Tel's number and make sure him and Stu are still tailing 'em,' Gary said, trying to take the onus off his brother's mistake.

'When he answers, pass me the phone,' Ed ordered.

'There's no answer,' Gary said seconds later.

'Ring Stu then, just keep trying the fucking pair of 'em,' Eddie screamed in annoyance.

'Stu's phone's on answerphone, so is Tel's now. They must be somewhere where there's no signal,' Gary said anxiously. He knew his father was about to blow his top and that was never a pleasant sight.

Ricky drove along aimlessly for another six or seven minutes, then finally his father's phone rang.

'Did you stay with 'em, Tel?' Ed asked immediately. He listened to what Baldwin had to say, ended the call and smirked.

'We've got 'em. Tel said they're living on what looks like a private bit of land off the A80, which is the road that runs between Glasgow and Stirling. First thing tomorrow morning, we'll head down there and grab the kids.'

CHAPTER THIRTY-FIVE

Frankie didn't know if she was coming or going the following day. Her dad had rung her late the previous night to tell her what had happened, and, even though she had been sure that Katie was telling the truth, the realisation that Jed was definitely still alive filled her with dread.

'I made you a coffee, Frankie, and you must eat some food today. Brett's been crying again, he say he wanna go a school with Kelvin,' Babs said, as Frankie came down the stairs.

'I wish he could go to school, but I daren't go against what my dad told me to do.'

Babs shrugged. 'I don't see what the O'Haras are gonna do if they in Scotland, and Brett gotta go back to school sometime. Why don't you have a word with his teacher? Tell her to be extra vigilant.'

Frankie shook her head. 'I think my dad's worried that the O'Haras might know what area I'm living in and what school Brett goes to. It doesn't matter if they're in Scotland, mate, they'll still have contacts locally, and if my dad snatches Georgie and Harry, they might have Brett abducted so they can get them back again.'

Babs shuddered. 'I think I'll keep Kelvin home today an' all, then. They can keep one another amused, can't they? What about Joey, is he coming round again?'

Frankie nodded. 'Joey and Dom have booked the rest of the week off work, so they're both coming round. My nan and grandad wanted to come over as well, but I told the boys not to pick 'em up. I love 'em and all that, but they do my head in at times and I can do without the extra stress of them two arguing.'

'I tell you one thing, sweet child, when them kiddies of yours arrive home safely, you have to show gratitude to that Katie girl. I always said she was OK, didn't I? I knew she were genuine.'

Frankie put her head in her hands to hide the embarrassment she felt. 'I know, and I feel so awful for the way I spoke to her in prison. She only wanted to be my friend and just because she was a traveller, I treated her like a piece of shit. I will never judge a book by its cover again, Babs, and as soon as I've got Georgie and Harry settled, I will make it up to Katie. I owe her big time.'

Over in Rainham, Joycie was extremely perturbed by Joey's refusal to make Dominic come and pick her and Stanley up. Since her husband had written off her beloved Jaguar, Joycie had got quite friendly with her local mini-cab firm and today she had no intention of missing out on all the drama.

'Hurry up with them pigeons, Stanley, then go and get yourself spruced up. Oh, and pack your overnight bag.'

'Where we going?' Stanley asked, perplexed.

'Frankie's. I told you the other day that Eddie was going to Scotland to find Georgie and Harry. Well, Joey rang this morning, reckons he might have found them.'

'Who's coming to pick us up, Dominic?' Stanley asked.

'No, we're getting a cab. I'll ask for that elderly man, Sid. He always does a special price for me, lovely chap he is.'

'Has Frankie actually invited us over?' Stanley asked suspiciously. He knew how Joycie had a habit of turning up at people's houses when she wasn't particularly welcome.

'Nope, don't think she wanted us there, but we're going anyway,' Joycie replied stubbornly.

'We can't just turn up uninvited, love. Frankie's probably at her wits' end, and she might not want people around her if she ain't herself.'

'Well, Dominic's going round there with Joey and he's not even related. Whether Frankie likes it or not, we're the only grandparents she has and we shall be there for her in her hour of need. Now, chop chop and get your arse in gear.'

* * *

Eddie Mitchell picked up his binoculars once more. He'd recognised Georgie immediately. She looked a lot older than her tender thirteen years, but her similarity to Frankie at a younger age was uncanny. Harry was a different kettle of fish. There were nine mobile homes on what looked like a private bit of land and Ed had seen at least five lads that could pass for Harry's age, but none of them had light-blonde hair.

'That fat slag Alice has just come out her trailer again. It's gotta be Harry who she keeps speaking to, surely?' Eddie questioned, handing the binoculars to Raymond.

'It don't look like him to me, Ed, but I suppose kids change in time,' Raymond replied sceptically.

Gary snatched the binoculars that Raymond was peering through. 'It must be him; Alice has just clouted him round the head.'

'I need a slash. Keep watch for Jimmy or Jed to make a move,' Eddie said as he stood up. He'd already seen Jed earlier and, unlike the previous evening, had recognised the little shit immediately.

Gary turned to Raymond as soon as his old man was out of earshot. 'We can't just fucking run on the site tooled up and drag them off by their hair. Have a word with him, Raymondo, he'll listen to you.'

'I will, but you know what he's like, Gal. That's definitely Harry; Jed's just given him some dosh. He must be on his way out, I reckon,' Raymond replied, eyes glued to the binoculars.

Eddie's legs were as stiff as a board as he walked back to the lads. They hadn't been able to drive the vans near enough to spot the kids clearly because the O'Haras were living on private land. Terry and Stuart were parked down the road, looking after both vans and watching the front of the site, while Ed and the rest of the lads had spent the past few hours crouched down and peeping around the side of an old barn.

'Jed's just got in a pick-up truck with a bird and a little kid, and Ray's just seen him give that boy we thought might be Harry some money. It's definitely gotta be him, Dad, although I must say he looks entirely different to how we imagined,' Gary said to his father.

Eddie snatched the binoculars off Raymond and studied the

347

lad in question. He was totally unrecognisable from the timid-looking blonde-haired boy he'd known as a child.

'So what happens now, Ed? We can't just steam in there like a load of loonies. There's a few blokes other than Jed and Jimmy living there, and for all we know, they could have shooters and all sorts,' Raymond said to his boss.

Eddie handed the binoculars over to Ricky and stood up again. Debating what to do for the best, he ran his fingers up and down the stubble on his chin. 'I don't think we've got a lot of choice but to go in there like headless chickens. I mean, I can't exactly imagine, by looking at Georgie and Harry, that they go skipping out the fucking site hand in hand together, can you?' Ed replied.

Raymond shrugged. 'Can't we just watch their movements for a couple of days? They can't spend their whole lives cooped up in there, surely, so perhaps we're better waiting for either of 'em to go out and snatch 'em individually.'

'Fucking hell, Dad, our Georgie's only got a boyfriend. Look, they're going for it hammer and tongs behind the beige trailer next to Jimmy's,' Ricky said.

Eddie grabbed the binoculars off his son and stared through them in complete and utter horror. Having seen enough of his thirteen-year-old granddaughter's breasts being groped, he threw the binoculars onto the ground in disgust. 'Right, seeing that has fucking made my mind up. Let's get back to the van and as soon as Jimmy goes out, we'll give it ten minutes or so, then in we go. Them kids are coming home with me today, 'cause if they don't, I'll end up killing every single pikey cunt that raised 'em.'

Frankie glanced at her brother as their nan took the embroidered handkerchief out of her handbag and began dabbing her eyes with it.

'Truly hurt, me and your grandfather were, weren't we, Stanley? Feeling unloved and unwanted at our age is enough to kill the pair of us off,' Joyce said in a sorrowful voice.

'Frankie wasn't being horrible, Nan. She didn't even really want me and Dom to come over today. Surely you understand what a difficult time this is for her?' Joey said, sticking up for his sister.

'It's a difficult time for all of us. Georgie and Harry were my Jessica's grandchildren and she'd want me to be here for their homecoming,' Joyce replied stubbornly.

Not wanting a full-scale argument to ensue, Dominic stood up. 'Now who would like a drink? Tea, coffee, something stronger perhaps?' he asked brightly.

'I'll have a cup of tea, please,' Stanley replied.

'And I'll have a large brandy and Baileys. After feeling like some decrepit outsider, perhaps it will cheer me up a bit,' Joyce added sarcastically.

Fuming with her grandmother's insensitivity over her plight, Frankie grabbed her brother's arm and dragged him out of the lounge. 'Nan is really getting on my tits, Joey, so either shut her up or get rid of her,' she hissed.

'I can't just sling her out, can I?' Joey replied uncomfortably.

Frankie glared at him. 'Well, I'm telling you now, one more word out of that drama-queen mouth of hers and I will. I'll drag her out the door by her fucking bouffant if I have to, so best you sort her out.'

After what seemed like an endless wait, Jimmy O'Hara finally went out at two o'clock that afternoon. He had a couple of other blokes who obviously lived on the site in his Shogun as well, which in Ed's eyes was an added bonus and a good omen.

'I'm sure Jed clocked me earlier, but Jimmy didn't even glance our way,' Stuart said as O'Hara's Shogun drove past them. Both vans were parked in a nearby layby, but far enough away from the site to avoid too much suspicion.

Ed took his mobile out of his pocket and rang Gary. He had sent him and Ricky back to the barn with the binoculars so they could keep a close eye on the kids. 'Jimmy's just drove past us. Where's Georgie and Harry?' he asked. The adrenalin was running through his veins now, the excitement had kicked in.

'Harry's riding up and down on a quad bike with that other lad he was with earlier, and Georgie's just gone inside the barn with her boyfriend. We hid behind it as they walked towards us, but then we moved and hid behind some trees,' Gary replied.

Eddie paused before answering. 'Right, we'll grab Georgie first, then Harry afterwards. Stay where you are, Gal, and ring me if anything changes. I'm on my way over to you now.'

'What about the boyfriend, though? He's bound to run back to the site and alert 'em,' Gary said.

'I'll deal with that little fucker, so don't be worrying about him. Just stay where you are and I'll be with you in ten minutes.'

Eddie put his phone in his pocket and turned to Raymond. 'Grab plenty of rope and the duct tape. You come with me, and Tel, you stay 'ere with Stu. I shouldn't think Jimmy will be back for ages, but if Jed returns, or anyone else, ring me immediately. Georgie's in the barn with that lad, so I'll nab her first, then we'll drive on the site and get Harry.'

'Be careful, Ed, if you've gotta drag her across that field, someone on the site might see you,' Stuart warned.

'They won't. I'm gonna take her the long way round behind all them trees. They won't be able to see fuck-all if we go the right way.'

As he was about to get out of the van, Ed's phone rang. 'What's up?' he asked Gary.

'Harry's drove up the road on that quad bike. We've lost sight of him, but he's heading your way.'

'Fuck,' Eddie said, ending the call. 'Right Stu, take them binoculars, get in the Renault and do not lose sight of Harry. He's heading this way on a quad bike. Tel, you wait here and stay in the van. We'll need to gel quickly. Ray, you got that rope and tape?'

Raymond nodded.

Eddie opened the passenger door. 'Right. Let's do it.'

Georgie O'Hara was becoming more sexually adventurous by the day. Kissing and cuddling Ryan Maloney was something she enjoyed immensely and whenever he pushed his erection against her or touched her boobies, it made her feel all excited and tingly down below. Ryan, on the other hand, was becoming more and more frustrated with the situation. He'd slept with a dozen or so girls in the past, all gorjers, and he wanted Georgie so badly it pained him. Obviously he respected her reluctance to entertain him. Any proud travelling man wanted to marry a decent girl, a virgin, but how he was meant to wait another three years without any sexual relief at all, he just didn't know. Becoming overly rampant once again, Ryan sat himself up. He moved Georgie's hand off his thigh and unscrewed the lid off the cider bottle. He took a few gulps, then passed the bottle to Georgie.

'You don't realise what an effect you have on me, Georgie girl. I know you said that you don't wanna make love till we're wed, and I respect you for that, but can't we do something else in the meantime?'

Georgie drank some cider, handed the bottle back to Ryan and smiled smugly. She did realise what effect she had on Ryan and the thought made her feel all warm and happy inside. 'I let you touch my boobies, don't I?' she said obstinately, as she flicked back her hair in the seductive way she'd practised in her nan's full-length mirror.

Ryan sighed. 'Yeah, I know you do, but can't you touch me as well, Georgie? Please, I beg you.'

'Touch you where?' Georgie asked demurely. She knew exactly where Ryan wanted her to touch him, but she loved playing the innocent when it suited her.

Ryan put the cider bottle down, took Georgie's hands in his and stared into her eyes with a pleading look in his own. 'Look, Georgie, I'm a lot older than you and a man has needs. All I'm asking you to do is let me get me cory out and I want you to rub it for me. I can't wait three years without any pleasure at all, and I don't wanna cheat on you, because I love you too much.'

The word cheat immediately wiped the self-satisfied smile off Georgie's face. The thought of Ryan kissing or touching another girl made her feel physically sick and for once she knew he had her over a barrel. 'OK,' she said nervously. She had never seen a willy in the flesh before and instead of feeling mature and sexually confident, as she usually did, she suddenly felt like the little girl she actually was.

Feeling so aroused that he thought his penis was about to explode, Ryan stood up and lowered his tracksuit bottoms and pants to his knees.

Georgie felt anxious as she stared at his erect willy. Instead of dangling downwards as she'd expected, it was sort of poking upwards.

'Just put your hand on it and I'll show you what you've got to do,' Ryan urged her.

About to do as her boyfriend had asked, Georgie let out a terrifying scream as four strange men burst into the barn. 'Leave him alone! He's my boyfriend,' she shrieked as one of the men ran towards Ryan and hit him over the head with a baseball bat.

'You shitcunts. My dad's gonna kill you,' Georgie yelled as she fought to stop two of the men from tying her hands and feet up with rope.

Ryan stood up clutching his head. He was very dazed and didn't even realise that his penis was still hanging out for all to see.

'Put the tape on her mouth and carry her outside,' Eddie ordered, as his granddaughter began screaming blue murder and swearing like a navvy.

While Gary, Ricky and Raymond carried Georgie out of the barn, Eddie swung the bat again and struck Ryan straight across his now extremely flaccid penis.

'You dirty, perverted little cunt,' Ed seethed, as he tied Ryan up with the rope.

Ryan was in such excruciating pain that he could barely speak. 'Who the fuck are you?' he managed to mumble.

Ed picked up the duct tape and cut a strip off with his Stanley knife.

'Hurry up, Ed,' Raymond urged him.

Debating whether to cut the boy's cock off and stuff it down his perverted little throat, Eddie decided against it. He had Gina, Aaron and Rosie to think of now and he couldn't risk another long stretch in prison. He put his knife away, bent down and put the tape across the boy's mouth. 'You ever go near my granddaughter again and I will fucking well kill you. She's thirteen, you nonce case. Oh, and when you see Jimmy and Jed O'Hara, you tell 'em from me, Eddie Mitchell said hello.'

Checking that the rope was tied tight enough around the

boy's arms and legs, Eddie spat in his petrified face, stood up and sauntered casually out of the barn.

Less than a mile down the road, poor Stuart was having trouble keeping tabs on Harry O'Hara. When he'd first appeared out of the site he'd driven up and down the main road on his quad bike with his mate hanging off the back. Twice he'd nearly caused an accident, and the second time, when a driver had stopped and got out of his car, both boys had given the motorist wanker signs. When the driver got out and chased them, Harry had driven the quad bike onto a nearby field. Stuart put the binoculars to his eyes once again. Harry was pretty far away now, but if he wasn't mistaken, it looked like both he and his mate were chasing chickens around a pen. Stuart's phone rang and, thankfully, it was Eddie.

'I'm still with him, Ed, but I can't get the van any closer. He's chasing chickens around some farm, by the looks of it. The good news is, he's left the quad bike halfway across the field, so he's gotta come back this way.'

'Where exactly are ya?' Ed asked.

'The direction the vans were parked in, I'm straight along that road, probably about half a mile down. Shit, I think he's running back towards the quad bike now. What do you want me to do?'

'Get out the van, run towards the bike and pretend you're trying to nick it, buy it or whatever. I don't care what you do, but keep him there. If he kicks off, clump him, but try not to hurt him. I'm on me way now.'

Stuart jumped out of the van and sprinted towards the quad bike. Harry and his pal were a lot nearer to it than he was, but he knew he'd get there first. At fifteen, he'd been the 100-metre champion for his school and the district. He reached the bike and, not knowing what else to do, sat on it.

A minute later, Harry ran towards him with a dead chicken under his arm. His mate was a short distance behind. 'Get off my bike, you cunt,' Harry ordered.

'I only wanna buy it off ya. How much do ya want for it?' Stuart asked in a friendly manner.

'It ain't for sale, is it, Sonny?' Harry said, as his friend caught up with him.

'Nah, get off it you wanker,' Sonny yelled.

Stuart glanced from boy to boy. Both looked angry, their eyes full of hatred and their skin looked extremely weather-beaten for their years. Harry was only eleven, Stuart knew that, and the other boy couldn't be that much older. Not knowing what else to do, Stuart tried the same tactic again. 'Go on, please let me buy it, I want it for me son. I've got plenty of dosh on me, look,' he gestured, pulling a wad out of his back pocket.

Harry dropped the dead chicken and smirked at his pal. Seconds later both boys lunged at Stuart with their penknives.

Eddie pulled up behind the Renault van. 'Stay in the back with Georgie,' he shouted at Terry.

Ricky, Gary and Raymond sprinted across the field. At sixty-one, Eddie could still run, but not quite as fast as he once could. Gary was the first to reach Stuart. He had both kids in a headlock, but was struggling to hold them. 'Well done, mate,' Gary said, as he grabbed hold of Harry.

'Get off me, you shitcunts,' Harry screamed, as he felt rope being tied around his arms.

Eddie was out of breath as he arrived at the scene. Harry's pal tried to do a runner, but Ed grabbed him by the neck. 'Keys to the quad bike,' he demanded, holding his hands out.

'Go fuck your grandmother,' the boy replied brazenly.

Eddie kneed the boy as hard as he could in the nuts. 'I said keys to the quad bike,' he repeated.

'Harry's got 'em,' the boy squealed, as he fell to the ground in pain.

'Check he's got the keys, Ray, otherwise that little cunt might be back at the site before we have a proper chance to get away,' Ed ordered.

Ricky found a key in Harry's jacket pocket. 'You little bastard,' he shouted as Harry spat a mouthful of phlegm in his face.

'What's that doing there?' Eddie asked, clocking the dead chicken. It had been squashed in the scuffle.

'Don't ask, you really don't wanna know,' Stuart said, as he stood up and brushed his clothes down.

Gary put some tape across Harry's mouth and lifted the boy over his shoulder. 'Should we tie him up an' all?' he asked, pointing to the other lad, who was still writhing on the floor in pain.

'Nah, he's going nowhere for a while,' Eddie replied confidently.

'I'll ring Terry, make sure the coast's clear,' Raymond said.

Five minutes later, both Georgie and Harry were safely trussed up in the back of the van.

'Well done, lads,' Eddie grinned, shaking both Stuart and Terry's hands.

'Your fucking grandson stabbed me in the side, look,' Stuart complained, lifting up his shirt.

'It's only a nick, you'll live. Right, I settled up with that nosy old fucker at the B&B. You and Tel got all your stuff out, didn't ya?'

Stuart nodded. 'Everything's in the van, including our sleeping bags.'

'Do yourself a favour, go find a supermarket and stock up on food and water. Once you get back to the site, don't budge. I guarantee you, by tonight or tomorrow lunchtime, Jed and Jimmy will have either done a runner or they'll be gunning for us.'

CHAPTER THIRTY-SIX

Alice saw Jed's truck pull up outside and breathed a sigh of relief. From the moment she had opened her eyes that morning she'd had one of her feelings of doom and when she'd tried to ring Jed earlier and got no answer, she'd been worried he'd had an accident or something.

'How's my Shelby girl?' Alice said, as she lifted her granddaughter off Lola's lap.

'Why did ya keep ringing me, Mum?' Jed asked.

'I just wanted to make sure you were all right. Why didn't you bloody well answer?'

''Cause I had me father on the blower. He's just found us a new horse-box and he wanted to run it past me before he bid the old mush for it. I'm a bit old for you to be checking up on me, ain't I?' Jed said, kissing her on the cheek.

'Had one of me bad feelings today, boy. I ain't had one of them for a long while. Makes me feel horrible, it do,' Alice explained.

About to take the piss out of her the way he used to as a boy, Jed opened his mouth and quickly shut it again. His mum had had one of her bad feelings on the day his son Luke had been murdered, and also when Sammy had died, so mocking her was out of the question.

'Where's Georgie and Harry?' he asked, feeling a bit anxious himself.

'Georgie's with that Ryan Maloney and Harry went out on the quad bike with that little toerag.' Alice didn't like Sonny Adams. He was two years older than Harry, and, in her opinion, was a bad influence on her grandson. It was only since Sonny

356

had moved onto the site that Harry had started thieving, being insolent and bringing home dead bloody chickens.

'Do you fancy a bite to eat, Alice? I bought a crusty loaf, ham off the bone and some of them Spanish tomatoes,' Lola asked.

About to reply, Sonny Adams' frantic yelling stopped Alice from doing so. 'Some men have took Harry away. I tried to stop them, but they beat me,' Sonny panted. He'd forgotten about the pain in his groin and had sprinted back to the site as fast as his legs would carry him.

'Dordi! I knew it. I feel ill,' Alice screamed.

Jed's face turned as white as a sheet. 'What did these men look like? Are you sure it weren't the gavvers?' he asked, his voice trembling with fear.

'No. They were big, bad men and there were five of 'em. I heard one call another one Ray, then they tied Harry boy up and put him in the back of a white van.'

When his mother became completely hysterical, Jed ordered Lola to take her and the baby inside the trailer. He turned back to Sonny. 'Where did this happen? How long ago was it?'

'About twenty minutes ago. We was on that old mush's farm. The quad bike's still there. The bad men took the keys and they drove off that way,' Sonny said, pointing to the left.

'Run over to the barn, see if Georgie's in there with Ryan,' Jed ordered him.

Sonny ran off and Jed's hands were quivering as he took his phone out of his pocket. 'Dad, come home now. Eddie Mitchell's snatched Harry.'

As Jimmy launched into a torrent of abuse, Jed's brother Billy drove onto the site in his Land Cruiser.

'What's going on? Mum just rang me sobbing her fucking heart out,' Billy said.

'Mitchell's found us; he's got Harry. Dad's on his way now, but I can't wait that long. I need your motor, but go get the guns first. Grab both of 'em, Bill, and you come with me.'

While Billy ran across the field, Jed relayed to his father what Sonny had told him.

'I'll be forty minutes or so behind you, boy. You go on ahead of me and I'll pick my shooter up on the way back. Leave it in the trailer under the sofa. What motor's Mitchell in, do you know?'

'It's a white Merc Sprinter with red writing down the side. I clocked it when I left the site earlier and the number plate starts with BJJ. There was another van behind it, a blue Renault Trafic with white writing on it, so keep your eyes peeled for that an' all,' Jed said. He might not be able to spell or read, but he knew which letters were which.

Alice ran out of the trailer. 'I can't get no answer on Georgie's phone,' she screamed in panic.

Seconds later, an out-of-breath Sonny reappeared. 'Georgie's gone. Ryan's tied up in the barn. The bad men beat him an' all.'

Jed kicked the tyre of his pick-up truck repeatedly. 'They've got Georgie an' all. Me and Bill are leaving now, Dad, and I swear on my Shelby's life, when I catch up with Mitchell, I'm gonna blast the cunt to pieces.'

Georgie O'Hara's eyes were wide open with terror as she stared at the four men from the back of the van. The one that was driving was called Raymond, but she didn't know the names of the other three and she now wondered if they were nonces. Her dad had always wanted her to be on her guard against those types of men.

Since the tape had been removed from their mouths, Harry had done nothing but shout and curse, but his brazen attitude had now wilted a bit and he'd just started to cry. Being snatched by the men had been a terrible shock, but seeing his sister already in the back of the van was an even bigger one. He was glad Georgie was there, though, as he wouldn't want to go through this frightening experience alone.

Eddie studied his grandchildren carefully. With Georgie, he'd felt a slight tug on his heartstrings because of her likeness to Frankie, but Harry hadn't had any effect on him yet. Both children looked, sounded, and behaved like gypsy kids, which he'd fully expected. What he hadn't reckoned on was their reluctance to calm down so that he could explain what was going on. Seeing tears appear in Georgie's eyes as well, Ed decided this was as good a time as any to have a little chat with them.

'Please don't be frightened because nobody here is gonna

hurt you. I'm sorry if we scared you back there, but we didn't have a lot of choice but to grab you the way we did.'

'Why did you grab us, then? Are you nonces?' Georgie asked, glaring at Eddie defiantly.

'No. I'm your grandad.'

Georgie and Harry glanced at one another. Both had stopped crying now, but neither knew if this man was telling the truth or not. Harry decided to test him. 'You ain't our grandad. Jimmy's our grandad,' he snarled.

'You've got two grandads. Jimmy's your dad's father and I'm your mother's,' Eddie explained. He was relieved he finally had their attention at last.

'I'm your Uncle Gary, that's your Uncle Ricky and the man driving is your Uncle Raymond. You'll see your mum soon,' Gary added, smiling at Georgie.

'So where is our mum, then?' Georgie asked distrustfully.

'Waiting for you at home. That's where we're taking ya,' Ed replied.

'I don't wanna go there,' Harry shouted.

'I can't leave my boyfriend. I love him and we're getting married when I'm sixteen,' Georgie said, bursting into tears.

'Don't you think we should untie their arms now, Dad? There's some cans of drink and crisps in the front, they might be hungry,' Ricky suggested.

'Go on, then,' Ed replied.

'Ain't you gonna ring Frankie and Larry?' Raymond shouted out.

'I'm not gonna ring Larry till the morning now. It's gonna be nearly midnight by the time we get home and I couldn't stand a houseful of Old Bill and social workers tonight. Let Frankie spend a bit of time with 'em first, and I'll call Larry first thing tomorrow.'

'You'd best tell Frankie we've got 'em,' Gary urged.

About to give his daughter the good news, Eddie dropped his phone as both his grandchildren made a lunge for the handle of the back door.

Ricky managed to grab Georgie and Eddie grabbed Harry, who then did his utmost to manoeuvre his way out of his grandfather's arms.

'Leave my brother alone,' Georgie screamed, kicking her grandad in the leg.

'Right, tie their hands back up and they can stay that way until they've learned how to behave themselves.'

'I hate you!' Harry yelled in protest.

Eddie put his phone back in his pocket. He'd ring Frankie in a while when the kids had quietened down a bit. He stared at his grandchildren and shook his head in disbelief. He'd fully expected them to be rough around the edges, but he hadn't expected them to behave like wild fucking animals.

Alice O'Hara was absolutely beside herself. She couldn't stop screaming, was in floods of tears and her whole body was shaking from head to toe.

'I've got some brandy in mine. I'll go get it, it's good for shock,' Linda Maloney said. She felt anxious as well. Her Mickey had gone off with Jimmy and she knew they'd taken a gun with them. As for poor Ryan, he was in bits, bless him.

'Bring your Ryan over 'ere. I wanna know exactly what happened,' Alice wept.

'I dunno if he'll come, Alice. He's frit to death, the poor little sod. His brothers are looking after him; he wouldn't even talk to me about it. Loves your Georgie, that boy does.'

When Linda went off to get the brandy, Sarah, Alice's best friend on the site, held Alice in her arms. 'Everything will be OK. Jed and Jimmy will get your grandchildren back for ya, I know they will, angel.'

Alice looked at her friend with a psychotic expression plastered across her face. 'They ain't my grandchildren, they're my babies. I brought them up. I was the only mother they had. Georgie and Harry belong to me.'

Stuart and Terry headed back to the site and parked nearby. It had taken them ages to find a supermarket, but eventually they'd come across one and had stocked up with enough food and drink to last them a week.

'Jed's truck's there, but Jimmy's still out. Do you reckon that poor little cunt's still tied up in the barn?' Stuart said to his sidekick.

Terry laughed. 'Yeah, he ain't gonna be found till tonight, I reckon. Someone's bound to go and look for the kids at some point and they'll probably find him then.'

'What is the time?' Stuart asked Terry. He'd left his watch back home in Brentwood and felt lost without it on his wrist.

'Half-past four. We've got a long night ahead of us, but I ain't that tired, are you?'

'Nah, I'm hungry again, though. I'm gonna have another sandwich, want one?'

Terry chuckled. 'Go on then, you greedy fucker.'

As Stuart and Terry jovially stuffed their faces with BLT sandwiches, neither man had a clue that both Jed and Jimmy were in separate motors on the M74. Worse still, they were getting closer to the Mercedes Sprinter by the minute.

Still unaware that Georgie and Harry were now with her father, Frankie was becoming more deranged by the second. Hearing no news was doing her head in, but having to deal with a houseful of people as well was literally driving her insane.

'Bleedin' starving, me and your grandfather are. When we gonna eat?' Joyce asked in her hard-done-by voice.

'Can we have McDonald's, Mummy, please?' Brett asked, jumping up and down.

'No, we bloody well can't,' Frankie yelled, at the end of her tether. She stormed out to the kitchen and was followed by a very worried Joey.

'Look, I know this is an awful time for you, but for fuck's sake chill out and have a glass of wine or something. You've been shouting at Brett all day and you can't take your frustration out on him. He doesn't understand what's going on, does he? He's only bloody seven.'

Knowing her brother was entirely right, Frankie felt guilty, then started to cry. Joey put his arms around her and hugged her to his chest. He couldn't begin to imagine the anguish Frankie was going through, but sometimes he had to be cruel to be kind.

'It's Nan that's doing my head in. She's been knocking back the brandy and Baileys all day as though she's at a fucking party. Can't you get Dom to take her and Grandad over yours

361

for the night? There's too many people here and I'm just not in the mood to socialise.'

'I know Nan's brain damage, Frankie, but her and Grandad are getting ever so old. They're in their seventies now, and they mean well deep down. Why don't I order us all a takeaway? I'm sure once Nan's eaten that and had a few more drinks, she'll be ready for bed anyway. We'll give her some wine, that should knock her out,' Joey joked.

Frankie nodded. Her brother always calmed her down, that's why she loved him so much. 'Pour me a glass of wine, then,' she said.

'Are you OK, Frankie?' Babs asked, poking her head around the door.

'I'm fine, mate. Go in there with Dom and entertain the kids and Nan and Grandad for me while I have a little chat with Joey,' she replied.

Joey handed Frankie her wine and poured himself one as well. He held his glass up and clinked it with hers. 'Here's to Dad working his magic and bringing the kids home safely.'

When the phone rang it was Dom who answered it. 'It's your dad, Frankie,' he said, running into the kitchen.

Frankie snatched the phone out of his hand and, as she heard what her dad had to say, dropped her glass of wine in shock.

'What's happened? Talk to me, Frankie,' Joey pleaded, fearing the worst.

Bursting into tears of pure joy, Frankie began jumping up and down like a loony. 'He's got 'em! My babies are on their way home.'

Forever the pessimist, Eddie ended the call to his daughter and rang Stuart again. 'Well?' he asked. He was trying not to say too much in front of the kids.

'Nothing to report, boss. Jed's truck still ain't moved, and we ain't seen hair nor hide of Jimmy,' Stuart confirmed.

'Do not take your eyes off the gaff, because they're bound to realise something's missing soon. Don't both fall asleep, for fuck's sake,' Eddie warned.

He put his phone back in his pocket and smiled at his

grandchildren. They'd calmed down a bit in the past hour, but he could still see the look of fright in their eyes.

'Want some Coke and crisps? If you promise to behave yourselves, I can untie your hands for ya.'

'I need to go a toilet,' Georgie said in almost a whisper.

'Pull over, Raymondo, somewhere that's got trees or bushes.'

Georgie wasn't amused. 'Why can't I go in a normal toilet?'

'In case you try and do a runner again,' Eddie replied, as he undid the rope around her hands.

'I wanna pee an' all,' Harry said.

'You take him, Gal, and I'll go with her,' Ed ordered, as Raymond pulled the van over.

'You ain't coming with me,' Georgie said, scowling at her grandad.

'Don't worry, I'll turn me back,' Eddie promised as he grabbed her by the hand.

Five minutes later, toilet duty was over and both kids were back in the van. Harry was munching on crisps and Georgie was sipping a can of Coke.

'So, what's our mum like then?' Georgie asked unexpectedly.

'Your mum's kind, loving, generous and pretty. In fact, she looks a lot like you,' Ed told her.

'Have we got any more brothers or sisters?' Georgie asked.

'Yeah, you've got a little brother called Brett. You'll meet him when we get home.'

'We've got a sister called Shelby,' Harry added in a stroppy tone.

'Do either of you actually remember your mum?' Eddie asked.

Harry frowned, then shook his head.

'I do, but only a little bit. Why ain't she ever come to see us?' Georgie asked. She was interested now, but also very confused at the same time.

'Tell 'em the truth, Dad. Don't lie to 'em,' Ricky urged.

Eddie took a deep breath. He wanted to be as diplomatic as possible. 'Because when you were young your dad ran away with your nan and grandad and he took yous two with him. Your mum looked for you, we all did, but none of us could find you.'

'How did ya find us now then?' Georgie asked.

'Because we kept looking until there were no more places left to look,' Eddie replied, not wanting to mention Katie.

Harry blew his empty crisp bag up and burst it with his hand.

'Fuck, that made me jump,' Raymond complained.

Harry grinned. 'Nanny Alice says our mum is a proper old shitcunt and she said our mum got put in prison for trying to murder our dad.'

Eddie stared his grandson in the eyes. Frankie was going to have far more aggravation with him than she was with Georgie, that was for sure. He decided to play the boy at his own game. His Auntie Joan had taught him a valuable rule when he was a boy: 'When in Rome, do or act as the Romans do, boy,' she used to quote regularly. He smirked at Harry.

'Your Nanny Alice is a nasty piece of work. She's an evil, twisted old hag.'

Harry dropped his gaze and looked at his hands instead.

'We're gonna need to fill up with derv, Ed. We're on the M6 now, so I'll stop at the next services. If anyone wants a piss or some food, sort it now,' Raymond informed everyone.

'What did Stu say?' Ricky asked his father.

'That truck's still there and the other tosser is probably still in a boozer somewhere.'

Gary rubbed his hands together and grinned. 'Lovely jubbly! Now we're on the M6, we're home and dry, lads.'

Jed O'Hara was absolutely seething as he drove along like a bat out of hell. His brother's Toyota Land Cruiser had a three-litre engine, was as nippy as anything, yet he still hadn't caught up with Mitchell.

'Ring the old man again, see where he is. Tell him we're on the M6,' Jed ordered his brother.

Billy rang Jimmy's number. 'He's still on the M74, he said he'll be on the M6 in about ten minutes,' he told Jed.

'Has he seen that blue van, ask him?'

'No, he ain't.'

'Tell him to put his fucking foot down, then,' Jed said angrily. Stuck in the fast lane behind someone who was only doing eighty miles an hour, Jed held his hand on the hooter. 'Get out the way you prick,' he screamed.

'What did you say that number plate started with?' Billy asked a few minutes later.

'BJJ,' Jed replied.

'I think their van's a few motors in front of us; it says BJJ on the plate,' Billy said pointing towards the middle lane.

Jed veered over to the empty slow lane, then put his foot down. He couldn't read, so had no idea what the red sign-writing said, but he recognised the layout of the lettering at once.

'Well?' Billy asked impatiently.

Jed grinned. 'Gotcha, ya shitcunts.'

CHAPTER THIRTY-SEVEN

Joyce was jumping around the lounge, punching her fists in the air like a deranged football fan whose team had just lifted the FA cup.

'I wonder if we'll recognise 'em. Did your dad say what time they'll be home?' she asked her granddaughter.

'He reckons between four or five hours. I'll have to tidy up, the place looks like a bomb's hit it. Babs, do me a favour, give the boys a bath and put 'em to bed while I clear their toys away.'

'I don't wanna go a bed. I wanna see my brother and sister,' Brett said sulkily.

Frankie picked her son up and swung him around. 'You be a good boy, have your bath, put your jim-jams on, and when you're done, Dom will go and get you and Kelvin a McDonald's.'

'I want Big Mac,' Kelvin shouted, leaping up and down on the armchair.

'Will Georgie and Harry be having McDonald's with us?' Brett asked. Kelvin was his make-believe brother, and he was very excited by the prospect of having a real one.

'No, not tonight they won't. They won't be here until very late, so you won't be able to see them until the morning. Now up them stairs, before Mummy changes her mind about the McDonald's.'

'Where's Jordan?' Frankie asked Babs as the boys ran up the stairs.

'Having a sleepover at his girlfriend's house, would you believe? He's at the age now where he don't need his mamma no more, but yours will need you. I can't tell you how pleased I am for you, Frankie,' Babs said, hugging her pal.

'I can't wait for them to arrive, but I'm ever so nervous about seeing them again. I bet it's not all plain sailing, you know. They're bound to have issues if they've been bought up by Jed, Alice and Jimmy.'

'They'll probably find it all a bit strange at first, but I bet you, within a month or so, they'll be in their element living with you. They are so gonna love their mamma.'

Frankie grinned. 'As long as they love me, I'll be the happiest girl in the world.'

Eddie rang Gina to ask after the kids and let her know he was on the way home, then focused on his grandchildren again. Georgie had the figure of a voluptuous young woman and it worried him. 'Who's this boyfriend of yours, then?' he asked her.

'Who's that you were on the phone to?' Georgie replied, ignoring his question.

'My wife, Gina.'

'So, is she my nan?' Georgie asked, knowing full well she wasn't.

'No, your nan's dead, unfortunately.'

Harry smiled. 'Grandad Jimmy says that you murdered our nan and went to prison, the same as our mum did.'

Seeing his father's eyes begin to cloud over, Gary butted in. 'What's happened to that mutt of Joey's, Dad? Is it still alive?'

'Yeah,' Eddie said, eyeballing his grandson with a look that could kill.

'Don't him and Dom take it out no more or what? They always used to have it with 'em, but I ain't seen it lately,' Gary asked. He knew he was talking a load of old bollocks, but a change of subject was desperately needed. Gary knew his dad well enough to know that Harry had been seconds away from getting a good wallop.

Eddie averted his eyes away from Harry and, much to Gary's relief, chuckled. 'The mutt spends a lot of its time in the neighbour's house now, by all accounts. Apparently, the old girl that lives next door recently bought a male Westie and it was love at first sight. Joey said every time him and Dom try and take Madonna back indoors, she goes ballistic, tries to bite 'em and then howls all night.'

'Who's Madonna?' Georgie asked. She briefly wondered if they were talking about the singer.

'Your uncle's Chihuahua,' Ricky replied, smiling at her.

'What's one of them, then?'

About to explain the breed, Raymond's intervention killed the conversation stone dead. 'I don't wanna worry you, lads, but I'm positive we're being followed.'

Jed O'Hara had done a lot of thinking since Georgie and Harry had been kidnapped earlier. He had another child; one he knew nothing about and had never set eyes on. He didn't even know what sex it was or its name, for Christ's sake.

Frankie had been pregnant with their third child when she had stabbed him and got sent to prison. At the time, Jed had had every intention of trying to get custody of the baby once it was born, but Sammy's murder, plus Frankie's threats, had changed all that. In the end, Jed had been left with two choices. Number one was live, do a runner and keep Georgie and Harry for ever. Number two was risk getting murdered, locked up, and lose his kids for good.

The situation was a no brainer and since the night Jed had left Rainham, he'd blanked his then unborn child completely out of his mind. His parents had done the same and the child had never been mentioned since, but now Eddie Mitchell had tracked them down, Jed's feelings had changed towards it.

'Move over then, the van's gone in the slow lane. You just nearly drove past it, you dinlo. What the fuck you doing?' Billly shouted.

'I'm thinking,' Jed said, as he put his foot on the brake and swerved into the slow lane.

Billy chuckled. 'What about? Getting the kids back or murdering that mug, Mitchell?'

'Neither, I was thinking about me other chavvie, you know the one I've never seen.'

'What you thinking about that for?' Billy asked bemused.

'Because it's mine and I've decided, once this is all over and we've finished off Eddie, that chavvie is coming home with me.'

* * *

Raymond looked at the fuel gauge and grimaced. 'We're on the fucking red. I'm coming up to Kendal services; we're gonna have to fill up,' he said anxiously.

'I bet it's Dad come to take us back,' Harry whispered to his sister.

Georgie nodded and squeezed his hand. Part of her had wanted to see her mother, even if it was only for a brief visit, but on the whole she couldn't wait to get home to Ryan. She'd only been gone a few hours and was missing him already.

'How we gonna play this, Dad?' Ricky asked.

Eddie had had his thinking cap on for the past five minutes. He'd had a feeling the O'Haras would come for the kids, which was why he'd ordered Terry and Stuart to stay in Glasgow, but he hadn't reckoned on it being this quick. 'Do you know anyone who has a silver Land Cruiser?' Ed asked his grandchildren.

Both glanced at one another and shook their heads. Their Uncle Billy drove one of those, but they'd been taught at an early age to keep their mouths shut.

'What should I do, Ed?' Raymond shouted out.

'Pull in and drive straight to the pumps. There's fuck-all they can do on a packed garage forecourt, is there?' Ed replied.

'Say they've got you-know-what?' Ricky asked his father. He didn't want to say too much in front of the kids.

'Then they shoot at us and probably blow themselves up at the same time,' Eddie said jokingly. He was acting more blasé than he actually felt and was cursing his decision not to bring any guns up to Scotland with him.

Desperate to be reunited with his father, Harry sensed an opportunity and clutched the crotch of his tracksuit bottoms with both hands. 'I need a wee again,' he said.

Eddie ignored his grandson and leaned over the passenger seat to try and get a look at the Land Cruiser in the wing mirrors. For obvious reasons, Ed had asked Flatnose to get hold of a van with no windows in the back, which was a bind now they were being followed.

'Right, we're at Kendal services. I'm pulling in now,' Raymond shouted out.

'You ain't gonna hurt my dad, are ya?' Georgie asked

tearfully, as Gary took two baseball bats out of a navy-blue sports bag and handed one to Ricky.

'We only ever hurt people who hurt us,' Gary replied quite truthfully.

'Where's it gone? I can't see it now,' Eddie asked Raymond, as he stared in the wing mirror.

'They followed us off the slip road, but I still couldn't see who was driving. It's too dark.'

When Raymond pulled onto the garage forecourt, Ed clambered into the passenger seat. He turned around to face Ricky and Gary. 'I'm getting out with Raymond. Yous stay with them two and watch 'em like a hawk.'

Jed O'Hara parked the Land Cruiser out of view at the exit of the service station. 'Give us the shooter,' he said to his brother.

Billy's hand shook as he handed him the gun. Unlike Jed, and his deceased brother Marky, Billy had always been the runt of the litter when it came to bravado and he knew it. 'You can't just shoot 'em in the garage. You'll get us both banged up,' he said.

'Just shut it and give me the bullets,' Jed ordered.

'The bullets are in the gun, ain't they?'

Jed glared at his brother. He was a sod for playing pranks on people himself, but Billy joking at a time like this just wasn't funny. 'Don't mess about, Bill. My chavvies are in that fucking van.'

'I ain't messing with ya. All you said was get the gun; you didn't say anything about bullets, did ya? I thought it was already loaded.'

Absolutely furious, Jed whacked his brother over the head with the now useless weapon. 'How's the gun meant to work without any fucking bullets, you thick, useless cunt? Dad keeps the bullets separate in case the chavvies ever find the shooters,' he screamed.

Billy held his hands over his head in case he got clumped again. 'I'm really sorry, Jed, but I didn't know that it weren't loaded. Dad might tell you everything, but he treats me like a dinlo and never tells me nothing.'

'That's 'cause you are a fucking dinlo,' Jed said, turning the key in the ignition.

'Where we going now? They ain't come out the service station yet,' Billy said, as Jed zoomed back onto the motorway.

'Ring Dad and give me the phone,' Jed yelled.

Billy did as his brother asked. 'You got bullets, ain't ya? Where are ya now?' he asked his father. On learning his dad's gun was loaded and he was only about twenty miles behind him, Jed breathed a massive sigh of relief.

Raymond was surprised to see no sign of the Land Cruiser as they left Kendal services. 'Perhaps we got it wrong,' he said to Eddie, who was now sitting in the passenger seat.

'Nah, whoever it is will reappear, mark my words,' Ed replied.

Two miles down the M6, Ed's wise words were proved right, as Raymond recognised the Land Cruiser sitting on the hard shoulder. 'What's the plan now?' he asked his boss.

'Turn the radio up,' Ed ordered. He had some ideas, but didn't want the kids to hear what he had to say. He leaned towards Raymond's left ear. 'It's gotta be Jed and Jimmy in that motor. I reckon we should lead 'em over to the salvage yard and finish the job tonight.'

'Do you still keep the shooters there? 'Cause I've a feeling the O'Haras might be armed,' Raymond whispered.

'Let me make some phone calls and I'll talk to you in a sec,' Ed replied.

He rang Gina first. 'You all right, Ed? Not at a disco, are you?' Gina joked, as she heard the sound of Destiny's Child blaring out in the background.

'I need you to pack some stuff for you and the kids and go and stay at your mate Claire's for a couple of days.'

'What?' Gina asked in amazement.

'Look, we've got a problem this end. Nothing serious, but I don't want you in the cottage alone tonight.'

'I can't go now. I've just bathed the kids and Rosie's in bed already. I'll go first thing in the morning,' Gina said.

'No you won't, you'll go tonight. Get your stuff packed and get out of there ASAP! Understand?'

'OK,' Gina replied. The seriousness of Eddie's voice told her all she needed to know and she began to panic. 'You will be all right, won't you?' she asked, trying not to cry.

'Don't worry about me, I'll be fine. Just do as I told you and ring me as soon as you get to Claire's, OK?'

Gina told Ed she loved him, ended the call and burst into tears. If anything happened to her wonderful husband, she just knew she would die of a broken heart.

Stuart was next on Ed's must-ring list. 'I take it there's no movement your end?' he asked, knowing deep down it was a dumb question to ask.

'Nope, been sitting 'ere like two stooges, me and Tel. Jed's truck ain't moved and Jimmy still ain't back.'

'Right, change of plan. Head back to Essex as fast as you can. I'll give you more instructions on the way,' Ed ordered.

'I thought you wanted us to stay up 'ere and follow Jimmy and Jed,' Stuart replied, bemused.

'Too late. They're already following us.'

The hardest phone call for Eddie to make was the last one. 'I wish I hadn't told Frankie I had the kids with me. She's fragile enough as it is and if she hears we're being followed, she'll lose the plot,' Ed whispered to Raymond.

'Don't tell her. Just say we've broken down or something,' Raymond suggested.

Eddie paused before he punched in the number. He had never involved Joey in anything underhand before but for the first time ever, he desperately needed his son's help.

Frankie was just writing down the order for their Chinese takeaway when the phone rang. 'Someone answer that,' she shouted, as she bent down to pick up Brett's Big Mac and fries. The messy little sod had just knocked his dinner off the tray and was now crying because it was scattered all over the carpet.

'It's your dad, Frankie, but he wants to speak to Joey,' Babs shouted out.

Frankie stood up and snatched the phone out of her friend's hand. 'What's wrong?' she asked her father.

'Nothing's wrong. Well, apart from the van playing up, that is. Put Joey on, sweetheart, I need him to ring a mate of mine who's a mechanic,' Eddie lied.

'Where are the kids?' Frankie asked suspiciously.

'In the back.'

'Put 'em on the phone. Please let me say hello to 'em, Dad.'

'They're both asleep, Frankie, and you'll have plenty of time to say hello to 'em when we get home. Now, put your brother on the phone, else we might spend the night on the motorway.'

'What's up, Dad?' Joey asked as he put the receiver to his ear.

'Keep smiling, and don't let Frankie know that anything's amiss, you get my drift?' Eddie said.

'Yeah,' Joey replied, in an unconcerned tone.

'The O'Haras are behind us on the motorway and I need your help, son. Is Frankie still standing next to you?'

'Yeah.'

'Right, when you put the phone down in a minute, pretend you've got to ring a mechanic mate of mine. Ask your sister for a pen and paper and I'll give you a false phone number. Then, end the call and ring me back out of Frankie's earshot on your mobile.'

'I need a pen and paper,' Joey told Frankie.

Joey's heart was beating rapidly as he took down the imaginary phone number. 'Right, I'll ring him now, Dad,' he said.

'If Frankie asks, I think the alternator's on the blink.'

'No probs,' Joey said ending the call.

'What's a matter with the van?' Frankie asked.

'Dad reckons the alternator's on the blink. He wants me to get one of his mechanic pals to ring him.'

'Why don't he just ring the AA?'

'Because the van isn't kosher, you div,' Joey replied jovially. How he was putting on such a convincing act he didn't know, but he could tell that his sister believed him.

Frankie breathed a sigh of relief. 'For a moment there I thought that something had gone proper wrong. I had visions of Jed and Jimmy following Dad or something.'

Joey chuckled falsely. 'You and your overactive imagination will get you into trouble one day, sis.'

CHAPTER THIRTY-EIGHT

After the conversation with his father, Joey's appetite had all but disappeared by the time the Chinese takeaway arrived.

'You ain't eaten enough to keep a bleedin' fly alive,' Joyce said, poking her grandson in the arm.

'I ain't a lover of Chinese. Want some of my spare ribs?' Stanley asked Joey.

'No, I'm fine thanks, Grandad. I'm gonna have to pop out in a minute. Dom's gotta drive me round to one of Dad's mates,' Joey announced.

'Have I? First I've heard of it,' Dominic said, laughing.

Frankie put her plate on the table. 'Who you got to go and see then?' she asked, with distrust in her voice.

'Dad said if his mechanic mate had his phone switched off, I had to go round to his house,' Joey replied, as casually as he could.

'Where's this bloke live then?'

'Dagenham,' Joey lied, looking his sister straight in the eyes.

Dominic knew his boyfriend better than anyone and he could tell that something was wrong. 'Shall we go now?' he asked him.

Joey nodded and stood up.

'You are coming back, ain't ya? I want you here when the kids get home,' Frankie insisted.

Joey grinned. 'Of course I am.'

Jed O'Hara had always been a big believer that things in life happen for a reason. Obviously, he was still a bit pissed off with his brother Billy, but now he believed that fate had played its part. If he'd have run around that service station brandishing a gun he might have got himself nicked and, seeing he was now on the M1 with his father and Mickey Maloney behind, Jed convinced himself that it was a sign from above.

'What you smiling at?' Billy asked.

'Do you know what Billy boy? I think you were destined to forget them bullets on purpose. We were meant to follow Mitchell and finish the job in Essex.'

'What makes you think that, then?'

'Because once me and Dad have done away with Eddie and his wanky little firm, I'm gonna find my other chavvie and kill that slag Frankie, an' all.'

Joey told Dominic to drive towards his father's cottage and then fell silent.

'What's going on, Joey?' Dom asked, minutes later.

Taking a deep breath, Joey repeated what his father had told him.

'So why are we going to his cottage?' Dom asked, confused.

'Because Dad's asked me to get something he needs. Later on, he wants us to park at the Brentwood junction on the M25 and pick up the kids from him. He's gonna ring us with a time.'

Dominic felt a shiver run down his spine. 'What exactly are we picking up from his cottage, Joey?'

'You really don't wanna know,' Joey mumbled.

Absolutely livid, Dominic mounted his Porsche onto a kerb. 'If you don't tell me, I'm not fucking driving you there, nor will I pick up the kids. What are we collecting, Joey?'

Joey glanced at his boyfriend's face. Dom was a laid-back sort of guy who rarely lost his rag, but on the odd occasion he did, he wasn't pleasant. 'He needs me to pick up a gun, if you must know. We need it in case the O'Haras know where Frankie lives and come to the house.'

Dominic shook his head in total disbelief. All this sounded like a scene out of the film *Pulp Fiction*. He glared at his partner. 'But you don't even know how to use a gun, Joey.'

'Yes I do – you pull the trigger,' Joey replied sarcastically.

'And what if I refuse to do this for you? I really don't like the sound of it all, you know. It's ridiculous and also fucking dangerous.'

Joey had never been interested in learning to drive, but for the first time in his life, he wished he had. 'Look, we won't have the gun for long. My dad's sending Stuart and Terry round to protect us and I'll give it straight to them. Please, Dom, just drive, otherwise my dad will go mental.'

Remembering the last falling-out he had had with Joey's father, Dominic pulled off the kerb and drove towards his cottage.

Noticing that her grandad and Raymond were in deep conversation in the front of the van and Gary and Ricky were doing the same in the back, Georgie O'Hara decided to have a little chat with her brother. Both children were well aware that their dad and Grandad Jimmy were now following them but, being the eldest, Georgie had taken it upon herself to think of a back-up plan if anything were to go wrong.

'Where's your phone?' she whispered in Harry's ear.

'Back at the trailer. Where's yours?'

Georgie sighed. Her mobile had been in her big silver purse and had been left at the barn when she had got taken away.

'Do you think Dad and Grandad will rescue us and take us back home?' Harry asked in a hushed tone.

Georgie squeezed her little brother's hand. 'Of course they will.'

Joey hid the gun in his overnight bag and put it on top of the wardrobe so it was out of harm's way. He didn't know how he'd react if the O'Haras came to the house, but it was his duty to stick up for his sister.

'What you being doing up there?' Frankie asked accusingly as he came down the stairs. Dominic was sitting in the lounge with a face like thunder and she wasn't stupid; she knew something was wrong.

'I went upstairs to put me sweatshirt on. It's turned bloody cold, ain't it?'

'Sod the weather, what's up with Dom?'

'Me and him have had a bit of a row. There's a gay guy that's started work in my office and he's rang me a couple of

376

times. Dom kicked off about it. You know how jealous he gets,' Joey lied.

Satisfied with her brother's explanation, Frankie smiled. 'Nan got up to go to the toilet while you were out and fell flat on her face. She's OK, but well pissed, so can you help me get her up the stairs? Her and Grandad can sleep in the spare room, and you and Dom can doss in Jordan's.'

'Come on, Nan, let's get you to bed,' Joey said as he walked into the lounge.

'I made her a coffee, but she won't drink it,' Babs informed Frankie.

'Always has to bleedin' well show herself up,' Stanley mumbled.

'What did you say?' Joyce asked.

'Nothing, dear.'

'I might be a bit tipsy, but there's sod-all wrong with me hearing, you know,' Joyce slurred as her grandchildren helped her off the sofa.

'You and Grandad are gonna sleep in the double bed in the spare room. It's freshly made up,' Frankie said, knowing how particular her grandmother was on the subject of clean sheets.

Joycie looked at Frankie as though she were mad. 'I ain't sleeping in the same bed as that cantankerous old goat,' she said.

'You'll have to. We've only got five bedrooms, Nan, and Georgie and Harry will need one of those.'

Stanley glared at his wife. She could be such an awkward old cow at times. 'I don't wanna sleep in the same bleedin' bed as you, either. You snore like a drunken sailor.'

'Well, I'm glad we agree for once, 'cause the thought of having you sleeping near me after you went off fornicating with that old slapper makes me feel physically sick.'

At the mention of Pat the Pigeon, Stanley himself felt physically sick at the memories.

'Babs can sleep with me – that's if any of us end up getting any sleep. You can have Babs' bed, Grandad,' Frankie offered kindly.

'Dirty old bastard,' Joyce slurred, as Joey and Frankie took one arm each and led her out of the room.

Stanley poked his tongue out behind his wife's back then, once Joycie was out of earshot, turned to Dominic. 'Hooked-nosed, evil old witch.'

Approaching Milton Keynes, Eddie began to have serious doubts about his original plan. Dropping the kids at the A12 junction off the M25 would have been feasible if they only had one motor following them, but now there were two, it was far too dangerous.

'Turn the radio up again,' Ed ordered Raymond.

As Raymond did so, Ed leaned towards him. 'We can't drop the kids off at the slip road. It's too dodgy and I don't want Joey and Dom getting hurt. Think of somewhere we can meet up where they'll be loads of people milling about.'

'It'll be gone ten by the time we get back, Ed, so there ain't many places gonna be busy. Surely we're better meeting Dom and Joey at a garage. I can't see the O'Haras pulling onto the forecourt, 'cause they're all camera'd up,' Raymond suggested.

'But what if they do?'

Raymond shrugged. 'It's a chance we're gonna have to take. Get Joey to make sure Dom parks up away from the pumps and turns the headlights off. I'm sure the O'Haras won't pull in behind us; they didn't at the service station, did they?'

Eddie rubbed the stubble on his chin. 'What garage do ya reckon's best to stop at? We can't use the one near Brentwood nick, as it's too near to Frankie's gaff.'

'I reckon we're better taking the 127 turn-off. If we stop at that garage opposite Palms Hotel, the O'Haras will probably pull up near Ardleigh Green lights and wait for us there. They definitely ain't gonna wanna create a scene where there's cameras, Ed.'

Eddie took his phone out of his pocket. 'Let's hope you're fucking right, Raymondo, 'cause if you ain't, Joey and Dom might be in shit street an' all.'

As the evening wore on, Frankie was becoming more suspicious by the minute. Joey's behaviour was odd, to say the least, and even though he was trying to join in the conversation, Frankie knew him well enough to know that something was wrong. Everybody had gone to bed now apart from Babs, Joey, Dom and herself and as her brother stared at his phone again, Frankie felt her hackles start to rise.

'Whaddya keep checking your fucking phone for? I know something's wrong, Joey, so you might as well just tell me what it is.'

Eddie had ordered Joey to say nothing to Frankie until he'd picked the children up so, as he was just about to lie, Joey was relieved as his phone burst into life. 'We'll leave now,' he said, after listening to his father's instructions.

'You ain't going nowhere until you tell me what's going on,' Frankie yelled, blocking the doorway with her body.

'I won't be long and as soon as I get back I'll explain, I promise.'

'You fucking tell me now, Joey, else I'm coming with you.'

'I'm going to pick the kids up, if you must know. Now, get out the way, else we're gonna be late.'

Frankie stood open-mouthed as her brother and Dominic pushed past her. When the door slammed, she turned to Babs. 'I knew something would go wrong. I thought it was all too good to be true,' she shouted tearfully.

Babs hugged her. 'You don't even know that anything's wrong yet. Perhaps your dad has to go somewhere afterwards.'

Frankie shook her head furiously. 'If my dad has involved my gay brother in all of this, then something is very fucking wrong.'

Jed looked at his fuel tank and ordered his brother to ring their father and pass him the phone.

'What's up?' Jimmy asked.

'I'm nearly out of juice. I reckon the cunts will take the next turn-off, but even if they don't, I'm gonna have to fill up. There's a garage not far past the Post House, ain't there? I'll fill up there, then catch you back up. Don't lose 'em, for fuck's sake.'

Jimmy chuckled. 'Me and Mickey are right behind 'em. The only place Mitchell's going is inside a coffin, boy.'

* * *

379

Georgie and Harry looked startled as their grandfather ordered their hands to be tied up again. 'What have we done wrong?' Georgie complained.

As Gary did the deed, Eddie looked around and leaned over the seat. 'In a minute you're getting out the van. Your Uncle Joey is picking you up and he's taking you home to your mum. We'll be round to see you again either later tonight or tomorrow.'

Feeling his chance of escaping slipping away, Harry glared at his grandad. 'What you gonna do to my dad? If you do anything bad to him, I'll tell the gavvers and get 'em to lock you up.'

'And if you ain't nice to your mother, I'll have you locked up an' all. Your mum loves you very much and once you get to know her properly, you'll love her as well,' Ed replied.

'Are you gonna hurt our dad and grandad?' Georgie asked nervously.

'No. I'm gonna send 'em back to Glasgow, that's all,' Eddie lied.

'Right, we're only five minutes from the garage now, Ed. We've definitely lost one of 'em and he ain't reappeared yet,' Raymond said.

'Bats ready boys, just in case we need 'em. Raymondo reckons they won't follow us 'cause of the cameras, hence the change of plan,' Ed explained.

When Gary and Ricky grabbed the baseball bats, Harry looked fearfully at his sister and began to cry. He'd always got annoyed with his Nanny Alice for fussing over him like an old mother hen, but he wished he could have a big cuddle from her now.

Georgie winked at her brother as reassurance that everything would be all right. For now it was the only comfort she could offer him.

Joey and Dominic were still barely on speaking terms. Dom was furious that Joey had sort of threatened him with his father and, not for the first time in his life, wondered what sort of family he'd got himself involved with.

'Are you OK?' Joey asked softly. His boyfriend's hands were visibly shaking and Joey felt terribly guilty for involving him, but he couldn't drive himself, so had had little choice.

'Yeah, I'm fucking fantastic,' Dominic replied, his voice full of sarcasm.

Joey glanced at his watch. His dad had told him to park by the bit of the garage where you put air in the tyres.

'Tell the cashier that you've got a puncture if he or she looks at you strange. Let 'em know you're waiting for someone who's bringing a spare and then we'll reverse up to you, get the kids out the back and shoot off. Give it a couple of minutes then you drive off,' were his dad's exact instructions.

'I wonder what will happen if the O'Haras pull in here as well,' Joey said nervously.

Dominic glared at his partner. 'Shame you never brought the gun with you. We could have shot them and got ourselves locked up for twenty years. It might not sound like much fun, but I'm sure it would have been better than us getting killed, which is what will probably happen now. Never again will I let you talk me into anything like this, Joey, and I mean never!'

'Right, 'ere goes, lads,' Raymond shouted as he swerved onto the garage forecourt at high speed. Breathing a sigh of relief as Jimmy's Shogun drove past, Raymond swung the van around and reversed up to Dominic's motor. Eddie jumped out of the front, opened the back doors and urged Gary and Ricky to get the kids out double quick.

'Why are they tied up?' Joey asked, horrified.

'Because they tried to do a runner earlier. Just get 'em home and untie 'em there. Do not let them out of your sight for one minute, OK?'

Joey nodded and jumped in the back with the kids. 'Wait until my dad pulls away, then drive off a minute or so later,' he told Dom.

Appalled that both children had their hands tied up, Dominic shook his head in disbelief. If the cashier had clocked them and written down his number plate, the police would be hunting for him, thinking he was a dangerous paedophile on the loose.

Joey smiled lovingly at both of the children as he digested their appearances. Georgie resembled Frankie, but looked a lot older than he expected. As for Harry, he was unrecognisable.

'Hello, I'm your Uncle Joey. Your Mummy's going to be so pleased to see you,' Joey said, his eyes welling up with emotion.

Harry stared at his uncle. His earlier upset had been replaced by pure anger and he was livid now he didn't have his family on his tail. 'We're still gonna live with our dad and yous can't stop us. We don't even wanna see our mum, do we, Georgie? We like living where we are, and that ain't gonna change, so why don't you shitcunts just leave us alone?'

'We hate you, you bastards!' Georgie screamed.

'Drive, Dom,' Joey ordered. He locked eyes with his boyfriend through the interior mirror and both knew exactly what the other was thinking. Poor bloody Frankie.

CHAPTER THIRTY-NINE

As predicted by Raymond, Jimmy's Shogun was parked on the pavement at Ardleigh Green traffic lights.

'Do a left here and head to Dagenham, Raymondo,' Eddie said.

'I'm sure the soppy cunts think we don't know we're being followed. Why else would they hang two or three cars back all the time?' Ray replied.

'Any sign of the other motor?' Eddie asked. He was worried it had headed towards Frankie's house.

'Ain't seen it yet, mate. Probably stopped for petrol, unless the bastard broke down,' Raymond replied.

Glad to be rid of the kids so they could now talk openly, Gary leaned his head over the front seat. 'So, what's the plan now? I take it the shooters are in the usual place?'

Eddie nodded. A couple of years back he'd had a new toilet built inside the scrapyard and it had been especially designed by a pal of his, with a false floor underneath. Ed had very few dealings with the salvage yard these days, so apart from the one handgun he kept at home to protect his family, anything else untoward was hidden there. Ed still had contacts inside the police force and if he ever got tipped off that the Old Bill were on his case, it wouldn't take him long to clear the yard of anything that could be incriminating.

'That's the only hitch we have. If the O'Haras are armed it's gonna take us a few minutes or so to get the guns out,' he replied.

'How about if me and Gal are dropped off, you and Ray continue in the van, then come back five minutes later?' Ricky suggested.

Ed's scrapyard was just off the A13 and because of where it was situated, he immediately shook his head. 'Too dodgy. If they're behind us they'll definitely see you get out. I think we're just gonna have to hope they ain't armed, and three of us can distract 'em with our knives and bats while the other makes a dash for the guns. Who's the fastest runner?' he asked jokingly. Eddie knew that if the O'Haras were armed, they could all be in shit street, and part of him now wished he'd got the handgun from Joey. The reason he hadn't was that protecting Frankie and Brett was top of his agenda and once Stuart and Terry were on home turf, he knew they would be absolutely fine. He dialled Stu's number again.

'Where are you now?' he asked hopefully.

'Just leaving Newport Pagnall services. We needed juice,' Stuart explained.

'Put your foot down as far as it will go. We've temporarily lost one of the bastards,' Ed explained.

'Where did you lose 'em?' Stuart asked, dreading the answer.

'The Brentwood turn-off, but don't worry 'cause Joey's got you-know-what and he should be at Frankie's about now.'

Stuart felt sick as Ed ended the call. As much as he liked Joey, in a situation such as this Joey was going to be about as much use as a chocolate teapot. He turned to Terry. 'We need to hurry. I think Frankie might be in danger.'

The nearer Joey got to Frankie's house, the more worried about how the children were going to adapt to their new life he became. 'We're nearly home now,' he explained kindly.

'But this ain't our home,' Harry spat.

'Is our mum gonna be there waiting for us?' Georgie asked, genuinely interested. She had no intention of ever living with her mother again, but still had a strange urge to meet her and see what she was like.

'Of course she is. Your mum's waited for ages for this moment.'

'Well we ain't! We don't love her. We love our Dad, Nan and Grandad Jimmy,' Harry said nastily.

With his sister's happiness in the forefront of his mind, Joey stared at his nephew. 'You'd better snap out of your foul mood,

Harry, 'cause if you say one thing to hurt your mother, I shall fucking hurt you twice as hard, you got that?'

Aware that his uncle was giving him daggers, Harry looked away.

'Pass me my mobile, Dom, it's in the front somewhere,' Joey said, as his musical ringtone came to life.

Dominic didn't answer, but did as he was asked. Tonight's events had absolutely petrified him and he was beginning to wonder if he and Joey now had a future together.

'What's up?' Joey asked his dad.

'You home yet?'

'Nearly. Why? What's wrong?'

'Just make sure you ain't being followed, boy. We've lost one of the motors, the Land Cruiser. If you see it sitting near Frankie's, get Dom to drop you off, then tell him to drive off with the kids still inside.'

Joey looked out of the back window. 'There's nothing behind us. If need be, where should Dom drive to?'

'Oh, hang on a minute. It's OK, panic over, the bastard's behind us again, Ray's just spotted him.'

Joey breathed a massive sigh of relief. He wasn't made of the same steel as his dad and brothers and the thought of pointing a gun at someone, even if it was to protect his sister, filled him with total dread. 'Please be careful, Dad,' Joey urged.

'Of course I will, but if you ain't heard anything from me in, say, four hours, ring Flatnose and tell him to come and look for us. You know where we'll be, don't you? And you've got Flatnose's number? If you have to ring him, just tell him the score, he'll know what to do. He sort of knows about what's going on anyway, I rang him earlier, but you're the only one I've actually told where we're heading.'

'I've got both his numbers, but if I ring him at two or three in the morning, will he be awake?' Joey asked anxiously.

'Of course.'

'What about Larry?' Joey asked.

'Don't ring him yet. I'll call him tomorrow. Look, try not to worry, boy, as I'm sure everything is gonna be fine, but if something does go wrong, never forget how much I love you and also promise me you'll always take care of Frankie for me.'

Aware that his eyes had welled up, Joey did his best to keep the emotion out of his voice. 'I promise and I love you too, Dad.'

Eagerly awaiting the return of her children, Frankie was glued to the window in the living room. 'Where are they, Babs? They've been gone ages. What if something's wrong?'

Babs put a comforting arm around her friend's shoulder. 'They've not even been gone half an hour yet; it seems longer 'cause you're so excited. Everything is gonna be just fine, and whenever Babbsy say that, she always right.'

'Keep watch for me while I go a toilet again. I've got the shits through nerves and look at my hands, I can't keep 'em still. Say they don't remember me, or even worse, hate my guts for taking them away from their father? I just want them to be happy, Babs, and I'm so worried they might not be able to settle into a normal life. Them travellers are such a different breed from us, they really are.'

Babs wanted to reassure Frankie that the kids would easily adapt, but from what Frankie had told her about the O'Haras, she knew she would only be lying to her friend. She chose her words extremely carefully. 'Whatever problems you have with them, sweet child, please remember that a mother's love will always shine through in the end. No person in any child's life can ever be more special to them than the woman that brought them into this world.'

Eddie felt quite emotional as the van hurtled towards Dagenham. Usually, when faced with any violent-looking situation, Ed was brimming with confidence, but because he knew it would take them a good few minutes to retrieve the guns from under the toilet floor, he wondered if he was making the right decision by heading to the yard. If he survived, but something happened to his sons or Raymond, he would never forgive himself. It would feel like a repeat of Jessica's death all over again.

'What's up, Dad? You ain't having second thoughts, are ya?' Gary asked.

'Nah, I'm just a bit worried they could be armed and we

won't get to the guns in time, that's all. We can't back out now, though, I've waited too many years for this fucking moment. Give your families a bell. Tell 'em you love 'em, just in case something goes tits-up.'

Raymond felt physically sick. If his boss had doubts, then they were all in trouble, and he so wished that he was at home with Polly and Chelsea. Visions of Jessica's mutilated corpse flashed through his mind and, feeling dizzy, he slowed down and leaned out of the window.

'What the fuck you doing?' Ricky shouted.

Raymond hadn't eaten much all day, so rather than actually be sick, he just heaved. 'Sorry, my guts have felt dodgy since that poxy sandwich this morning. I'm fine now,' he lied.

Gary was fuming with his old man for putting the fear of God into everyone. He knew his father's words had caused Raymond to feel nauseous. 'Are you going soft in your old age or what? Them thick pikey cunts have been following us all the way from Scotland yet they're still hanging way back. They're that dense they don't even think we've clocked they're on our tail. As for ringing our families, saying our possible goodbyes, I've never heard such a load of old bollocks in all of my life. We're the Mitchells, for fuck's sake, and I, for one, ain't scared of no bastard.'

Eddie digested his son's words and, feeling embarrassed, nodded. 'You're dead right, Gal. Come on, let's fucking finish this, lads.'

Frankie could barely breathe when Dom's car finally appeared outside. Her legs felt like jelly as she ran out to the drive.

'My babies, my little babies,' she sobbed, as she approached the car.

Joey got out, shut the door, and held his tearful sister in his arms.

'Let me see 'em. I wanna hold 'em,' Frankie screamed hysterically.

'Calm down, you'll frighten them. They're nothing like you remember them, so don't act too shocked, eh? They're going to need plenty of time to settle; they've had a hard life, remember?' Joey warned.

387

'Georgie! Harry!' Frankie yelled, as her brother opened the car door.

'Say hello to your mum,' Joey urged the kids.

Georgie stared at her mother. Harry didn't want to look at the woman who had taken him away from his beloved family, so looked at the gravel instead. Neither child said a word.

'Why are their little hands tied up?' Frankie cried.

'They tried to do a runner earlier. Now, let's get them inside, they must be hungry and thirsty by now,' Joey said sensibly.

Frankie couldn't help her tearful reaction to her children's homecoming but, not wanting to startle them further, did her best to pull herself together. The last time she had seen them was in 1993, on the day that she'd stabbed Jed. She'd gone to prison straight after that and had never set eyes on them since. Joey untied Georgie and Harry's hands and told them to sit down on the sofa. Frankie knelt down next to her children and tried to hug them both.

'Leave us alone. Go away!' Harry shouted angrily.

Georgie sat frozen to the spot. She was staring at her mother as if she'd just seen a ghost.

Babs turned to Joey and Dominic. 'Let's go rustle up some food and drinks. Frankie needs time alone with her babies.'

Frankie grabbed the leather pouffe and sat down opposite her children. She could barely believe they were home and she couldn't take her eyes off them. They looked so grown up, both of them.

'I can't believe how old you both look,' she whispered.

The kids glanced at one another. Being in a big house was strange enough on its own, as neither child could remember setting foot in one before.

'Do you remember me at all?' Frankie asked. She was shocked by how mature for thirteen Georgie looked and Harry she would never have recognised in a million years. His hair had darkened so much from when he was little.

Georgie nodded, then grasped her brother's hand.

When Harry was around his dad, grandad, and especially Sonny Adams, he was brazen and never scared of anything. Today, however, had really put the fear factor into him and being separated from all his family, bar Georgie, he couldn't hold it together any longer. 'I don't wanna be here. I want my dad and my nan,' he cried.

When Frankie tried to physically comfort him, he angrily pushed her away. 'Get off me, you fucking shitcunt. This is all your fault – I hate you,' he screamed.

'Harry, I'm your mum, don't you understand that?' Frankie asked tearfully.

'Leave my brother alone. You tried to kill our dad. We both hate you,' Georgie yelled protectively.

Frankie stared at the two children she no longer knew or recognised. Memories of their childhood came flooding back. Their births, their first steps, Georgie's favourite doll, her first day at school. She could even picture Harry toddling around with his beloved teddy bear under his arm. How he'd cried when he thought she'd lost it that time, when she'd planned to put it in Jed's motor with the tape recorder hidden inside. For years, Frankie had dreamed and planned this reconciliation, but it was never meant to turn out like this. She wasn't stupid. She'd hardly expected the children to gallop into her arms and then they all live happily ever after, but she'd thought they might have missed her, or would at least be pleased to see her again. Instead, they'd been reared to hate her. They'd been brainwashed by their father, Alice and Jimmy and how she was meant to change their perception of her, she really did not know.

Unaware that his kids were no longer in the back of the Sprinter van, Jed was full of beans as he and Billy drove through Elm Park. He was no longer angry with his brother for forgetting the bullets, he was too excited about what was about to happen to be bothered about that now.

'Ring Dad and pass me the phone,' he ordered Billy.

'All right, boy. I was just saying to Mickey, I think Mitchell could be heading to his salvage yard. I bet the prick keeps his guns there, unless they've already got shooters on 'em, or Frankie's living over that way.'

'Do you reckon they know we're following 'em? Me and Bill don't.'

'I should imagine so. Mitchell might be a lot of things, but he's no dinlo, boy. What I suggest we do is catch right up with him now. He's bound to stop somewhere soon and when he does, we'll be ready. We don't want the chavvies involved, so we get them out the back and get Billy to drive 'em straight back to Glasgow. I've rang your mum and she's OK now, she just wants us all home safe and sound. We're gonna have to move off the site though; I've already made a few phone calls and sorted us somewhere.'

'Why we gotta move? Surely if we finish off the cunts tonight, we're safe where we are?'

'Your mother wants to move, says we don't know who else the Mitchells have involved. I think she's right. The quicker we get out of Glasgow, the better.'

'Fuck all this talk about moving. What I wanna know is how we're gonna play this. We know Eddie and Raymond are definitely in the van and you can bet his cunting sons are with him, and probably some other mug that works for him. I don't just wanna blast 'em all away. Let's kill any deadwood, and then torture Eddie,' Jed suggested.

Jimmy chuckled. He and Eddie Mitchell had been at loggerheads since 1970 and he certainly wanted to give him the most agonising death possible, but there wasn't the time to torture him properly. 'I dunno if we'll have time to arse about, Jed. We'll make sure we send him out in a bit of style though, I promise. Now catch up with us 'cause we're just approaching the A13.'

When Jed started to laugh manically, Billy looked at him as though he had lost his marbles. Unlike his brother, he was shit-scared over what was about to happen and he couldn't work Jed's mind out at times. 'What's a matter? What you laughing at?'

'When Mitchell's gasping for his last breath, I've got a big surprise for him and Dad.'

'What?'

'I'm gonna tell both of 'em who killed Harry Mitchell.'

'What, you gonna make something up?' Billy asked confused.

'No, I'm gonna tell the truth. It was me that killed the old cunt and I can barely wait to break the good news.'

* * *

390

Eddie Mitchell's heart was beating nineteen to the dozen as they approached his salvage yard. He'd wanted Jimmy O'Hara dead for as long as he could remember and now he finally had the chance to do something about it. 'Let me take Jimmy out. Gal, Raymondo, yous two make sure Jed cops it, then go for whoever else is with 'em. Ricky, you get the guns. Right, lads, get your hands on that door handle 'cause we're pulling up in less than a minute or so.'

Ed had rung Big Pete, who managed the yard for him, hours earlier. The gates were made of wire mesh, and Ed had told him to just pull them to and put the chain or padlocks on one gate. 'I've lost me key and need to drop a hooky motor off later,' Ed had lied.

'Right, hold tight, in case Pete's fucked up and we smash ourselves to pieces,' Eddie said, as Raymond put his foot full on the accelerator.

When the gates flew open and the van screeched to a halt, Eddie yelled his adrenalin-filled orders. 'Go, go, go!'

CHAPTER FORTY

When Jimmy and Jed both screeched to a halt, all hell immediately broke loose. Baseball bats, knives, even a hammer was used in the tussle that followed.

'Grab the fucking gun, Ray,' Eddie screamed, as he managed to knock the sawn-off out of Jimmy's hand.

About to comply with his boss's orders, Raymond was whacked over the head with a hammer by Mickey Maloney and fell to the ground in a heap.

Jed picked the gun up and immediately fired two shots. He'd spotted Ricky running towards the left-hand side of the yard and guessed he was up to no good. 'Gotcha, you shitcunt,' he said, as Ricky's body hit the ground with a dramatic thud.

'Jed, help me. I've been stabbed,' Billy pleaded.

Jed glanced at his brother, saw no blood, so turned his attention to Ricky instead. 'Let me sort these cunts out; I need to check they ain't got phones on 'em. I'll be back in a minute, Bill,' he promised.

Gary was running towards where Ricky had taken a tumble. 'You ain't going nowhere, cunt,' Jed shouted, as he took a couple of pot shots at Gary as well.

'Fuck,' Gary screamed in agony, clutching the back of his right leg as he fell to the floor.

Jed took Gary's mobile out of his pocket, smirked, then ran over to Eddie's van. He flung open the back doors, fully expecting an emotional reconciliation with his children and was shell-shocked to find that, apart from four sports bags and some rope, the van was empty.

'You fucking cunt. Where are my chavvies?' Jed shrieked as he ran over to where Eddie Mitchell lay.

Eddie was in agony. Between them, Jimmy and Mickey had managed to overpower him somehow and not only had they twisted his right arm until it had broken, they'd also smashed him across both kneecaps with a hammer.

'I said, where are my fucking chavvies?' Jed repeated, his eyes bulging with anger.

As ill as he felt, Eddie had never been a man to disclose important information. 'Somewhere where you'll never find 'em,' he spat.

'This is all your fault. I told you not to let him out of your sight, didn't I?' Jed shouted at his father. He was almost crying with rage, and aimed a kick at Eddie's head.

Jimmy hung his head in shame. If only he had known that the tear-up would take place at the salvage yard, he'd have driven into that poxy garage. He'd been worried it might all go off in a public street where neighbours might be able to give a description of him, and he hadn't wanted to be caught on any cameras, just in case. He could just imagine an image of him on the garage forecourt ending up in the papers or on the news. The police had never looked very hard to find the children, but they'd look for him if he was wanted for murder, Jimmy was sure of that.

He put a comforting arm around his son's shoulder. When they'd left Essex, he had never kept in touch with any of his old pals from the manor because they were on the run. He'd known Pat Murphy most of his life, and how he now wished that he'd kept in contact with him. He would have known where Eddie lived and he could probably have given him Frankie's address as well.

'I'm gonna fucking kill him, Dad,' Jed yelled, pointing the gun at Eddie once more.

'Keep an eye on him, Mick, while me and Jed check on the others,' Jimmy instructed, leading his son away.

'On my Shelby girl's life, if that shitcunt don't give me an address in the next five minutes, I'm gonna blow his brains out,' Jed spat.

'Give me that gun,' Jimmy ordered.

Jed shook his head, so Jimmy slapped him hard around the face to knock some sense into him.

'Killing Eddie at this point ain't gonna get you them chavvies back, you dinlo. Now pull yourself together. Let's get everybody tied up and we'll torture the answers out of 'em. Now, where's Billy?'

Jed felt a pang of guilt as he remembered his brother had said he'd been stabbed. 'I dunno. It's proper fucking dark now,' he lied.

Jimmy ran to his motor and grabbed his torch and some rope. 'Jed, over there. Look, one of the bastards is getting away,' he said, spotting Gary moving towards the far end of the yard.

Gary was only seconds away from where the guns were kept when Jed tussled him to the ground. His right leg was bleeding profusely, but even though he couldn't put his foot to the floor, he'd still managed to drag himself towards the newly built toilet where the shooters were kept. He'd found Ricky lying in a puddle of oil on his travels. His brother was still alive, but had been shot in the back and looked in a really bad way.

'Where were ya going?' Jed asked Gary, with a menacing expression on his face. He knew he wasn't heading towards the exit, and Jed's guess was he was trying to retrieve a gun from somewhere.

Instead of pointing towards the toilet, Gary pointed to the big building on the left-hand side of it. It was an old warehouse that was now part of the salvage yard and it was where all the tyres were kept.

'Got guns in there, have ya?' Jed snarled.

'Nah, I was gonna see if there was a phone in there,' Gary lied.

'Jed, get back down this end, boy. Your brother's in trouble, I think. We might have to get him to a hospital,' Jimmy shouted out.

Kneeing Gary as hard as he could in the proverbials to ensure he wouldn't move again for the foreseeable future, Jed legged it down to the other end of the yard. He paused as he saw Ricky lying face down on the ground and, unable to stop himself, gave him a sharp kick in the side of his head. He then checked on Raymond, who was still out for the count, before he ran back to his father.

'There's hardly any blood. He'll live,' Jed said, as he inspected the two small gashes on his brother's stomach.

'He don't look good, boy. Keeps shutting his eyes and talking rubbish like he's delirious. He might have internal bleeding or something. Mickey's gonna have to take him to A&E in case it's bad,' Jimmy said anxiously.

'And what's he meant to say when he gets there?'

'Mickey'll have to say he got stabbed in a fight and tell the nurses his name's Billy Smith. He can tell 'em he's a traveller and give 'em the name of the site in Tilbury. If the Old Bill are called, Mickey'll have to give a false name an' all.'

Jed nodded. 'Get Mickey to drop him at Basildon Hospital then, the further away from 'ere the better. There's a building down there on the left, looks like a warehouse. Let's tie the others up, drag them in there and torture some answers out of 'em. As soon as we get the truth, we'll kill 'em all.'

'Jimmy, Jimmy!' Mickey yelled.

Jimmy and Jed ran over to their pal. Eddie Mitchell had his left hand around Mickey Maloney's throat and was doing his best to strangle him.

Seeing a baseball bat lying nearby, Jed picked it up and smashed Eddie over the back of the head with it. 'Give me that rope, Dad. Let's tie this piece of shit up first,' he said as Eddie fell helplessly to the ground.

'I'll tie him up,' Jimmy said. He was worried his son would go too far and actually kill Mitchell before they got the information they needed.

Eddie Mitchell was a man who had too much pride to have ever considered defeat in the past, but as Jimmy smashed his mobile phone, then tied the thick rope around his hands, he feared the worst for the first time ever. Images of Gina, Rosie and Aaron flashed through his mind and he felt like fucking crying. He'd wanted to ring his family earlier, tell them how much he loved them, but Gary had stopped him from doing so. Now he would probably never have the chance to speak to them ever again.

* * *

395

Frankie smiled at Georgie as Harry wolfed the last of the chicken sandwiches. When Georgie was young she'd had strange eating habits, gorging on food for days then starving herself. Seeing Harry eat a whole tray of sandwiches by himself, Frankie wondered if her son was of the same mould.

'Are you still not hungry, Georgie? You should really eat something. Do you remember when you was a little girl you used to be addicted to them Heinz bangers and beans? I've got some in the cupboard. Shall I get Joey to open a tin for you?'

'I ain't a little girl no more and if I say I ain't hungry then I ain't. I've got a boyfriend who I'm gonna marry as soon as I'm sixteen, I'm a grown-up now.'

Frankie was appalled, but tried not to show it. At least Georgie was talking to her now. Her children's accents were absolutely awful. They sounded just like their father and the way they pronounced their words and some of the things they said brought back terrible memories of her time with Jed.

'So what's your boyfriend's name? Is he the same age as you?' Frankie asked pleasantly.

'His name's Ryan and he's fifteen. I really love him and he loves me. Look, he bought me this,' Georgie said, flashing the eternity ring her boyfriend had given her for her birthday.

Frankie felt sick as she stared at the ring. When she had last seen Georgie, she'd been an adventurous, fun-loving, four-year-old girl. Now she had massive breasts, a gypsy accent and was discussing her bloody wedding. Wishing more than ever that she had succeeded when she'd tried to kill Jed that time, Frankie forced herself to smile. 'Is Ryan a travelling boy?'

'Yeah! I would never marry him if he weren't. All gorjers are scum; Nanny Alice and Dad taught me that.'

'And what about you Harry, have you got a girlfriend yet?' Frankie asked, trying to include her son in the awkward conversation.

'Mind your own business,' Harry replied, glaring at her.

Frankie had sadness etched across her face as she stared at both of her children. In all honesty, Georgie had always had a slight wild streak in her. When she was young she used to have a habit of running away and she had never been able to suffer the confinement of a classroom when she'd started school. Georgie looked like her father, had his mannerisms, and Frankie knew she only had herself to blame for that.

'Can we go home now? You can't make us stay 'ere,' Harry said bluntly.

Feeling her eyes well up again, Frankie bit her lip to stop herself from crying. The change in her beautiful, loving, timid son was the one thing that was literally breaking her heart in two. Gone was the happy, fresh-faced, polite little boy whose smile could light up a room. In his place was a sullen, dirty, scruffy lad who had an attitude problem, terrible language and front teeth missing.

'So, what hobbies have you both got?' Frankie asked awkwardly. She felt as if she was conducting an interview with two complete strangers.

'I like shopping for clothes and I like music. Harry likes quad bikes and thieving,' Georgie responded, nudging her brother.

'You like drinking cider and playing with Ryan's cory,' Harry chuckled, joining in with the fun.

Unable to stand one minute more in the same room as her children, Frankie let out a stifled sob and bolted.

Jimmy and Jed led Eddie to the warehouse where the tyres were kept, and laughed as they pushed him violently onto the concrete floor.

'Tie his legs up while I bring the next one in,' Jimmy ordered his son. Mickey had now taken Billy to the hospital and Jimmy insisted that his son wasn't to be left alone until the extent of his injuries were known.

'If he were to die, I don't want him dying alone, Mick,' Jimmy had told his friend.

Jed picked up the rope and smirked at Eddie. 'What's it feel like, knowing you're gonna die soon?'

Aware that Mickey had taken Billy to hospital, Eddie knew, with Jimmy outside, this might be his last chance to get to the guns. He waited until Jed bent down to tie his feet up then, with all his might, kicked him full in the face with his right foot. Jed flew backwards, clutching his chin and cursing.

'You fucking wanker,' he mumbled, as he stood up and spat out a mouthful of blood. Eddie's kick had caught him completely by surprise, so much so that his teeth had nearly severed the end of his tongue.

Aware that Jed was in shock, Eddie leaned his back against the wall and tried to heave himself up by crawling up against it. He needed to get outside to see if one of his lads was in a fit state to untie his hands.

In excrutiating pain, Jed put his hand inside his mouth. The tip of his tongue was literally hanging there by a thread. Aware that Eddie was back-crawling up the wall, Jed forgot about his own predicament, and grabbed the hammer.

'You ain't going nowhere you fucking piece of shit!' he screamed as he repeatedly smashed it against Eddie's legs. When Ed fell to the floor, Jed ran over to where the tyres were kept. He picked up one that was attached to an alloy wheel and ran back over to where Eddie lay. 'Tell me where my chavvies are, you cunt,' he slurred, repeatedly smashing the wheel against Eddie's left leg. The injury to his tongue was stopping him from pronouncing his words properly.

Eddie winced as he felt his shin snap in two, but he still didn't groan or utter a word. The O'Haras might be capable of breaking his arms and legs, but they would never break his spirit.

Joey held his inconsolable sister in his arms.

'Can yous two sit in the front room and keep an eye on the kids while I have a chat with Frankie?' Joey asked Dominic and Babs.

Dom and Babs both nodded and Joey shut the kitchen door. He opened a bottle of wine and poured two glasses.

'What the hell am I gonna do, Joey? They've changed so much I don't even feel like their mother any more. I knew they would have been brought up badly, but they're worse than my wildest dreams. I don't like either of 'em, especially Harry – I think he's horrible. What type of mother does that make me, eh?' Frankie sobbed.

Joey sat his sister down at the kitchen table and handed her a glass. 'Drink that, it will make you feel better,' he said, before downing his own in one. Joey put his empty glass on the table and let out a worried sigh. Apart from the day that his mother had been murdered, this was probably the worst and most stressful day of his entire life. His dad's life was in danger along with his uncle's and stepbrothers. He'd rowed with Dom and, unbeknown to Frankie, had a gun hidden upstairs.

'Where's Dad? I can't cope, Joey. I think he should take 'em back to Jed. They'll never acclimatise to living here with me; they hate me,' Frankie wept.

Forcing himself to be strong, Joey took his sister's hands in his. 'Don't you dare fucking give up, Frankie Mitchell. Getting them kids back was never gonna be a bowl of cherries within hours of their return, was it? They're victims of Jed, just the same as you are. They'll settle in and grow to love you eventually, but it's going to take a hell of a lot of patience and hard work, on your behalf especially.'

'I don't think I can do it, Joey, and what about poor Brett? It's gonna be awful for him living with them two, I just know it is.'

'You can't surrender at the first sign of problems, Frankie. Brett will get used to them being around, and me and Babs will both be here to help you.'

'I wish Stuart was here. He would know what to do. Ring him for me, Joey. I haven't heard from him today.'

'He rang earlier, just after the kids got back. I told him they were home and he said he'll call you back later,' Joey told her.

Frankie stood up. 'I'm gonna ring him back now. I need his advice.'

'No,' Joey insisted grabbing her by the arm. He knew that she would start firing questions at Stuart about where her dad was and he didn't want to put Stu in an awkward position. His dad had told both of them that under no circumstances were they to breathe a word of the O'Haras following them to Essex.

'What's going on, Joey? I know something's wrong. Where's Dad?' Frankie asked with suspicion.

Joey had never lied to his twin sister in their younger years. Even when she'd first suspected he was gay, he'd admitted the truth immediately, but just lately, because his dad had encouraged him, he'd become good at fabrication.

'Don't start worrying. All it is, is Stu was with Terry and

their van broke down on the way home from Scotland. Dad couldn't send the AA 'cause the van's a ringer, so he had to get his own mechanic and send him up the M1. You know, the phone calls I told you about earlier.'

'But you said that Dad's van was the one breaking down and I thought Stu was staying in Scotland for a bit.'

'Nah, it was the other van, and Dad told Stu to forget about staying in Scotland, he said there was no point. I think the vans belong to a mate of Dad's and he can't leave one on the M1 in case he gets the guy in trouble. The mechanic is gonna drop Stu and Tel back here and when Dad and the boys have burned the vans, they'll come back, too,' Joey fibbed.

'Thank God for that! I had an awful feeling that Jed and Jimmy might be following Dad. There's something I need to tell you, Joey, something I should have told you years ago, but I was so worried about Dad getting hurt or banged up again that I kept it all to myself. Please don't have a go at me when I tell ya, 'cause I was gonna tell you when I was in prison, but when the O'Haras did a runner with Georgie and Harry, I didn't want them caught up in the crossfire. Now we've got them back, it's the right time to tell you, I know it is. I want you to decide whether we should tell Dad or not, because the burden of keeping it from him is tearing me apart.'

Joey felt a shiver run down his spine. He had no idea what his sister was talking about, but he knew that whatever it was, it was going to be bad news. 'Tell me, Frankie,' he demanded in a hushed tone.

Frankie took a deep breath. 'It was Jed that killed Grandad Harry.'

Joey looked at his sister as though she'd gone mental. 'Don't be so ridiculous. If Jed told you that, he's a liar. He was winding you up, Frankie.'

Frankie felt her eyes well up once more. Apart from Babs and DI Blyth, she had kept the secret to herself for so long, the guilt of revealing it to her brother was almost unbearable.

'He wasn't lying, Joey. Me and Kerry planted a tape in Jed's Shogun; we heard him talking about it with our own ears. Sammy was with him. They both murdered our Grandad.'

Joey counted back the years and shook his head. Jed would have only been about fifteen at the time, how could he have been the one to kill his gangster of a grandfather? 'You're wrong, sis, you're so fucking wrong. Jed was only about fifteen. I bet you any money you like that he saw you and Kerry plant the tape and because he wanted to split up with you, he said all that on purpose.'

With tears now streaming down her face, Frankie crouched down and clutched her brother's hands. 'We only planted the tape because me and Kerry knew that Jed and Sammy were cheating on us. That's why I tried to kill him, Joey, it's true, I swear it is. You ask DI Blyth if you don't believe me; I even told her.'

Taking four deep breaths to stop himself from losing it completely, Joey pushed his sister out of the way and and ran upstairs to retrieve the gun.

'Joey, I'm sorry. Come back, please,' Frankie wailed.

When Joey ran back down the stairs, he bore a look on his face that Frankie didn't even recognise. 'Dominic!' he screamed.

'Whatever's the matter?' Dom asked as he came out of the lounge.

'I need you to drive me somewhere. It's important,' Joey said, his voice as cold as ice.

'No way. I've had enough of driving you about today to last me a lifetime,' Dom replied sarcastically.

Grabbing his boyfriend by the neck, Joey slammed him up against the wall. 'You either drive me or we're finished for ever, and I mean that.'

Dominic stared at the coldness in his partner's eyes. He didn't even recognise the man he'd been in love with for the past twelve years. Knowing he only had a split second to decide whether to stand by his man or lose Joey for good, Dominic made his choice.

'Come on, let's go,' he shouted, as he grabbed his leather jacket.

As the front door slammed behind her brother and his boyfriend, Frankie guessed the truth and let out the most piercing scream her voice could reach.

401

CHAPTER FORTY-ONE

When Babs ran out of the room to tend to Frankie, Georgie turned to her brother. 'I've got a plan. I think we should start being nicer to Mum, because if we do that, it will make it easier for us to escape.'

'I don't like her, though. Can't we just ring Dad? He'll come and get us.'

'I don't know Dad's number off by heart, or Grandad's. Do you?'

Harry shook his head. 'Don't you know Nan's number or Ryan's?'

'No. They're all stored in my phone. Try and remember some of the numbers, Harry. Don't you know your own?'

'No, don't you know yours?' Harry asked.

'I knew my old number, but not the new one,' Georgie replied.

'How we gonna escape if we can't ring anyone? I wanna go home,' Harry whinged.

Seeing that her brother was about to cry again, Georgie hugged him. 'We will go home, I promise you that. Dad and Grandad will definitely find us, but in the meantime let's try and be a bit nicer to everyone, because that way they'll leave us alone a bit more. If we need to escape, we don't want them watching us all the time and if they think we're unhappy, they will.'

'But say Eddie hurts Dad and Grandad. They won't be able to come and get us if they're ill,' Harry wept.

Georgie had the same fear, but being the eldest, put on a carefree attitude for her brother's sake. 'Dad and Grandad are far too clever to let anything bad happen to 'em. Now, just be strong for me, Harry, until I can sort something out. We won't have to stay 'ere long, I promise you that, but while we're stuck 'ere we might as well get to know Frankie a bit better. She is our mum, after all.'

Babs was having little joy calming Frankie down so, at her wits' end, rang Kerry. 'It's Babs, Frankie's friend. I'm sorry to ring you so late. Did I wake you up?'

'Yeah, but not to worry. Has something happened to Frankie? Is she OK?' Kerry asked worriedly. She had been furious with Frankie when she'd all but told her to stay out of her life, but they had been through so much together, she could never hate her or wish her any harm.

Babs explained that the kids were home and that Frankie was in pieces. 'She's upstairs crying now. I ain't told her that I were gonna ring you, but I know she could do with your help. Georgie and Harry have been real nasty to her. If you could ring her over the next couple of days and lend your support, that would be wicked.'

'OK, I'll call her first thing tomorrow.'

Joyce thought she was having a bad dream when she heard someone sobbing uncontrollably. Rubbing her eyes, she sat up and turned on the light. No, she couldn't have been dreaming, someone was crying. Joyce got up, put her dressing gown over her nightdress and went to investigate.

'Whatever's the matter?' she asked as she spotted Frankie sitting on the landing, rocking to and fro.

'Joey's in danger, so is me Dad, Raymond, Gal, Ricky and Dominic. Jed and Jimmy have followed 'em back from Scotland and now Joey's chasing after 'em. I've tried to ring Stuart, but his phone's dead. Say he's been hurt an' all?' Frankie sobbed.

Joyce felt her heart start to pound at double its usual pace. She had already lost her beautiful daughter because of Eddie's feud with the O'Haras, and the thought of losing her Raymond as well didn't bear thinking of. She crouched down next to her granddaughter. 'Who told you all this, your dad?'

'No, it was Joey's reaction when I told him a secret that gave it away. I had a feeling Dad had been followed, that's why he kept ringing Joey earlier. Jed's evil, Nan, he murdered my grandad.'

'What?' Joyce asked incredulously.

Frankie fell into her grandmother's arms. 'Jed killed Grandad Harry, Nan.'

Overcome by sudden tiredness, Harry had fallen asleep on his sister's lap.

'Wake up, Harry. Someone's at the door – it might be Dad,' Georgie said, poking him in the shoulder. They'd been in the lounge on their own for ages now. Her mother and the black woman had both disappeared.

'Frankie, it's Stu and Tel,' Georgie heard a voice say.

'Can't we nick some money and just run away?' Harry asked, rubbing his tired eyes.

'No. We must wait for Dad to come and get us, in case the gavvers find us and lock us up.'

Frankie ran down the stairs and threw herself into Stuart's strong arms. 'I was so worried about you, Stu. Have you seen my dad and Joey? Are they OK?' she wept.

'I ain't seen 'em. Your dad told us to come 'ere to look after you and the kids. Where's Joey gone, then?' Stuart asked, enjoying Frankie's warm welcome. He'd missed seeing her so bloody much and he'd only been in Scotland a couple of days.

'I need to speak to you alone,' Frankie said, dragging him into the kitchen by the arm.

Upstairs, Stanley was having one of his recurring nightmares about Pat the Pigeon. In this particular dream, she had his John Thomas in her mouth and she was laughing as she snapped the end of it off with her teeth.

'Stanley, wake up, Stanley,' Joycie said, shaking him furiously by the shoulder.

'Get off me, leave me alone, you old slapper,' Stanley mumbled.

Absolutely livid, Joyce punched her husband as hard as she could in the side of his ugly bald head. 'How dare you call me that after what you did! I have never been so insulted in my entire life.'

Stanley sat up, clutching his sore head in his hands. 'That bleedin' hurt. What did you do that for?'

'Because you called me an old slapper. You no good, philandering, bald-headed, old bastard.'

'No I never. I didn't even know you was in the bleedin' bedroom.'

'Get up. The kids are back home and there's a drama going on downstairs. Apparently Jed killed Harry Mitchell and Frankie reckons our Raymond's life's in danger. Jimmy and Jed followed the lads home from Glasgow, by all accounts, and no one knows where they are now.'

As his wife dissolved into tears, Stanley forgot about the pain in the side of his head and jumped out of bed to comfort her. 'Our Raymond will be fine, love. He's a big boy and he knows how to look after himself. Now, go outside while I get dressed and I'll come downstairs with you.'

'Just hurry up and put your bleedin' clothes on. You ain't got nothing I ain't seen before, Stanley. We produced two kids, you senile old fool.'

Stuart felt his blood run cold as he listened to what Frankie had to say.

'You know what your dad's like, Frankie. If this is true, he'll never forgive you, so best you don't tell him you knew about it. When I was inside with him, all he ever spoke about was how much he loved your mother and how he needed to track down his father's killers. If this comes out, he'll disown you,' Stuart said truthfully.

'But I've already told Joey and me nan. I can't keep it secret now, can I?' Frankie wept, feeling totally sorry for herself.

Stuart stood up. He was furious with Frankie for burdening him with her knowledge. How was he meant to keep schtum to Eddie about this?

Frankie clocked the look of disappointment on Stuart's face and threw her arms around his neck. 'Please don't go, Stu. Stay 'ere with me.'

405

'I need to carry out your dad's orders, Frankie,' Stuart said, loosening her grip from around his neck.

Worried that if Stuart left, she might never see him again, Frankie looked at him in a totally different light. He'd always been a great mate, a rock who offered a strong shoulder to cry on, but realising his life might now be in danger brought Frankie's true feelings bubbling to the surface. For the first time ever, she admitted to herself how handsome Stuart was, how when he held her in his arms his touch made her feel safe and womanly. Jed had destroyed her faith in men, but Stuart wasn't Jed. He was the total opposite of her ex and, as Frankie let her barrier slip, she realised just how much she loved him. With no time left to mess around, Frankie grabbed Stuart by the arm.

'Do you love me?' she asked him bluntly.

'You know I love you. I wouldn't bleedin' come and visit you every day if I didn't,' Stuart replied.

'I don't mean a friendship kind of love. I mean, are you in love with me, as in, do you want to be with me?'

Unable to look Frankie in the eye in case his answer repulsed her, Stuart stared at his feet. 'Yeah, I am in love with you, Frankie, and I do wanna be with you.'

Frankie punched him gently in the chest. 'Why didn't I wake up and smell the coffee earlier? We've wasted so much time.'

Stuart looked at her in amazement. Was she trying to tell him that she felt the same way? 'What you trying to say, Frankie?'

'I'm trying to tell you that I love you as well, you dickhead.'

Aware that Frankie was crying yet again, Stuart held her in his arms. 'Why didn't you let me know how you felt? You never acted like you wanted to know.'

'Because I brainwashed myself that all men were like Jed and I also didn't think you'd be interested. I lived with a pikey who just happened to kill my grandad. My mum's dead because of me and so are my uncles. I've got three gypsy kids, two who seem to be uncontrollable. What decent man would want me, eh?'

Stuart held her tearful face in his hands. 'Frankie, none of those deaths or anything that happened was your fault. The feud that your dad, grandad and uncles were part of with the O'Haras started long before you ever entered this world. You never caused it, babe, you're the victim of it.'

As their lips met romantically for the very first time, Stuart felt as though he was in seventh heaven but remembering the promise he'd made to Eddie, pulled away from Frankie's grasp and opened the kitchen door. 'Tel, grab the sports bag on top of the wardrobe in Jordan's room,' he shouted.

Terry ran upstairs, grabbed the sports bag and threw the contents onto the floor. The gun had gone.

'Stu, we've gotta go out again,' Tel shouted as he pushed past Joyce and Stanley and ran down the stairs.

'What did Joey hide upstairs, Stu? Please tell me, was it a gun?' Frankie cried.

Instead of answering the question, Stuart kissed her gently on the lips. 'Lock all the doors and if anyone knocks, don't answer it. My battery's gone dead, so ring me on Tel's phone if you need me.'

Joyce and Stanley had been standing at the top of the stairs earwigging and had heard the conversation between Frankie, Stuart and Terry.

'Who's got a gun? Please God, not our Joey,' Joycie screamed at Frankie.

Stanley put his head in his hands. From the first moment his Jessica had brought home Eddie Mitchell, he'd known he was trouble. He'd told Joycie his fears at the time, he'd known the Mitchell family's reputation, but she wouldn't listen, and instead of warning Jessica to steer clear, she'd encouraged their relationship. With panic in his eyes, Stanley shook his head in despair.

'If only you'd have listened to me, Joycie. If only you'd have bloody listened, woman.'

Back at the salvage yard over in Dagenham, Eddie, Gary and Raymond had spent the past fifteen minutes sitting in the warehouse where the tyres were stored, being tortured for answers. Like Raymond earlier, Ricky was now the one in and out of consciousness and Ed was desperately worried about him. He was still breathing, but had lost so much blood since being shot that Eddie knew he could die if they didn't get him to a hospital soon.

Gary took a deep breath as Jed put the gun to his temple once more. He was more frightened of his brother dying than getting killed himself.

'You've got one more chance to tell me where my chavvies are, otherwise I'm gonna blow your brains out. Now, what will it be?' Jed jeered, his voice full of evil.

Gary stared at his father and Raymond. Both men had their hands and feet tied up and were sitting opposite him, their backs against a wall. Ricky was lying next to them, in a bloodied heap. Winking at his dad as a sign of letting him know he was OK, Gary answered Jed's question. 'Blow me brains out then, you cunt.'

Realising they were getting nowhere fast, Jimmy urged Jed to follow him outside the building. 'Look, boy, this technique ain't working and we can't go home without them chavvies, 'cause your mother will lose the fucking plot. What I suggest we do is kill one of 'em. That should then give the others a kick up the arse to start talking,' Jimmy suggested.

Jed spat a mouthful of blood on the floor. His tongue was still throbbing, but the pain was bearable.

'Let's kill Gary first. Can you imagine how Mitchell will feel, seeing his trappy cunting son die in front of him?' Jed replied.

'Nah, let's kill the other son. He's virtually out for the count, so can't give us no answers anyway. We need to keep the ones alive that can still talk, Jed.'

'Can't you drive over to Pat Murphy's and see if he knows Ed or Frankie's addresses? He's only ten minutes down the road and I can take care of these dinlos until you get back.'

'Sonny Tyler told me that Murphy sold up a year or so back. Moved to Norfolk somewhere, he did. We'll get the info we need once we start pulling that trigger, boy. The mouthy one ain't gonna tell us nought, neither is that shitcunt Raymond, so what I suggest we do is blow Ricky's brains out, then see if Eddie falters. If we've killed one of his boys, then he knows we're capable of killing the others, so he might just start blabbing.'

Jed smirked. 'I've got something to tell him that's gonna really get his goat.'

'What?' Jimmy asked intrigued.

Jed chuckled. 'You'll soon find out. Call it an early birthday present.'

'Be brave and say nothing, boys. If we're gonna die, let's do it with our heads held high. I know it's hard, but let's try not to think of our families. We know they're well provided for and we know they'll never forget us. We're fucking legends, always remember that,' Eddie said, trying to keep everybody's spirits up, even though he knew deep down they were all goners. Eddie had always lived his life with a certain style and if he was going to croak it tonight, then he would die with style as well.

'What yous cunts whispering about?' Jed asked, as he walked back into the warehouse with a sadistic expression plastered on his face.

'We were just saying what fucking knob-ends you and your father are,' Ed replied smirking.

Jimmy strolled over to where Eddie was trussed up. He bent down and ran his fingers across the scar on Ed's left cheek. It was the one he'd put there back in 1970. 'If you thought I left you with a reminder of what I was all about then, Mitchell, that's nothing compared to what I'm gonna do to ya now.'

Eddie sniffed, collected whatever phlegm he could from the back of his throat and gobbed it into Jimmy's face. 'Mug,' he said forcing a grin.

Absolutely seething, Jimmy wiped his face with his sleeve, then grabbed Ricky by his lifeless neck. He knew what it felt like to lose a son and now Eddie would know what it felt like, too.

'Where am I?' Ricky mumbled. He was in cloud cuckoo land.

When Jimmy grabbed the gun off Jed and put it to Ricky's head, Eddie shut his eyes. *He's all but dead, anyway, and at least he won't be suffering no more*, he tried to convince himself.

'Fucking pikey cunts,' he heard Gary scream as the gun went off.

Eddie opened his eyes again. His wonderful son was lying on the floor with the left-hand side of his head blown away. His eyes were still open, so was his mouth and he had a look of shock on his face rather than one of peace. Images of Ricky's childhood flooded through Eddie's mind and he quickly shut his eyes again.

Gary was crying, not out loud, but Ed was aware of his pain.

'Snap out of it,' he mumbled, before Jed and Jimmy dragged him across the concrete floor.

Jed smirked as his father perched Eddie on top of the two tyres they were using as their execution chair. After all these years, it was the perfect time for him to reveal his little secret. He crouched down in front of Eddie and grinned at him.

'I think it's high time I spilt the beans. Would you like to know the real reason why your Frankie tried to kill me, ya mug?'

'What's he going on about?' Gary whispered to Raymond.

Raymond said nothing. He was too upset to speak. All he could think about was Polly and Chelsea. His beautiful daughter was so looking forward to the big party he and Polly had planned for her seventh birthday and now he wouldn't even be alive to celebrate it with her.

Eddie focused his eyes firmly to his right. Ricky was lying to his left and if he looked at his dead son's body, he was worried he'd crumble.

'I said, do you wanna know why Frankie tried to kill me?' Jed screamed, punching Eddie in the face.

'Because she thought you was a cock,' Eddie replied sarcastically.

Jed laughed out loud. 'Never caught the geezer who murdered your father, did they? Ever wondered why, have ya? That's why Frankie stabbed me. She found out I was the culprit.'

Eddie stared at Jed. It couldn't be; Jed had to be winding him up. 'You weren't fit enough to clean my father's shoes, let alone kill him,' he snarled.

Jed grabbed Eddie by the chin and manoeuvred his face so it was only inches away. 'I killed your shitcunt of an old man, and do you know what? He begged me for mercy. Fifteen years old I was and I beat him senseless. Cried like a baby, the old cunt did, so don't tell me I weren't good enough to clean his shoes.'

'You're a fucking liar. My Frankie would never keep something like that from me,' Ed yelled.

'You fucking scumbag cunt,' Gary shouted. He would have killed Jed with his bare hands, if only they weren't tied up.

Raymond shut his eyes. He just wanted to die now, get it all over with as quickly as possible.

Eddie was turning redder and redder in the face. 'You fucking spineless piece of shit. I'm gonna kill you,' he yelled, as he tried to thrust his incapable body towards Jed.

Jed laughed at Eddie's feeble attempt to attack him and turned to his father. 'I'm sorry I never told ya, but I did it for me Grandad Butch. He was never the same man after Harry shot him. I waited and waited for you to do something about it, but you never did, so me and Sammy took it into our own hands. It had to be done, Dad. Revenge had to be taken.'

Eddie took deep breaths to calm himself down. He knew he had mugged himself off by wriggling about like a deranged eel, but his reaction had been spontaneous. He wasn't even thinking of his dead son or Gina and his kids any more; all he could think about was his dad and how Frankie had betrayed him. He was so annoyed with his father, absolutely fucking seething. How could a man of Harry Mitchell's stance be battered to death by a boy who was barely out of nappies? For years Ed had looked up to his big bad gangster of a dad, and now he'd lost all respect, even though he was about to die in a not dissimilar way himself. As for Frankie, her actions were despicable and if by any chance he came out of tonight alive, she was out of his life for good.

'Dad?' he heard Gary say.

With tears of disappointment in his eyes, Eddie looked at his eldest son. The O'Haras were still busy talking among themselves.

'Keep your chin up. Don't make yourself look a cunt,' Gary mouthed.

Eddie nodded. He would not beg for mercy like his father had. He would die like a man.

* * *

Dominic's hands were visibly shaking as he tried to turn the steering wheel. He couldn't believe this was happening. It was like a bad dream, totally surreal.

'Please don't do this. Let's go to the police, I beg you. If something happens to you, I'll never forgive myself for giving you a lift. You're a lover, not a fighter, Joey,' Dominic pleaded.

Stony-faced, Joey ignored his boyfriend's little speech. He took the handgun out of its cloth and stared at it. When his dad had first given him a key to his cottage, he had shown Joey where the gun was kept and Joey, having never seen one before, had been interested to know how to use it. Unbeknown to Dom, Ed had given Joey a lesson in shooting. 'You're a natural, boy. You never know, it might come in handy one day,' his father had joked at the time.

Dominic stopped at the traffic lights and shivered as he glanced at his partner. His earlier anger at Joey for involving him in the drama had now all but disappeared. Whatever Frankie had said to Joey in the kitchen earlier had turned him into a person that Dom barely recognised, and that scared him.

'Joey, I beg you one more time, please don't do this to me. If you truly love me, you wouldn't be putting me through this.'

Joey looked at Dom and felt no guilt when he saw the pain and tears in his boyfriend's eyes. 'When you turn onto the A13, drive past the scrapyard, then pull over on the left. Wait five minutes then, if I ain't back, drive straight back to Frankie's. I love you, Dom, I always will, but don't make me choose between you and my family, because you won't like the fucking answer. As much as you probably won't understand this, blood is a very special tie, and at the end of the day, I'm a Mitchell.'

When Jimmy held the gun against his temple, Eddie shut his eyes. He couldn't look at the fearful expression on Gary's face. Ricky had been so badly injured he hadn't really known what was going on, but Gary had only been shot in the back of the leg and although he must be in pain, he was very much in a state of awareness. Ed took a deep breath, wondering if it was going to be his last. After all these years, his colourful lifestyle had finally caught up with him.

'You've got one more chance to give us an address, lads,

else Steady Eddie 'ere gets his head blown off,' Jimmy said to Raymond and Gary.

Eddie opened his eyes and stared at Gary and Raymond. One looked near to tears, the other petrified, and Eddie knew it was his duty to be strong for them. He wasn't afraid of death, never had been, but he was very afraid of never seeing his wife and kids again. Who would be there to protect them after he had left this planet? No one, that's who. He turned to Jimmy. Jed had popped outside to try and locate his phone, which he'd lost in the earlier tussle, and Ed guessed he was hoping to have heard from Georgie and Harry.

'Come on then, shoot me you two-bob cunt. What you waiting for, Christmas?' Ed jeered.

Furious with Eddie's brave and obstinate attitude, Jimmy pushed him onto the concrete floor. He balanced the gun on top of the tyres and punched Eddie three times in his smug face. 'Where are my fucking grandkids?' he hollered.

Jed reappeared. He had managed to find his phone, but was gutted that there were no messages from the kids. 'You not killed him yet? What you waiting for?' he asked.

'I was waiting for you. I thought you'd wanna see the cunt take his last breath an' all,' Jimmy replied, picking up the gun again.

'I found the phone; no joy. Time for some torture, methinks,' Jed said.

'I think we're best to finish 'em all off now and get the fuck out of here, boy. We need to find out if Billy's OK.'

Gary and Raymond glanced at one another, then both clenched their eyes firmly shut. They couldn't watch Eddie die, it was far too horrendous to even contemplate.

Ed closed his own eyes as he felt the steel of the metal barrel push into his temple. This was it now, the end, and with all the past sins he'd committed, he fleetingly wondered if God would accept him in heaven or banish him to hell.

Hearing four gunshots, Eddie said a prayer. He was no Bible-basher, had never really believed in God, but what choice did he have other than to put his faith in Him now?

'Dad. Are you OK, Dad?'

Ed's body froze as he heard the familiar voice. Was he

already dead? Or was he fucking dreaming? Frightened to open his eyes in case he came face to face with the devil, Eddie kept them closed.

'It's me, Dad. Please be alive.'

Hearing Gary and Raymond laughing, but also crying at the same time, Ed opened his eyes and took in the scene around him. Jed and Jimmy were both lying on the floor next to him with blood gushing out of their backs and standing over him, with a stunned expression on his face and a gun in his hand, was none other than Joey.

'Thank you, God, and thank you, son. Untie me, there's a knife over there, I need to check they're both dead,' Ed croaked, instinct taking over.

Joey's whole body was trembling as he cut the rope off his father's arms and legs. He then headed over to where Gary and Raymond were tied up and set them free as well.

Even though he suspected he had a broken leg and arm, Eddie had always had an uncanny knack of being able to rise above pain and still managed to crawl over to where the O'Haras lay. He picked up the gun that Jimmy had been using and slid it across the floor towards Gary. He checked both of their pulses and let out a sigh of relief. 'They're goners,' he shouted, as he crawled over to where Ricky was lying. 'God bless you, boy,' he said in a choked-up tone.

Raymond and Joey walked over to where Ed was sitting, and stood over Ricky's body. 'Rest in peace, mate,' Raymond said, wiping away a tear.

Overcome by shock at what he had done, Joey couldn't speak. He couldn't even cry.

'I don't wanna see him like that, I can't face it. Cover him over so I can say my goodbyes,' Gary said with a sob in his voice.

'Put your jacket over him, Ray. I can't take mine off 'cause of me arm,' Eddie ordered.

Desperately trying not to cry himself, Ed took deep breaths as Gary limped over and grasped his brother's lifeless hand. When he'd left Beverley all those years ago, he knew his boys would be OK because they had such a strong bond between them. Inseparable as children, their closeness had continued into adulthood and Ed knew that Ricky's death was going to hit Gary harder than anyone else.

'I love you, Rick. You were the best bruvver that anyone could ever wish for and I'll look after your Amy for ya, I promise you that,' Gary wept.

Eddie felt distraught. Seeing Gary's raw pain was breaking his heart. He knew he had to be cruel to be kind, for all of their sakes. 'Gal, snap out of it, son. I know you're devastated, we all are, but we really do need to sort this mess out now. We don't want Ricky to die in vain, do we? The last thing he'd want was for all of us to get life.'

Gary wiped his eyes with the cuff of his jacket and nodded. His dad was right. Ricky would hate to see them all go down.

'You'd best ring Flatnose,' Raymond said, suddenly finding his voice. He'd been so disturbed earlier that he hadn't really been able to speak. Not only had Ricky's death brought back awful memories of Jessica's demise, but the thought of never seeing his daughter again, the child he'd waited so long for, had all but torn him in two.

'Someone needs to go out to the van. One of us must have left a phone in there,' Ed suggested.

Joey took his phone out of his pocket and handed it to his father. All that had happened had somewhat traumatised him, but not in the way it should have done. He'd not shed a tear when he'd stared at his dead brother, nor was he bothered about killing two men. The thing that had shocked him the most was his ability to behave in that way. He'd never thought himself capable of being involved in any type of violence, let alone murder.

Instead of calling Flatnose Freddie, Eddie dialled Larry's number. If Ricky hadn't died and Gary didn't have a bullet lodged somewhere in his leg, Flatnose could have mopped up quite easily. Raymond was now over his earlier concussion and Ed could have just turned up at the hospital and pretended he had taken a good hiding from someone. Bullet wounds were different gravy, though. The Old Bill would start sniffing around like there was no tomorrow.

'What's up, Ed?' Larry asked, half asleep.

When Eddie told him the score, Larry had never woken up

so quickly in his entire life. 'So, did all this happen where the tyres are kept?' Larry asked, trying to catch his breath. He could barely believe what he had just heard.

'Yeah. We're still here now.'

'Right, get yourselves out of there and get rid of any incriminating evidence you might have on you, and I mean everything. Once you've done that, set fire to the warehouse with the O'Haras still inside. Then call an ambulance, followed by the police. You tell the authorities that you went up to Scotland to get your grandchildren back, and then you got followed home. Tell them the truth about Joey picking the kids up from the garage – it's probably on camera anyway – and say you drove straight to the yard because you didn't know where else to go. You tell the police that you have no idea how the fire actually started. Say that you overheard the O'Haras talking and you think that they were planning on burning you alive. Your injuries and Ricky's death should cement your story and do not involve Joey in the end part.'

Eddie sighed. 'I'd rather just ring Flatnose, Lal. I can't be doing with all the Old Bill's questions; I've just lost my son, for fuck's sake. Ain't there another way we can sort this without involving them? And what about the forensics? Say they discover that the O'Hara's had been shot? We'll all be in shit-street then.'

'Now listen to me, Ed, and listen very carefully. The O'Haras have killed not only your father, but also your son, and if you loved Harry and Ricky as much as I know you did, you wouldn't want their deaths to be in vain, would you now? What you've just told me about Jed murdering your father has literally knocked the stuffing out of me. Harry wasn't just one of my clients, I classed him as one of my best friends as well. You must honour your dad's and Ricky's memories, Ed. Fitzgerald Smythe is the best QC I've ever worked with, but even he couldn't get you out of this one. Even Einstein would falter on a case such as this. Please, just do as I say, Eddie. It's the only way out this time, I can promise you that. As for the forensics findings, we'll have to cross that bridge when we come to it.'

'OK,' Ed said ending the phone call. He turned to Gary, Joey and Raymond and repeated the conversation.

'I can't drag my brother's body out of 'ere like a lump of dead meat. You're gonna have to do that,' Gary muttered.

Eddie nodded, then turned to Joey. 'How did you get here?'

'Dom brought me. I told him to wait five minutes in case yous weren't here, then drive back to Frankie's.'

'You'd better go and check he ain't still sitting there. If he is, jump in the car and go back to your sister's. Say nothing, though, Joey, I'll do all the explaining later.'

'Nan and Grandad are at Frankie's an' all,' Joey informed him.

'Oh, for fuck's sake! You're just gonna have to try and act normal, boy. I'll get there as quick as I can.'

When Joey left the building, Eddie tried to stand up, but couldn't. 'We need to get rid of everything now, boys. Rope, knives, baseball bats, the gun, the whole fucking caboodle,' he ordered, as Raymond helped him up.

'How we gonna do that? Ray, you'll have to dump all our props somewhere; I can't drive with this leg,' Gary replied.

Eddie looked at his son's dead body. It was lying only a couple of feet away from him. The mess they were all in was suddenly getting to him and he felt ill, really ill. How the hell were they meant to clean up after themselves, then burn the place down when only Raymond could fucking walk properly?

'Look who I found,' Joey said, as he reappeared with Stuart and Terry by his side.

For the second time that day, Ed thought how his prayers had been answered. He briefly explained to Tel and Stu what had happened, then told them what Larry had said.

'Come on, mate, let's get you up,' Stu said, as he and Terry bent down to help Ed.

'Tel, you get rid of the gun and any shit in the back of the van. Look near the Portakabin for a knife, 'cause O'Hara's other son got stabbed. When you've done that, go straight back to Frankie's,' Eddie instructed.

Terry nodded and ran from the building.

'Stu, you help Raymondo take Ricky outside, then I want you to take Joey home for me. Say nothing when you get there, not even about Ricky. I'll do the talking when I get back from the hospital or wherever the cunting Old Bill take me.'

Unable to watch his brother's body being dragged along the floor like an animal carcuss, Gary half limped and half ran out of the building. Stuart and Raymond picked Ricky up by his arms and legs and, instead of torturing himself by watching, Ed distanced himself by focusing on the hero. Joey had been such a disappointment to Eddie as a child, the runt of the litter, and when Ed had found out his son was gay, he had all but disowned him.

'Come and sit 'ere, boy,' Eddie urged him.

Joey did as he was told. As a kid and a teenager, all he had ever wanted was his father's acceptance, but he hadn't wanted to gain it this way. He put his head in his hands. 'I'm still in shock, Dad. Don't get me wrong, I'm glad I saved your life and Gal's and Ray's, but I can't believe that I did what I did. How can I go back and work up the City next Monday? I feel like a different person. As for Dom, we ain't gonna survive all this, I just know we ain't.'

Eddie put his arms around his saviour's shoulders. For years Eddie had wanted to wipe the O'Haras off the face of the earth, and now Joey, the most unlikeliest of heroes had just achieved what Ed had previously failed to do himself. 'You'll need to take some time off work to get your head together, but don't worry about you and Dom, you'll be absolutely fine. Match made in heaven, yous two.'

Feeling himself about to falter, Joey did his best to stop himself crying. 'You always said that shooting lesson would come in handy one day, didn't ya?' he joked tearfully.

Eddie ruffled Joey's blonde hair then, with the arm that wasn't broken, held his son more tightly than he'd ever held him in the past. 'I love you, boy, and I'm so bloody proud of you.'

'I love you too, Dad, but I'm not very proud of myself at the moment,' Joey said honestly.

Eddie tilted Joey's chin upwards, so he could look him in the eyes. 'Do you wanna know why you did what you did today?'

Joey nodded. He knew why he had done what he had deep down, but he could never tell his father that Frankie had known about his Grandad Harry's death. That would always have to remain a secret between the two of them, as Joey knew that his father would go apeshit if he ever found that out.

Eddie stared at his son intensely. 'You might have been a softie as a child and then turned all gay on me, but you can never change the stock you were reared from. What's bred in the bone will one day come out in the flesh, Joey, and you proved that today, boy.'

Joey was confused. 'And what is that supposed to mean? That I killed Jed and Jimmy just 'cause I'm a Mitchell?'

With immense pride in his eyes, Eddie smiled. 'No, Joey. You didn't kill them just because you're a fucking Mitchell. You killed them because you are Eddie Mitchell's son.'

DISCOVER
MORE FROM

Kimberley
CHAMBERS

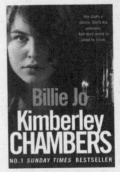

The Mitchells & O'Haras Trilogy

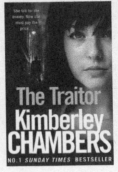
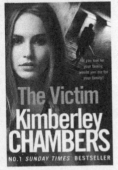